MEMORY'S EYES

MEMORY'S EYES

A New York Oedipus Novel

Cordelia Schmidt-Hellerau

International Psychoanalytic Books (IPBooks)
New York • http://www.IPBooks.net

Published by IPBooks, Queens, NY
Online at: www.IPBooks.net

Cover design by Karola Schmidt-Hellerau and Kathy Kovacic using two
photos from the series "Father and Daughter", courtesy of WLC Ltd.

ISBN: 978-1-949093-62-9

For my late parents and my sister,
And for my psychoanalytic colleagues,
And for my former and current patients,
And for the man I love,
And for all my dear friends,
And for the parents who once were children,
And for all the children within us:

MEMORY'S EYES

This is a story older than time.
A Greek master told it first.
It starts out almost as sappy as a movie romance,
Or as quirky as a New Yorker cartoon.
However, as you continue, you are bound to sense some
discomfort.
And soon you'll find yourself puzzling over a mystery.
It's fun, and it's dark.
This is the only warning you'll receive...

TABLE OF CONTENTS

SOPHOCLES

A Prologue

One late afternoon about 2,500 years ago, Sophocles was sitting on the white steps of the Acropolis—still under construction at the time—looking down over the temple's surrounding olive groves and their folds of silver-green-gray that were flickering in the sunlight's blinding glance. What a sight: centuries before and many more to come, it would always be like this. It was a momentous, albeit very private hour for Sophocles. While a light breeze from the Aegean shifted the strands of his hair over his forehead, Sophocles' mind got wrapped up in a daydream that took him by surprise: he fantasized of having a daughter. A daughter? He was lucky to have three sturdy sons, Iophon and Sophocles by his first wife Nicostrata, and Ariston by his second wife Theoris. Three healthy boys were enough to consider himself a proud father. Still, he wanted to have a daughter—a daughter who would sit with him and share this wonderful moment of solitary contemplation. His daughter...! She would be beautiful, for sure, but above all she would be a sweet and tender soul, attuned to her father's mind while independent and free, upright in her character, firm and bearing—without presenting herself as boisterous and feisty, as his sons often came across. All this fighting! She instead would understand to savor this quiet moment at sunset, tracing her thoughts in silent connection with those of her father, who for once didn't want to be the hero, the celebrity, the politician and arm-twister, nor the husband, lover and seducer of vanity, always successful, always responsible, always victorious—none of this for now, enough just to be her father! How was he doing? She wouldn't tell, but somehow she would let him know that she valued and respected him, that she cherished all they had experienced together, and that she would forgive his failures and shortcomings—always, and come what may...

Thus musing along the ripples of his reveries, Sophocles at once thought of Oedipus' daughter Antigone: she stood by her father until he died! The index finger of his right hand started to twitch around the writing utensil (some sort of quill) he always carried with him in order to comfortably scratch his back or, more often, to write down a few words, a fleeting idea, or an unusual expression caught in passing—material for new plays that would flow, a ceaseless stream of poetry, from the small wax tablet in his pocket to the stages of all times.

Sophocles would write 123 plays throughout his long life, but he would become most famous for his three Theban tragedies, portraying Oedipus and the characters of his family ensnarled in the twists and turns of their destinies and personal struggles. Had he followed the myth's chronology, he'd have first written *OEDIPUS REX*, then *OEDIPUS AT COLONUS*, and finally *ANTIGONE*. But at that point, in 441 BC, Sophocles wanted to create a daughter, and so he started out with the myth's endings, where the spotlight is fully on Antigone, presented as a strong figure, clear and loyal, brave and unyielding—and somewhat rebellious. Wonderful, Sophocles thought, fascinated with this fantasy. She would be his dream daughter—and he titled the play *ANTIGONE*.

Only 12 years later, in 429 BC, Sophocles travelled back on the mythological timeline, now fully diving into the core of the tragedy: *OEDIPUS REX*. No other play would grip Sophocles more profoundly in the process of writing than this one. Even though it won only second prize in the competition at its original performance, it became a big success. The audience was deeply affected; many cried or lowered their heads in grief and dismay. Sophocles immediately felt that this would forever be his masterpiece.

Another 23 years later, in 406 BC, shortly before Sophocles passed away at the age of 90, he wrote *OEDIPUS AT COLUNUS*, portraying Oedipus, the old man, guided by his devoted daughter

Antigone to his final resting-place. Oedipus was to die and so was his author. As the tale goes, an unknown young woman cried at his burial. Five years after Sophocles' death, one of his grandsons brought this third Theban play to the stage, a grand praise of Oedipus' daughter and a not-so-subtle condemnation of Sophocles' sons, who some years before his death had aimed and failed in court at declaring their father insane.

* * * * *

The myth of *Oedipus*[1] reaches far back into the early years of *Oedipus'* father *Laius*, who as a young man abducted and raped his disciple *Chrysippus*, the son of his foster parents. For this misdeed he was punished with a curse: were he to have a son, this son would kill his father and wed his mother! *Laius* tries to escape his fate; he resists impregnating his wife *Jocasta*. However, she makes him drunk, manages to conceive, and gives birth to a son. Scared and furious *Laius* threatens *Jocasta* with throwing her out of the royal palace, and she agrees to give up the infant. They pierce one of his feet to have him pinned to the ground somewhere out there in the wild. But a *Shepherd* pities the baby and brings him to the King and Queen of Corinth, *Polybus* and *Merope*, who adopt the foundling and name him *Oedipus* (swollen foot).

---

1   All persons in this myth whose names here are printed in *italics* play a role in this novel.

Many years later *Oedipus* hears someone call him a bastard. The insult startles him and makes him wonder: *who am I, and who are my parents?* In order to answer these questions he goes to Delphi and asks the oracle: *who am I?* He learns that he is doomed to kill his father and wed his mother. Horrified, *Oedipus* decides to protect his parents and never return to *Polybus* and *Merope*. Instead he takes the road towards Thebes. Meanwhile *Laius* too is on his way to question the oracle in Delphi because rumors have it that his son will come to kill him. On his way to escape his fate, *Laius* runs right into it: At a crossroad, he clashes with a young man; *Laius'* servants demand that he gets out of the chariot's way; *Oedipus* refuses; they get into a fight, *Laius* hits *Oedipus* over his head, whereupon *Oedipus* kills *Laius*, the man who unbeknownst to him is his father, and all but one of his minions, who will deliver the news of *Laius'* fall to *Jocasta*. Continuing on his way to Thebes, another obstacle bars *Oedipus'* way, the *Sphinx*, a fabulous creature with the head and breasts of a woman, the haunches and abdomen of a male lion, and the wings of a large bird. The *Sphinx* challenges everybody passing to solve a riddle: *Who walks on four legs in the morning, on two at noontime, and on three in the evening?* Nobody so far had been able to unravel the mystery. Yet *Oedipus* responds: *It's man, who crawls on four legs early in life, stands upright as an adult at noontime, and needs a cane in the evening of life.* This is the right answer. Deprived of her enigma's power the *Sphinx* hurls herself into an abyss. *Oedipus* proceeds to Thebes where *Jocasta's* brother *Creon* rewards him for freeing the city from the monster's terror by wedding him to *Laius'* widow, who unbeknownst to him is his mother, and enthroning him as the king of Thebes. Over the years *Oedipus* and *Jocasta* will have two sons, *Polynices* and *Eteocles*, and two daughters, *Ismene* and *Antigone*.

This is the foundation from which the drama of *OEDIPUS REX* arises. Concerned about a terrible plague in Thebes, King *Oedipus* decides to consult the oracle in Delphi and learns that the plague won't end unless the murderer of *Laius* has been found and punished. Hence *Oedipus* commits himself to uncovering the truth, whatever it may be, even if it were to implicate himself. He forces the blind prophet *Tiresias* to say whatever he knows about the unknown past, and learns that it was he, *Oedipus*, who murdered *Laius*. This incredible revelation is corroborated by the *Shepherd*, the man who once rescued the abandoned baby. With the horrible truth laid open, publicly exposing *Oedipus* as the murderer of his father and the spouse of his own mother, *Jocasta* hangs herself in the palace, and *Oedipus* blinds himself, piercing his eyes with a golden pin from his mother-wife's robe.

Decades later we meet the old hero again in *OEDIPUS AT COLONUS*. He has spent many years hidden away in his former palace from which *Creon* and *Oedipus'* sons eventually force him out. Again abandoned and scorned by everybody who knows about his horrible misdeed, he is left to stumble through a hostile world, a blind beggar at the hand of his daughters *Antigone* and *Ismene*. *Oedipus* has thought long and hard about his crime and guilt. He has felt remorse, but he has also held on to his right of self-defense when attacked by his father—old scores that can't be settled anymore. Eventually he has come to terms with his past. Now finally, at the beginning of the play, *Oedipus* arrives at Colonus, a small village near Athens (where Sophocles was born). Here *Theseus*, the king of Athens, offers *Oedipus* a safe and dignified place to stay and end his life. However, *Creon* as well as *Oedipus'* sons, *Eteocles* and *Polynices*, fighting over Thebes' throne, arrive to lure or drag *Oedipus* back home, alive or dead, because the oracle grants eternal protection to whoever owns the final resting place of his body. Despite this hoped-for benediction, *Creon, Eteocles,* and *Polynices* do not intend to give *Oedipus* the proper burial rites in Thebes. *Oedipus* recognizes that they prey on him solely for their own advantage. Therefore he refuses to comply and curses his sons to die from each other's hands. When *Creon* persists in trying to blackmail *Oedipus* by abducting his daughters, *Theseus* steps in and ends this brazen assault. After promising *Oedipus* to forever protect his daughters, he brings him to an undisclosed location to peacefully die.

The myth then goes on as told in Sophocles' play *ANTIGONE*. *Oedipus'* daughters have returned to Thebes. The battle over the throne has left both brothers dead. *Creon* has ordered a state burial for *Eteocles* only; *Polynices*, however, who attacked Thebes with the help of six hostile captains and their armies in order to defeat his brother, shall be punished by remaining unburied and rotting outside Thebes, grub for the vultures. Undeterred by the threat of the death penalty, *Antigone* defies *Creon's* order and manages to throw a handful of dirt on

Polynices' body, symbolizing his burial. *Creon* punishes her by locking her alive in a tomb of stone. The blind prophet *Tiresias* urges *Creon* to reverse his sentence, but by the time *Creon* has changed his mind and ordered *Antigone* to be freed, she has already hanged herself in her grave. Grief stricken *Haemon*, *Antigone's* fiancé and *Creon's* son, stabs himself when he finds her dead body, whereupon Eurydice, *Haemon's* mother and *Creon's* wife, also kills herself after having cursed her husband.

PART I

HOW IT ALL STARTED

A Family Romance

SCENE AT NIGHT

*W*ho are you? Hayden asked. *I don't recognize you,* he said. *Do you know who you are?* It was dark but not dark-dark. Didn't he see me? *Ann, is it you?* he asked again. He cowered on the floor, submerged in shadows, his back against our bed and his open hands floating through the air like white-faced ghosts, ready to fall upon and muffle his cryptic request. *Yes, it's me, Hayden, it's me!* I had only been out for a few hours. *It doesn't feel like you, or maybe it does—just stay where you are, give me some time!* I sat down right next to the door, the floorboards softly creaking, then silence again. *Hayden, are you okay? What happened? Can I switch on a light?* He pulled his knees up to his chin. *No, stay, don't move, I'll tell you!* It was past midnight, and I knew that Hayden had met up with some friends that day, and maybe they had smoked marijuana. *I'm not on drugs, Ann,* he said, as if he could read my mind. *I had an insight: I'll go on this trip, and it pains me to leave you; but I'm also leaving myself, staying here, because I will be on*

11

your mind, won't I? And as you'll stay here in New York, I'll take you with me—right? I'll talk with you in my thoughts, see you in my dreams and in the windowpane of the train when I look into an unknown landscape and find you out there. But then—doesn't that mean you are everywhere? So who are you? I mean, can I just make you where and how I want or need you to be? And do you know who you are and want to be, for you and for me, and are these two different? What then is yours, and what is it that your parents made you think you are, or your friends, or I? Don't you think that matters? He was right, I didn't know, and looking back I think his question was like a paper cut, thinly slicing me open. It hurt, and I wanted to pull away, but I managed to stay. *It does matter*, I finally said, *but I don't know how to answer.* Hayden sighed. *Me neither*, he admitted. *Will you come back, Hayden, will you come back to me?* He kept silent for a while. *I told you, I can't leave you, so no, I can't come back to you either; and who would I be anyway, not knowing who you are?*

The next day Hayden went on a concert tour around the world for many months. We left it open whether we would email or speak on the phone throughout this time. But as soon as he left, I began to write: facts and fantasies, ideas and images, memories and daydreams surged in pursuit of his parting question, and eventually lined up to a story about how it all started...

EDDIE

One of my favorite stories my father told me when I was little was the one in which he first arrived in New York. Tell me how you came to New York, I would ask and would not stop bugging him until he finally agreed and said, Okay, Ann, here we go...And while he was wandering in this tale of all tales through the streets of this great city, describing the things that he remembered, I imagined every little detail he mentioned and more. At that time I only knew the familiar places of my hometown, the old city of Cologne. Thus, even the name *New York* sounded awesome, and to think of my father as a young man, alone between these densely packed skyscrapers of Manhattan (I had seen them in photos), was exciting and a bit scary. I admired him for being so adventurous, and listening to him I felt I was *really there*—at least as long as he was talking to me, but maybe even a little longer...There were many things he didn't tell me, and these, I guess, I simply made up to fill in the picture of this mysterious world across the Atlantic. I can't clearly recall how I thought of my father as a young man at a time when I wasn't even born. So now again I have to make up things in order to complete my narrative. I'm thirty-two, and I live in New York. Knowing life in this city quite well, my stories seem so unduly romantic—not unlike the family romances of the serial novels in my mother's fashion magazines, which I loved to read as a child—but at heart they still hold the truth of the five-year-old I then was and maybe of what I became over the years...

So this is my story: My father, Edward O. Stark, or just Eddie, as everybody calls him, comes to New York one ordinary afternoon with a small bag in one hand and a street and subway map in the other, comes in by train from Philadelphia, where he had lived with his Aunt Margret in her fine apartment for as long as he could remember, and gets out, finally, at Grand Central Station. Now here he is in the middle of a totally amazing moment: new and free. He looks around. What an energetic crowd of people, he thinks, racing and zipping back and forth between trains and stairways and all the blinking and sparkling showcases in this huge hall of Grand Central Station—*Grand Central Station!*— and everybody's calling, chatting, yelling and laughing, and all so useful, earnest and determined like Eddie himself hasn't felt in a long while if ever... This is it, he thinks, watching a group of seven impressive men in dark suits with black briefcases hanging strap-wise and neatly polished from their shoulders, energetically hurrying ahead, just cutting his way and already gone, devoured at once by the bubbling, scurrying hell of the crowd. Yes, instantaneously he knows, this is my City, this is where I want to be! He has a bit of money in his bank account, his inheritance from Aunt Margret, not much, but enough to comfortably risk a new start and move into a B&B or a cheap hotel for as long as it will take to find a more decent place to stay, a place where he has his own bed and fridge and can do his own laundry.

My father said that he loved New York at first sight, and strangely enough, he had this distinct feeling that he belonged here. He wasn't naïve. As protected as his small world had been up to this point, he always was a smart observer and somehow knew about the difficulties of settling in a new place. His habit was to scan things carefully, and only then decide. So I see him leaning against a big post next to a coffee shop, looking around. What now, he wonders. The total freedom of choice intimidates him in its enormity. Every step he will take from here can easily lead his life in a different direction, and there is no way to foresee the consequences or to make a reasonable decision. On the other hand, this is the adventure of life! Eddie has finally arrived in New York!

Searching for some good whereabouts he meanders through the rest of the afternoon and half of Manhattan. Fortunately Eddie is a good walker. At that time he had already run the Boston Marathon twice. Thus, trekking block after block and scouting out the smaller hotels throughout the Village for him is a piece of cake even with his travel bag in hand. He is briefly tempted to take a room at *The Inn at Greenwich Corner*, which is located in the middle of the bohemian scenery of cafés, bistros, and second-hand shops, but the room is too expensive and the surrounding street life too noisy, and it's only late afternoon, so Eddie keeps moving. Anyway, his joy lends him wings and lifts him up, and the longer he flies through the streets with his eyes everywhere, from the people on the ground to the architectural design at the top of the highest buildings, the more he likes what he sees. Already he feels at home in the city.

Eddie gets his first New York stay in a romantically run-down SoHo inn, the *Ever Lodge*. A small room smelling of the multilayered history of previous guests, slightly moldy mixed with a sweet odor of detergent, it costs a fortune compared with what he had calculated. There is a richly ornate chest of drawers, a dark wooden closet for the suits he hadn't brought, a wrought iron desk with a scratched glass tabletop, and Eddie immediately thinks that he would see his feet next to his plate if he were to eat at this table, but anyway the chair is too low to comfortably sit there. Jesus Christ, he softly mutters, but doesn't want to appear picky and behave like a spoiled brat in the eyes of the lodge's concierge, an elderly woman who has climbed up with him to the third floor and now suspiciously scrutinizes each and every one of his moves, as if ready to snub him and push him out. Okay, Eddie thinks, and shows some interest in the bed, which he briefly examines with a bobbing trial; the bed has a worn-out mattress, soft like a cotton cloud, and the khaki-colored comforter looks so heavy that Eddie breaks into a sweat—he doesn't like it, for sure, but as long as there are no bed bugs, hopefully, who wants to make a big fuss...? I'll take it! he says, pulling a fifty-dollar bill from his inner jacket pocket, and tries to look happy. He is too tired to search for another place; now it's already past 9 PM! So if it wasn't fate, that's why he decided to stay, at least for the night. The concierge grabs the bill and disappears.

My father said it was in 1974, and he was twenty-two when he came to New York. At that time he usually wore corduroys and woolen sweaters—I have seen him in old photos, a friendly looking man with dreamy eyes, sensitive skin in his beard area and a blond shock of hair only to be tamed and combed back with lots of pomade. When he was little, Aunt Margret would stroke him over his scrubby head singing, *Brylcreem, a little dab will do you,* a dumb phrase she got from an advertisement; it would stick in his mind forever. Over the years in the morning when my father would look in the mirror, it would often come up: *Brylcreem*, he would think...and at first it would annoy him, but then he could smile and let go. In some pictures this *Brylcreem* makes him look well behaved; but I've seen others where he looks more wild and heady, actually a bit like a young Marlon Brando. Anyway, in the few photos he kept from these early years in New York, I see my father's self-confidence and a certain pride. I always thought he knew what he wanted, no matter what. And he was good-natured. My mother sometimes poked fun at him, declaring, When I met him, Eddie was a sweet young man with a pale face flat like a plate that everybody could put their things on, and then they started shining and sparkling, and people would think: wait a minute, is this really what I thought it was? Thinking about it or saying it made her laugh. Well, that's why you married me, my father usually responded, grinning crookedly; it was a familiar banter between them.

Still, it's true, he has this talent to relentlessly look at the bright side for everybody, and this gift got him stuck with Aunt Margret, who gave him a lot to work on. According to him, she was an almost genial complainer: foremost the weather, too hot or too cold, too dry or too wet; the mail too late; her hips hurting; the wrong president; Eddie not here; Eddie not there; and if only she and everybody else had done things differently, everything actually, from the beginning of her and her parents' and her grandparents' lives on. Who gave him the patience to endure her so long and always cheer her up? He often wonders...

It was a mistake to have you, Aunt Margret told Eddie many times, and I picture her, shaking her big round head with the blue curlers bulging under the headscarf she used to wear in the late afternoons, so my father told me. It must have looked a bit odd to him. But despite all the concern she meant to express when she once again prepared herself for her big speech about his parents, there was always a funny smile on her lips. Your parents weren't made to be parents, she would say. They were dreamers, romantics, idealists; they spent all their time reading Marx and Engels, or Hemingway and Henry Miller, discussing social justice, the price of freedom and the like. Who could buy

18

a box of cornflakes for that crap? They ended up on the blacklist, lost all their opportunities—oh my god! In their early years they were successful screenwriters, even thought of moving to Los Angeles. They could have had such a good life with the big money they made before the devil struck them to give it all up and live in a commune with people half their age, hanging around all day plotting against the system—what good was that for? And then, one day, out of the blue, they decided to have a child, just like that! They had no idea what it meant to raise a child. It came from their ideas about existentialism, they told me, existentialism! And there you were, not a flimsy idea, no, a real crying baby crawling on the floor in dirty diapers, eating the ants and butts from the ground while they were discussing socialism and Sartre! I told them, this is not going to work for this kid, but they just laughed me off, thought I was hopelessly old-fashioned and conservative. What could I do? I think you were real lucky when they crashed their car one night on their way back from a bar—lucky you, they had forgotten about you, can you imagine? They forgot that they had wrapped you in a blanket and put you to bed on the floor under a corner-bench in the CAVE—that's the bar they called their home, fine name for a home, CAVE! Forgot about you sleeping on the floor while they drove their lives off a highway bridge falling down 300 feet deep, and that was that! The cleaning woman found you in the morning. You were sitting between two chairs sucking your thumb, she said. At that time your parents were already dead. Cutting them out of their wrecked car took hours. When they were done they called to say that my sister and husband had died.

And the kid, I immediately asked, what about Eddie? I liked you. From the first moment I saw you I liked you. So I agreed to take you. That was good. That was right. But anyway they shouldn't have had you. I had told them, but they wouldn't listen.

Even though Eddie didn't like when Aunt Margret talked like this about his parents, he always felt drawn to hearing every single word of her longwinded tale of fame and blame, as if one day something new would grow out of this lullaby, something he hadn't asked for and couldn't even imagine. Still they were fine people, Aunt Margret sometimes added. Crazy people, but they loved each other, they really did, and they worked together so well—your parents! Then Eddie saw them shining in the mysterious light of their hopes and dreams: his mother concentrating on reading his father's manuscript with a pencil in her hand, ready to write her little remarks and corrections between the lines; and his father, in his best Sunday mood, affectionately sitting next to her, softly whistling and curiously peeking over her shoulder to catch what she was doing while he rubbed her back with one hand and chased the summer flies with the other. Were they happy and in love till their very end, Eddie wondered, or did they grow more and more disappointed with the cultural climate, and discouraged about the lack of opportunity to make their voices heard? Had they come to a point where they felt the best part of their lives was over, and only suicide could make sure that this special feeling they'd always had for each other wouldn't dwindle away and get lost, unnoticed and irretrievable? Eddie was always sure that his parents had shared an extraordinary, unique love—such love, he dreamt, more important than anything else, in the end more important than politics, art, or even little Eddie, their baby. Yes, too bad for the child, they might have said when they decided to end their lives. What a sweet boy he is! However, it was his life, and he would have to make it. They thought Eddie would be able to fend for himself, at least eventually. That's how Eddie imagined their worldview. They didn't forget about him on this last morning of their life, they purposefully left him, safe and sound in the CAVE, when they went to their deaths together, just the two of them, his parents. They were racing through the highway's boundaries, holding hands, and in midair they were looking at each other smiling and saying it one more time—I love you!—as they were flying, trundling, or shooting high-speed and slow-motion towards death. They were looking into each other's eyes until they crashed black, as black and mute as only death can be. That's how it was, Eddie thought.

Meanwhile Aunt Margret would continue to mutter and mumble and feel sorry and sad about his and her destiny and all the luck that had gone down the drain. Eddie understood that there was something in her that wouldn't give her a rest. Maybe she felt bad for having these mixed feelings about them. Or maybe she had an old grudge with her sister that wouldn't heal. It's okay, Eddie sometimes said to her, or: You did good. He would say this even when he was little, maybe at the age of four or five, and it might have sounded somewhat odd for a child to speak like this to an adult. But his aunt would let him and seemed to get some relief from it. Are you sure? she then would respond and smile, and when he nodded earnestly, she would say, Come, let's go for an ice cream! And while they were peacefully sitting next to each other in front of the ice cream store and silently licking a big scoop of vanillafudge, Eddie pictured his parents in a darkish tavern with a group of friends smoking and drinking, laughing and talking about important things, while his mother's foot in a woolen sock would softly stroke his belly as he lay under the bench she was sitting on...But now he is in New York, and nobody wears those woolen socks anymore.

In the morning, when Eddie gets down to the Ever Lodge's small breakfast area, there is a woman sitting and reading the Art section of the *New York Times*. Her dark curly hair—still entangled and befuddled from a short and agitated sleep, I imagine—loosely falls over the slim bones of her shoulders, completely covering her face. Who is she, Eddie wonders? The woman is so involved in the paper that she doesn't even look at Eddie when he sits down at her table. There is only this one table in the small dining area, and all the hotel guests are supposed to eat here between 7 and 9 AM. So he looks around, feels slightly allergic to the red and pink roses on the wallpaper, the frayed plush on the chairs, the lace cloth on the credenza, all of this an offense to his taste and style—my father has a very fine sense of aesthetics—and so he starts doubting that he will stay here for another night, when all of a sudden he notices the woman's sleeve: the sleeve is hanging down from her hand holding the newspaper, which she is slowly lowering either because her hand is following her eyes as they near the end of the article at the bottom of the column, or because she is so disappointed with what she is reading that all her day's energy is momentarily seeping out of her—anyway, the sleeve of her brocade-embroidered dressing gown is dipping like a thirsty tongue into her cup of black coffee, greedily sucking it up and licking it off and drowning in brown the features of an idyllic Chinese country life that had just been pleasantly playing and dancing along her soft, silken forearm. *Madame—your sleeve*, Eddie cautiously says, and it might have sounded like *your slave*, because the woman moves her newspaper to the side and looks at him with utter surprise.

How beautiful she is! Even though maybe in her forties, she radiates a youthful, even girlish freshness, but also a loving maturity, a thoughtful depth, a sweet manner, and such a harmonious soul that Eddie falls head over heels for her, loses himself in her eyes, these gorgeous eyes—when has he last, or ever, seen eyes like hers, so open to him, so clear and calmly focused, so interested and intelligent—she looks as if she has gone through all kinds of human issues, from energizing to destructive, and enjoyed and survived it all. Eddie is speechless. As soon as he has recovered his wits he reiterates, Your sleeve— sleeve, I mean, and points at what he's talking about. Oh, says the woman, now realizing her maladroitness, and a shadow of regret glides over her eyes like a raincloud, which gets Eddie fired up. I actually know how to completely eliminate coffee stains, he has the presence of mind to come up with. I am something of a magician with regard to coffee stains! The woman smiles, possibly comforted, perhaps amused, and certainly curious. Are you! she responds. Yes, Eddie confirms, and has no idea where this will get him, but he is so pleased to see his breakfast partner smile again. I'm Eddie, he introduces himself, advancing his hand towards hers while lifting himself up a bit to produce an elegant bow. Hi Eddie, I'm Joyce, Joyce responds and hands him her hand, which he delicately takes, barely touching it, only to breathe on it, or rather, indicate an old-fashioned hand-kiss. Nice to meet you, he gallantly says and sits down again. This is what our heroes get to live out in our fantasies, and my father was my hero—for many years he was, and maybe he still is.

Joyce was an actress, that much I know, actually in her time a very famous actress. She was not any Joyce, my father told me, she was *the* Joyce—and I guess, on this decisive morning, Eddie cannot understand why it hadn't occurred to him right away who she is, because now he can see it so clearly. But why is she in this remote place and not somewhere better, he wonders, for instance at a Palace Hotel or a Park Tower suite? Instead, here she is, and soon he will learn that her mind has some odd wrinkles quite like his, or everybody else's—what a relief! The previous night was the premiere of her current engagement on Broadway, Sophocles' *Oedipus Rex,* she tells him, and of course she is Jocasta, Laius' widow and Oedipus' mother and wife—A perfect casting, Eddie instantaneously agrees—But a draining role, Joyce confesses with a saddened smile, adding that all her life she'd wanted to perform it, but it had taken her until now to finally play it on stage. When Eddie sat down opposite her, she'd just been reading the *New York Times* critique, which savaged the production, to put it mildly. "Why do we need to see this play performed like a two-thousand-year-old relic?" the theatre critic angrily denounced the director. "In times of global research, when we can easily trace the genetic parents of foster children, the question has to be answered: what does the Oracle *have to* tell us *today*?"

Joyce had handed Eddie the critique in order to share her disappointment, and Eddie, as he reads it, cannot help but blurt out, What an idiot, that's totally beside the point! Joyce, cautiously but firmly squeezing and kneading her sleeve like dough to be recast as a fine pastry, nods approvingly. Encouraged, Eddie continues to read aloud, "Joyce as Jocasta might have made for a good enough widow but certainly not for a seductive wife, not even by way of a hint." That stings! Eddie meant to express his dissent and outrage when quoting this with a sneer—but he should have known that it would hurt Joyce to have this verdict thrown in the open, right into this breakfast area, where it seemed to linger and reverberate, even bounce back and forth between the two of them, noiselessly but with a razor's sharpness and no mercy—and Eddie would give a lot to take it back and make it unsaid and unheard, but he can't, and so he has to see again this tiny tinge of a raincloud sailing across her beautiful eyes, darkening them and revealing for a moment an unfathomable pain, something that always elicits his Moirae's call, now sealing his fate: Without really knowing it, he devotes himself to making Joyce happy. What a task!

I always felt I knew Joyce, but really I didn't. She died shortly after I was born. She was my father's friend, but I think of her as my granny, and even though babies probably don't love yet, I might as well have loved her. There is one photo that shows her holding me in her arms: my head is leaning on her bosom while I'm looking at her, and she looks at the photographer and has this smile on her lovely face, such a mysterious smile, sweet, sad and sympathetic—what can I say: not unlike Mona Lisa's. I have this picture in an Art Nouveau silver frame. Maybe my mother took it; I think she gave it to me when I was little, because it was always there, it had a place in my room, sometimes on a windowsill, other times hanging on the wall, and later I put it on my desk. As a kid I complained to her about the things that bothered me. I looked at the photo, and in my mind I would say to her, My mother won't let me go with my friends, can you imagine? Everybody goes! You would let me, I'm sure! Or I would say, It wasn't my fault that I lost my sweater, I didn't want to wear it in the first place, and anyway I had too much to carry! She was my imaginary confidant for the little troubles of my days. At other times, when I was more curious, I would ask her, How was it for you when you met Eddie? How was your friendship? And why did you die so early, at age 49?

This is the one story my father never told me. I asked him many times. Tell me, what did she die from? Were you with her when she died? What were her last words? Then my father's face would always draw wrinkles. I told you, when I came home she was gone, he would say. But gone where...? I insisted. Leave it, Antje, my father would respond. He usually calls me Ann, but when he addresses me by my full name, Antje, he is very serious and really means it. You know that I don't want to talk about it, it hurts too much. Most often his eyes then fixated on some distance to get lost in, and I tiptoed around him, knowing that I had touched his sore spot. Her death was his secret. I gave up asking him about it. But why would it still hurt him after so many years? We all lose a friend sooner or later, don't we? I sensed there was something tragic that I've wanted to reveal as long as I can think back. That's why I've started to make up stories; it's the best tool with which to poke around in the fog. I enjoy it, and I will do it until I can make sense of it all.

So, I imagine, on that morning in this poorly kept *Ever Lodge*, when the shadow of this unflattering quotation swept over Joyce's eyes, to his own surprise, Eddie hears himself saying, I want to make you laugh again! to which Joyce—what would she say? Perhaps something sibylline like, You want to play? Both are free that day, unconcerned about what's coming, for once as if in the shining droplet of their present, this small magic ball in time that had just rolled their way, nudged along by the secret hands destiny played for them. Over the creaky wooden steps he follows her up to the fourth floor, and through the long-winding corridor, to her room, number 429. He enters without hesitation. The bed folded from last night's wrinkles still seems untouched, and while Eddie gives in to a rising wave of desire, not knowing whether it is his or hers, Joyce is looking at him—she looks at his eyes as if they were two knobs to hold on to, or as if they gave her the right to love him in some way or other—until he closes and buries them in her arms. Hours pass. In the late afternoon, when the sun comes sparkling through the blinds' cracks, they finally decide they are hungry. Joyce has only the evening gown from last night's premiere party to wear—so what! And Eddie in his brown corduroys feels a bit out of place next to her—but so what! Giggling like kids they stumble down the stairs, totter past the concierge's reception desk, and reel into the open air of King Street, dive into the creamy crowd, stroll past the galleries, peeking in here and looking in there—what time is it actually?— amazing!—and end up in a small Italian restaurant with two big heaps of Spaghetti Bolognese on their plates and two glasses of Chianti. To you, Joyce says. To us, he responds. That's how I got my granny.

This is the version that is most compelling to me. I can't get it out of my mind. It feels obscure but strangely right. Issy, my sister, objects. She stubbornly wants to believe that our father never slept with Joyce. They were friends, just friends, she protests. You always have to make things up, she accuses me. It's just your fantasy that wants to make them lovers, just for the thrill of it or what? I don't know what to say to that. It's too bad that she gets so tense in this particular area. Romantic relationships raise a red flag for her. Issy believes that things started out quite simple: my father needed a room, Joyce had one to spare, he rented it, they became roommates, and eventually they grew a lasting friendship. But how lasting, and how at all?

Joyce is an enigma. Eddie, searching for her eyes in the morning, would easily grasp his task for the day. He is very good at that. Seeing her drink her warm milk with a splash of coffee, slowly dipping her raisin muffin in her big cup, all lost in thought or last night's dreams, and softly pushing and steering around a flaked-off crust or a swimming crumb like an ocean liner in a bath tub, he would read correctly what she needed. Sometimes it was just to be left alone; other times, to keep her company in silver silence. And then there were days when she was more vocal, loudly yawning, laughing about something she was reading in the newspaper, or banging the pan on the stove to sizzle some eggs sunny side up and inviting Eddie in: What are we going to play today?...Good question!

She loves to roam through second-hand shops, loves to endlessly try on costumes and suits from decades ago—Eddie, Eddie, look at that!—loves to put on hats and throw scarfs around her neck— Eddie!—while he patiently sits on a small stool amongst hat stands and clothes racks, watching how Joyce playfully dresses up to be a Mrs. Hardtforth, who sold all her last-year's dresses, suits, and evening gowns to this *Second Time Around* store because she suddenly discovered that her husband had accrued a gambling bill so huge that it eclipsed at once the sun, her fortune, and their future altogether—Joyce shuffles around like a drowned rat. Eddie looks at Mrs. Hardtforth and shakes his head. This is part of the game. Joyce nods and says, Anyway, I would never walk around like she does. But what about this? And off she goes, and comes back from the fitting room wearing a fur coat, huge and bulky, a monster made of raccoons; two of these beasts with their tiny ears and stiff snouts sharply pointed like ancient weapons are snuggling around Joyce's neck and staring at Eddie from black, maliciously gleaming, glass eyes. Ugh! Eddie says, You scare me, and Joyce laughs.

Sometimes he was her slave, carrying her purse, holding her umbrella, saying the required lines and opening the doors for her to graciously walk through. Other times he was like a little poodle scuttling behind her. Then again he approached her like the prince waking up Snow White with a magic kiss and holding a red rose hidden behind his back.—I saw it! No, I didn't.—He also was her stage companion, reading her partner's lines when she was preparing for an audition or practicing a new role. Or he played her doctor and nurse when she got a bad cold, needed to stay in bed and have her breakfast brought in on a white tray. I think in those years Eddie was patient, always patient, trying out variations of the roles she had assigned to him, most often without knowing about it herself, and he gave everything a chance for as long as it would take to find what felt right or would surprise her and make her smile. And with him she smiled and giggled and laughed—it was as if Eddie's mere presence tickled something in her that she couldn't resist.

30

Already, previously, she had felt comfortable and calm in the presence of men, she told Eddie, but with him she could even be enthused, excited, and out of bounds. Thank you, Eddie, she often gasped with beaming eyes when she had laughed herself to tears, thank you, oh what a funny guy you are, thank you, I love you! Then Eddie would hug her. It made him so happy to make her happy. It was then as if the whole world was swinging.

But my father is also playful in his own right. Already in these early years, Eddie started to collect toys—a passion that later morphed into a hugely successful business, his toy company FIXIT. While Joyce roamed through second-hand clothing stores, Eddie looked for little oddities: a tiny rabbit made from sheet metal sitting on a crocodile, a wooden jumping jack with a broken and bandaged leg, an iron racing car with four square wheels, a snow globe enclosing the Statue of Liberty raising her left arm, a necklace made out of tiny glass monkeys. He found these items in the ashtrays on the shopkeepers' desks, or next to the cash registers, or in the corner of a window, or hanging on a doorknob. He had an eye for these things. Joyce enjoyed herself by rummaging through piles of fleece, feather, and fur, and he loved to find a small ragdoll that had been sitting for decades on a shelf, placed there by who knows whom, never having been dusted, sitting obediently and with an unnoticed smile, waiting for a parent to pick her up, until Eddie discovered her, slipped her into his jacket pocket and brought her home. There she still is. In the hallway of our house in Cologne we have a big glass cabinet with my father's toy collection; a few pieces were probably high priced when he bought them, but mere preciousness was never his objective. He is interested in the odd and the weird, all the things that are somehow garbled, wrong, or unfitting. He really gets a kick out of these strange creatures, and once in a while I would see my father standing in front of this cabinet, all lost in thought, looking at these toys or taking one of them out, softly chuckling. They mean something to him. I don't know what. I'm no collector, and I don't play with toys.

Eddie moves in with Joyce, who lives comfortably in a small but elegant apartment on Fifth Avenue. Eddie's room doesn't have a window, but since he really shares the whole place with Joyce, this doesn't matter much. Only his little toys are kept in the dark, and for a long time Joyce, who is always preoccupied with something of her own, doesn't even notice them. The first item Eddie purchases is an old, seemingly Greek horse wagon with a coachman on the box seat and a removable passenger in the richly decorated carriage. He brings it home, sits down at his desk and slowly drives it around, softly humming *broummmm...*, which gives him a strange thrill. Joyce is on stage that afternoon, the place is all his, so he gets totally lost in some dream that places him in a remote countryside, a rural landscape on a cool, windy day with heavy clouds hanging down over the reaped, scrubby cornfields as he is trotting or maybe rather floating home. Home? He has never been to this place but still seems to know his way around. Anticipating something particular, he doesn't clearly know what, a subtle melancholia tugs at his heart with gnarly fingers. Hasn't he done everything right? When he enters the darkish hut through its low-cut wooden door, it feels as if there hasn't been anybody for decades. The narrow hallway is barred by a fallen coat-rack—hats, jackets, and winter garments sprawling all over the scuffed floor carpet. The doors to the kitchen and the living room yawn open, offering a bleak glimpse into a long vanished life. Is it here that he should have been raised? A local newspaper, opened to its Arts section, indicates the 10th of January 1930. Eddie drives his little wagon around the empty coffee cup. The sun sends dusty bands of light through the splintered shutters pointing all the way down the hut's hallway, where a closed door attracts his attention—the only closed door in this half decayed house. His little wagon wobbles over to it, ripping through densely tangled spider webs artfully spanned throughout this abandoned universe. He has to open this door! But the door is jammed. For unknown reasons Eddie feels a sudden surge of fury rising from the pit of his stomach. Now that he's here he wants to open this damned door, once and for all! He launches himself as if against the gates of heaven, his whole weight crashes at the dusty planks, bending the door at its upper half—but it remains stuck down at the bottom. So he steps one step back and boots it with a full-speed kick—ha!—and the wood splinters, cracks open, his foot races through and—ahh!—Eddie angrily pulls back, rips open his ankle—ugh!—blood shoots out of a piercing wound, thick and red on his pale skin—quite telling! But something behind the door has moved; now he can open it a crack, and looking through the small gap into the dark interior of this chamber he spots a skeleton, dressed in a leather suit stiff and bulging like armor with wanly shining metal buttons, a skeleton with a skull grinning at him, grinning!

Eddie bumps the wagon against the lamp, switching it off. For a while he remains frozen in this uncanny spot. What was that all about? He wants to go back to this hut, back through the door he has managed to open a bit, but the image is fading, there are still the adumbrations of the living room, the grin, the newspaper, the kitchen table, the coats in the hallway, and then all is gone... But there is also the key in the door and Joyce coming home, calling, Eddie? and switching on some lights. Where are you? And he's looking up from his desk. What are you doing? Joyce is baffled, but only briefly. Look, someone gave me this big bunch of roses, isn't that nice, she says, and Eddie nods and fills a vase with water.

This old-fashioned horse wagon always had a special, spotlighted place in my father's collection—and now it reminds me of something else. My father is a sleepwalker. As Aunt Margret told him and he told me, it started when he was little, about four years old. At the time he still slept next to Aunt Margret in her big wooden bed that she once shared with Pablo, her husband of a few months, who she had met on a Caribbean cruise on the occasion of her 30th birthday. Pablo had waited on her table, she told little Eddie when he asked her about the wedding picture hanging over their bed. He was a handsome man, she said, in fact gorgeous lad, and he showed her around the facilities on the big boat. Also, he was very funny, and after hesitating for a moment—or was she pondering what she should or shouldn't tell the child?—she added that she was smitten by his charm. At night when he was done with work and the captain wasn't looking from the command bridge, Pablo danced with her through the moonlight all over the upper deck, crooning right into her ear, this lovely fellow! Soon after her return to Philadelphia they got married.

I was adventurous when I was young, and I was so in love, Aunt Margret admitted, softly sighing over the loss of her life's zest and spark. We had these wonderful weeks, she raved. But Pablo was Mexican, and one day the police came and took him away. He was an illegal...What's an illegal? little Eddie wanted to know. It's when you are where you aren't supposed to be, Aunt Margret explained. Anyway, they took him to some sort of prison where all the illegals were put, and eventually they deported him to Mexico, with no allowance to reenter the US. Never ever?! I complained to the authorities, but they said Pablo used fake papers, our marriage certificate was not valid, null and void. That may have been so for them, but not for me. What could I do? At first we were writing letters back and forth, but over time, you know, eventually we lost contact. I could have travelled to Mexico, but I wasn't sure that I would be allowed back into the US. That was stupid on my part! Of course they would have let me back in. Yet there was also my mother, who was still alive and bedridden at the time. She sure didn't want me to go to Mexico! What good does it do to see him again, if he will never be allowed to live with you here in Philadelphia, she argued. This is how mothers are, Aunt Margret sadly concluded and folded her hands over the pink cotton of her nightgown. In prison? Eddie whispered. Yeah, Aunt Margret confirmed, nodding her heavy head, that's what they do! And I...? In my view I was married, even though they said I wasn't. That's the story of this picture, that's Pablo—forever my sweetheart! And Eddie wondered if Pablo spoke English or Aunt Margret spoke Spanish, but he didn't dare to ask.

Anyway, he understood that this was why she remained single in her big master bed—until he moved in with her. Many times she said how much she loved to watch over him, loved to see him sleep like a little angel. But then, around the age of four, he started to walk out of her bedroom. One morning she noticed that the bedroom door was open, and she was sure she had closed it when she went to sleep. Eddie was sleeping. So she must have forgotten after all, she decided. But it kept happening, not every night, just now and then, despite the fact that she paid extra attention to closing the door. It was uncanny, and she couldn't explain it until she saw it happening. One night when the moon, full and bright like a white paper lantern, had just come around to glaringly shine onto her pillow and into her eyes, and she just wanted to turn around, she heard Eddie's comforter swishing, and peering over to him she saw him slip out of bed, get up, silently walk over to the door, which he opened and left the bedroom. Of course she followed him, at first thinking he needed to use the bathroom. But instead he walked into the living room, mounted a chair, and sat on the windowsill looking out into the night. Eddie, what are you doing here? Aunt Margret asked him. He looked at her and calmly said: I'm searching...What are you searching for?...My horse-drawn buggy, he answered. What horse-drawn buggy? You don't have a horse-drawn buggy, Aunt Margret said. It's out there, Eddie insisted, pointing into the dark park in front of their house. Then he slipped off the windowsill and quietly went back to bed. The next morning he had no recollection of it. Maybe he wants a horse-drawn buggy, Aunt Margret thought, and wants it so badly that he dreams of it. So she went out of her way to find him a horse-drawn buggy. When she was finally able to give it to him, Eddie didn't like it. The horse is supposed to be black, he complained and pushed it away. They only had brown horses, Aunt Margret defended her purchase, and what does it matter? Brown horses are as good as black ones...It needs to be black, Eddie mumbled. We can paint it black, Aunt Margret suggested. Then it'll still be brown, just pretending to be black, Eddie insisted, and that was that. Another night, Aunt Margret found him in the kitchen sitting in front of the open refrigerator. Eddie, are you thirsty? What are you staring at? she asked him. Sugar, he murmured, there is no sugar in my pocket...Come to bed, Aunt Margret told him, the sugar is in the kitchen cabinet. Tomorrow I'll show you. But the next morning Eddie wasn't interested when she wanted to show him where she kept the sugar. He just said I know and continued building a complicated castle with his Lego blocks. And so it went on.

Eventually, on the occasion of a yearly check-up, Aunt Margret brought this up with Dr. Spitz, his pediatrician. Does he also wet his bed? Dr. Spitz wanted to know, deeply embarrassing Eddie, who stood there in his underpants waiting to be allowed to get dressed again. No, no, Aunt Margret responded. He just gets out of our bed, mostly at full moon—he might even talk with me, it's a bit weird—and the next day he can't remember anything. Dr. Spitz looked concerned. He sleeps with you in the same bed? Aunt Margret felt unjustly criticized. It's two separate beds, just next to each other, she clarified. Well, you know—there are children who actually do better when they have their own room to sleep in, Dr. Spitz then said. Do you have another room for him? Eddie listened carefully. Maybe I could arrange that, Aunt Margret considered. There is a small room, where I have my sewing box, do the ironing... I could make it Eddie's room, if you thought it would help...? Dr. Spitz seemed pleased. I think it's an excellent idea! Try that, and let me know if it helps. And so she did despite some regret of again being alone in her bedroom. I think thereafter, Eddie liked the doctor—even though I just made this story up. The only thing I know from what my father told me is that he got his own room and bed when he was about four or five years old, which was a good thing, for sure. He said the day he moved in, he felt like a captain on a big boat.

However, he remained an occasional sleepwalker. It's mysterious, this sleepwalking. It must be a state between dreaming and waking, neither one nor both at the same time. My father once sleepwalked into my room. I was about ten years old at the time,

38

and he woke me up because he tried to take down the curtain and loudly joggled and jerked the curtain rod. Waking up, I first thought he was a ghost coming in through the window, and I screamed in terror. My mother came running in and turned on the light. My father must have woken up by then, because he apologized and went back to bed with my mother. The next day he told me that he didn't mean to scare me. He said that he sometimes sleepwalks—not very often, he reassured me, yet it happens, and there is nothing he can do about it. There were a few more episodes like that, and knowing what it was, I didn't mind too much, even though it remained spooky.

Hayden, I'm not sure, did I write this for you or for myself? What if I sent you this strange mix of early fantasies and later ideas in their current makeover? Would you read and understand them as stories about my father, or would they instead tell you something about me? Because I made up most of it. Before you left you asked me who I am, and whether I believe I am who I am because of me or because my parents raised me to be like this. How could I tell the two apart? Everything is intertwined, I suppose, my own traits and my parents' guidance, all of it came together, and here I am. But you made me wonder about my family, first of all about my father. Who was he when he first came to New York, at the time even younger than I am now? What were his dreams, his ambitions, his beliefs, and how did they make their way into my mind as he raised me? He cared a lot about being honest and reliable. Don't lie, he would say to me, even if something is uncomfortable or embarrassing to admit. We all make mistakes, and that's okay. But if you lie, you lose yourself, at least for a bit; you pretend to be different from the person who made the mistake. Is it worth it? No, nothing is worth not standing up for yourself and facing who you are!

As an adult I came to value his advice. But as a child it was hard, despite the fact that he wasn't big on punishment. He reasoned rather than scolded. Let the truth be your friend, he used to say. It won't be an easy friend, but one that keeps you out of trouble. He had read the old Greek classics and Kant, and whenever it fit he would throw in the famous lines: *gnothi seauton!* and *sapere aude!* which he was happy to translate for us into *know thyself* and *dare to know*. It impressed me, made me curious, and my father liked that about me. He always encouraged me to think, to ask, to learn, to find out, to not content myself with little; he wanted me to try harder, dig deeper, to not avoid but enjoy working on something. Now I am grateful for that; it helps me to be patient when something is difficult and to not give up on what I want. But when I was little it cost me quite a few battles and angry tears. Good that he didn't shy away from my screaming and yelling. It showed me that he too didn't settle for the easy way. Yes, he is willing to fight. He sticks to what he thinks is right. He appreciates a good argument. Education was always important for him. He could be very generous with Paul, Issy, and me, as long as we progressed well in school. He regretted not having tried graduate school and insisted that we did. And when I told him that I wanted to study psychology in Munich, he immediately agreed. Freud rose from the grounds of enlightenment, he said. If I were young I might study psychology as well.

Later, though, he had a much more muted reaction when I told him that I wanted to do psychoanalytic training in New York. It surprised me. I thought he would be delighted. Was it because he wanted me to live near to Cologne, not far away in New York? I told him that I wasn't sure yet whether I would become an analyst, or just get some training here and continue with it later in Cologne, or use what I learned during my training when teaching at a university, perhaps in Germany. All seemed open. He stayed neutral and didn't say much about it. And so I didn't talk much about it either. I love my father, but we are not very close. We walk our separate ways. In particular, since I moved to New York, we don't see each other too often. Sometimes we don't speak on the phone for weeks. It's not that I forget to call him, but he has these periods of withdrawal, when he doesn't pick up the phone and doesn't respond to my messages on his answering machine. Then I wonder: where is he? Is he involved with a new girlfriend? Or is he depressed, still mourning my mother? Unlikely!

Sometimes I imagine that he longs to be back in his early years in New York, when he was free, and the whole future seemed to be open. What a moment in life! He went to the *Ever Lodge* in SoHo, and his whole life unreeled from there! But what if he had instead stayed at *The Inn at Greenwich Corner*, the small hotel in the Village he had liked but considered too expensive and too noisy. Tired as he was, he would have slept through all the cars' honking and the bars' music, and all the night's activities. He would have slept like a rock. In the morning he would have gone to one of the nearby coffee shops. While waiting for his scrambled eggs on a bagel, he would have read the small handwritten notes on a bulletin board near the cash register, and maybe he would have found a little ad for a one-bedroom apartment in the neighborhood. He would have called them up, would have stopped by, would have liked it, and that would have been his first rental apartment in New York, just as he had imagined it. He had never thought of moving into an elegant building on Fifth Avenue. He never would have been able to afford that. So there he'd already gotten ahead of himself. He couldn't resist the temptation. And once he gave in, things followed their own spin. That's fate, it rears its head and roars like a lion, yet the streets are too noisy, nobody hears it...But then again, had he stayed in the Village, he wouldn't have met Joyce, nor my mother, and I wouldn't be here. Maybe part of me would be here, sort of, somehow in another person, another combination, and the other part of who I am would have remained something virtual forever, just potential, or not even that...So I'd rather have Eddie get to the *Ever Lodge*, meet Joyce, and later my mother, and all that followed from there. Eddie... It's strange to write about my father as *Eddie*—it's a bit like I would write about an unknown young man, Eddie, not my father—and in fact, in those years, he wasn't my father yet, and little did I know...Well, it's just writing, a fantasy on paper...

JOYCE

Once my father mentioned that Joyce was superstitious. For instance, on a day that she had to go to the doctor, she would wear a sweater inside out and count it as a good sign if nobody noticed that there was something wrong with her. Or before each of her performances, just when the curtain lifted, she would briefly tap her nose three times with her pinkie. Superstition is very common amongst actresses, my father said, and it's best to leave it alone. Still quite extravagant was that after each of her premieres, Joyce had to spend the night at the poorly maintained *Ever Lodge* on King Street, where my father first met her. She hoped she could trick fate into showering her with praise by returning to the place where she had started her career many years ago as a young acting student who was picked, heaven knows how, to play Romeo's Juliet on Broadway. At that time she lived right around the corner from the *Ever Lodge*, where she knew the old doorman from chatting with him when time and weather permitted, and where she had some of her best conversations with the bartender when stopping by once in a while for a glass of sherry before going home.

For Joyce, at the time home was a small rented room in a battered two-story flat, which she shared with a young, still unsuccessful artist, Larry, who was madly in love with her, and Maggie, an agoraphobic spinster, the tenant, who spent most of her time on house cleaning and clashing with Larry over their divergent philosophies about the order of things. Anyway, Joyce premiered with Juliet, and the next morning, when she was anxiously sitting in the kitchen, her knees drawn up to her chin and her head buried between her arms, all stiffened in anticipation of a public ripping, with the shreds thrown freely to her envious colleagues—Larry stormed into the kitchen waving the New York Times, as if to chase away the swarm of nasty flies in her mind, and smashed the paper on the kitchen table, trumpeting: fantastic, glorious, awesome, fabulous! His outburst probably startled Joyce, but without taming his voice, Larry read—or rather screamed out aloud—the critique's opening line: Last night a star was born: Joyce, an eighteen-year-old, first-time appearance on Broadway, became the emotional and spiritual magnet that centered all the other performances in this play and moved the viewers to tears. Joyce was incredulous, stunned, and finally overwhelmed with joy. Tears streaming down her cheeks, she hysterically thanked Larry for the good news—*thank you, thank you*—as if *he* had written this review, jumped up and hugged him and danced through the kitchen like a mad cat, wildly fidgeting around and eventually tripping over an electrical cord or something, lurching side- and backwards, thereby pulling Larry with her to the ground, where she ended up rewarding him with sex, something he'd always and she'd never wanted. But he had made her so happy, how could she have shown her gratitude better than by making him happy too? And anyway, this was what everybody did at the time.

It had been a singular act of passion on his and of ecstasy on her side. However, it resulted in an unwanted pregnancy. Joyce was at the beginning of her career and couldn't afford to be a mother. Larry felt divided: on one hand, he thought this baby would tie Joyce to him, and that was just what he wanted; on the other hand, he was afraid that this baby would ruin his relationship with Joyce, complicate his life, severely restrict his freedom, and altogether just be a pain in the neck. So there were more good reasons not to have this child than to have it. But rather than saying so, he claimed to be concerned that as an artist he might never sell more pictures than Vincent van Gogh, who, as is well known, interested only one buyer for one single painting in his entire life. With this sad example, Larry argued that he might not be able to provide for a family. Joyce nodded. They didn't discuss it a lot. Almost instantaneously they came to the conclusion that even though it was a shame, they couldn't raise this child.

Joyce was lucky: the heavy, visible months of her pregnancy occurred during a long summer break on Broadway, hence none of her colleagues really noticed anything. As soon as her son was born, she gave him up for adoption to an unknown couple who couldn't conceive. She did see and hold him though, at least for half an hour. He was lying on her chest, tiny and wrinkled, darkish and heavily breathing, and while she softly stroked the wet hair that densely covered his big head—*look at you*, she reverently thought, amazed that such a miracle had just slipped out of her, *look at you*—he looked at her with his wide-open, watery-blue eyes, looked as if to absorb and gulp all of her in at once, and his look—his look was like a scalding drop that singed a tiny hole in the middle of who she was. Or was it no more than a mere blip in her life, without any trace? No, impossible that it was lost on her in a flash what a high price she was paying for her freedom, non-refundable as it were—but this was the deal. Is this right, she wondered, am I doing the right thing? Then the lady from the adoption agency came and took him away. That was a strange moment! But life went on. It had just gone through a shock, a secret shakeup, imperceptible for most everybody, like an inexplicable absence that briefly ripples the surface awareness of our friends, and then everything glides back to the familiar places where we don't think too deeply about anything. For Joyce it might have been something like an inner earthquake that briefly connected her with the most ancient fears of mankind, but then, as soon as the glasses on the kitchen counter stopped tinkling and jangling, she took a deep breath and moved on, sort of forgot about it—but not totally. For a while she still wondered: How is he, and how will his new family be? And in the following years, once in a while, when seeing children on the streets right around where she lived, she thought: what if this little boy were my son? But even these thoughts faded away in the dimming light of the day. And who wants to speculate so much about the things that aren't there, when life is exciting, difficult, busy, and a challenge altogether?

Of course, Eddie didn't know about all of this when he first met Joyce at the Ever Lodge. And even Joyce might not have fully realized that there was more than her early successful review as Juliet that pulled her back, time and again, to the area where she had lived in her early years. Anyway, here is what I think could have happened: Larry was convinced that thanks to his support, Joyce was becoming a famous Broadway star, who eventually would be able to cash in a ton of contract money and connect with all sorts of wealthy celebrities—potential clients of his art. So he made plans to go big, to rent a studio and splash or sprinkle lots of oil-paint on large canvasses, anticipating that he would soon be known as a great artist, which he felt he had the potential for, and it's possible that he did. When I grew up there was a little oil painting signed *LB 1952*, so this could be one of his that he gave to Joyce, who then left it to Eddie, who still has it hanging in his kitchen. It shows a slaughtered rooster whose feathers seem to explode in all colors, racing across the canvass and even bursting over the frame, spattering disorderedly all over the wooden casing. It is a small square picture that frightened me when I was little; later I came to enjoy its unbound, albeit somewhat morbid, vibrancy.

Anyway, Larry had some talent and dreamt of himself as a painter, who would exhibit in some of the world's major galleries. Hence he paraded himself with his spirits flying high as an eagle, so high that at first he didn't notice that Joyce wasn't flying with him. Only slowly did it dawn on him that she was spending more and more time away from home—and Larry didn't know why or where or with whom, for heaven's sake! When he finally fully realized that she wasn't with him anymore, he totally freaked out and crashed. So much did he hurt that he threw fits and fists, violently shook her by her arms, smashed Joyce's favorite vase (a round one made of watery blue glass, what a beauty it had been...), and then threatened to stop painting forever, with Joyce being held responsible for the waste of his genius, and finally, after nothing, really nothing, helped to turn her around, he started to drink. A terrible, vicious cycle set in: the more Larry drank, the further he drove Joyce away, and the more she withdrew, the more he drank. He who had been an interesting man with great knowledge and good talent, I would think, was now hanging like a wreck in a rotten chair, gesticulating with a dried out paintbrush, continuously sticking it into the open air like a conductor who wants to orchestrate a whole range of howling feelings while babbling to himself or mumbling to a non-existent world, gibbering something about the decline of the Occident, the maxim of refusal, the resurrection of zealots—and more and more empty wine bottles gathered at his feet.

Was Larry just a goddamned narcissist, an obnoxious parasite who felt entitled to exploit the first, nearly accidental blossoms of Joyce's early fame? Or was he, somewhere deep down where nobody, not even he, could hear it, in a shrieking uproar of anguish, a blazing fire of total despair over having just foolishly lost and recklessly abandoned his son, the only son he would ever have? Joyce didn't know, nor would he care. They simply were too young for these kinds of thoughts and questions. Joyce looked at him, and yes, she felt sorry and sad to see him so broken, but it also angered and disgusted her quite a bit. No way could we have raised this child, she kept thinking over and over, while feeling relief about her decision and deep gratitude for the unknown adoptive parents who would love her son as much as he deserved to be loved, and help him grow up in the safe environment of an orderly family. As the trash between Larry and her piled up higher and higher, she decided to leave him and move out. On September 30th she gave notice to the spinster and departed before Larry had slept off his drunken dreams.

Here I have to make up another small, though decisive, detail about something that helped Joyce a great deal. There was a man, I know there was, but I don't know anything about him, so I call him Jack. This Jack would have been totally mesmerized by Joyce's performance as Juliet, and after having watched her he began to send her flowers in what bordered on an obsession, evening after evening, until he finally summoned up the courage to step into her cloakroom and into her life. He knew he had no right to do so, but he couldn't help wooing and courting her in the smartest, most charming terms. He listened to her and said the right things at the right moments when she was nervous before a performance. He complimented and encouraged her when she had doubts about her life, the adoption of her son, and her future as an actress. He helped her negotiate new contracts, took her out for dinners, brought her little presents like a poetry book, a little sewing bag, a box of dark sweet chocolates, and finally a moonstone pendant on a golden necklace. All of this stretched over several weeks, so that it never felt overwhelming or out of place. Finally he knew that he had fallen in love with her. However, he was 47 years her senior and, with most of his assets entangled with those of his wife, indissolubly married. So he didn't confess.

One night, just when Joyce had moved out of her small SoHo room and was dwelling in the interim on a friend's sofa, Jack told her that he wanted to buy her a nice condominium on Fifth Avenue. It's an incredibly favorable opportunity, he declared, a place owned by a former friend-turned-enemy or rival. This idiot was finally down on his knees in the middle of a horrific bankruptcy—serves him right, Jack added—and now was begging him to buy his Fifth Avenue condo for as little as he was willing to pay, so that later, when all was settled, he could buy it back—which Jack of course would never allow to happen. This is a once-in-a-lifetime chance, Jack said, and explained that for various reasons, he wanted to buy this condo but didn't want to figure as its owner. Hey, he said to Joyce, I'll buy it for you as your gift for tonight! No dinner in addition, you see? And I won't ask for anything in return, I promise. What could be wrong with that? Joyce smiled in disbelief. Where was the hook, she wondered, and fleetingly she felt sorry for this unknown, desperate man who would be evicted and driven out of his home as soon as she nodded her head. Was that right? Was that how she wanted to be? But there she was, the spinster had quickly swept up the broken pieces of her ruined relationship with Larry, and her few things had already been stuffed for short-term storage into the theatre's basement—it would have required the resistance of a giant to say no to such an offer! Still cautious, she said, Okay, I will look at it, can I see it? Ho-ho! Jack hollered, totally taken aback. Are you picky? Joyce blushed and shamefully lowered her eyes.

Of course, life on Fifth Avenue was quite different from the cozy SoHo bohemia—a bit like in a fairy tale castle. This is how I pictured it as a child: The building had a doorman who opened the door for Joyce and greeted her by her name. Stepping into the elevator must have felt like rising up into a mahogany-paneled sky in which the brass buttons of each floor sparkled like shining stars. To get to her condo, Joyce had to push star number 10. Then, stepping out of the elevator, she would walk on a light gray carpet that carried her softly while muffling the sounds of her heels, so that it was almost like she was floating through a corridor of silence to her condo's door, which opened with this soft and distinct *click* she soon came to recognize as the sound of homecoming. The spacious living room looked right into Central Park, reaching out to this incredible, ever-changing view over the trees and lawns, the lake and the impressive silhouette of Central Park West! Farther on, there was a small bedroom with built-in closets, a windowless guestroom that she could use as a garage for her bicycle, a narrow kitchenette—she wasn't big on cooking, anyway—and an oldfashioned, romantic bathroom with a four-legged tub and a shell-shaped sink with two ceramic-handled silver faucets for cold and warm water. What a lovely place! For Joyce, who had just moved out of a slanting garret, it must have felt like the peak of a palace. When she first entered with Jack and his friend's lawyer, who carried the key and the contract, when they came in just to have the look she had asked for, she felt so reverent and incredulous that she could only whisper *how beautiful* over and over, *how beautiful!* And shyly looking at Jack, the businessman, she asked, Are you sure? Are you really sure?

Oh, Jack was sure! His certainty was not only an outgrowth of his love for Joyce, but also an act of revenge launched against his friend-turned-enemy, who many years ago had deeply hurt and almost killed him by seducing his—Jack's—wife at the end of a long, drunken summer night's party when he—Jack—had been pretty much knocked out by the host's generous and unlimited offer of *Château Latour*—who could renounce such an opportunity?—and had lost track of his wife Wendy, only to find her the next morning naked and blissfully asleep in his old friend's hairy arms! The horrendous image instantaneously erected a concrete wall between them that would stay there forever. Wendy was unfaithful only this one time, but once was already too much. Jack continued to love Wendy—albeit now with a splash of regret—and Wendy loved Jack, but he could never touch her again. What a loss and deprivation in his still young and, up to this night, harmonious life. At times it made him bitter and grim; however, in most situations he took on a casual attitude of bonhomie and treated Wendy as respectfully as any other family member. He often wished it could be different, but it wasn't, and there was nothing he could do about it. All of this briefly welled up in him as he entered his old friend's place. When Joyce signed the contract for the condo at the price of one-tenth of its worth, a tired smile of satisfaction flitted through the gray stubble on Jack's cheeks, indicating the final settlement of the bitter dispute he had been carrying out over all these years in his otherwise deserted heart. It was over! Was it over? At least he had been able to do both—resentfully act on an old grudge and generously create a magic moment for his beloved Joyce. That's how life is, over-determined, not so unlike our dreams.

Of course Jack recovered his male passion once the Fifth Avenue condo was made homey. He and Joyce had carefully picked several pieces of nice furniture that made the place so comfortable that Jack could get out of his jacket, open his shirt and tie, and put his feet up on the coffee table. Whenever they discovered that something was missing, Jack would take care of the bill. Time and again Joyce tried to contribute with the income from her engagements on Broadway, but Jack strongly objected. Save the money for later, he suggested, and wouldn't tolerate any opposition. In this sense he behaved like a father determined to take care of his daughter, and Joyce felt safe in his shadow, trusting that he knew what was best for her. But in another sense she sometimes felt as if she had to take on the role of a mother, helping little Jack come to grips with a whole lot of conflicts that enraged him because they made him so anxious. As young as Joyce was, then in her early twenties, there seemed to be a calm and grounded wisdom woven through her thoughts and language, which allowed Jack to relax; she could even have a funny take on all the things he struggled with, and he wouldn't mind. Thus time and again she succeeded in opening him up for some sort of peace with how his life had played out; because despite his stunning economic success—good luck played a big role in it—things had turned out very differently from how he thought they would. And rather than keeping his ideas and dreams high up in the clouds as something to occasionally look, wave, and smile at, Jack was determined to go for them, and when he stumbled he blamed it on everything except his lofty ideas. Nobody could change his attitude, since he hated all objections and could become quite obnoxious, demeaning, and quarrelsome when things didn't go his way. At those times, Joyce kept her mouth shut and patiently waited until he was out of his testy mood; she knew that sometimes it was better to address things later—if at all. Then they would talk about it while strolling through Central Park or sitting on a sunny bench, and when they were done with talking, they would crawl into bed and become lovers like once upon a time...

Mondays and Thursdays were Jack's days. Sometimes as early as the afternoon, or in the evening, he would come to her Fifth Avenue condo or pick her up on Broadway and would stay till she had fallen asleep after midnight. On weekends he was with his family, starting Friday night. Tuesday nights he played tennis with a junior partner at his law firm, and Wednesdays—who knows what he did on Wednesdays, he just didn't come to see Joyce on Wednesdays. On the days he wasn't with her, she was usually busy, performing on stage, learning a new role, doing some household chores, but sometimes she just sat in her living room on the window sill, looking at life in the park, following with her eyes the strollers and runners, the kids and the dogs, and thought about Jack and about her life. She knew it wouldn't go on like this forever, it couldn't, but she had no idea how it would or should change. Everything seemed to have come to a momentary halt that felt slightly numbing but comfortable. The future was elsewhere. Time and again she thought: for now it's just what I want! She plunged into reading Shakespeare and the Greek tragedies, the European classics and Beckett's plays, and of course Arthur Miller and many others, and she was going to every new show on Broadway, seriously studying the actresses' performances in order to learn how to do it and how not. It was a fascinating and fulfilling life.

One Thursday when Jack came for dinner, she surprised him by having put up bookshelves over one wall of her living room; she had done it all by herself and was rightfully proud of this proof of her technical skills. On her new bookshelves she had organized the piles of her readings, and now she would have every book handy whenever she wanted it. Jack struggled a tiny bit with her independence, she noticed, but he said he loved it, and with slightly nervous laughter, he added, You're getting so smart and cultured, soon I will feel like a dumb jackass next to you, to which she gave him a big hug, and beaming at him with her beautiful eyes, she said, Now you really talk like a jackass!

And then one Monday night after more than six years on Fifth Avenue, Jack didn't show up. He wanted to be there for dinner, and she had prepared a nice bouillabaisse and put a bottle of Sancerre in the fridge, but he didn't come, neither as announced at 7 PM, nor later by 9 PM, as sometimes happened when he had difficult negotiations with his clients. He didn't come at all, and Joyce intuitively knew that he would never come again. Still, she was hoping, was feeling upset and concerned, couldn't stop fantasizing about all the possible and impossible reasons for his being held up, and struggled with wanting to call his home or his office the next day. But knowing that Jack had kept her out of his life—or rather a secret in his life—she did none of it. She just stayed home and waited, even called in sick for her performance on Broadway—despite the fact that Tuesdays weren't Jack's days—simply to be there for him if he called or came anyway, maybe, but of course he didn't. She was there and waited.

It wasn't until Wednesday that she learned from the newspaper that Jack had died from a heart attack in his home on Monday morning with his wife Wendy at his side, as the journalist meant to mention in comforting terms. He was gone. Jack and Joyce hadn't been able to say goodbye to each other. They had never talked, hadn't even thought about death—yet death had its own agenda, and no one could object to that. Joyce, who only wore the brightest colors, bought a black raincoat and mixed in with the huge crowd at Jack's memorial service. With amazement and alienation she listened to the speeches given by his cousin, his business partner, the chair of a charity, and the Deputy Director of Finances of New York City. They talked about a man she felt she didn't know. Her Jack was another Jack, and of course she thought she knew the true Jack. She also caught a glimpse of Wendy, actually of not much more than a heap of black fabric, and even guessed to have discovered his friend-turned-enemy, a lone, emaciated man in the last row who sobbed so heartbreakingly that Joyce thought losing any chance of reconciliation might be one of the worst pains a life could bear. She got up and left with everybody else in the middle of the mourning crowd.

Strangely enough, Joyce's career really took off after Jack's death. First she played Cordelia in *King Lear*, and she played her so convincingly that one critic speculated: In order to play this role with so much emotional depth and authenticity Joyce must have profoundly loved her own father! Well, maybe, who knows? What Joyce did know at the premiere of *King Lear* was that playing Cordelia was her very private goodbye to Jack. It was a deeply calming and settling experience for her, and when King Lear carried her dead body onto the open stage wailing *Cordelia, Cordelia! Stay a little!* she had a comforting sense of reunion that released a simple thought of closure: we had our time, and it was good. Then the curtain fell. When she stood up from the floorboards to get ready for an enthusiastically applauding audience, she felt lifted and liberated, as if she had just ended the first big chapter of her life, during which she had still needed a father to lean on and learn from.

The year went by and another spring came. The old dirty mounds of snow in Central Park started to murmur, whisper, and giggle as they melted and trickled along the muddy pathways and down the hollow hallways of the public drainage pipes. Joyce had played Maria in Chekhov's *Three Sisters* on Broadway and travelled with this role around the country for four further months—Boston, Chicago, Atlanta, Dallas, and San Francisco—and everywhere she enjoyed people, premieres, and parties, and with only a bit of additional press work, she was able to add to her growing celebrity status. Still, sometimes she longed to simply hear her special homecoming *click* and be all by herself for a while. She had these strange moods that once in a while quietly pulled her into the blurry drifts of her inner world, where she would float with strange ease and comfort along the maze of secret images, thoughts, or mere sensations—she couldn't say what they were, just something vaguely sweet to get lost in. Then she would sit for hours on her bed, gently stroking her little toes without even noticing it, until a sense of peace allowed her to give it a rest or fall asleep.

A few times she had gone back to the pubs where Larry and his buddies used to hang out, but he had been so nasty to her that she had given up on wanting to keep any friendly contact with her past. Also, she liked being on her own. Some lovers had come and gone, a few stayed only for the night, others wanted more, even marriage, but she wasn't sure. For a little while she was in love with Alberto, a young actor from Venezuela. They met in a coffee shop on Broadway where the actors and actresses hang out with their friends. Alberto didn't have an engagement, he didn't have much of an income, and since Joyce really liked him, she asked him to move in with her on Fifth Avenue. They got along very well. But after a few weeks a friend from Caracas called to offer him a position at the National Theatre, and Alberto accepted and decided to leave. Joyce was upset, so upset that it surprised her. Alberto was sorry to hurt her, but he had to follow this promising career opportunity. When he parted, Joyce sobbed on his shoulder, hard and dry. He stroked her back and waited till she was ready to let him go. Then he picked up his backpack and sunglasses and walked out the door and through the quietness of the hallway, at the end of which the elevator took him in, and after a long moment in which it seemed that time stood still and everything could have taken another turn, the door closed and cut off his last wave goodbye. For a few months Joyce and Alberto exchanged postcards. However, their work and separate lives were demanding, and more and more they drifted apart and finally let go for good. But sometimes when she went to bed, Joyce slipped into Alberto's yellow t-shirt that she had found in the laundry basket, and hugging herself, she imagined his arms all around her, which helped her fall asleep with a funny smile on her face.

Then one year, on the first of January, when everybody in New York was still pondering whether to sleep in or wake up, Joyce got a call from movie director Woody Allen, who asked her if she wanted to play in his next movie an outrageous and self-absorbed, totally inconsiderate hippie and drop-out girl, Maggie, who lived in an oak tree in Central Park, much to the chagrin if not horror of her sister Karen, a successful and renowned psychoanalyst—a role assigned to Diane Keaton—who practiced in an elegant office on Park Avenue and would of course fear for her reputation, since her obnoxious little drop-out sister shamelessly took to holding very personal and revelatory lectures from high up in the oak. Maggie would speak with great delight and enthusiasm, Woody Allen explained, in particular because Karen's analytic patients would regularly visit after their sessions, and on weekends flock to the tree, sitting cross-legged on the lawn around the big trunk, and looking up to Maggie, as if she were a priest on a church's pulpit, they would hungrily absorb the words that she sprinkled down on them like breadcrumbs: for instance, she would make up what a mean sister Karen had been—everybody could relate to that—how much money her sister earned—something everybody was interested in—how her love-life was or rather wasn't—which everybody was even more curious about, and so on. Whatever occurred to Maggie as the insight of the moment, she would freely share with her fans, and she would also answer every question raised, no matter how odd or peculiar—and Karen's patients were peculiar. Woody Allen said that the details of this role could still be discussed and partly created on scene. He also said that he was inspired by Italo Calvino's novel *The Baron in the Trees* as well as by a great scene in Fellini's *Amacord*, namely the moment when Titta's crazy uncle Teo is up in a huge tree screaming *Voglio una donna!*—what an unforgettable moment! In his movie it would be the other way around—the crazy people on the lawn, the woman in the tree—and in this sense, Woody Allen said, his movie should be more comical than Calvino's novel, more an homage to Fellini. He hadn't decided yet whether to call the movie *Maggie in the Oak* or *The Oak Treatment*. He also mentioned that he didn't have a lot of money, but he thought Joyce might be great in this particular role, which he actually had written with her in mind. So, would she consider? How high is the oak? Joyce cautiously asked, and explained: I cannot promise I won't get dizzy up there! Woody Allen immediately understood. I'm acrophobic too, he empathized with her, so I can assure you that I'll be most sympathetic should you get scared or dizzy up there. By the way, the movie will end with me, playing one of Karen's patients, climbing up the tree to move in with the hippie-sister, and to be honest: thinking of acrobatically extending myself to get up to Maggie, already gives me nightmares! Fair enough, Joyce said, I'll do it.

The movie became a big success in many countries, and particularly in big cities like New York and Buenos Aires, where half of the citizens are either analysts or in analysis, and for them Woody Allen's picture was a true feast. Some years ago I saw it on DVD, and I liked it a lot! It's fun to trace how over the years Woody Allen has taken on psychoanalysts, always in a teasing way, which I think is a declaration of love. But of course, most of all I was curious to see Joyce in the movie. I hardly recognized her, dressed as she was in some sort of Neanderthal costume, cowering on a big oak branch (my father told me the branch was actually placed only three feet above ground in the movie studio, which made things much easier for everybody); she looked wild, dirty, and like a snotty-nosed brat, not so esoteric and sensitive as in other pictures. Anyway, for Joyce this role was a blessing because it was her entry into the world of movies, and even though none of her later movies were really a hit, she would have some exciting experiences in and around the hills of Hollywood, and get on safe ground financially, which allowed her not to worry about how to maintain her Fifth Avenue condo, and how to live a good life without bothering all that much with realities—and this was crucial for her, because, I think, Joyce was a dreamer.

Altogether life went quite well for Joyce. But why had she cut all ties with her family? My father said Joyce didn't like to talk about it. What she did tell him, though, was that her father had been a watchmaker and her mother a piano teacher. Both were openminded and seemed to have supported her interest in the arts, which was rather unusual for the time and place she grew up in, some small town in Georgia in the late thirties and forties, where life was governed by the simple and strict rules that drove all color out of her days and her suspicious neighborhood. She had told my father that she had a brother, Craig, 13 years older, who she had missed out on getting to know very well before he left home, so she had nothing much to remember about him, except that over the span of several years, he starred for her in an abundance of fantasies, in which he became the romantic hero of her secret daydreams, a guy she fashioned for herself as not unlike Humphrey Bogart, alone in some unknown and faraway place like Casablanca—and Joyce had always wondered how Bogart's story could have continued after Ingrid Bergman took off with her husband. In reality Craig had gone to Los Angeles, from which he had once sent her a birthday card letting her know that he was working a number of jobs in order to earn the money to later go to college. Then he stopped writing her, and she sort of forgot about him. Joyce also told Eddie that she'd had a little sister, Leslie, who died at age 11 by either mistakenly stepping or else voluntarily jumping into the street when the school bus drove by. Joyce said that Leslie's death completely arrested her family life. Nobody dared to wonder openly whether Leslie had killed herself, a possibility only corroborated by the fact that she had burned her diary on the day before the accident. But why would an 11year-old want to kill herself? Eddie once spelled out this simple question, but Joyce shrugged him off. So he let it go. But she maintained that it was only after Leslie's death that she became a shoplifter. When Eddie first saw it happening in a grocery store, he thought it was a joke, a kind of typical Joyce-thing. Out again on the street, he laughed and said, You are a lovely thief, but I am an equally fabulous detective, so I saw you slipping the small jar of olives into your pocket. Why didn't you choose the pâté two steps further down the row? That would have made for a perfect dinner! His words were nothing but a tender tease, but Joyce didn't react as if she enjoyed her stealthy misdeed. Without a word of response she turned around, hastily walked away, and not granting it a single look, she threw the olive jar into the next trashcan as she steamed by.

PAUL

And then at some point—I'm really confused about the times...what year was that? I think my father always remained vague about it, or maybe I haven't paid attention. It seems they had already lived together on 5th Avenue for a couple of years—anyway, I know that at some point Paul arrived in the picture. It could have been on a Saturday afternoon. Jim, the doorman, called them up while they were having a late brunch, both still in their bathrobes sitting at the window table looking out over Central Park. Joyce had her feet on Eddie's lap, and Eddie softly stroked her soles while they discussed a new product idea for Eddie's young toy company *FIXIT*, which had taken off with amazing speed—and he hadn't even found a fitting logo for it. So there was this phone call with Jim saying a woman and a little boy had asked to speak with Eddie. A woman and a little boy? She doesn't want to give her name, Jim said, but she looks pleasant and has promised she won't bother for long. Eddie sighed and wanted to get dressed to go down to meet them in the lobby, but Joyce didn't want their brunch to end so abruptly; also she was a bit curious about this nameless woman. Stay, she suggested, let them come up. You look fine in your bathrobe. Both thought the visit had to do with *FIXIT*'s first toy on the market, the *Magic Man,* which had become so popular that it had sold out several times in its first ten months. The *Magic Man* was a colorful plastic figure, which could be taken totally apart and remade into lots of other figures, for instance it could become a woman, a monster, a car, a gun, a dog and lots of other fabulous things—it really was amazing, and Eddie had been smart to patent it before starting its production. Guess the kid wants a *Magic Man*, Eddie said, and went to the dark room to pick one up and have it handy as a present when the two of them arrived.

However, when he opened the door, he was struck! The woman standing in the doorframe—a slim lady, tastefully dressed in a beige outfit with a white silk blouse, purse, and high heel shoes in light brown—was his college teacher! She looked at him with a shy though calm smile and simply said, Hi Eddie! At her hand, one step behind her, the little boy of about five or six years fearfully stared at Eddie, as if he already knew his fate and was desperately trying to avoid it. But his mother stayed firm. This is Paul, your son, Eddie's teacher said, and looked straight into Eddie's eyes. Then there was silence, the silence of shock, a shock that momentarily shut down all of Eddie's thoughts and feelings. He looked at the little boy, the *Magic Man* lamely dangling from his hand, and felt incredibly helpless and dumb. Joyce, who had stayed sitting at her fauteuil rubbing her feet and watching the scene from behind, got up and cautiously stepped closer. Eddie managed to awkwardly introduce the two: Joyce—Judy. Hi, Joyce said, and suggested that the two come in so that they could close the door to the hallway. She pulled two more chairs to the window table, invited everybody to sit down, quickly removed the dishes, cleaned the table with a few strokes, and placed a fresh cup of coffee in front of Judy and a glass of orange juice in front of little Paul. I didn't know... Eddie eventually tried to say something. I know, Judy interrupted him, I didn't tell you, I'm sorry, I should have. But I didn't want to make it public, and when Paul was born, you had already graduated and left. Would it have made a difference? Eddie didn't say a thing. I figured the child was my responsibility, Judy continued. Don't get me wrong: I'm not here to complain. Actually, we had some very good years! My parents were willing to help out, they were all crazy about Paul, she added with a smile and tenderly shifted some strands of hair from Paul's eyes, thereby removing his last hideout. Really good grandparents, she added, and he loved them. Unfortunately they passed away last year—in quick succession, only six weeks apart from each other. They had been married for more than sixty years, so when my father died, my mother didn't want to live on any longer—even though she wasn't alone, Paul and I were living with her.

For a while they were quiet, all four sensing how every word now would bring them closer to the end of their former and the beginning of a new and totally unknown life. Luckily I read

67

about you in the newspapers when the *Magic Man* came out, Judy continued. Paul got one, even from the first edition—he called it his *Magic Dad*, some kind of a superman, I guess—right Paul? Paul didn't move. When I read about you, I started to tell Paul about his father, how we met when you were in your last year of college and how we sort of dated for a little while...I told him what a sweet and funny man you are, what a good basketball player—Paul too is already quite good at making baskets, aren't you, Paul? Paul remained frozen in his chair. Last month I was diagnosed with late-stage metastatic pancreatic cancer, Judy finally said with her voice dry and factual, as if she were reporting a new scientific discovery. There isn't much one can do about it, and therefore I don't think that I even want to go through any treatment except of course palliative care at the end—which might come very soon. That's why I'm here. That's why we came today.

At this point the afternoon sun would push through the big white clouds, dramatically pouring a gush of red light over the four pale faces. My goodness! What challenging news on what had been an ordinary, unsuspecting Saturday afternoon! Eddie looked at Judy, who now appeared to him so much older than she had when for a short while he was her student with a total crush on her. She had come in as a replacement for a colleague who suddenly had to take a leave of absence, and from the moment she entered the classroom he had felt electrified, he couldn't say exactly by what—maybe by her smile when she looked at them, or the slow swing of her movements when she walked from the door to her desk, where she put down her purse and some books, or was it the Italian ring of her name that she wrote on the blackboard, Judy Salentino, or her joyous laughter when someone made a funny comment, or her cute gesture of repeatedly pushing her long black hair out of her face? He hadn't been able to concentrate on anything she was teaching. After a few days of being totally out of sorts and in sheer amazement whenever he saw her in class, he made use of her office hour, pretending to discuss a difficulty with his paper, but actually only to be near her, a request that was granted to him and more—it hadn't taken long for this consultation to heat up, so much so that Judy decided to lock the door to her office in order to prevent anybody else from consulting her. Had he loved her? Looking at this fine lady in her silk blouse and designer suit, he briefly wondered about this before drifting back to the luscious, exuberant, vibrant woman in his arms, who had cooed and gasped under his juvenile passion—while he had the most amazing lessons of his college years before the regular teacher resumed her work and Judy vanished without prior notice. How strange that they never said goodbye to each other or explicitly ended their affair, Eddie now thought. One Wednesday morning the old teacher simply showed up again, naturally replacing Judy. He remembered how his first surprise had quickly turned into a subtle mix of disappointment and relief—*it was over!* For the following few weeks he nervously kept watching out when walking through the building's corridors, hoping and fearing to run into her and not knowing if she still expected him to come for further consultations. In fact he had only once seen her again from afar walking across the campus, but hadn't dared or even wanted to catch up with her—he thought it was better for both of them to just let it go. Maybe she already knew at the time that she was pregnant, he now thought, maybe she had already decided to not tell him when he was still around, he now wondered, and maybe she had only allowed him to have sex with her because she wanted a baby no matter how and from whom? This latter thought snuck up on him as something ugly—the terrible suspicion of having been harvested and the fruit secretly stolen from him. He suddenly felt shabby. But then again: hadn't he pushed for it and ignored all concerns, not even thought of any consequences? Eddie slightly shook his head as if to shake off these troubling ideas—and looked over to Judy. What would Judy be thinking?

Maybe Judy thought: Here's Eddie. living on 5th Avenue, and again with an older woman! That first! Then she would wonder if Paul could live here with Eddie and Joyce and how this would be for him, and trying to imagine him sitting at this window table in what would become his home, her heart painfully contracted to a small fist that wanted to pound on her mean cancer, pound it and smash it—she took a deep breath. If only she could live long enough to bring Paul up! If only she knew anybody else to take care of her son. But maybe she had no right to decide this for him. Paul had a father, and whether she liked it or not, Eddie was the father he had. They would have to manage and get along, one

70

way or another. Paul was a smart kid and would make it. Would Joyce be good to him? Were they married? Could an actress be a real person? She looked at Joyce, who seemed so much more normal in her bathrobe than in the photos of her various roles. Strangely enough there was something about Joyce that Judy liked, she couldn't say what, but she felt sympathetic toward her.

Joyce noticed Judy look at her and smile. Poor woman, she thought, she has to give away her child—like I did; but for her it must be worse. She is deeply bound to her son, she loves him, while I...? Where is my son now? How might he be living? Did his foster parents take good care of him? Is Judy asking us to take care of Paul? It seems as if Judy is saying Eddie is his father and now, since she won't be able to carry on, he has to take over. Joyce looked at little Paul, who in fact looked like a carbon copy of Eddie—no doubt, he was his son.

Paul was sitting on the edge of his chair like a stone in the Holocene, thinking: It's not going to happen! It's not going to happen! It's not going to happen! It's not going to happen! It's not going to happen! But his magic wasn't working so well, at least not immediately, because instead of getting up to leave with him, his mother continued to explain that she had no further relatives except a cousin who had lived his whole life in a mental institution and didn't even recognize her when she visited once in a while. Also from a legal point of view there shouldn't be any problem or need for adoption and the like because, when Paul was born, she had taken the liberty of putting Eddie's name as the lawful biological father on the birth certificate, not with the intention to raise any claim of support from him but in order to honestly state whose son he was, so that Paul could seek out, find, and contact his father, should he wish to do so. Further, she said that Paul wouldn't be without means because she had established a life insurance policy with Paul as the beneficiary, and he would also inherit her house, which had been the house of his grandparents, and given that it was situated right next to the campus of the University of Pennsylvania, it should sell for a considerable price, and this money would go to a trust fund in Paul's name; all that would certainly pay for his whole education, including possibly a boarding school and later an Ivy League college and graduate school. Judy's points were thoroughly thought through, the plan totally fleshed out with no loose ends to pull at, and there wasn't much Eddie could think of saying at the moment, except how sorry he felt that Judy had gotten so sick, for which Judy thanked him politely. Before they finally left, Judy placed a little lavender colored card with her address and phone number next to her untouched cup of coffee, and said: Please be in touch soon! Eddie nodded and walked them to the door. Paul briefly glanced at Joyce but didn't deign to look at his father. His head lowered, he left the room as if he had just been sentenced for life.

Four months later Judy died. Joyce and Eddie had visited her and the child three times in Philadelphia, each time on their way back taking the car's trunk full of Paul's clothes, books, and toys so that he would have something of his own at the 5th Avenue apartment on the day he arrived there for good. A week before Judy died, Eddie went to Philadelphia and stayed with her in her old-fashioned mansion, the place where Judy had grown up and where Paul had spent the first years of his life. Eddie put his few things in the guest room facing right onto the university campus, and in a flash he saw her again walking across the green lawn and briefly wondered what different turn his life would have taken had he called and caught up with Judy back then. Would she have told him about her pregnancy? After college he had stayed three more years in Philadelphia. It would have been easy to find him had she tried. She hadn't. Or he could have seen her with a baby carriage somewhere in the streets—would she have told him then? No, he didn't think so.

Judy called, and Eddie went downstairs to the living room where the hospice had put up a medical bed for her that made her more comfortable and facilitated her care. Judy was very weak and often dozed off from the morphine, but Eddie and she had some good and important conversations. Most of all Judy wanted to tell Eddie all he needed to know about Paul. She asked Eddie to read the diaries she had written for Paul starting on day one of his life. Also she went with him through the photo albums and shared her pleasure and her tears of farewell in explaining all the different events in the pictures that she had documented so carefully and that Eddie now needed to know about as well. She wrote down a list of Paul's likes and dislikes, noted his few allergies, the names and phone numbers of his friends and beloved Kindergarten teachers. It clearly comforted her to talk about all of this at great length. However, when Eddie wanted to talk with her about the end of their affair, she declined. Let it be, she said, but she took his hand and held it for a while, and later she leaned her cheek against it in what seemed like a tender moment, only to abruptly withdraw when Paul walked in—still, Paul had seen it, responding with a hostile glance at Eddie and quickly climbing onto her bed and snuggling into her arm. Eddie understood, got up, and left the room for a while. At one point Judy lightly asked him about Joyce, who would become Paul's stepmother, and Eddie told her that he wasn't married to Joyce but loved her and that she was a good and generous woman. That was all Judy wanted to know. She also asked him a little about him, why he hadn't gone to graduate school and what he planned to do with *FIXIT*, but she really couldn't concentrate on much other than Paul and her concerns for his upbringing. In the evenings Eddie called Joyce; he spoke with her a bit about the day and told her how important it was for everybody that he spent these days with Judy—the days that according to her doctors would be her last.

In the afternoon before she died, Judy had been restless and somewhat confused. When they had dinner, with Paul sitting at the left side of her bed and Eddie at her right, she had asked Paul three times about his homework, even though Paul was only in Kindergarten in those days; repeatedly demanded the medicine she had already taken; and wanted to make a phone call first to her mother and then to the medical director of a research center in Dallas that she had once contacted when she was first diagnosed with cancer. She also didn't want to eat and dropped the glass of orange juice she had requested, and the sweet, sticky nectar spilled over her comforter, which then needed to be changed. Finally, after 10 PM she fell asleep, and Eddie told Paul to go to bed, promising he would watch over his mother and wake him up if needed. Reluctantly Paul walked to the door, his anxious eyes glued to his mother, who at that point slept with her mouth open, heavily breathing. As it seemed that Paul had trouble detaching himself from his mother, Eddie got up and wanted to take his hand to walk him to his room, but Paul furiously pushed him away, ran down the hallway to his room, and slammed the door. Eddie understood but felt weary and unsure how he would manage the child without Judy. When he returned to Judy's bedside, she slept quietly, and Eddie sat down next to her thinking of all the things he would have to do once she passed away.

Later a nurse from the hospice came to check on her, and since Judy was sleeping and didn't seem to need more morphine, she left, wishing Eddie a good night. Not a moment later, Judy opened her eyes, now all clear, and said: Is she gone? Eddie nodded. Lock the door, Judy demanded. I have locked it, don't worry, Eddie responded. Come here, Judy said, patting the side of her bed to indicate what she meant. Eddie got up and sat down at the end of her bedside. Come closer, would you, please? Eddie moved a bit closer. Judy obviously wanted to say something, for which she seemed to struggle to find the right words, but finally she took his hand, and squeezing it hard, she said: I wanted to thank you for giving me Paul—you know Paul—Paul was the best thing in my life! Her face drew a painful, crooked smile. Thank you—thank you—thank you, she reiterated with increasing urgency that made Eddie uncomfortable, but feeling the poignancy of the moment, he tried to reassure her: It's okay, Judy, everything is fine, relax! Yet instead of calming down, Judy became more agitated and struggled to rise, spurred by a desperate surge of desire to hold on to her life and lover, her bygone lover, who once had changed everything and now should do so again, in the here and now, right now. She gripped him with bony fingers, with a raptor's claws, in this confusing hunger for sex that grabbed him by his neck and pulled him down, down on these dissolving contours of her sweat-damp nightgown, closer, closer, here, here, she panted, and forcing the terror into his eyes, and squeezing an anxious scream out of his chest: Leave it, Judy, leave it—she gave it all and all to him, and as much as he instinctively tried to wrest himself free, she sank and fiercely dragged him onto her, drowning him, mouthing her kiss of death between his open lips—this kiss that freed her from all that her comforter had muffled, while he, in the grip of his agony—or was it hers?—tried to struggle himself out of this blue-ringed octopus' thousand bruised arms and legs clutched all around him—let me go!—but behind her back the pillow now reared up to two big bloated wings as if to powerfully rush down on him and bury him under the passion of death. All fractured. All flew in pieces. Paul, she mumbled, Paul...! Then she let go, softened and weakened all of a sudden, sinking back onto her pillow, which now framed her thin, haggard head with its deep-seated, dark-circled eyes in their cavernous crypts like in a coffin, while her dry, sunken lips murmured Paul, and once again Paul...before her eyes turned upwards and elsewhere, blank, and her left hand fell off his shoulder, while her right hand still clung to his arm—then she stopped breathing. Judy had passed away. A pillbox dropped to the floor and rolled somewhere, slicing the sudden silence with its loud and mundane clunk. She was dead. With the horror of death in his heart, and choking from an overwhelming disgust, Eddie got up and away from her and her dead body that lay there, strangely obscene in the final defeat of its futile desire, disorderedly sprawled over the bed, this medical bed—her deathbed. *Oh god...!* Eddie thought. And in his effort to smooth over the assault of death, he rushed to rearrange her sheets and straighten her comforter, so that it would look as if she had peacefully died in her sleep—when his eyes caught the door and little Paul standing there in his pajamas, icily staring at the scene that he had watched in most of its entirety, and it hit Eddie right away that Paul would never forgive him for what he had seen. Eddie stood rooted to the spot, not knowing what to say. I hate you! Paul hissed, turned around and left.

Maye *hate* became part of Paul's mission. When I once asked my father about the time when Paul moved in with him, he only dryly said: It was difficult, clearly understating his assessment.

Paul came to 5th Avenue, obdurate and with a big *NO* written on his forehead as he was struggling with an endless stream of fantasies, in which he wielded his knife against Eddie, slashing his throat, piercing his chest, all to retaliate against him for his loss and restore his mother's innocence. He relished trashing his *Magic Dad* not without having him first thoroughly dismembered and destroyed, the pieces demonstratively displayed on the window table above Central Park. He refused to eat with Eddie and Joyce and refused to eat at all unless he could take his plate into the dark room, which had become his room, immediately closing the door and, since Eddie had taken away the key to lock it, he pushed his bedside table in front of it in order to bar anybody from coming in. This has to stop, Eddie said to Joyce. Give him time, it's part of his mourning, Joyce responded. But Paul's angry grief raged on, and finally Eddie took him to a child psychoanalyst close by on Park Avenue, so that Paul would be able to attend his sessions by going there on his own. Dr. Mesmer, who agreed to work with Paul, was a nice lady about the age of Paul's late mother, and that might have helped to get Paul to agree to go to her office five times a week. It cost a fortune, but Eddie took it from Paul's funds, justifying it as part of his education. In fact, soon the tension around Paul slightly decreased, and when Dr. Mesmer came up with the idea to enroll Paul into a private Boarding School in New York, one of the few who even took first graders, so that he would be at school during the week and only join Eddie and Joyce on the weekends, all three breathed a sigh of relief.

On the evening of Paul's first day at the Boarding School, Eddie came home with a bottle of champagne, a big jar of Russian caviar, and a French baguette to celebrate their renewed freedom. To us! Eddie said when they touched glasses, to which Joyce rejoined with: To love and life! Not having to be on guard for the first time in weeks, they realized how much they had felt taken hostage by Paul's mere presence, and how afraid they had been of the hostile looks he used to fling at them like deadly missiles from the corners of his dark room. Now all doors were open, and the place was theirs again. I'll be our disk-jockey tonight. Let's hear what The Mamas and the Papas have to teach us, Eddie joked, and before the needle went down on the record, he sang: Monday, Monday, so good to me...! Well that sounds just right! Both laughed, hummed with the music, and later they enjoyed hearing more of their favorites: Eric Clapton, Diana Ross, Cat Stevens, and of course The Beatles (my father still likes to play this music once in a while, now from his CD collection). Sometimes they spontaneously got up and danced. Joyce put her feet on Eddie's lap, and he stroked her soles. Thank you for being so patient with Paul, Eddie said. I didn't mind this whole mess with him too much, Joyce replied. You didn't? Eddie was surprised. I sure did, he emphasized. Joyce thoughtfully smiled—and there it was again, Eddie could see it right in front of him: the hint of some mystery, something like the shadow of an obscure ache that probably attracted him when they first met and that he had set out to completely disperse—and for a long time he believed it had vanished, only to see it now reemerge in her flickering eyes. What is it? Eddie cautiously asked. What's troubling you, tell me...!

This was a moment of choice. Joyce somehow felt the danger of bringing this up—and had she decided not to answer, everything still might have sunken back into the graveyard of history. Yet she felt an urge to tell her story, a force so compelling that she gave in. Joyce told Eddie what she had been thinking about in all these weeks since Paul's arrival: that she too had a son but didn't know anything about him or his whereabouts; that she was very young and had just started her career as an actress when she got pregnant; that at the time she felt she couldn't raise a child, and that therefore she gave him up for adoption shortly after he was born! Eddie was surprised and wondered why she had never told him about it. Joyce said that she had sort of forgotten about it—but of course not really; so when Paul moved in and was so angry at them, she felt he had a right to be angry, and she wanted to make up with him for what she had missed out on with her own son. She had started to become increasingly obsessed with thoughts about her son, she said, it was as if he continually looked at her wherever she was, whatever she did, at night before she fell asleep, in the morning when she woke up, during the day when she walked to the theatre, and on stage when she was waiting in the wings, sometimes even while she was acting her part on the stage. She said, sometimes he looked sad, and sometimes he looked angry, or he seemed lost or anxious or helpless—he made her feel terrible! She was wondering whether her son knew that he was adopted; and if he did, did he hate his unknown mother for giving him away? She said she didn't even know his name or the name of the couple that adopted him; at the time she had been told that she shouldn't be in contact with them, and that it would be better for all if she didn't even try. Your ways will part here, the adoption agent had stated, forget that you had this child; you have no son anymore.

Eddie was slightly shocked when he heard this, not as shocked as he was when Paul turned up at his doorstep, but still he felt amazingly numbed by the news. Finally he said: It was a good and brave thing for you to have this child and give him up for adoption. You just were young, too young to be a mother, I understand that. But these words didn't seem to carry much comfort to Joyce. I'm not so sure anymore that I was too young to have this baby, she responded. And see—I never got pregnant again, and now I sometimes miss having a child, to hold it, to see it growing up...There was nothing more to say. The lightness of the evening was gone. While the champagne slowly warmed and fizzed out of their glasses, both looked over to the magically illuminated skyline of Central Park West right onto the Dakota Building where John Lennon had been killed a few weeks earlier, at gunpoint, something they still hadn't been quite able to fathom.

Maybe this is the secret my father doesn't want to tell me: maybe Joyce died from missing her son...a mother's broken heart kind of thing! Once the bottle was opened, this nameless ghost billowed hugely and spread everywhere, pervaded their normal conversations with a sense of banality, intruded their lovemaking with the shadow of wrong, and stained their previously enjoyable commonplace activities with a whiff of transience. First Eddie had thought that perhaps Paul could replace the son Joyce had missed out on, which in turn could help him to develop a sense of being a father, a good father if possible. He put some effort into joining Joyce in her weekend activities with Paul. They went to the zoo, took a boat ride in the harbor, attended sports events at school, and so on. However, as the months wore on, Eddie felt that Joyce's preoccupation with Paul on the weekends was exaggerated, really beyond normal. As soon as Paul walked through the door on Friday afternoons, her face lit up, and from that moment on she seemed to only have eyes for him. She did include Eddie in her *kid's-fun-plans*, as she called them, but more as the provider of tickets, organizer of gatherings, or chauffeur to events than as her partner in the experience. In Eddie's view Joyce wanted Paul just for herself, and Paul only wanted to be with Joyce. He felt excluded.

But this wasn't the full picture. My father once told me that in the beginning he didn't quite know how to be a father. When speaking to Paul, his voice often sounded harsher than intended; he didn't hesitate to occasionally slap his son over the back of his head; he didn't care that Paul winced when he gave him suggestions that came across as orders; and he was unmoved when Paul cried because Eddie had yelled at him. Did he think this boy needed to toughen up? I wonder if paternal tenderness grows on the grounds of first caring for an infant? Paul had marched into his father's life already grown to an oedipal rival, and there was little that could soften the unavoidable clash between the two.

At his first Christmas in New York, when Paul presented Eddie with a broken fire engine that he had tried to fix with cardboard, Eddie gave it a depreciative look, and his first thought was: Paul just gives me what is broken, the things he cannot use anymore. But maybe Paul gave him what was broken because he hoped that his father could fix it? In fact Paul had carefully studied Eddie's toy collection and noticed that all the items were crooked, broken, or oddly fixed, and he had taken great care in patching his fire engine to fit Eddie's standard. Somehow Eddie must have liked it anyway, because it ended up in his collection. However, more often than not Eddie got irritated with Paul, in particular when Paul acted against the basic rules of family life. For instance, Paul left his dirty sneakers and filthy socks wherever he took them off, dropped half of his clothes that were supposed to go into the laundry basket on the living room carpet, and stacked the bathroom and kitchen corners with his tattered comic books and kids' magazines, thus edging the ugly trace of rebellion in Eddie's need for an orderly, comfortable, and aesthetic world. Knowing how allergic Eddie was to this mess, Joyce hurried to pick up after Paul, collected, folded, organized, and piled up what he dumped down—only to see the whole place cluttered again shortly after. Eddie hated how Joyce enslaved herself to Paul's obnoxious behavior and told her to stop it. Joyce defended her actions by putting forward that she only did this because Eddie was such a control freak, and she wanted to avoid getting into a fight about it, which, however, was exactly what they did. He should clean up his own mess, Eddie stated. Give him a break! Joyce demanded, he is little and has to adjust to a lot of changes right now. Eddie wanted to counter that Paul wasn't her son but his, so he should be the parental authority, but he managed to bite his tongue, because he didn't want to remind Joyce that *she had no son anymore.*

When they got into these fights, Paul seemed to gleefully watch them argue. With an air of innocence he then would ask Joyce if she could help him with his schoolwork, and when she agreed and sat down with him at the window table, Paul would slowly shuffle his chair close beside hers, and eventually—Eddie had no idea how—manage to sit on her lap, leaning his head at her bosom and rubbing his naked foot at her thigh, seemingly lost in thought. To see the two of them enjoying their homey intimacy under the pretense of doing schoolwork needled Eddie with jealousy. He is nearly eight years old, he reprimanded Joyce later, it is totally inappropriate that he would sit on your lap like a baby! But Joyce only laughed at him and called him prudish, which offended Eddie, since it seemed to be Joyce who had grown distant and prudish over the weekends ever since Paul had walked in on them one night when they had been having sex. He seemed to have stood there in the door watching them for quite a while before his cold feet betrayed him with a sneeze, and Eddie and Joyce discovered the intruder. Eddie was furious! He could have killed Paul right on the spot, and he would at least have belted him one, hadn't Joyce, despite her nakedness, held him back, and scantily covering herself by pulling the bed sheet around her—a move that momentarily exposed Eddie and his still erect penis to Paul's hostile inspection—she rushed over and brought little Paul to his room, staying there for a long time softly talking with him until Eddie was so frustrated that he got himself a beer, lit a cigarette—something they actually had agreed on not doing when Paul was with them—and flipped through the TV programs in search for an action movie. *Fuck it*, Eddie thought, *fuck it!*

Later Joyce joined him, and for a while they watched this boring movie about a serial killer who slaughtered prostitutes in the neighborhood of where he had grown up and was chased by a gang of pimps as well as a squad of police detectives—just the usual thing. When the movie stopped for a commercial break, Joyce said: I'm sorry for the interruption. It wasn't you who interrupted, Eddie retorted. I know, Joyce said, but I stayed too long. I wanted to talk with him. I think I understand him. So what do you understand, Eddie charged. Let's not talk about this now, Joyce cautioned. Silently and without touching they continued sitting next to each other, lonely and hurt, staring at the TV screen, both lost in their own meandering worries. For sure, some weekends went by on a lighter note. But when they clashed like this, it often took Eddie and Joyce several days to recover some natural sense of intimacy and trust, and then they dreaded Friday coming about and again having to walk on eggshells throughout the weekend.

Soon Eddie figured that Paul, rather than being the remedy and replacement son for Joyce, had turned into a bigger challenge than he was prepared to handle. Joyce withdrew more frequently into her own world or was swayed by waves of melancholia and cranky moods. Despite all the passion and charm Eddie employed, at times he didn't manage to win her back, and when he failed and continued to fail, he could get so furious that he would simply demand her attention or even force himself on her, for which he later apologized, only to get this sad smile in response that made him feel bad and mad and altogether unfairly blamed and abandoned by Joyce, whose heart and mind seemed totally hijacked by something—a memory that nearly wasn't, but now was all she cared about. In his desperate struggle to recapture his central place in her life, he finally gave birth to an elaborate project—and as is typical for my father, once he gets an idea in his head, he doesn't let go until he has realized it. That's probably why *FIXIT* was so successful. The project he secretly developed was to find Joyce's real son, or at least to find something out about him or the couple that had adopted him. If Joyce could somehow reconnect with her own son, Eddie thought, she might stop obsessing about Paul, which was his main objective—besides his wish to make her happy and win her back. All he had was the name of the agency Joyce once had mentioned in passing, but that was already a good start.

I don't envy my father for that phase of his life, but I also think Paul wasn't just a nasty kid, and my father, who always wants things his way, definitively was too hard on him. I don't know how Paul understood all of this. He was so young! He had learned that dead people don't show up again, but he couldn't really fathom that his mother was one of them. At the memorial service when her white coffin with a big bouquet of white roses on top stood in front of the altar, he first thought that she was in it, and he would have liked to look at her and find out how she was doing. While people were giving speeches and the organ was playing the kind of music his mother liked to hear on Sundays after breakfast, he came up with some smart ideas about how he could open the lid without making the rose bouquet slip down, and how he would check on her as soon as the others were gone. But when the iron door behind the altar opened, and he saw the coffin being rolled right into the blazing flames of the crematory, he decided that his mother was still in the hospital and that the coffin contained her sick sheets that needed to be burned. Hence at the end of the memorial service he wanted to go to the hospital, whereas his father resolved to drive back to New York, and it was right then and there, in front of the church where everybody still lingered to share sadness, memories, and concerns before leaving, that they had their first big fight. To the pitying looks of all bystanders Paul screamed and kicked and threw himself on the wet ground when Eddie wanted him to get into his car, because Paul was used to going to the hospital by train; but when Joyce asked him why he wanted to go by train and not in the car, he wouldn't tell her, since he didn't want to betray his mother and give away where she was hiding.

From that day on he often had a dream: He is taking the train to the hospital, but then the doorman doesn't want to let him in, and when he finally manages to sneak past him, he cannot remember what floor he used to go to, and then he gets lost in the long corridors stuffed with empty beds and blinking machines and plastic cans filled with explosive liquid, so even though they block the doors he needs to open, they cannot be removed. It is night and nobody is there, all the patients are sleeping, the nurses have gone home, and the doctors are at a conference. Then the lights go off, all is dark around him, but he clearly hears something like a door opening or a window closing, and he knows, this is his mother, who just woke up and is going to the bathroom.

Paul goes to the bathroom, picks up *The Amazing Spiderman*, his favorite comic book, sits on the toilet, and starts looking at the pictures of his hero. Eddie knocks at the door. How long are you going to take? he asks, and since Paul doesn't know how long it will last, he cannot answer, so he hears Eddie swearing and walking away towards the kitchen. Paul hurries to get up and leaves the bathroom with Spiderman under his arm. From the hallway he sees Eddie peeing into the kitchen sink. Paul sneaks back into his room and silently closes the door. His head feels empty today, and his belly is strangely bloated. He walks as if on cotton. What can he do? The pressure in his belly increases, and he can barely breathe, which makes him anxious—will he die now? He is confused. Maybe he needs a bit of fresh air. He opens the door of his dark room and peeks over to the living room, which is empty. Then he hears Eddie talking on the phone, and through the open door to the bedroom he sees his father's feet on the bedspread bobbing to the rhythm of his conversation. Paul hesitates. If only he could breathe better. He has to open a window to get some fresh air. He is not supposed to open the windows because they say it is dangerous—they live on the tenth floor. But he needs, needs some fresh air to breathe! With his eyes carefully watching Eddie's shoes bobbing, Paul creeps over to the new white leather sofa that was delivered only last week; Eddie had picked it because it was white, and white would light up the room and give it a lighter feel. Paul feels heavy, bloated, and squeezed in his jeans with his belt strangulating his bowels. The sofa stands right beneath the window. Climbing up and standing on it, he can easily reach the knob. He opens one wing of the window without making any noise. Fresh air streams into the room and cools his burning face. If only he didn't feel so dizzy and stuffed. Paul gets hold of the sofa's armrest and sinks down. Sitting there with the cool white leather under his head and hands, he feels somewhat better. But then a new wave of dizziness seizes him, everything is tumbling around him, his belly swells up like a balloon, he barely can breathe despite the cold air flowing in from the open window, his head is swimming and everything's spinning about him, and he tries to hold his ground on the sofa, but now the sofa starts swimming and swelling too, soon it is close to bursting—unbearable it is, unbearable—and he has no idea where this knife comes from, this knife that he has in his hand, sharp silver steel, it'll help him breathe, he feels, it'll give him relief, he is sure, and Paul closes his eyes and lowers the knife in his right hand, and dips its point into the white and soft but bulgingly tautened skin, pffffhhh, and the blade glides through the skin as if it were butter, pffffhhh, and the skin opens, a thin, fine hairline, a slit straight through it all—and from the inside red dust is welling up and spurting out and trickling down on the carpet—out, out—and then nothing. An incredible relief is streaming through his body, a total relaxation is smoothing his arms and legs and softening his abdomen, his throat opens and his breathing eases, his head calms and clears up—Paul feels exhausted but safe. His heart starts beating again.

JANIS

The first photo Janis took when she arrived at JFK Airport in New York showed a little girl, not taller than the luggage next to which she was standing, sticking out her tongue at a customs officer hugely towering over her and her family's belongings. My mother loved this photo. For many years it hung in our hallway next to the front door, and when she left it was one of the few items she took with her. She told me that she hadn't wanted to go to New York. And when she arrived, it turned out that Sally, the exchange student she was teamed up with, had already left by the time her plane landed. I'll explain later, Sally's father simply said when he picked her up at the airport. Janis was puzzled. How would school and how would all the rest go without Sally? What a mess! Silently she sat next to Mr. Moore, who briefly pointed at various buildings of Manhattan's skyline, naming and explaining them as they slowly creeped along in the middle of the pack of hundreds of cars pushing their way towards the Triboro Bridge. Janis felt uncomfortable. But since she was already here she didn't want to return either. At home she had suspended her memberships and subscriptions for the next six months, and she didn't feel like reversing all of this. Lucky me: had my mother turned on her heels and traveled back, she wouldn't have fallen in love with my father, and I would not be here.

Anyway, here is what I imagine happened: Just before Janis arrived in New York, the Moores, who lived two floors above Joyce and Eddie, had run into an awful family crisis. By some accidental revelation, Mr. Moore was forced to admit that he was gay and in love with Ben, a young saxophone player. Mrs. Moore was so abhorred and outraged over this shocking news that in a fit of panic she had packed a few things, including Sally and her little brother Noam, determined to move two and a half thousand miles across the continent to San Francisco, where she would stay with her mother until a divorce had clarified all the legal issues. This whole family drama had exploded in the forty-eight hours before Janis' arrival, and everybody was so upset and frantic that nobody had thought of her until the very last moment. They were scrambling to get their stuff into the cab for the airport, Noam was crying and clinging to his father's hand, and all of a sudden Sally gasped: Oh god, Janis is supposed to arrive today! For a moment everybody froze on the spot as if time stood still. Then Mrs. Moore got carried away by a new wave of bitterness and sarcastically remarked: Too bad for poor Janis, but don't you worry, Sally, your father won't harm her, for sure! And off they went. So there was Mr. Moore, a fine man, lawyer by profession and jazz pianist by passion—that's how he'd met Ben—standing on the street, looking past the yellow cab that carried away his family with Noam's little hand desperately waving out of the side window. He still couldn't believe that this was happening. However, as the cold wind blew into his face, he finally felt he could breathe again. The traffic noise sounded soft, steady, and calm compared to his wife's shrill voice cutting through these last hours as their marriage was breaking down so rapidly that he was left stunned. What a nightmare! It was over! Was that right? Was it good? Or was this the biggest mistake of his life?

Eventually he went back to his condo in order to call first Ben, second his law firm, and third a divorce lawyer he knew from the tennis courts. Things would need time to be sorted out, he thought. And just when he entered the lobby, Eddie stepped out of the elevator. Hi Tim, Eddie said when he saw Mr. Moore. They had become somewhat friendly since Eddie had hired him to help patent the *Magic Man* and set up *FIXIT* with its small headquarters in Times Square. Hi Eddie, Tim responded, and was immediately struck by an idea. Do you have a moment? he asked. Sure, Eddie responded. Why don't you come up with me, Tim suggested, I want to ask you something.

Eddie went with him, and while Tim fixed two espressos, he looked around the marvelous five-room-condo and wished Joyce had such a spacious place; then he wouldn't feel so crowded when Paul was hanging around on the weekends.

With a few strokes Tim outlined his current situation. Eddie felt sympathetic. Then Tim explained that Janis, a German exchange student, was about to arrive, and since Sally was gone, he didn't know what to do with her. She has to attend a few classes, he said, but that won't fill her days. Could you use her for some light work in your office? I would pay her salary, that's not the issue. I just want her to have a good time while she is in New York, and working in a young toy company should be great for a student from Cologne. Sure, Eddie said again and thought that in addition Janis could babysit for Paul on the weekends and during the upcoming school vacation. There is always something to do! Both men were pleased with the arrangement. Janis would sleep in Sally's room but would mostly spend her days upstairs with Eddie, Joyce, and Paul. Eddie was happy that he could do Tim a favor, and Tim felt grateful for Eddie's unprejudiced support. Both had the sense that they could become friends.

Time and again I've wondered what exactly it was like for my mother when she first came to New York. I was so young, she usually said when I asked her. She was seventeen, and *so young* sounded like *too young*. At the time she struggled at school, more than she had confided to her parents, and she was at risk of not passing her final exams. Her grades were down since she had ended it with her first boyfriend, Peter, who wanted to have sex all the time, every day, whenever they saw each other, and that really was too much. When she said *no* for the first time, Peter angrily walked out on her. Janis didn't understand why he didn't get it. Was he only going after sex and not interested in her? Had he nothing else in mind? Even though she was heartbroken, she wrote him that she didn't want to see him anymore. It's just the perfect moment for you to go to New York and forget about him, her mother had said, trying to finalize things. But Janis still hoped that Peter would call and say that he was sorry for behaving like an idiot—or something along those lines. I don't like Sally, she declared. Not true, her mother countered, last year when she was here you got along just fine. How would she know, Janis thought but didn't say. Can't I cancel my flight? she asked her father. Her father aligned himself with her mother. You won't chicken out, will you? he replied. Think of all the great pictures you will be able to take, he tried to entice her. Janis was strongly into photography. Only a few months earlier her parents had given her a sophisticated camera as a birthday present—not exactly the one Janis wanted, but definitely a very good one. Her father was right. Janis had already thought of strolling through New York with her camera ready at hand. Still, she remained reluctant. So her father partly conceded: If it doesn't work out over there, you can come back sooner. Anyway you should travel to the States in order to renew your passport. Janis had an American passport because she was born in Chicago during an extended business stay of her father's in the sixties. But what was that good for anyway, Janis thought. She felt dumped by Peter and abandoned by her parents.

Silently she sat in the back of the car that her father was driving to the airport. Her mother was giving her a ton of useless instructions for how to behave in New York. Her younger sister

Sabine was sitting next to her listening to some music on her headphones while looking out of the window. When they arrived at the airport, Janis threw her backpack with her camera, her passports, her books, and her little diary over her shoulder; lifted her small luggage out of the trunk; and decided that she wanted to say goodbye right there! Her parents were reluctant at first, but given the hassle of finding a parking spot in the airport garage, her father quickly agreed. Well, now you're on your own, big girl, he stated cheerfully, as if shooting the starting gun, and briefly hugged her. Her mother got teary. Take good care, she whispered, and stroked her hair. Sabine briefly said goodbye and grinned. Janis in her thin jeans and light anorak shivered a bit when the cold wind ruffled her hair and stuck its moist fingers into her sweater's open collar. Bye, she said, and pulled her luggage towards the big glass door, at which she briefly paused and turned around to wave. Her father was still standing at the open trunk looking over to her. Her mother was busy untangling her seatbelt, and her sister seemed to be changing the radio station. Janis looked at her father, who looked at her and smiled, and she smiled too. This would be a great picture, she thought. But the sudden idea that she might never see them again left her a bit bewildered when she finally entered the departure hall.

Moore's place looked cut out of a movie, my mother told me. Tasteful modern-style furnishing, lots of contemporary art, and all the lights of Manhattan flickering through the windows from three sides with Central Park right in front of the living room—

quite something! Janis was awed and said: Cool! Compared to this place, how small her family's house in a suburb of Cologne seemed, how modest their garden with the swimming pool and a terrace for two sun chairs! Mr. Moore—Call me Tim, he had offered when he picked her up at JFK, and she had thought, *Tim, how weird to call this man Tim!*—took her anorak and showed her Sally's room where she would be staying. Are you hungry? he asked her. Not much, Janis responded, and felt clumsy with her English. Okay, I'll fix us a small bite, Tim responded, and produced some deli sandwiches together with a bottle of Prosecco out of the fridge. Guess after your long trip you'll go to sleep early tonight, he suggested, so why not celebrate your arrival with a glass of Prosecco! Janis sheepishly nodded, thinking how upset her mother would be if she knew that she was alone with Mr. Moore, drinking Prosecco in the middle of a Hollywood set. *Dear Ma*, she thought of writing her, *shortly after I arrived, your friend Fred Astaire stepped in, and I had a great time with him. He called me "little Miss Ginger," we had Champagne and were dancing on a balcony high above the roofs of New York…*

How do you like the corned beef sandwich? Mr. Moore asked. Good, Janis answered, and put it down on the paper plate in order to lick some mustard off her fingers. She felt embarrassed when she realized that Mr. Moore had watched her. But he didn't seem to care. He leaned back in his armchair and said that unfortunately Sally had gone with her mother and brother to San Francisco. He didn't explain the exact reasons for their departure other than calling it a *family crisis*. Then he outlined how he thought Janis could organize her days: she would go to school in the mornings—a secretary from his office would bring her the first day, and would always be available if she needed to call for help or advice—and in the afternoons she could work at *FIXIT* in Times Square; he would introduce her to Eddie and Joyce the next morning. Okay, Janis said, and thought, since she was already here, at least she could give it a try.

Later she was lying in Sally's bed with her eyes wide open, tired and drifting in and out of sleep. She didn't miss Sally but felt like an intruder in her room. The closet was filled with Sally's clothes, the desk and drawers stuffed with her personal things. Why couldn't she have the guest room? Then she heard the doorbell and Mr. Moore's steps as he went to open the door. He seemed to have a visitor. Muffled voices and brief laughter seeped into the darkness around her. Without really meaning to, Janis found herself eavesdropping on the conversation outside, but she couldn't catch more than a few words. At least she decided that the visitor was a man, and surprisingly enough he had a voice like Peter's. What if Peter had followed her to spend these six months with her in New York? He would enter her room, she would pretend to sleep, and he would kiss her or something like that. She wouldn't go to school. Together they would crisscross the city, and at some point they would take a small apartment for a low rent in Greenwich Village; Peter would play the guitar and she would take pictures and write a *New York Diary* chronicling her experiences with a short story for each picture. They would make friends, all artists, musicians, writers, maybe stay there, and she would never go back to school, never back to Cologne. But then instead she saw Mr. Moore coming in...she couldn't clearly see him because it was so dark, but somehow she knew he was sitting at her bedside and slightly stroking her arm as if to indicate that he wanted to have sex with her...Angrily she pushed him away—her hand banged against the bedpost: *ouch!* And there was nothing other than the mystery-laden black of her first New York night with her room's ceiling sparkling from the lights coming in through the cracks of her window shades.

Janis needed to go to the bathroom, but she didn't clearly remember where it was. The clock on her bedside table showed 01:35. Cautiously she opened the door and looked through the dark hallway—nobody there. Slowly she tiptoed over to the big living room window to take another look at Manhattan by night. How beautiful, she thought, all these little illuminated window-spots—all these people still awake! Now she felt like plunging right in and discovering everything! Could she take a picture? She got her camera, positioned it on the windowsill and calmly pressed the shutter release. The lens widely opened and slowly took in the image with a subtle, extended buzz. Then Janis heard a noise, a brief soft slapping or jolting, then a sigh, then silence again. She decided to try to take a photo of the room, which she later titled *Living in the dark*. She turned and positioned the camera, and while she was holding the shutter release down, a door on the other side opened, a person walked by, briefly brushing a veil of shadows across the silver salt, and soundlessly disappeared in the next room. Who was that? Maybe she should just find the bathroom and go back to bed, Janis thought. Sneaking through the dark hallway her heart was pounding.

You know, Hayden, up until now I could simply write along, dreaming up my family's prehistory. Now I feel stuck! Is it because you never responded? I miss you. Without your response, it's no fun to write. But I know at some point you will say something to me, and so I continue. It's strange, but I have the hardest time with getting my father and mother together! I just can't picture how it was when they first saw each other. I've tried various ways—nothing seems right. So I have to jump ahead and continue a bit later when Janis was already working in the afternoons at *FIXIT*. Most of the time she was just babysitting the telephone, and there were not many calls, because at the time the orders for the *Magic Man* usually came in by mail. She then typed the bills, packed the New York orders in padded envelopes and the bigger orders in cardboard boxes, which she brought to a nearby post office. The out-of-state orders were forwarded to a big distribution center in Connecticut where they would be bundled, joined with other items, and sent out in big trucks all over the country. Janis liked to do this simple work that didn't require much thought and still gave her the feeling of having accomplished something useful at the end of the day. While working she listened to a radio station that played pop songs, many of them just newly released—it would take weeks before her friends in Cologne could hear them—nice thought!

Usually Eddie was gone at least for a couple of hours, in part because he only had one desk and chair in his office, and when Janis was working there, it was a bit awkward for him to sit on the couch with just a little coffee table in front of him— two pieces of furniture from Joyce's early years that had almost been forgotten in a storage room on Broadway, and were now happily retrieved for Eddie's new *FIXIT* headquarters. When Eddie was gone Janis took pictures. She photographed every angle of the office and the view out of its window that opened to a corner of Times Square. She also took pictures on her way to the post office and at her favorite coffee shop where she usually went after school to have a sandwich for lunch. Since she had the unexpected addition of a nice paycheck for her afternoon work, she had enough money to get her films developed at a small photo shop that she had found on her way to the post office. She was very critical when scrutinizing her photos and had committed herself to selecting only the best and not more than three shots from each roll for enlargements. Carefully she documented all her contact sheets in a big folder, writing the date and location on each of them and putting down a few related thoughts in her New York diary. I know it's there, I found it in the attic, and maybe next time I go home I'll look for it.

One day, when Eddie came back from his business ventures, Janis had arranged a small exhibition of her photos in his office. She had placed a photo of the desk on the desk, a photo of the couch above the couch, a photo of the book shelf at an empty spot in the middle of the book shelf; a photo of the window besides the window, a photo of the door next to the door, a photo of the coatrack right under the first of its five hooks, and a photo of a crack in the wallpaper right above this crack. Eddie was stunned! Without saying a word he walked from picture to picture, closely looking at each of them before he finally sat down on the couch. Looks great, he then said. Janis quickly picked up her camera and took a picture of Eddie sitting on the couch next to the photo showing the couch. Stop it, Eddie said and laughed, and Janis took another picture of Eddie laughing. So you are into photography, Eddie then said in an effort to somehow regain the upper hand. He never liked to be surprised; I think it made him aware of something going on he had no idea of, and that always seemed threatening to him. Janis nodded and shrugged her shoulders. Yes or no? Eddie demanded. So she said yes and put her camera down. Do you have more photos? Can I see them? My mother was rather shy; she did a lot of things just by herself and rarely shared with anybody what preoccupied her at a given time; but when Eddie wanted to see her pictures, she wanted to show them and hear what he would say. So she pulled out the small folder containing about a dozen enlarged prints and handed it over to him. Then she took another picture of him looking at her pictures. Eddie slowly leafed through her collection, calmly scrutinizing each picture. He was impressed, and told her so. He said she seemed to have talent and a very particular way of seeing things. He also wanted to know where she had developed her film and ordered the enlargements. You should work with the negatives, he then suggested. There are many different ways of turning a negative into a positive, and the outcome is dependent on a variety of things, like the length of the process, the character of the paper, and so on. You should experiment with these things! Janis of course knew all of this and much better than Eddie, but she was so pleased with his reaction that she simply listened to his words as if each of them could reveal another compliment for her. After so many months, for the first time she was happy. Eddie said he had kind of a friend who had a darkroom, and he would talk with him and ask if she could use it. Now Janis really loved being in New York!

There is a photo series of Paul at the 5th Avenue condo: Paul as he is coming out of his dark room with a toy gun in his hand, Paul in his pajamas at the open fridge, Paul kneeling on the white sofa looking out the window, Paul's lost items as they trail him on his way to the bathroom. Janis loved to take pictures of Paul, and Paul loved to be photographed by Janis. Right from the start, Janis and Paul got along very well. When Janis gave him the Swiss chocolates she had brought for Sally, Paul gallantly said: Merci! Where did that come from? Janis laughed, because it was so surprising and sounded cute, and Paul laughed too. They always had something to laugh and giggle about, and when Janis had to babysit because Eddie and Joyce were going out, they usually had a very good time with each other. On premiere nights when Eddie and Joyce stayed at *The Ever Lodge,* Janis and Paul even huddled together in his bed, because she felt uncomfortable sleeping in the living room, and it was much more fun to snuggle under one comforter. Of course they didn't tell Eddie and Joyce. It was their secret. Had Joyce known about it, most likely she would have been angry with Janis, because Janis was seventeen and Paul seven, which made their sleeping together inappropriate. I don't know how Paul felt about it, but I believe my mother could be like a kid with Paul, she enjoyed it. Maybe she was not yet ready to be an adult.

Joyce also had a close relationship with Paul, as documented in another series of photos, showing the two of them together: Paul sitting on Joyce's lap, several takes of Paul looking over Joyce's shoulder while making faces, Paul huddled in a corner with Joyce's fur coat all around him, and Joyce lying on the floor laughing with Paul standing above her in a victory pose. There are two pictures showing Eddie with Paul: one shows little Paul sitting on the floor hugging his father's big black winter boots while Eddie's hairy legs, their feet in white socks, stand sturdy like tall pillars to the right and left of the squatting child; the other shows Eddie and Paul, each with an ice cream cone in their fists on a park bench. No further pictures of the two together. It proves how hard it was for them to fit in one frame. Eddie continued to make all the responsible moves to get Paul a good education and whatever he needed besides that; and on good days they even bonded for a while, mostly over shooting baskets on Sunday mornings, or biking through Central Park, or watching a game on TV. But deep down, I think, my father held on to his belief that Judy had seduced him just to get pregnant, and Paul had to pay the price for the sham. Paul, on the other hand, might have kept blaming Eddie for his mother's death, maybe just unconsciously, because at the time when Judy gave him the *Magic Man,* she started to talk about his father and about her illness, a coincidence that seemed to reveal to him some kind of cause-and-effect relation. Anyway, even though Eddie and Paul didn't really like each other, Eddie's relationship with Joyce normalized about a year after Paul had moved in with them, probably thanks to Janis, who didn't mind spending a lot of time with the difficult kid.

Eddie and Joyce resumed their old cherished habits like sifting through second-hand stores, lingering in galleries, discussing the plays Joyce was acting in, or developing new ideas for *FIXIT,* many of which were not meant to be realized but served the purpose of fun. They went to the movies and saw friends at dinner parties while Janis was babysitting Paul. Thus it seemed as if their old playful and lighthearted attitude towards life had returned to 5th Avenue. However, Eddie kept sensing a slight absence in Joyce's moods, a subtle distraction in her attention to what they talked about, a shift away from him when they made love. When he asked her about it, she claimed not to have noticed it, or it not being true, but he was keenly aware of it all the time. Eddie was as passionate and tender as ever, and at that time Joyce seemed to be sexually even more responsive than she used to be—if I interpreted correctly what my father mumbled once when he was tipsy. So Eddie sometimes doubted his senses and wondered if his perception was accurate or merely a trick of some residual jealousy or his suspicious imagination. But clearly he felt the need to get Paul off Joyce's heart and his back. That's why he decided to dig up some valuable news about the son Joyce had given up for adoption.

Indeed, the whereabouts of Joyce's son became Eddie's foremost preoccupation. In the afternoons when Eddie was busy meeting sellers, producers, advertisers, journalists, or the like, he often went to the adoption agency that Joyce had once mentioned. When he first got there and asked directly, if there was any way, *any*, to learn something about a child whose adoption had been arranged by this agency in the early 50s, the agency's director, Miss Clark, had flatly denied his request. No way, she said once and for all. These documents are and will remain sealed!

But my father never takes *no* for an answer. So he may have returned the next day, lingered in a coffee shop opposite the agency watching what went on by its front door, and when Miss Clark finally left the building, he got up and went over to the agency, now armed with a neat story. The young secretary, who wore a nametag reading Susan Turner, raised her eyebrows in unwelcoming surprise when she saw him again at the reception desk. But Eddie smiled his most winning smile and explained that he decided to come back because this was actually a very important matter! He said that his mother, Joyce Anderson, was very sick and would soon be dying, and all she wanted was to be sure that her first born son, whom she had given for adoption to this agency, was doing okay. She didn't want to contact him, he promised, she just ached to know that things had turned out well enough for him—because otherwise she wanted to anonymously bequeath him with a considerable amount of money. She just wants him to be okay. Then she'll be able to peacefully die! Eddie said this, apparently concerned and to his own surprise truly sad. Miss Turner skeptically pierced him with her gray eyes and firmly shook her head. However, Eddie had noticed a brief hesitation, a mix of doubt and sympathy, and that was all he needed that day. He would build his strategy on this split second of doubt.

In the weeks to come, he would run into her as if by accident, cautiously call her, and eventually casually invite her for coffee. Please think about it, he suggested with no more urgency in his voice than he thought she could tolerate. I understand that you have to discuss this with your colleague, Miss Clark, he said, purposefully denying the seniority and hierarchy of the office. I do appreciate and honor her for denying my request. I know there are rules. But all I ask you is to please consider and—please!—put a good word in on my, that is my mother's, behalf. I'll be back. And back he came, always politely apologizing for bothering her again and thanking her for her precious time or wishing her a good start to her week or a wonderful weekend. Each time he placed his business card anew next to the small pot with yellow violets that was sitting somewhat forlornly on the proper blankness of the agency's reception desk.

In the meantime Janis had started to work in Morton Schwartz' darkroom. Morton was old—my mother said he seemed to be at least hundred, so most likely he was in his seventies—a man with a good eye for pictures and a grumbly voice nobody really understood when it bubbled out of his scrubby mustache and trickled into his weird conversations with clients. In the evening hours before he closed his small shop on W 44th Street, Janis was allowed to experiment with the machines and chemicals and the various papers he had shown her by briefly pointing with his hands here and there as if talking to an expert. Janis had never seen them for real, but she had read a lot about photo techniques, and she was gifted in figuring things out on her own. So Morton was right in trusting that she could eventually do it or else would ask him, and since Eddie had promised that he would pay for whatever costs would arise, it was a good deal for him. Janis was glad to be left alone. Happily she turned on the *No Entry* sign next to the door and disappeared into the dimly red world of the images that emerged under her carefully probing hands. Intuiting the length of light exposure, waving shadows across the field, and prematurely lifting the paper's edges out of the basin, she created surprising effects. When she came out of the darkroom, Morton usually looked over her production and made some suggestions for how to technically improve the results. Sometimes Janis went right back and tried it again, often successfully. Eddie was impressed. Beautiful! he said, and took her to an Ansel Adams exhibition at the Met. He meant to be encouraging, and Janis was interested and scrutinized each picture for a long time, but she also felt intimidated, and she declined when Eddie wanted to buy her the catalogue at the end of the show. Later, though, she went back and got it anyway.

Then one day Eddie came to his *FIXIT* office and gave Janis a Hasselblad 500 as a present! It was a used one, but in excellent condition. He had seen it by chance in the window of a pawnshop, and he had negotiated a good price, twenty-five percent down from its listed price. Janis was stunned and in disbelief. It was her dream-come-true camera. Are you sure? she asked, knowing how expensive these cameras were. Try it out, Eddie simply said, and was happy to see how impressed she was. She warily lifted the precious Hasselblad, gingerly took it out of his hands as if he would claim it back any moment, and since Eddie didn't interfere and simply stood there with his open hands, calmly looking and smiling at her, she finally believed that it was hers. Thank you, she said. Thank you so much! Eddie pulled a small, worn manual that had come with the Hasselblad out of his pocket and put it on the desk. He suggested that she stop working in order to go out and try it out. But it was a rainy day that day, and Janis felt too anxious about her new camera to take it outside. So it was Eddie who left for the rest of the afternoon, knowing that Janis would want to just be alone with her Hasselblad. Janis placed the camera her parents had given her on the bookshelf and looked at her new Hasselblad. What a beauty it was, seemingly simple, yet fabulously sophisticated! Then she discovered that film was in it, obviously left there by its previous owner, with three more pictures to be taken. How long had it been in there? Would it still be good? What would be the first photo she would shoot with it?

As I know my father, he certainly was quite a bit curious in the following days. How is your Hasselblad working out? he repeatedly asked. I'm not sure yet, Janis responded. Can I see something? he would pressure, and Janis would shake her head and say: Not yet! What Eddie didn't know was that Janis had started a series of photos of him sleeping on the couch of his *FIXIT* headquarters. At first it seemed like a mere convenience. It continued to rain, so she didn't feel like going out, Eddie was there, and Janis was itching to take her first Hasselblad picture. Maybe that's how she chose him—and eventually fell in love with him? She never told me how it happened. Eddie had come in after a business lunch, and after asking her, as he usually did, Do you mind? and her responding as always Not at all, he had lain down on the couch to take his afternoon nap. When Janis looked up from her desk and over to him, he was already deeply asleep. Amazed, she thought: *He looks like a King!* His head was bent backwards comfortably resting on this old silk pillow that shimmered golden and dull on the absorbing softness of the sofa's dark red velvet. His glasses, the New York Times, and an unopened letter were lying on the small coffee table next to his shoulder. His left hand was buried in the pocket of his corduroy pants, his right hand placed on his chest right above his heart. He had slipped out of his shoes, which had toppled on top of each other next to the sofa's heavy wooden leg, and his large feet, one still in its woolen sock, the other naked—where was the second

110

sock?—were freely hanging over the end of the couch. This was the first picture she took with her Hasselblad: *Eddie sleeping I.* How exciting it was to look from above through the view finder, adjust the cutout, hold her breath, and then press the shutter release! Janis put the camera down and savored the moment.

Then she stepped a bit closer to the couch. Two more pictures to go. Looking through her Hasselblad she narrowed down on Eddie's face slightly bent to the side, placing it diagonally in the square frame; his blond hair had fallen backwards and freed his forehead, which was shining from a thin film of moisture; his short eyelashes densely hemmed his firmly closed lids, under which she saw his eyes flitting back and forth as if following a fleeting dream; his long and straight nose, a black point in a big pore at its tip, divided his face into a light and a dark side; as he was lying on his back, his smoothly shaved cheeks had fallen somewhat inwards, the right more than the left; his mouth was just slightly opened, showing parts of his upper teeth; a blond hair stuck on his lower lip, shivering there as he breathed in and out; his chin was comfortably resting on his neck's small bulge of round flab that cozily snuggled into his soft turtleneck. *He looks like a baby*, Janis thought with some surprise, and pressed the shutter release. This was *Eddie sleeping II.*

One more to go! Janis wavered for a moment, but then she opted for the architecture of Eddie's shoes and feet at the leg of the couch and kneeled down: at the bottom of the right half of the picture's frame she saw his black shoes piled up, one heel sticking in the other's opening, both right below and in front of the sofa's lathed wooden leg, which oddly seemed to jut out from under the velvet cover's dark rectangle, on top of which Eddie's strong feet rose high into the open air, remarkably comfortable and unabashed, monuments of a forward motion in unconscious recklessness, to which a small heart-shaped birthmark below his right big toe offered a strangely cute contrast; the left side of the picture remained rather empty, showing nothing other than the blank, beige carpet running straight into the white painted wall, disrupted only by an open old-fashioned socket. Janis thought this composition looked interesting and pressed the shutter release. It would become *Eddie sleeping III*. She felt elated and simultaneously exhausted, almost as if she had accomplished a difficult task. Carefully she rolled back the film. Now she wanted to see how these pictures had turned out. Softly, in order not to awaken Eddie, she took her coat and went over to Morton's darkroom.

It could have been around this time that things at 5th Avenue got complicated. Joyce had participated in an actors' strike demanding higher wages, and together with the other protesters she had been kicked out of her theatre and her most recent role on Broadway, where she had played the mistress of a corrupt politician, a play that had gotten rather bad reviews and, under these conditions, was advantageously canceled from the program. The loss of her contract with the theatre, her home base, was a big blow to Joyce and made her upset, insecure, and anxious. Unfortunately, it also caught Eddie in a tense moment.

Instead of comforting and holding her, he just dryly remarked that the whole thing had been unwise on her part, to say the least, since *her* pay had been steadily raised in all these years and was actually pretty great at the time. Joyce was hurt by his lack of compassion and thought of kicking Eddie out, but instead she just called him cruel, selfish, and cold-hearted; then she disappeared for three days, and nobody knew where she went.

This could have been the moment my father and mother got involved. For instance Eddie, being alone and with no plans on a child-free Monday night, would have invited Janis for dinner and thereby discovered not only her interesting and funny mind but also the charms and beauty of her young, skinny figure—so different from Joyce's more complicated psyche and her womanly body features. And Janis would have been impressed with how much Eddie knew about the world of art and photography, literature and philosophy, much more than her father or any boyfriend she'd previously considered suitable. So that's perhaps how it clicked between them. Did Eddie have qualms when he started an affair with Janis? Did he initially think of only a short fling or was he serious about it? Was he ready to tell and leave Joyce? Whatever he might have pondered, Joyce reappeared, didn't say where she had been or with whom, Eddie didn't ask or say anything, and life went on.

Meanwhile Paul had gotten into a fight with David, an older boy at his boarding school, who at the height of the debate had offended him with a stupid slur, something casual like *bastard*, and after simmering in Paul's heart for a few days, during which he brooded over all sorts of revenge options, this stupid little word *bastard* had all of a sudden propelled him into a meltdown, an unexpected eruption of hatred so deep that he had popped open a switchblade—to the horrified gasps of the surrounding kids in the schoolyard—and wielded it against his offender, who barely managed to jump two steps backwards, thus abruptly bumping into Miss Enderlin, the school's principal, and knocking her down, whereby she broke her ankle. Paul, who really had aimed at David's heart, at least succeeded in slitting open the sleeve of David's anorak—piffff—before being wrestled down by some stronger kids. Because of this violent assault, Paul was temporarily suspended from his boarding school while a commission was formed to investigate the slur, the provenance of the switchblade, the attack itself, and the damage all of this had done to the school's reputation, because David's father had gone to the press to report his outrage over these events. Paul hated to be confined to 5th Avenue, and Eddie hated Paul being home. Joyce was unnerved that both didn't get along. And Janis felt uncomfortable—and maybe guilty—in the midst of all this tension and wanted to withdraw, but didn't like being at the Moore place either, because Ben had sort of moved into the guest room, and despite the fact that Tim and Ben were very nice to her, she felt awkward and like an intruder when she spent time there while the two men were chatting, cooking, playing Jazz or whatever…So she had asked Eddie if she could sleep at the *FIXIT* office. There is no shower, he had cautioned, and Times Square at night is not a safe place for a girl like you! But

Janis remained undeterred. Trust me, she demanded, and Eddie finally agreed. So in some sense, Janis moved in with Eddie while Eddie still lived with Joyce.

I wonder—was it because of all this turmoil that my father turned away from Joyce and fell in love with Janis? Or was he flattered when he discovered that Janis had taken all these pictures of him? Was that the way they had gotten close, literally close? She snuck these photos during his naps, scrutinizing his face, and he had no idea about it. Over time she took hundreds of shots, slinking around in order not to awaken him, working as if in a fever, totally obsessed with her subject—or was she looking for something, something that would only reveal itself in these close-ups? Countless moments she immortalized, displaying his sleeping face, some in full, studies of strain, sorrow, or restful relaxation, but also bitterness, hard and alarmingly cold, revealing traces, it seemed, of an ongoing inner fight against whatever might once have crossed his path. Other photos show only details: the ear, for instance, with a ray of sunshine illuminating a brush of hair spiking out of the black of its caving abyss; or one of his eyes, closed by its lid and mute like a dune in the desert; or the texture of his skin, rough and cratered, a foreign planet with nowhere to go; or one picture of his mouth with its fissured lips closely tightened and chapped resembling old discarded pipelines; or his lips looking moist and naked and lusciously open like a woman's waiting to be kissed. I've seen many, and there is something disturbing about them, in particular about these close-ups stripped of their human context, each one an alienating mystery in itself. Later all these photos were collected and printed in a book, titled *EDDIE SLEEPING*.

Did my father sleep with Janis on this couch in the *FIXIT* office, the couch that everybody could see in her photo book? Did my mother fall in love with Eddie? Or was she merely in love with the object of her passion—photography? Anyway, something must have happened between them because I was born in May of the following year—so my mother must have become pregnant with me in the fall. I think her stay in New York was supposed to end in September. I know that she spent part of the summer on Nantucket at a place owned by the Moore family. Were Tim and Ben with her, or did Sally join her with her mother and brother for a summer vacation? Or was she alone with Eddie? Or were they all together there, Tim and Ben, Joyce, Eddie, Paul, and Janis? Then she went back to New York.

When did she realize that she was pregnant? Maybe she woke up one day and felt a bit strange, nothing much, just something seemed different. She needed some air. Walking out right onto Times Square as early as 5:15 in the morning was wonderful. The streets were wet from the previous night's rain, the shops and bars still closed with their shutters down, a few homeless people bundled up in their belongings sleeping in the entranceways and niches along Broadway's crooked frontline. Janis was thinking about Eddie. He was so generous. He always knew what she needed or wanted. He was funny but difficult to talk with. With her he seemed more relaxed—with Joyce he behaved as if on guard, subservient. Returning to the subtle shift she'd felt inside, and lingering on a picture she'd taken a while ago, showing Eddie's back as he was sleeping on his side, curled up into a fetal position with his white shirt slipped out from under his black sweater and hanging down, limp and exhausted like a peace flag at the end of a long war—why did that thought come up?—she slowly walked against the fresh breeze in search of an open bakery or coffee shop, when suddenly, just as she was turning the corner to W 40th Street towards Bryant Park, the thought struck her: *what if I'm pregnant?*

The fact is that Janis didn't return to Cologne. She declared she wanted to stay in America. How adventurous! Of course there were fierce disputes on the phone with her parents who wanted her to first finish school. Janis didn't tell them how much she doubted that she would pass her final exams. She was now eighteen years old and had the right to decide for herself. I just want some time off, she explained, I may decide to finish school next year. But right now I want to stay in New York! Eventually her parents gave up. I bet she didn't tell them then that she was pregnant! And when Eddie offered to pay for her tuition if she wanted to go to the Rhode Island School of Design to study photography, her mind was made up: she would become a photographer! Yes, that was exactly what she wanted! All of a sudden things had to hurry up. The deadline for class enrollment at the Rhode Island School of Design had already passed, but Eddie talked with Tim, and luckily Tim knew a few influential people there on the Board; and since the Moore family had been donors of the institution for many years, things worked out well for Janis. On August 31st she sat next to Eddie driving up to Providence with all her belongings in the trunk and her most precious one, the Hasselblad, on her lap.

LARRY

Tall and determined Lawrence Bonnet paces the space at the front of the classroom—at least that's how I picture him—his black straggly hair tangled and as usual unkempt for days, his dark blue eyes energetically blazing out from under his bushy brows, piercing his students—though without really seeing them, it seems—his beige short-sleeved shirt disorderedly stuffed into and partly hanging over his baggy brown pants that clump into his big black boots—all of which are supposed to signal: *I don't care about conventional codes, I'm an artist*. Call me Larry, he had demanded, marching through the door on the first day of his seminar, and throwing his jacket and briefcase from afar at his desk next to the blackboard, he got right into his subject matter, as if there were no other world to be in than *photography*. The whole semester it had been his show: always this forceful entry, always high speed through the hour, and always at the end a baffling question, some loosely connected words he flung at his students, almost as an attack on their focus carefully hatched **during the lesson** only to be shattered in doubt by this last throw-in, which left them stunned, stirred, and upset until he would jet in again a week later to repeat this cycle in continuation of his stride.

Janis was sitting at her desk in the third row watching Larry Bonnet wildly gesturing while vaguely explaining Diane Arbus. Her classmates were taking notes. She just watched. The legendary Professor Bonnet: standing now upright, a massive, bulky character and type of a man, the broad case of his chest bulging and shrinking with the push-and-pull of his rattling breath that exploded every few moments in a thunderous coughing fit, thereby shamelessly spattering splashes of steam over his desk and the projector's cast of the famous photo *A Jewish Giant at Home With His Parents in the Bronx*. You see—you think you see—but you don't know *what* you see, Larry declared. Is this just a bunch of freaks? What's the story playing out between these little parents and their gigantic son? Is he ashamed of his height, of being so out of and beyond any acceptable shape and proportion, troubled by his mother's helpless looks and devastated by his father's saddened resignation, ready to explode, the monstrous balloon he is, and then implode, all out of steam, to shrink to the size of a baby? Or on the contrary: is he just about to channel all his unfathomable rage and ever boiling heat of fury to finally murder his dwarfish parents, snatch them by their throats, one in each hand, lift their little bodies, shake their tiny limbs, squeeze and squash them—and drop the bloody pulp on the carpet? You may be spinning off trail—*I do*—but

120

that's not even it! Decisive is what you sense but don't see inside yourself when you look at it: That's what all photography is about.

Larry Bonnet never failed to impress them, never hesitated to be crude and direct. *Bullshit*, he would say, or *Baloney*, when a student tried to be smart. He wanted the real thing—but it had to be his. Other opinions were immediately kicked off stage. Still, as much as his students felt bruised by him, they did revere and like him, and when he was sitting down with them in one of Providence's noisy pubs, he could be charming and relaxed, poke fun at himself and show some humility that almost matched the humiliations he dished out in the classroom.

Larry had announced that he was organizing an end-of-semester exhibition of the students' photographic works that would determine their final grades. Each of his nine students was asked to select ten photographs to express a theme, and he, Larry, would also present ten pictures from his own work. All photos had to be twenty-five by thirty, black and white, and needed to be developed and enlarged by the students. It would be a public exhibition, titled *100 Shots 1982* and would have its opening at the end of the semester. At first, Janis had thought of making a portrait of Larry and each of the classmates, herself included, but several of her colleagues had declined to be photographed, so this idea didn't work. Maybe then she thought of showing the progress of her pregnancy in ten steps—by the end of the semester she must have been close to her due date with me, and somewhere, a long time ago, I saw contact sheets with pictures of my pregnant mother, so it could have crossed her mind...but since she was as shy as ambitious, I guess she discarded that one too. What she would end up showing was her series *Eddie sleeping*.

Did Eddie visit Janis on the weekends? Did he on Fridays drive up from New York in his blue Oldsmobile Cutlass and stay with her till Monday morning—thereby leaving Paul to Joyce and avoiding the whole complication of their all being together in one room? My mother never said anything about that. I think it's strange that she would have spent most of her pregnancy alone in Providence, but it would fit. She was so secretive; she liked to do her things by herself, and when she finally came out with something, she never said much about it. So here is one of my secret thoughts: sometimes I wonder if not Eddie but Larry was my father—even though that would make me a prematurely born baby, which of course can happen. But I do remember that my mother occasionally said that she was very fond of Larry. Once she mentioned that he was bisexual. As a child I didn't know what *bisexual* meant, and that's perhaps why I never forgot her remark. She said Larry had lots of boyfriends and girlfriends, who usually were quite stunning. I thought Janis looked beautiful, not like a fashion model, but in her smart and idiosyncratic appearance very attractive! So he might have at least tried to seduce my mother. Did she have an affair with him? It's almost impossible—yet not completely unthinkable, because as rude as Larry was, he could also be very convincing and certainly overpowering. It flattered his students if they could withstand his assaults in good spirits and drink a beer with him thereafter. Mona, who wore her curly red hair long, down to her butt, once stood in front of the classroom drawing a sketch of a photo on the blackboard, and in only the blink of an eye, Larry had grabbed her hair from behind, lifted it up, kissed her neck, and let it down again. Nobody said anything. Mona continued to finish her sketch. Did it happen? Was it just a flash of fantasy? Pete had the courage to raise his hand and ask: Why did you do that? And Larry shot back: What? Pete blushed. What did I do? Larry challenged. Did I do something? Or did you think I did what *you* actually wanted to do? Lisa, who had been taking notes, lifted her eyes and asked: What happened? Exactly! Larry snubbed. Garry grinned. Janis was fascinated and thought she understood. Then Mona turned around, smiled, and started to explain her sketch, and those girls who believed that they had seen something envied her.

At the beginning of the semester all students had to submit a project that Larry would discuss with them in a one-on-one session at his home near campus. Janis had submitted the plan for a series: close-ups of broken toys. This idea was certainly inspired by Eddie's toy collection. However, Janis wanted to focus on the ordinary, cheap toys she found on the street—a dented doll, a busted ball, a rusty whistle, a ragged plush bear, a battered police car, or a tattered picture book—and she would photograph them exactly where and how she found them: in a garbage bin half drowned in trash, on the sidewalk lost out of a toddler's stroller, or picked up and pinned upright on a newspaper box, or cast away next to a gumball machine, or crushed and flattened by cars on the streets' asphalt. I've seen these pictures a million times because Eddie later used them for an advertisement series: *Fix it with FIXIT* was the slogan.

Janis' appointment was at 4 PM. When she rang his doorbell, Larry bellowed: *come in!* The door was ajar. He was standing in front of his bookcase, entangled in an angry dispute on the phone. Why the hell would you do this! he shouted. We've agreed on that, I counted on you! Dammit!—I could be ready in a week! I told you!—*No! No! No!*—You would think that, you would???—After all these years?—Don't!—Listen, I can come over, right now!—No?—What?—No!—Oh fuck it—fuck it, and fuck you! He smashed the receiver on the cradle. Janis waited. Larry stood and stared, simultaneously helpless and furious, his shoulders hanging down, his hands balled into fists as if he was ready to punch his gods into mercy. I just lost my gallery! he murmured.

His study was a mess! The sofa was loaded with books and newspapers; a big wooden box with apples covered the small coffee table, next to which there was an opened case of Coca Cola cans, half empty. Grab one, Larry vaguely offered, but Janis didn't move. Still holding her briefcase with her project, she looked at Larry's desk, which was stacked with folders. The desk lamp's glass shade was cracked, the ashtray overflowing with butts, a potted plant drooped its wilted leaves. Behind his desk, the window opened up to a nice view of an overgrown garden, framed by some gray curtains, parts of which had detached themselves from the rods and were lumping down on the carpet, where a black cat had made its bed in its folds.

Asshole, son of a bitch! Larry hissed and started to walk up and down the small open aisle between his desk and the bookcase. Can you believe it? It's unfair, so unfair! he howled, and Janis saw that he was in a fight with his tears and would lose it in a moment. I can't bear this! It's too much, I really can't! Larry moaned. Janis felt uncomfortable. Professor Bonnet, I'm sure you'll find another gallery! she offered. Call me Larry, he growled, pacing past her to pour himself a whiskey. Want one? No, thank you! Fine, Larry barked back, that's exactly what Clyde said: No, thank you! What an obnoxious little fucker he is! *No, thank you!* Janis cautiously moved towards the door. Wait, wait, Larry yelled, I will look at your project, I'm reliable, you'll see, I'm there in a moment! This damn thing just took me by surprise! Sit here! Let me see! And with one angry stroke of his fist he swept his books, magazines and newspapers off the couch in order to clear some space for Janis. Sit here, I'll just get myself another drink! Sure you don't want any?

Then he sat down, close to Janis, too close she felt, and so close that he put half of his weight on her shoulder when he opened her folder, pretending to look at the outline of her toy series, but all he saw was Clyde. Janis wanted to explain what she had in mind, but he wouldn't let her. I love him, he stammered, I love him so much! And now he has dropped me. Why? Why? Her folder slid out of his hands, unseen and totally useless to him, and Janis didn't dare to move and pick it up. I've never loved anybody as much as I love him! I would give him anything, anything! And now he kicks me out? Just because I'm a few days late? That can't be it! Oh god, I can't bear it! Larry dropped his head on his hands on his knees and moaned. He is gorgeous, boy, is he gorgeous! And look at me! I'm old. I'm getting fat. Baaahhhh, that fat old faggot! Tearing at his hair now, Larry covered his head with his hands as if to protect it from the blows that were raining down on him. I'm not so quick anymore, but only lately. Still, I got two or three good shots a month, really good ones, I mean. That wasn't enough? That wouldn't do?— At first he admired me. I helped him, didn't I? He was so insecure in the beginning, that's what he was: shy, not knowing how these things work, with whom to talk and stuff, and I helped him. It's because of me that he got this gallery! Real fine place! Have you been there? *C. Man's Gallery*? You have to go! He had the money, but I had the knowhow! That's why it worked! Larry remained silent for a while, shaking his head, then he resumed: But he got cocky, my little boy, finally he knew all these fancy people, people with big bucks; he was invited to cocktail parties, and these so-called artists crawled up his ass— those suckers! I called him, invited him over, and he had no time! Friday? No. Saturday? Unfortunately not. Sunday? I'm afraid... So what about Monday? Maybe! That's how it went. Who was he fucking around with all that time? Larry stared at Janis. Then he broke into tears. God, did I love him, I adored him—and I still love him! What shall I do, what, tell me, what…?

Janis must have felt very uncomfortable, but she had a good idea: Perhaps today's just a fluke! Tomorrow everything might be different, she suggested. And now I don't know what to think, because one storyline would go that here Larry would hug her in relief, grateful for what she said, as if she had become his fortune-teller and would be a good oracle for him, just the comfort he needed; or, Larry would be struck with a sudden insight of lunatic power, namely that he actually loved Janis, by which all his love that had crashed at Clyde's locked door suddenly and only momentarily wallowed over to my mother, who he liked, sort of, and this would have made him hug her and press his face and lips to her neck and lick her ear— *ugh!*—and urge her down on the couch—why not, he would have whispered, working himself up as he touched her all over and checked her out in order to forget and undo this terrible, terrible blow. And Janis, relieved that he had stopped sobbing and howling, paralyzed and confused, would have allowed him to rape her, against but maybe not totally against her will, yet still she would have let him take advantage of the pity she felt for him and the horror and unacknowledged disgust in seeing him, the famous teacher he was supposed to be, so pathetic, so broken, so totally devastated as no man should ever be, she felt, and in a bit of a funk she would have accepted that he would do what she didn't want him to do and what he was never allowed to do—and that could have led to her becoming pregnant with me.

For sure, she wouldn't have told him, neither him nor anybody else, and neither Larry nor Eddie would have guessed anything.

Another more lenient possibility, though, would be this: When Janis offered that all Clyde had shared was just the whim of the moment, Larry reacted as if awakened from a bad spell. He raised his head and looked at her, still somewhat bewildered but already reenergized, and stammered, Really? And shaking his head he reiterated, Really? Do you think so? Really? Is that right? As if she could know! And when Janis smiled and shrugged her shoulders, with a slight nod to validate his hope, he suddenly jumped up and decided: You are right! That's what it is! He just freaked out on something! Okay! Okay! Now your project, it's okay! It's great! Broken toys trashed away, great! Just go ahead. And walking her to the door he added: Thanks, by the way, we weathered that one, didn't we? Now we have a secret, you and I, don't we? And Janis with her folder would go as softly as she had come, because Larry was already back on the phone, and she certainly didn't want to witness his next conversation, and anyway knew what to do.

This was in the fall. Soon Larry Bonnet seemed to have recaptured his old peculiar self while hardly showing any dent from the catastrophic blow he had suffered, almost as if it hadn't happened, Janis thought, and whether he was back with Clyde or not, she didn't care to know. Had she asked him about it, he might very well have gazed at her with a puzzled look, not really knowing what she was talking about. Passion comes, passion

128

goes, that's what he used to say. He continued to be the character everybody knew.

Meanwhile Janis had enjoyed walking around the streets and fields in and around Providence in search of broken toys, and over the weeks she had amassed an amazing collection of 47 photos that counted for her semester's work. Now with the end of classes and the date of the exhibition approaching, she put a lot of thought into selecting and organizing her series *EDDIE SLEEPING*. She had a small number of really good pictures, and then there were some photos she thought were also good but didn't quite fit the theme, while other possible shots that did were not her best. As much as she shuffled and shifted the photos back and forth, she only came up with nine photos, a block of three by three, and that was it. What about the tenth? She lingered on that question.

Did she tell Eddie that she planned to exhibit the pictures she had taken of him? Probably not! Would he have come to the opening of the show had he known that he would be on display? Maybe not. She was afraid he wouldn't, yet wanted him at her side. So it needed to be a surprise. In general my father wasn't searching for the spotlight, but neither did he always shy away from it. Over the years I've watched him many times when he was introducing a new toy to the market. He usually invited a big crowd of journalists, educators, child therapists, retailers, parents, and kids, to whom he presented the new item, and asking for their opinions, he would joke, chat, and laugh with everybody throughout the afternoon. He gracefully did this with his slightly edgy charm, treated the press generously, and always got good reviews. But whenever my mother had a photo exhibition, he often missed the opening. Sometimes he would not arrive till late in the evening, when most people had already left, and when he did show up, he seemed awkward, staying in the empty corners, slipping out of the crowd to smoke a cigarette outside or engaging in a long conversation with the caterer, who didn't understand a thing about photography. This was really odd if not offensive to my mother. She tried to draw him into conversation, introduced him to the owner of the gallery or to some of the guests or potential buyers, but then he would stay only for a bit, just enough to show the necessary minimum of politeness, before finding a silly excuse to drop out. As little as I was then, I watched it, and I didn't like that he did this to my mother. Why don't you stay? my mother asked him more than once, to which he would reply: I don't like the crowds! She challenged that: At your events you manage even bigger crowds, and very skillfully! to which he would counter: Yeah, just because I have to. But I don't like it. This doesn't have anything to do with your photography; it's just not my thing. So why don't we leave it at that: I do my events, and you do yours. I think my mother felt hurt, abandoned, snubbed and unpleasantly exposed by his absence—it made her lonely. Photography was such an essential part of her life! Eventually, I think, she was more comfortable when he didn't show up at her shows, rather than having him show up in his typical way: sneaking in and out, always along the sidelines, where he could be spotted by her colleagues yet was never willing to converse, merely an odd presence that muted the excitement, something like a shadow of hers that had detached itself from where it should be and would wander, a lost soul, to the strange shores of arbitrary distraction. But at the time, when she prepared for her very first exhibition in Providence, she did not anticipate any of this, nor did he. I'm sure she was counting on Eddie to come and help, and yes, I know for sure that he came to support her at the opening of *100 Shots 1982*.

She wore a black velvet jacket, a black silk blouse, and big silver earrings, and when I look at the photo a journalist took of her that night, I'm still mystified by her natural beauty and the pensive look in her sincere eyes. How young she was and already so sophisticated! It was a warm early summer day. The windows of the institute's foyer, where the photo show was taking place, were wide open. The students were busy hanging their pictures. The previous night, Larry had already installed his series on the big wall right opposite the entrance: ten close-ups of an orchid starting from the small bud, to its bursting open, to the orchid's full blossom seen from various angles, to its shriveling down and wilting away, till it had fallen off and only the stem remained with a small swelling where the loss had occurred looking almost like the coming about of a next bud. He had organized the ten pictures in a big circle surrounding his signature, *Lawrence Bonnet*, with its letters fabricated from artfully crumpled silver tin foil that seemed casually attached to the wall on long thin pins or needles. In passing Janis had only briefly looked at it as she was pushing the cart with her ten framed pictures to her place farther down the hall.

Eddie was early, Eddie was there, and Eddie helped lift the pictures and adjust them in horizontally and vertically equidistant order, so that they all accurately hung three by three—it looked great! Janis' cheeks were glowing. Do you like it? she asked Eddie. Well, yes, all but the fact that it's me, Eddie responded. I guess I'll wear sunglasses tonight, but given the way you photographed me, nobody will even notice. That's right, Janis said, and actually it's not meant to be about you—it's more about something universal. Then she unwrapped her solution for the tenth picture, a section of a torso, part of a naked human body, probably but not distinctly male, with two hands, barely visible, holding a Hasselblad in front of the genital area as if taking a picture of the viewer. Eddie was taken aback. What's that? he wondered. I don't know, Janis responded. It was on the film that was in the Hasselblad you gave me. Eddie grimaced painfully. You can't use this, it's not you who took it! I developed it, that's enough for this show, Janis countered. I attribute this one to *Nobody Unknown.* She held it to the left of her three-by-three photo block, and in fact it did add intrigue to the whole. With a deep sigh, and shaking his head, Eddie struck the nail for the hanger. Then Janis pinned a small panel beneath it that carried the title: *BEFORE EDDIE SLEEPING.*

People were streaming in, walking around, looking at the photos, chatting and laughing, drinking Prosecco and nibbling on little salt pretzels. Can I buy this one? a young man asked, pointing to *EDDIE SLEEPING IV*. Janis shook her head. They all belong together, and I'm not selling. Eddie inserted himself into this brief exchange: How much would you be willing to pay? The man pondered for a moment. Well, say a hundred bucks—I mean, for all of them. Janis turned away. She didn't like this conversation. You see, Eddie whispered, there is already a potential buyer. Lisa came over to introduce Janis to her brother, and Janis briefly thought that she hadn't sent an invitation to her parents. Would they have come across the Atlantic to attend her first photo exhibition? Probably not. Relations between them were a bit strained since Janis had decided not to return home to finish school. This also meant that she had decided to make me a surprise baby—and I wonder how she thought that would go...?

Then came Larry. Janis saw him walking through the front door dressed in a strange purple-colored, cape-shaped jacket over black tight leather pants—like a costume, she thought, watching how he shook hands with everybody and hugged some of the younger women. He seemed to be in a good mood. Slowly winding his way through the crowd, he walked from wall to wall, briefly talking to his students about their displays, always smiling, politely nodding, patting their shoulders—he wouldn't grade their work that night, they knew that, yet still they were nervously watching his reactions.

Finally he strolled around the corner to Janis' display with Garry and Mona close behind him, because they wanted to be in the photo if one of the local journalists took Larry's picture. Larry stopped and looked at Janis' arrangement, first, it seemed, at the three-by-three photo block, quickly catching the idea, and then at the single photo, *BEFORE EDDIE SLEEPING*—and he froze on the spot, clearly shocked, no, horrified…He turned red, then pale, then started to tremble as if close to breaking down; his mouth open, gasping and searching for words, he stared at Janis and stared at this photo that was hanging there, more a quote than a statement, and not meant to be a menace to anybody. Where did you get this? he finally hissed at Janis, and Janis, alarmed and confused by Larry's reaction, could only stammer: It was in my Hasselblad when I got it. Your Hasselblad? Larry screamed, Your Hasselblad?—It's *my* Hasselblad, *my* Hasselblad, *mine, mine, mine*! And in one big bound he jumped forward to the wall, grabbed the picture and ripped it off its hook. The frame crashed to the floor, the glass splintered into big pieces, cutting through the photo and slitting it apart. The bang shut down all chatter. People gasped, turned around, hesitant, anxious but also curious to not miss something special going on; slowly they crept closer, eventually surrounding the spectacle in a big circle. This is mine, Larry whined, it's me! Clyde took it! Then he started yelling: You have no right to use it, no right to hang it here, you obnoxious little brat, you are fired, leave, out with you, *out, out*! And just as he wanted to grab Janis by her hair to drag her out, Eddie inserted himself and punched Larry in the face. Back off, he shouted, Leave her alone! Larry floundered, totally surprised to be confronted by this unknown man coming out of the blue to throw himself in his way. Larry raised his

134

fist, threatening Eddie, but simultaneously he had to struggle to regain his balance and composure. A piece of the torn-up photo stuck in his right hand like a sword. His purple cape had slipped from his shoulder and sagged down to the floor, unbeknownst to him, and just when he stepped forward, maybe to stick his paper-sword-knife in Eddie's heart or somewhere else, Larry stumbled, got one of his feet caught up in the long folds of his cape, and fell lengthwise into the glass shards. The photo knife crinkled, bespattered with Larry's blood, now gushing from his cheek, cut open by one of the crystal-gleaming daggers on the parquet. Embarrassed people retreated two steps; only Garry and Mona quickly jumped forward to crouch down to the right and left of the wounded colossus, just in case—and in fact there were some camera flashes lighting up and documenting the scene. Larry glanced at Eddie, speechless. Then he picked himself up and slowly gathered the shreds of his self as it was: dispersed, dissolved, and displayed to everybody in its splintered glory.

And here—I don't know what got into Eddie. He could have left it at that. He had fought for Janis, protected her from Larry's violent fist, and had won this fight. But Eddie couldn't let go. So while Larry was still on his knees in front of him, with one hand holding his bleeding cheek and the other pressing at the floor in support of his effort to get up, Eddie positioned himself, legs apart and arms crossed, in front of Larry and said aloud and full of contempt, slowly pronouncing every word so that everybody could hear it: Who are you! A professor, we thought, but a clown, that's what we've learned, dressed up like for the circus! You want to impress these people—but they are smarter than you, they are not awed by this ridiculous masquerade, they don't buy this crap, they know about *The Emperor's New Clothes*. What a pathetic imposter you are: your flowery photos are nothing original, no, they are stolen ideas, poorly done copies of Mapplethorpe's recent photo exhibition. I've seen it: stunning, genial shots of blooms! You've just tried to copy them, and you didn't even do it well! Shame on you! You are disgusting! Then Eddie turned away. Janis stared at these two men, unable to fathom what was going on. Garry and Mona stepped back, antsy and uneasy. Aching to his bones, Larry got up, cautiously and with shaking hands picked up his cape, pressed it to his heart, and started to walk, walked with swaying steps, teetered through the crowd that silently stared at him with a hundred eyes, lurched through the narrow aisle they opened for him, an outcast and leper now, who stumbled as if in a maze, upright yet strangely removed from himself, without seeing anybody, maybe even without feeling anything, walked with a slight limp because one of his heels had detached itself from his boot, probably when he fell, hobbled albeit with his head held high, approached the door, and left into the warm evening dusk onto the still heated street, straight ahead though, without looking and without noticing that just then, in that moment, a truck came driving by, not faster than permissible, but too fast to stop when Larry, still in his funk, began to cross the street, and the driver hit his horn, and the brakes squeaked, and the truck spun and slung and finally came to a halt, with the metal mudguards scratching and screaming on the asphalt and the rubber fuming and stinking, and with a part of Larry beneath the left double tire wheels, from which his purple cape still fluttered for a bit before it sank down, deflated and crumpled, yet gently covering his saddened heart, his pained soul, his lost mind, and his deadened bluish eyes.

Of course Janis had to leave the Rhode Island School of Design. After the police had interviewed everybody, and the men from the fire engine had lifted Larry's body off the street and driven him away, bagged in black fabric, zipper-closed and so small a package that some people might have wondered whether it was really him, the huge man he used to be, or whether he had managed to secretly slip away, merely leaving his purple cape behind—yes, whether he had miraculously escaped this *locus horribilis* of defeat in order to restart his life someplace else, where he would be appreciated and admired as an artist and loved as a man and human being—after all that and the unvoiced presumption that it was not only Eddie's scorn but first and foremost Janis' brazenness to pin her teacher up on the wall that had driven Larry to run his course all the way down to death—from that point of view it was clear that Janis couldn't stay any longer in Providence.

Eddie and Janis took *EDDIE SLEEPING* off the wall, wrapped the pictures in bubble plastic, stacked them on the back bench of Eddie's Oldsmobile Cutlass, and only briefly stopped at the dorm, where Janis collected her few items and left a short note for Lisa on the table saying *Sorry and good luck! Janis*. Thereafter she silently sat next to Eddie driving, not able to think, not willing to talk, and the ride was long, her dreams were gone, and the night was black all the way down to New York. I gather it was hard for both of them. But it was good that she went with him. It must have been right before I was born. Maybe Eddie wanted to bring her home anyway, just didn't want to tell her in advance while she was so focused on preparing her first exhibition. Anyway, I'm glad that I was born in New York, because whenever I mention Providence, people in Europe think I'm speaking of France. New York is good, a good place to be born, everybody knows where that is. I'm still strangely blank about picturing my birth or imagining how my mother came home with me—and where was home anyway? Where did she live? Life and time seem blurred about that, which might be only natural. We can't remember the experience of our birth, and who would want to anyway? However, I do know that at some point, maybe soon after, Joyce died, and we all lived in her 5th Avenue condo, Eddie, Janis, Paul, and I.

But I still don't know how Joyce died. What struck her down? Did she have a heart attack? Was it an accident? A suicide?— When I was little and asked my father about my granny, and he wouldn't tell me, I sometimes thought of her as a white bird: she just flew away one beautiful summer day, through the open window straight towards the shining sun, merrily flapped her wings, freely zipped out and lightly floated through the warm air that surged from Manhattan's street canyons heated by its tall buildings' summer walls, drifting up from deep down the chimney shafts, a breeze that carried her upwards, upwards, where she at first was hovering for a moment in the skies around 5th Avenue and Central Park, then smoothly gliding over to the Dakota, curiously looking from above at all the places she had gazed at so often from her living room, and then…I don't know where she would have gone then, but I always hoped she would have found a nice place to go. My father once said it was too bad that she died. He had just received a letter from the adoption agency that would have finally brought her news from her son. He had worked so hard on Susan Turner to get her to do what she was not supposed to do, under any circumstances, and when she finally agreed to provide the strictly forbidden information—it was too late, just one day too late. When he came to bring Joyce the letter, she was already gone, he said. Maybe she would have stayed, he thought, had she received it in time. But since she was already gone, he left it sealed as it was, because he felt he had no right to snoop around in her affairs. He had briefly thought of opening it to find out about her son and inform him of Joyce's death, but what good would that have done—at that point it was to no further avail. Before she was cremated, he put the sealed letter with the news about her surviving son in her folded hands, he said. When he dispersed her ashes from the Staten Island Ferry into the Upper New York Bay—as she had always wished for, should she ever die—they might very well have come together, she and he, or simply the dust they were and would always be—so there she was flying, I imagined, white and light like a short piece of thread in the wind, like a lingering thought, or like the strange bird that carries the soul of ancient tragedies to the all-embracing horizon of life in the middle of New York, in the middle of our hearts.

PART II

OUR ITALIAN JOURNEY

Musing Along

SCENE AT NIGHT

It was past midnight, and the phone rang. *Hello? Who is it?* The line crackled as if grit were trickling in from far away. *Hayden, is it you? Hayden?* I failed to find the light switch, I couldn't see. *Hello?* And then I heard him: *Ann?* It was Hayden. *Hayden! Where are you?* There was a pause. My words took time to reach him. *I'm here,* he then said, *I'm in Sydney.* I had thought by now he would be in Europe—I was a bit disappointed. *We had some additional gigs in Melbourne and Adelaide. Tomorrow we'll fly to Singapore, and next week to Tel Aviv.* These first phone moments after more than eight weeks—what could I say from halfway around the world? *How are you?* I asked him, and simultaneously he seemed to have said *I miss you,* but I wasn't sure. We both kept silent waiting for the other to talk. Finally Hayden said: *I didn't want to call. I had made up my mind to not contact you throughout this whole trip. But today I thought: this is just stupid! What do I want to find out? What do I want to prove? I got worried about losing you!* I smiled, but he didn't know. I was relieved, but I didn't say so. *Did you get my emails? I've already sent you five stories.* I was so curious to hear what he would say! He was silent for a moment. *Yes, I did receive your emails. But I didn't read them. They are all still unopened in my mailbox.* His response threw me, and even though thousands of miles apart he seemed to sense that. *I wanted to know how you would remain or change in my thoughts if I wasn't in contact with you.* Hayden has these complicated ideas. *And did I change?* I asked. *I don't know yet—I have to think about it some more. But I'm done with this. I wanted to hear your voice—and now I will read your emails.* I smiled. *Will you write me?* I wanted to know. *I've written you every day,* he said. *Endless letters I've sent you—in my thoughts that is, but still: did you receive my thoughts?* No, I hadn't, and only then I realized: I hadn't thought much about Hayden at all. I had lost myself in my stories. I thought I was writing for him. But maybe I had really written them for myself. Hayden had been present but only vaguely in the play's audience while the drama unfolded on stage. Now Hayden seemed to become anxious about my not answering him. *What have you been doing, Ann,* he asked, *Are you there, are you still there?* So I finally said: *No I wasn't there yet. When you read, you'll see.* Hayden seemed puzzled. After a while he said: *Let's be in touch, at least once in a while.* The crackling grew louder. *Yes,* I said, but I wasn't sure that he heard it before the connection got lost.

OCTOBER

Eddie was standing at the window warming his back in the afternoon sun—he always liked to do that. When I entered he smiled. Is it you, Ann? he asked. Yes, dad, it's me. Tenderness and concern flooded over me, or was it just the recognition of something familiar that soothed my fears about our estrangement? There was my father, it had been more than two years since I'd been able to bring myself to see him, and still he was the man who made for an extra beat of my heart. I was a bit surprised—an unknown woman was sitting on the sofa. With a big sigh she crossed her legs and raised her brows. Do you want a cup of tea? she asked me. My father said: Welcome home, Antje. Thank you for coming! This is Leonore, a friend. I'd rather have had this friend Leonore be elsewhere and felt a bit inhibited to hug my father in front of her scrutinizing eyes. But this wasn't my call, he's my father, and this odd situation wasn't new to me either. So I went and gave my father a hug. Hi, I said, and looked into his eyes, these eyes that are about to lose their light—or their fire, as he had told me, and I wasn't sure what he saw as he looked at me, briefly, before he lowered his lids. How are you, I softly asked him, and he made this clicking noise with his tongue, something he does when he is embarrassed, and said: It could be worse!

Leonore got up and came over to us, which immediately annoyed me: couldn't she just leave us alone for a moment? Instead—and totally uncalled for—she put her hand on my shoulder and said: Can I take your coat? She treated me like a foreigner, like a guest, as if I didn't belong here, and in some ways I don't, because I moved out many years ago, but I still have my room under this roof! It'll always be yours, my father had promised, and he also wanted me to keep a key so that whatever happens I could always come home. In fact it had felt nice to take out my key and open the door to my father's house, to enter the way I used to come home over so many years—and it is still more home to me than any other place, home of my childhood and of most of my memories, and that's why I didn't want to be treated here like a guest by any unknown Leonore. But I handed her my coat expecting that she'd bring it to the hallway, and that would give me a moment alone with my father. In fact, it worked, and as soon as she had left the room I said: Can we have dinner, just the two of us, tonight, I mean, after such a long time, I really would like that. My father nodded and said: Let me see what I can do.

He has aged. His hair has thinned out, his eyes seem smaller now, bedded as they are on top of two softly swollen tear sacs, which I briefly felt like touching, dabbing, as I did when I was little—sitting on his lap, I sometimes cautiously pulled up the skin of his eyelids or pinched his cheeks between two fingers, only a bit, probing, I don't know for what, but for some reason I enjoyed that. Father! Now he is untouchable, he looks frail to me, and I don't want him to know how concerned I am about what he told me.

I was surprised when he called. My father never asks for help. He takes his coat from the hook, the loop breaks, and the next day he brings it to the cleaner and gets it fixed. He would never ask my mother or me: Can you fix it? No. He knows how to help himself. Once his car got stolen, and I would have been happy to give him mine, which anyway was mostly sitting in the garage, but he'd rather take a rental than ask me: Can I use your car? What a shame! And when his partner left, and he nearly lost his company to the banks, he came up with a solution without asking any of his wealthy friends to help with the transition. There was little we could do for him. So it was a stunning first when he called and asked me for help.

It happened on a rainy day in early October. For the past few weeks I had been dragging my feet on writing an article on a survey about "The Oedipus Complex in Contemporary American Psychoanalysis," for which I had to type excerpts of thirty-five interviews. This was a boring task anyway, but I felt particularly listless, since only three of my interview partners had emphasized an interest in Oedipal fantasies; the majority had answered in rather indecisive, wavering terms; and twelve analysts stated that they were beyond Oedipus (if not Freud) and thought that this concept was greatly overrated, at times even detrimental to the analytic relationship. At first I was puzzled, then disappointed. I had set myself up to write a paper about a lack of enthusiasm, and I lacked the enthusiasm to write it.

Then my father called. Hi, it's Eddie, he lightly said. Hi Dad, I answered, immediately alarmed, because he rarely calls me. It is mostly me calling about once a month, just to check in and hear how he is doing. I had distanced myself a bit recently. Last time I saw him was for his sixtieth birthday. It had been *his* suggestion that I come see him that day. However, as it turned out, he never thought that I would make the trip from New York to Cologne just for the weekend. But there I was, arriving mid-morning with my carry-on and a box of Cohiba Cigars as my birthday present to him—and my father was sitting in the kitchen, still in his bathrobe, looking awful, un-showered and unshaven, dark circles under his eyes, as if he had a hangover. He snarled at me: What are *you* doing here? A young woman was sitting at the other end of the kitchen table, covered with only a long T-shirt, and she seemed to suffer from the same hangover that clouded my father's wits. Imprecisely waving his hand in her direction he introduced her as Sara. He calls me Zarah Leander, she explained and giggled. What was funny about that! I was totally taken aback. It was awkward to be standing there looking at these two unkempt people who seemed to have just dropped out of bed. I should have announced my arrival! Surprises are not for adults. Finally I put the gift-wrapped Cohiba-Box on the kitchen table and said: Happy birthday, dad! I brought you some cigars...and my father responded with *Wanna kill me?* The Cohibas had cost a fortune, and he thanked me with sarcasm. Typical him! Why does he have such a hard time accepting a gift and showing some appreciation? We got off to a very bad start, and so the weekend went on. I announced that I would go to sleep for a couple of hours, assuming that meanwhile my father would clear the deck, but when I came down again, he was still in a grumpy mood, and Sara instead of being sent off to the moon continued to hover over my father and dominate throughout the weekend. On Monday morning I left, irritated and depressed. Of course he later apologized on the phone, and of course we put it behind us. But for a long time after, I felt strangely hopeless and resigned.

I talked about it with my analyst, but I'm not sure that he understood what I was struggling with. He only poked for my anger, and sure, I was angry, but I knew that, and it wasn't the heart of it. When he kept bringing it up—you must be angry, he reiterated as if enthused about his discovery—I dropped the issue. Leave me alone! But still I wondered: why couldn't my father settle with one good woman—anyone would have been fine with me, just make a good choice! I kept making my phone calls. All was fine. We didn't tell each other too much about our personal lives, but we wanted to keep each other posted. When he occasionally mentioned that Sara had left him, I didn't ask for details, and he didn't volunteer any. One more had left. He seemed a bit sad thereafter. That was always the case, and each time it pulled me back in. Whenever I sensed his loneliness, I felt sorry for him and wanted to be at his side. But only a short time later he mentioned a new girlfriend in passing, Chantal from Bordeaux, who was a fashion designer in training at a Cologne-based institute—so she too would leave, I immediately thought, she would go back to France. These starts and stops keep my father going, and for most of the time he is too busy to call me.

But then he called. What are you up to these days, he asked me. I'm trying to make progress with my article, I lamely said, how about you? Someone talked in the background, and he seemed to put his hand over the mouthpiece, muffling this voice and his response. Then he came back: Listen, I've been diagnosed with age-related macular degeneration: AMD they call it. So I'm going to go blind—that is, I'm about to lose my eyes' fire. I was shocked! Isn't there a cure? There must be a cure! My father cleared his throat. No, there isn't. So I thought—I would like to see you—before I can't anymore. Immediately I felt bad for not having seen him for so long. Of course! I hurried to reassure him. But still—I can't believe it! Yeah, he slowly said, it's difficult for me as well. Now what I want to ask you is this: can you help me with the transition? You know I bought this house in Monteriggioni. Most of the restoration is done. But the house needs some finishing touches—appliances, furniture, and so on—and I thought we could do this together over the holidays. You could work on your article in the mornings and in the afternoons you could help me get around—just until I am used to walking in the fog. That was his proposal, and yes, I wanted to help him! And yes, I felt, I could do this. Yes, I said to my father, I can do this. Let me figure it out, and I'll get back to you shortly. I'll be with you soon, I promise.

I closed my eyes. My father wouldn't see anymore, wouldn't be able to read, to go to the movies, to spot a beautiful woman—to look into my eyes. He would get up in the morning and fumble for the socks that he had put on the chair or dropped on the floor the night before, and he wouldn't be able to find them, and a wave of anger would rise in him, which he would only be able to keep at bay by deciding to simply get a new pair from his closet. So he would get up, walk a few steps, and run into the open closet door, the door he hadn't been careful enough to lock the night before, so that it had slowly swung open, pulled out by its gravity, and now he would run into this open door, and it would hurt, hurt his nose, ouiiih, and he would swear: Fuck! Fuck! and be furious and desperate, feeling attacked, as if malicious spirits were out to trick him. Alma! he would scream, but Alma wouldn't be there yet, it would be too early, she only arrives at nine o'clock, so he couldn't blame her for not having his socks in reach. He would be alone in his house with all the silence around him—and anyway he was convinced that nobody wanted to hear him scream for anything or any reason. Biting his teeth, my father would stretch out both of his arms to avoid further collisions with all this stupid furniture barring his way— it needed to go, for sure—and reaching the railing to his left and touching the wall with his right hand he would now feel with one bare foot for the steps down to the first floor. But what if he slipped on the stairs, fell down, and broke a hip, a leg, an arm, or his back? He would have to learn to be cautious like a child, very cautious and courageous! Groping his way along the railing downstairs, he would head for the kitchen to start the coffee maker when suddenly the phone would ring, just that, but the shrill sound of its unexpected alarm would startle him and make him tremble...What! This was just a phone call! But how would he do this, how, and all on his own? How could he walk through the prospect of his aspirations without holding on to the solid fixtures of his grown world and another's reassuring glance that would determine the end of his nightmare and the beginning of a good, banal, better, oh-so-comforting reality? And how would he dress over time, not seeing what he looked like? Would he end up looking like a clown, like a slob—he who despite his standard of corduroys and sweaters always had a neat, classical elegance to him, an air of subtle, understated taste...? What if he, because he couldn't see, would dribble the soup from his spoon, let a strand of spaghetti slip off his fork, end up stained and spotted, having messed up his pants without even knowing it, without being able to notice and take care of it? Everybody around him would be so damn generous: don't say anything, they would whisper to each other, he can't see, don't embarrass him, what difference does it make? Who cares, they would think, it's just these few spots, nothing. Wrong, it was everything! It was what made him part of his culture, and its lack would set him apart from the civilized world he used to belong to. He would shuffle and stumble about like a cripple, like a rundown decrepit idiot! This fear, I thought, would torture his mind and push him into solitude. Then I thought: there must be a woman who would care for him, there always was. But he hadn't mentioned any. Maybe he was on his own right now, or had withdrawn for as long as he would need to transition into this new phase. It would be just him and me! Destiny wants me to help my father step by step to find his way! We would have a lot of time, time to talk. Maybe there would never be any better time for us to be together...So I had immediately booked my flight.

Leonore was nowhere to be seen when we left my father's house to have dinner at a nearby restaurant. The street was dark and slippery, it was drizzling and about to freeze. With his padded leather coat, a brown cashmere shawl wrapped twice around his neck, and his favorite green felt hat, he looked curiously old-fashioned. In order to protect his eyes from the cold wind he wore sunglasses, which must have prevented him from seeing the little he is still able to see. Instead he linked arms with me, and we walked slowly, uncertain and unsafe, a bit like an old couple, walked cautiously with respect to his diminished sight and in anticipation of these unknown weeks ahead of us. The small Italian neighborhood restaurant he had picked was only a few blocks away; its flashing sign, *Pina's Pasta,* projected its red letters all along the wet lane's gleaming cobblestones. This sign will make it easy for my father to find this place, I thought, he just has to walk towards the red light.

I often go to Pina, he said. The food is simple and good, and I like her, she's a fabulous woman. In fact, she was the first one I told about my AMD, just when I came from the hospital, and you know what she said? First she said: *Porca miseria!* And then she said: Well, by now you're able to find me with your eyes closed, aren't you? I'll make sure you'll have your table here, and I'll cook for you! So you'll be fine. My father paused, and I felt a brief sting because he hadn't told *me* first! Then she gave me a hug, he continued, And I tell you—it felt so comforting, it took all the scare away, at least momentarily. Of course, since then there have been days when I feel anxious, or furious; I lament, I complain, I bargain over I don't know what. But whenever I think of Pina's hug, I feel: it'll be alright, somehow it'll be alright—maybe it's as simple as that! I was stunned. Had I ever heard my father talk about being scared? What a moment! Yeah, I said, and briefly pressed his arm.

We had reached the restaurant. I tried to open the porch door, but a strong wind pushed against it, and in the end it was my father who opened it. Thank you! Inside was a quiet room with about ten tables, white paper covers over green-and-white-checkered tablecloths, a lamp hanging down over every table giving each space a private shine. And there was Pina. Ciao Eddie, she shouted, rushing through the kitchen door into the restaurant. She hugged my father. And you are Eddie's daughter, she immediately continued, and hugged me too! Welcome Ann, she said, Your father has told me a lot about you. He is so proud of you. Now you'll see that I take good care of him, and you

154

don't need to worry! And off she went, and we sat down at my father's special corner table, and soon we had two big heaps of Spaghetti Bolognese on our plates and two glasses of Chianti Classico in front of us. To our Italian adventure! my father said. To your health, I tentatively responded.

Silently we rolled our spaghetti around our forks. There was only one other couple sitting at the other end of the room, people my father seemed to know, because they briefly nodded when we entered. He easily makes friends with strangers, and he likes doing so. As a child it often annoyed me when he simply turned away, forgot about Issy and me, forgot about having promised to take us someplace, and instead bonded with some folks we didn't know, asking them where they came from, what they were doing, and soon he offered some help or invited them to join our table; and if these people had kids, he went to his car, opened the trunk, and got out some toys, the *Magic Man* or the *Mad Box* or whatever seemed suitable, and gave it to them as a gift. All these amazed faces around him, these beaming eyes, this air of disbelief that there was someone, a complete stranger, showering them with presents, attention, compassion, and advice! *He was the magic man!* But not for us! Usually, my mother, Issy, and I sat there like mute background actors in a repeated play, my mother more patient than we kids, who sometimes just left the table and went elsewhere; we knew, by the time my father was done chatting, charming and helping, it would be too late for whatever we had planned to do. But now I wonder: how will he go on doing this without seeing people around him? Will he just follow their voices when he hears them nearby, decide whether he likes them, listen to what they're talking about? Now I want him to be able to continue to do what he's enjoyed doing all these years. It always gave him deep satisfaction.

One summer day when my mother, he, and I were on a trip through the countryside, we came to witness an accident. It happened right in front of our eyes. A tractor had slipped half off the street, thereby knocking down a little girl, about my age, who was picking flowers by the side of the road with her parents only a few steps behind her; the tractor's big back wheel rolled over the girl's little legs, surely breaking them into pieces. It was awful. The parents were yelling and howling in a panic; the farmer, in shock, said time and again that he didn't mean to go astray and didn't know what happened; and the little girl lay on her back, her face paper white, her eyes and mouth wide open, like a doll, stiff and clean, the bunch of flowers still tightly held in her fist. No cars, people, or houses anywhere near, only cornfields stretching to the horizon and the glistening noontime sun brooding over the dusty asphalt—and of course, no cellular phones at that time either. So my father immediately offered to transport the girl to the nearest hospital. They put her in the back seat of our car, her head in her mother's lap, her father sat next to my father, and off they raced, leaving me with my mother and the terrified farmer at the site of the accident. Finally we mounted the tractor and slowly rumbled behind them. Of course my father did the right thing. But then he continued to stay involved with these people; he visited the girl in the hospital, and when there wasn't enough money in their healthcare plans, he chipped in, paid for an additional surgery and then for part of her rehabilitation, and then he went on taking care of her financially and otherwise and didn't stop before she was grown up and had settled into a job he had helped her find. He became the big man of this family, a kind of godfather or house-holy hero, at least in the eyes of the girl and her mother—I don't know how her father felt about all this...

Pina was chatting and laughing in the kitchen. This is my father's home, I thought; he feels comfortable here. I could see it in the way he sat at this table, leaned back in his chair, his small belly gently bulging out of his jacket, his firm and well-groomed hand simply resting on the table. Here he'll have dinner, here he will talk with Pina when she's done with work; together they will drink a glass of wine and chat about the things that happened during the day, and my father will know all about her and her family and will have good advice for everybody, and Pina will trust him, so much so that she often will first ask *him* about a problem before she even talks it over with her husband or her adult children. So there will always be a chance for my father to jump into gear and steer Pina's family carriage out of life's uneven ground and through her luscious, earthy, full-hearted world.—I realize I'm still a bit jealous, but actually, it's alright. For my father Pina is home, and I am not—or am I? In her warm and simple hug he finds what I can't provide, being so far away in New York. So I should be grateful and consider myself lucky that there is someone he can rely on, right here. The pasta is great, I said, and my father suggested: Next time you should try Pina's Saltimbocca!

Then we were silent again, and just when I wanted to ask him about the state of his sight, he said: Tell me, how you are doing over there in New York? So I told him that I am in the fifth year of my psychoanalytic training, and that I see my control cases in an office, sublet to me by an older colleague. When you called, I reassured him, I would have come no matter what. But it happened to also be a good moment in my practice for an extended break. My first control case, a math student, had just terminated his brief analysis in order to start a job on the West Coast; my second, a lawyer, was going into a twelve-week maternity leave; and my third training case, an Egyptologist, was currently working on excavations at Abusir and has scheduled to start his analysis with me in March. I didn't tell my father that I also had to interrupt my own analysis, because I didn't want him to know that I hadn't terminated yet. My father seemed pleased. Oh, then you are quite advanced with this! What are you planning to do next? I told him that I didn't know. I'm fascinated with psychoanalysis, but I am not sure if I want to stay in New York or if I'd rather return to Germany. I like New York, I said, but after five years I still don't feel at home there. Funny, my father responded, it's the same with me, just the other way around. Despite living in Cologne for more than thirty years now, it has never become home for me. I miss New York, I always do. It's weird: Janis wanted to stay in New York. It was me urging her to move to Cologne and settle here. Of course her parents were very happy about that, and probably the conditions for developing *FIXIT* were better here at the time than in the US. But still...My father gets melancholic when he talks about his time in New York...Would I end up like him, yearning for the past and not accepting a new place in my life, be it New York or anywhere else? The really weird thing is that in all these years my father never went back to New York, not even once for a visit. Why not? He wouldn't tell. I'm okay, he'd just say, don't worry! You can come with me when I fly back, I now suggested lightly and watched his face, which remained unreadable.

My father changed the subject: And what about a boyfriend, if I may ask, are you seeing someone? He would have accepted had I not wanted to tell him, but it felt nice to share a bit of my life with him. So I told him about Hayden, told him that he plays the jazz piano, that I met him at the *Blue Note* when he was playing an interesting jazz adaptation of Bach's *Art of Fugue*, how I had noticed that there was a strange fight going on between him and the trumpet player who, whenever Hayden wanted to start his piano solo, interfered and literally blew him away! Eventually Hayden came to terms with this guy's need to outshine him, he even smiled at him and responded to his trumpet solos with short, lovely piano echoes. My father looked somewhat skeptical. He is not a fighter, he said. The piece was Hayden's, I countered, it was more important to him that it came across well than that he engage in this stupid fight for attention. Hayden is so mature, I explained, he is serious, present, interesting, but also a bit mysterious... Mysterious? my father asked. I trust him, I said, and felt a bit defensive. He just moved in with me a few weeks before he left with his band for a tour around the world. He'll be back sometime in the spring, and only then will we really live together and see how that goes. Hayden...? Sounds like Haydn, my father said. Is he American? No, he is Austrian, I responded, but he has lived in New York for more than fifteen years. Then Pina brought us two more glasses of Chianti Classico.

I couldn't even speak German when we arrived here, my father reminisced. I had my private lessons, but it took me a while. So in the beginning I was sitting there, Janis had gathered all her friends, basically kids from school, and they were chatting and giggling, and I didn't understand a word. But I thought she should have that, she was so young, out of school for only a few months, so I wanted her to have this kind of fun—not needing to be too much of an adult right away. Imagine, she was eighteen and already a mother with two kids, what a challenge! And you were a colicky baby, crying every night! I always got up when you cried. I wanted Janis to sleep. So I put you on my arm, belly down, and walked with you through the house. Sometimes I threw a warm blanket around you and went out, strolled with you through the old parts of town. Nobody there, say at three o'clock in the morning. Usually you had calmed down by then, and I turned you around, and you were just lying on my arm, and if you weren't sleeping you were looking up to me with your big eyes. I told you a lot during those nights, babbled at you whatever was on my mind, my voice seemed to calm you down, and eventually you fell asleep.

After a brief silence my father went on—now as if talking to himself: One night I was sitting down on a park bench. I was tired and wanted to rest a bit. A woman came up to me, dressed all in black: black dress, black jacket, black shoes, even a black hat and scarf. She asked if she could sit with me on this bench. It was the only bench around. Sure, I said, and asked her what she was doing so late at night alone in this park. She said she couldn't sleep. Since her husband had died a few weeks ago, she couldn't sleep anymore. She said he was killed in an accident at a crossroad when he ran a red light. It was late at night, she said, and there was barely any traffic. But just when he missed this one red light, there was a cyclist riding home, a student of history, and her husband catching eye of him at the very last moment immediately tried to steer away from him, which caused his car to flip over, twice as they reconstructed it, and slam into the concrete socket of a signpost. The crash killed him instantaneously, she said. Unfortunately he didn't manage to fully avoid the student. With the back of his trunk he slashed into his bike; the poor kid was torpedoed out of his saddle, flew across the street, and landed on her husband's car. Now he is a quadriplegic! This terrible accident crippled him for life, she said, what a horrible moment—this one brief mistake took everything, all gone, all lost, all ruined! And she couldn't get over the fact that they'd fought earlier that night over having or not having children. She said she wanted a baby, and he wasn't up to raising a child. It pained her to think that she pushed it too far, that she should have dropped the issue when she saw how angry he got. So he stormed out on her and killed himself, albeit hours later and drunk by then, as they found out, but still, she felt, that was a terrible thing to do! The accident happened over there, she said, pointing across the park, and that's why she felt drawn to return to this place again and again. Each night she went to this crossroad and watched the lights turn red, over and over, as if she could undo it, stop it, if only in her head—but it never stopped, never. She had visited the student who was in rehabilitation at the time. She was amazed, she said, that he didn't seem resentful. He simply said: Shit happens! But how could he say so, she wondered? She didn't understand! This woman was talking more to herself than to me, a bit monotonous, as if she was saying the rosary. Meanwhile I was rocking you in my arms, and you were sleeping. All of a sudden the woman asked me if she could hold you for a while, she just wanted to feel what it's like to have a baby in her arm. And I needed to pee and agreed and handed you over to her, and told her I was briefly going behind the bushes. And so I did. But when I came back she was gone! I looked around and saw her on the other side of the lawn quickly walking away, the black scarf flapping behind her. So I screamed at her, *HEY!*, and started to run, and she turned around and saw me and started running too, and I got furious and sped up after her as she was approaching this damn crossroad—and I thought, what the hell...? Finally when she must have heard coming close, she threw you on the lawn and kept running, and I let her run away and knelt down next to you—you were awake, you whimpered a bit, not very much, and I picked you up and held you, held you, I was totally shocked, but you were fine, my god, you were fine, you were fine...My father had tears in his eyes. You've never told me...I said, and after a while he said: I know it happened, but it was also unreal, just like a nightmare. When I came home, Janis was asleep, so I didn't tell her. I've never told her nor anybody else, and now I don't even know if it really happened—or was it only a dream? What a nightmare!

Had it really happened? What if my father had taken a bit longer behind the bushes, and by the time he came back, the woman in black would have been gone? Gone and taken me along, determined to have a baby, incidentally me, stolen from a park bench...the way someone quickly grabs a package of meat at the grocery store, right? But who would have realized? She would have gone first to the Dome to cross herself and thank God for having sent this baby her way, or at least to settle her conscience, then briefly home, waiting for the busy morning traffic to start, the whole time nervously checking her watch and keeping me tight, oddly wedged between her bony knees, *uugggh!* Then at seven she would have hastened over to the train station—*Köln Hauptbahnhof!*—cleverly and inconspicuously mingled with the crowd, bought a ticket to Hamburg, and off we'd have gone, a couple of hours by train, I on her lap, increasingly fussy and anxious—feeling something wasn't right, something was different, maybe most strikingly her sweet and sharp perfume, sweet like her dreams of having a baby, and sharp like the knife with which she cut her losses and turned mine into a prize for herself. What's the difference for this baby, she would have thought, I can be

163

a mother as good as any other! From then on I would have breathed in this stinging mix of sweet and sharp through all these long years till my eighteenth birthday, when I would finally be free to go...But first she would have settled with me in Hamburg and raised me as her daughter. I would have grown up thinking she was my mother even though she wasn't! Would I have noticed, sensed, guessed anything? I would have heard the story about my father, who wasn't my father, heard that he was killed in this crossroad accident a long time ago in Cologne when she was pregnant with me— such a lie! Why did you move to Hamburg, I would ask my false mother, and she would have given me the wrong answer, namely that she couldn't bear to ever come across the site where my father died. What a lie!

All these thoughts! It is strange, but lying in my old bed in my old room right under the roof, I felt like a teenager again! So many nights I had been lying here, awake and unhappy or angry or worried about something—difficult years! The moon was shining in, and there was the silver frame with my granny's photo sitting on the windowsill. *Hi granny!* She smiled. She always smiled at me. *Do you want to come with me to New York?* I will take her with me! And then I sail over to New York, sail as if on some escalator that ends right at the door to my flat, and the door is open, and Hayden is there. I am surprised that he has returned so soon. But I still have to go with my father to Tuscany! I don't know how to explain it to him. He makes a sign with his hand showing that he wants me to stay, and I want that too, but I have promised to go with my father. Suddenly I feel pulled, or am I gliding away? I am falling, but I'm not scared, it is as if I am held or carried or transported on some rolling chair, or what?

Abruptly I sat up. It was still dark night around me, only the moon cast a stinging streak of light on the floor next to my bed. I should sleep! Early tomorrow morning we would drive to Tuscany. I hadn't even unpacked my luggage, it was sitting there in the bright moonshine, open like a treasure box with all the precious gowns, robes, costumes, pearls, and diamonds sprawling out of it, but really only my jeans, shirts, socks, and sweaters were scattered around. I could get some books from my father's library to take to Tuscany, I was sure there would be times when I would want to read—great idea! I opened the door and wanted to go downstairs to the living room, but then I heard voices—first Leonore's and then my father's voice. They seemed to be in the living room. So Leonore came back! She wasn't here when we returned from *Pina's Pasta*. What were they talking about? Their words were muffled but the tone was tense, they seemed to be arguing about something...can come with me...my father said a bit louder, defensively, or did he say ...*can't* come with me...? I held my breath. Leonore seemed to object. All of a sudden I felt a tremendous anger surging in me: If my father asked Leonore to come with us to Tuscany, I would quit! I would not take this whole trip only to cater to these two people! If my father needed my help, that was one thing. If he planned to spare his Leonore any trouble and have me bother with it instead while she painted her nails or whatever, I was not going to be part of this party! I felt like swearing—yet simultaneously I was surprised by my reaction. My father clearly said that it would be just him and me. What was I doing here? Was I trying to eavesdrop on this conversation between my father and Leonore? How stupid of me, how childish, impossible! To secretly stand in the dark staircase holding my breath! Jesus! I couldn't believe it! I went back to my room and softly closed the door, but my heart was pounding, and I didn't like this Leonore, for sure!

In the morning the street was still wet, the bushes were dripping, it was creepy cold, but the sky was blue, and I was in the mood to get going. In the foyer my father was circulating around his luggage, repeatedly tapping every piece with his hand, as if to make sure that it all stayed together. Leonore was nowhere to be seen, excellent! Maybe she ran off in a huff after last night's argument, I didn't care! My father's blue Mercedes was idling right in front of the house, all four doors open like wings spread wide to fly away. So he did steer it out of the garage, I couldn't help thinking, he wanted to feel one more time how it felt to be behind the wheel and drive; and while the machine was humming and the car slowly rolled and crackled the few yards over the driveway's white gravel, he may have waited for something, some special feeling to come up, yet there was nothing, just disappointment thinly dispersed over the lack of any excitement, zest, or arousal—oh well!

Then my dear Alma, our old housekeeper, arrived with her white apron, still the same style, flashing brightly from under her unbuttoned woolen coat; she hugged me, and she still smelled of cinnamon, mint, and the warmth of her strong, soft body that I knew so well! How often had I buried my face in her chest and smelled her love up close! I had hoped to see her before we left! Seeing me she got teary, and I welled up too. So nice to see you! she said. How long has it been! I missed you. How are you doing, big girl? I felt like sitting down with her and having coffee for hours. I'm good, I said, and scrutinized her face when I asked her how she was doing, because she always says fine. Fine, fine, she said, and stroked and rubbed my shoulder just to be in touch with me a bit longer. I've known her forever. Do you want to come with us to Tuscany? I asked her with a wink. She smiled and shook her head. I can't, you know, Otto isn't well, he needs me, and your father's house needs me too!

We got in the car. I sat in the driver's seat, where my father used to sit, and he sat next to me, where I used to sit—what a reversal of roles, I thought. I felt a little clumsy behind the wheel of this bulky limousine, but I would get used to it. It was fun to wind my way through Cologne, to see again these old streets I used to ride along on my bicycle, and I still remembered where to go, except for a few of them that had turned in the meantime into one-way streets and required a detour. My father was happy to give me guidance. We both followed our inner maps.

When we were on the highway, my father said: It's been quite a while since you've been in Tuscany. Do you even remember Monteriggioni? Tuscany! When I was little we went there many times. On our last trip, about fifteen years ago, Helene, my father's girlfriend at the time, was with us. She was only ten years older than me, and we became good friends. She introduced me to a lot of things about boys and showed me how to use eyeshadow, and how to paint my fingernails without going over the cuticles. But then she went off with some Lorenzo, whom she had met in a bar. It was a big drama. She just disappeared, and we got worried that something bad had happened to her, that she'd got lost or hurt, or was robbed or kidnapped. We even contacted the carabinieri; they cautioned us to wait for a few days, and sure enough, three days later she called my father and asked if he would mind sending her luggage by cab to Siena where she had moved in with this Lorenzo. My father was in the darkest mood. I felt betrayed by her and sorry for him. But we did stay for the rest of our vacation in Florence at the Hotel Lungarno and went for day trips to the countryside.

So I do remember Monteriggioni: a small medieval town, sitting like a bird's nest on top of a hill peacefully overlooking the corn and sunflower fields, the olive groves and vineyards, a fortress of tenacity, insurmountable now as ever, since nothing much seems to have changed there throughout the centuries. In its center there is a big piazza with a small collection of buildings, all huddling as if to frame what looks

168

like a theatre's stage—the perfect place for an old drama to play out. My father had sent me pictures of the house he purchased. It was built into a row of old houses in a narrow street, Via G. Matteotti, and looked over a small garden with a huge thyme bush in one corner and a tall cypress in the other right onto the town's old stone wall. It's actually fortunate that I found this place in Monteriggioni, my father said. You know, at first I was looking for a place in the middle of the vineyards and hills, something remote and quiet. But given my decreasing sight I would have been totally lost there. In Monteriggioni I can get around on my own. Everything I need is close by: a grocery store, a bar, a restaurant—even a church, he added with a chuckle.

So finally I got my chance to ask him: How is it for you, growing blind? There was a pause, and I was already regretting that I splashed this out so directly. But then my father said: You know, I've seen so many things in my life, and I still see some...I think it will work. I'll just have to develop a few new skills. For instance, I've signed up for training sessions in peripheral vision, starting when we get back from Tuscany. I also will try the Braille system, even though people tell me that it's hard to learn at my age. Maybe I'll purchase a dog to guide me— actually it could be nice to have a dog. So don't worry about me. It will be a different world I live in, literally a world at the edge, where the marginalized things reside, those we used to overlook because we are so focused on what seems important at any one moment. But in the end—what is important? Maybe it's what we've neglected or pushed to the side all along. That's what I will start looking at from now on.

And then in Zurich the hotels were completely booked because of some mega-event, and I was dead tired from all the driving, and the last room we could snatch was a double: one room with one bed for the two of us! Was that real or some bad joke? I couldn't believe it. Usually my father was so well organized. Why hadn't he made hotel reservations for us? No way could I share the bed—a queen-size—with my father—*no*! He noticed my discomfort and said he would sleep in the car, which I insisted he would *not*! You need to sleep as much as I do, I proclaimed, maybe even more so, because you are older. Oh! he said, and went to the hotel bar for a beer in order to give me some privacy while I undressed and went to bed. Don't worry, he said as he left, you know that I can't see much, and even less so in the dark. But I thought, it wasn't as much the *seeing* that I dreaded than the *feeling*: to even involuntarily make contact him with any part of my body as he lay next to me in bed, or have his naked foot touch mine by chance, or to sense his sleeping breath, uughh! The mere idea of lying in one bed with my father made my hair stand on end. And how uncomfortable would it be to later associate to this in my analysis—no, thanks!

When my father was gone, I cleared the floor of useless items and pushed our luggage to the wall, so that he wouldn't stumble across anything upon his return. Then I turned off the lights and tried to settle in for the night, crouched and huddled in an upholstered armchair with all the decorative pillows stuffed under my back, neck, and head, my legs wrapped in a blanket and my feet hanging somewhat forlorn over the small footrest. It wouldn't be comfortable, but it would work. I closed my eyes and wanted to relax, but my body was still driving, vibrating from the hundreds of miles we had travelled. People were laughing outside in the hallway. I heard the elevator going up and down. Some cars were honking on the street. The traffic slowly died down. A church clock rang midnight. And then I heard a noise at the door, the keycard inserted in the lock-slit, the door slowly opening, allowing a dim shine from the hallway to enter, just flitting by, then dark again and the swishing of clothes rubbing against each other in motion, and in the gloom of the night there was my father or merely a shadow of him, shoes in one hand, the other extended into space, feeling for what might be in his way, halting, unsure but cautiously trying, soundlessly tiptoeing forward in his socks, almost gliding through the air, then hitting the short sofa, bumping into this vulgar two-seater that blocked his way, a full-throng wall demanding him to stop— and he stopped. Without the slightest sound he put down his shoes, placed them on the mushy carpet at the end of the sofa, and then mounted the loveseat from behind, swinging his right leg over the backrest and coming to sit on its velvet bolster, like a rider on a horse; then he briefly bent forward, his chest on the bulk and his cheek briefly down as if tenderly streaking the seam of its dark wrap, before he rolled, willfully rolled over, hurling his left leg high up, whereby it seemed to be shaking or shivering until he was losing his balance, falling, plunging deeply down, plump, heavy, finally abandoning himself to the folds of his fatigue and the wrinkles of the night that was flashing, once in a while, with an image, a wandering face, and these eyes, again these unforgettable eyes, glued to a smile—and then all gone, all gone. He would sleep on this old creaking piece of furniture, crookedly, contorted and curved. He wanted me to sleep in the queen bed, comfortably stretched out and undisturbed in my dreams. And I wanted him to take the queen bed and forget about all the trouble, at least for the night. But the sheets would remain untouched. In the morning we would wake up, and looking at the clean, glossy, plain linen, unruffled by the inner struggles that remain almost unbeknownst to ourselves, we would regret, each for ourselves, not having made use of the pleasures of sleeping in a nice bed; we would think we were just stupid and childish. Mature adults should be beyond such precautions, shouldn't they? We are never beyond...! Or would I wake up in the middle of the night as I used to when I was little, a child with an uncanny sense of direction, who secretly tiptoed into her parents' bedroom, crawled under their wonderfully broad and warm comforter, and snuggled between those two sleeping giants in order to finally fall asleep with a funny smile on her face, not knowing if she would wake up with her cheek on her father's hand or her hand on her mother's breast...

NOVEMBER

The day after my eleventh birthday, my mother left. No! Issy left first. At some point—I think she was only nine at the time—she declared she wanted to go to boarding school. *What?* I remember how I stared at her in complete disbelief. Maybe I didn't even really know what *boarding school* meant. I want to go to boarding school, she repeated and pinched her lips. Why? My mother asked, equally surprised. Because! Issy stated. We waited. When she noticed that we weren't convinced, she added: And Olivia goes too. We'll go together. My mother sat down at the kitchen table right next to Issy, who listlessly pecked at the food on her plate, and put her arm around her shoulder. Issy angrily shook her off. But my mother said what she wanted to say: Olivia goes to boarding school because her parents are divorcing. I know she is your friend. You can visit her. During school vacation she can come here and stay with us. And you can write her. Also, you'll find many other friends in your life, Olivia isn't the only one. Maybe she shouldn't have added that last piece. Anyway, Issy wasn't in the mood for negotiation. I'm not going because of Olivia. I'm going because *I* want to go! No, she couldn't mean that, I thought, she wouldn't leave me. But we are friends too, aren't we? I interjected. No, we are not, Issy declared, we are sisters, that's different. I sensed my mother becoming annoyed. You can't just decide to go to boarding school. It costs a lot of money! I'm not sure that your father wants to put that up, since schools here in Cologne are actually very good. Issy didn't look at either of us. If you don't let me go, I'll kill myself. I'll jump out of my classroom window on the fourth floor, she said. My mother slapped her in her face. Don't you ever say this again! Yet Issy confirmed right away: I'll do it, I swear, I'll do it! And that was that. Sure, my father tried. My mother tried. They had many conversations with her behind closed doors. And I tried, I pleaded and begged her—all to no avail. Only Paul stayed out of it. He shrugged his shoulders and said: I don't care! I cried. I didn't understand why Issy wanted to leave me. We had done so many things together. What was wrong?

I think only at that point I realized that she had been withdrawing for quite some time; she hadn't been so open and engaged anymore; one day it was a headache; another day she had too much homework, or she was working on some project, or she was tired. Again and again there was something, anything, and she retreated to her room. At dinner she was more silent, no longer participated in our debates in her lively way. Was she depressed? But depressed about what? And then she had these brief temper tantrums, much to my surprise. Out of the blue she could throw a fit for nothing, run out and slam shut the door to her room. When she came out again, often only on the following day, she would be brooding and moody. It's true, she had been no fun to be with for quite a while, but why?

My father said her hormones were kicking in somewhat early. What was that supposed to mean, since I was a year older than she, and my hormones didn't throw any fits? I asked her many times: Did I do something wrong? Are you angry at me? Issy just turned away. It has nothing to do with you, she said. Just leave me alone! I asked my mother, who said she didn't know. So we had to let her go. She took only a few clothes but all her favorite books and her stuffed teddy bear, and she took down all the posters from the walls in her room—it really looked shockingly naked, completely deserted when she walked out the door. She gave me a brief hug, sat in the car next to my mother, who would bring her to the *Internat Schönfeld*, and didn't look back once as the car rolled out of the driveway.

It was quiet after she had left, very quiet. Our house was filled with silence. Silence also in the garden, as if all the birds had flown away, the whole place seemed deserted, lonesome, boring, with no spark to play anywhere, the swings hung stark and stiff. I missed Issy. In the late afternoons I sat on our garden bench under the weeping willow and thought of her. I ached for her. I resented her abandoning me. I blamed her for all I ever missed blaming her for, and yelled at her a thousand times. But then, when she came home for her fall vacation, I was overjoyed to see her. Issy too seemed happy to see me and to be home again. However, she stayed a bit distant. I remember how she and I strolled through the nearby woods on the day of her arrival. All of a sudden we saw a big flock of wild turkeys and at some distance a single one with a broken leg that strangely stuck out to the side. This turkey tried to stand up, each time hovering awkwardly for a bit in its effort to hop towards the others, but inevitably fell, collapsed on its chest, then spread its big dark wings, fluttered in order to get up, and fell again. It was painful and scary to watch, and I remember thinking that this turkey was as apart from its family as Issy was from us. Most striking for me was that I couldn't share this thought with her. That's when I understood that she had left me for good. At first I wrote her nearly every day, and sometimes she wrote back. It was difficult to call her because there were no phones in the girls' dorms, so she had to be found and brought to the office if someone wanted to talk with her, and then the secretary would be sitting right next to her—what could we say in these awkward moments?

I asked my mother why she thought that Issy had gone off to *Schoenfeld*. You know, at times people are incomprehensible, she said, we have to accept them as they are, everything else would be presumptuous. At that time she was pregnant with Theodore, who was born about half a year after my sister had left. Did Issy leave because she knew that there would be another child? *I* certainly didn't know it at the time! Or did my mother want another child because Issy planned to leave? Or was it a so-called accident? It was an exciting time when Theo was born. The midwife came, my mother gave birth at home. She didn't want me to be in the room during her labor, but right after he came out, I was allowed in, and I saw him all red, wet, wrinkled, still a little smudgy. I heard his first scream, what a scream, I still can hear it! Cleaned up, wrapped in a white towel, and lying on my mother's chest, he looked—just amazing! I was so in awe of this little baby, his tiny fists, his huge yawn, I couldn't take my eyes off him! I loved to watch when my mother nursed him, changed his diapers, comforted him, I was proud and happy when she allowed me to take care of him and carry him around, I couldn't get enough of looking into his round face with those chubby cheeks and big blue eyes—he looked around and looked at me as if he was thinking about everything—my smart little baby brother! For a moment life seemed to have returned home. I was so focused on Theo in these first months of his life that I forgot a bit about Issy. But then again, it didn't last very long, and he too left, as did my mother and Paul. When they were gone, silence fell back upon us like a heavy blanket muffling our previously joyous voices to nothing more than a dark murmur— *where are you—where are you—where are—where?* They were gone—or rather they stayed with us as this unfathomable loss that populated the emptiness of our home, a void screaming beyond comprehension.

So again: the day after my eleventh birthday my mother left. Yes, she did! I was standing in front of our house with the present she had given me, a yellow plastic bucket filled to the top with tulip bulbs and a small trowel with a red wooden handle. I wanted to plant the tulip bulbs near our garden fence, close to the front gate where the sun came in first thing in the morning and stayed throughout the longest hours of the day. Twenty yellow tulips. My mother came out of the house with her jeans and her rain jacket on, her long red hair bouncing in the wind. She carried Theo, who was five months at the time, all bundled up in pink, because she had decided that he could wear out mine and Issy's old baby clothes. He'll grow out of them so fast, let's save the money for something more durable, she had explained. She often tried to save money in those days. Theo peacefully looked at me while my mother came closer. What a cute little butterball he was, confident, it seemed, of whatever was ahead. My mother kneeled down next to me. Are you planting these bulbs now? she asked, and I noticed that her eyes were in tears. Yes, I answered, pointing to the garden door. I thought of planting them right here, ten on each side of the entrance. My mother nodded. That'll look nice! she said.

Then I discovered that she was carrying Paul's gray backpack on one strap thrown over her shoulder. Where are you going? I asked. Hold this, she said instead of an answer, and showed me how to hold open Paul's backpack. I held it open. My mother picked up Theo with her big hands under his little armpits, his small legs dangling down in my old pink romper. What are you doing? I asked her when she cautiously sank Theo into the backpack. She had never done this before. She didn't answer, just focused on lowering Theo into the open backpack, filling

178

the dark empty space with his little body and sitting him down on the few items she had already placed at the bottom of it, forming a kind of baby seat. What's your plan? I tried again. Look, she said, making Theo more comfortable by stuffing one of his sweaters behind his back, he fits right in. Only Theo's head and arms stuck out of the gray bag. Theo briefly complained, and then accommodated, again quietly looking at my mother. I've cut two slits here on the right and left, my mother explained, so he can stick his legs out. And while I was still holding the now heavier backpack filled with Theo, my mother reached her hands through both slits and pulled his little feet out. I noticed that he wore the yellow sneakers with the *Curious George* motif that I had picked out for him a few days earlier. Help me, she then said, turning around, exposing her back, and stretching her arms towards me so that I could slip the straps over her shoulders. And I did slip the straps over her shoulders.

When she turned again towards me I saw a tear running down her cheek. Mommy…I said, is Theo comfy…? She hugged me. He'll be fine, she whispered, and you'll be fine too. Then she abruptly moved a bit away from me, grabbed me by my arms and looked straight into my eyes. I have to go somewhere, she said with unusual gravity in her voice. You're my dear Antje, she added, you'll always be. You'll be smart and brave, won't you? *Antje,* she said. Somehow I must have understood that she needed to talk to me like the adult I would be some day. But I didn't understand what she wanted to tell me. I saw how she struggled to say more and waited, but then Paul came around the corner on the big Harley Davidson that my father had given him when he turned eighteen. How mysterious he seemed to me, Paul, in these black leather pants and this zipped-up black leather jacket, black leather gloves, laced up boots, all in black except for the silver helmet on his head. The Harley roared when he stopped next to us; his booted feet slid over the gravel, throwing up dust onto the three of us. Theo pinched his eyes. Paul's motorcycle radiated heat. Hey girly! he said, looking at me from above through his sunglasses. I've got something for you, a late birthday present. Here! And on a green cord he dangled his little silver whistle in front of my eyes, the one I had wanted to play with many times. He had never given it to me. You'll just spit into it and it'll be ruined, he used to say. Now he gave it to me for good! Really, I asked, I can really have it? Reluctantly I took it in my hands, expecting him to just tease me and take it away the next moment. Don't spit into it, remember? Paul said and grinned.

My mother got up with Theo in the backpack. You have to water the bulbs after you've planted them, she said. Not too much though, just so that they get moist. I nodded. You'll be back for dinner, right? I asked. Take care, sweetie, she answered, and swung her left leg over the Harley. Tonight I'll show you exactly where I planted the bulbs, I said, anxiously trying to pressure her into a commitment. She was already sitting on the Harley's back seat, with her arms around Paul's chest and Theo's little head resting on her shoulder. Go, she said to Paul. The Harley howled. My mother looked back at me, one more intense, piercing look, a look that hurt—then Paul lifted his foot, the Harley roared and jumped forward, yanking all three briefly back, then swinging around the bend of our driveway past the mailbox and the light post and onto the street that stretched from our house to the end of my world—off they raced. I followed them with my eyes as they rode away, quickly shrinking, my mother's red hair flickering in the wind over the black bulge of Paul's shoulders, and for a moment Theo's little head was still visible, a tiny light spot that quickly melted into my mother's jacket before all three fused into one single scheme. There was no helmet small enough to protect Theo's head, I remember thinking, and my mother never wore a helmet, nor a hat or cap, nothing, she just couldn't stand having anything on her head. Would they be safe? Would they return? And when? And where were they going? And why? I stared at where they had been just a moment ago, and where others now were busily crossing the road in passing. I looked and looked until my eyes were burning—and still I had lost them.

Where did they go? For some reason I always thought that they first went to Amsterdam, maybe because it is not too far from Cologne. So I see them arrive in the late afternoon, exhausted from all the wind on the ride. They pick the first restaurant that looks okay. Janis tries to disentangle her hair and makes painful faces as she tears at the knots in her felted strands. Theo has been nursed and sleeps on the corner bench in the free space between them. They have ordered steak with fries and beer. *Now what*, Janis thinks, and drinks half of her big glass of water in one thirsty gulp. Paul nervously plays with his keys and softly swears because he is hungry, and they haven't gotten even a piece of bread. With a growling sound he picks up one of the cardboard coasters that are neatly stacked on their table next to pepper, salt, and ketchup, and bites into it. Janis laughs. I'm starving too, she says.

Later they settle into a small hotel on Prinsengracht. Janis stands at the window and looks down to the street where Paul is smoking a cigarette talking with three men in the shine of an old-fashioned lantern. I have to wean Theo, she thinks, or else I'll always be trapped with him. Later, I imagine, she lies down and closes her eyes, but sleep won't come. She feels tired yet stirred and simultaneously numb.

Her eyes wander home, watching me as I dig one hole after another to place the tulip bulbs in. How careful she is, Janis thinks, she always takes such good care of things—she'll do well in life. Then Janis thinks of Eddie, who is sitting in his study behind his heavy desk staring at her picture—it was taken by a street photographer on their first trip to Italy, in Florence, on the Ponte Vecchio, right after Eddie had bought her a leather bag for all her photo equipment, and she was beaming with joy about this wonderful piece. That was the moment the photographer caught; they bought the picture for 10,000 Lire. Eddie loved it, it had made him happy whenever he looked at it, but now it almost kills him. The photo sits right next to the phone. Maybe I should call him, Janis thinks, but no, Eddie will never forgive me.

Theo is breathing heavily, and she worries that he caught a cold on the ride. Her hand wanders across the bedspread and touches something cold and soft. Is this Paul's jacket? What am I afraid of, she wonders, and watches how the light patterns on the ceiling above the hotel bed move as a car slowly drives by. From a certain angle the shadows come together to look like the sharp profile of her father at the end of his life when he was lying on his back, emaciated, his eyes closed, his mouth a bit open, half asleep, half dozing. *Here, I have a joint*, Paul had said the other day, *try it, it won't kill you. On the contrary, you'll see: it'll loosen you up, help you dream, make you happy*. I don't need a joint in order to dream, Janis thinks, and did it make me happy? She had taken a picture of her father in the last hour of his life, and in that moment he had opened his eyes and looked at her. *Oh, you're still here,* he had said with deep surprise, as if he felt he had left long before and only briefly come back to pick up some forgotten item. *Yes, father, I'm here*, she had answered, almost equally surprised that he had come back. *Janis?* He wanted to say something and Janis had put her camera down and reached over to his white hand on the white sheet. *Don't do it*, he suddenly said, but he looked away, up to the ceiling. *What?* Janis responded, *what, father, do you want me not to do?* But her father wouldn't respond anymore. He continued to breathe for another half hour or so and then at some point simply stopped— so subtle was the loss of his breath that Janis sort of missed the moment he died, because holding his hand she had trailed off to think about her mother who had died the year before after a long struggle with kidney cancer, and then she had thought of Joyce and of New York and had felt how much she missed it, and thought she wanted to go there, with or without Eddie, at least for a break, a vacation, at least three or four weeks. My mother mentioned it to me several times. Can I come with you? I immediately had asked her. I'm an American too, I have an American passport, don't I? And my mother had stroked my hair and replied: Yes you do. Maybe I'll take you with me...What did her father want to tell her, Janis kept wondering. Had he seen that she was about to take his picture and didn't want her to do so? She wasn't sure that he had noticed it but didn't dare to take another shot after he had spoken. Or maybe he didn't want her to go back to New York?

I think my mother took a ship from Amsterdam to New York—or had she taken a plane? Janis had kept in contact with some of her friends from the Rhode Island School of Design; they had invited her to teach a course on photography, but Eddie was against it. You can't just go and teach in Providence. Who would take care of the kids? I heard him say that. But Janis longed to go, she didn't know why. Maybe my father should have allowed her to go. Had she been able to go, at least for a few weeks, maybe she wouldn't have wanted so badly to be back in New York. My father can be so rigid! At some point I screamed at him: It's all your fault! She wouldn't have left us, she just wanted to go to New York for a bit, just for a vacation, but you wouldn't let her. And Issy wouldn't have left us either, if she could have taken those horseback riding lessons! Why are you always against everything, everything! My father had looked at me for a long, difficult moment, pained or angrily, I couldn't tell. No, it's not my fault, not at all, he then said, it's Paul's! And off he went and wouldn't talk with me for the rest of the day.

Why Paul, I wondered, why? I knew my father had the hardest time with Paul, and Paul openly disrespected him. Why do you hate him so much? I once asked Paul, and Paul just screamed at me: Because he is an asshole, a fucking asshole! I was undeterred. No, he's not! I said in a challenging tone. Yes he is, Paul snapped at me, he beat me up, with his belt, many times; he locked me in the basement with no food or water for 24 hours, for nothing, *nothing*! And he cut off my ponytail with some garden clippers—remember? Why? Because he is an asshole! And already at the doorstep he added: And you know what else he did, your dear daddy? He killed my mother—and your mother as well! I knew he was speaking metaphorically, because at that time my mother was still with us, and I knew that his mother had died from cancer, but I was shocked to feel how much hatred he carried. When he and my father were in the same room, I often felt like I was walking on lava. So in this regard it was a relief when Paul left, it eased the atmosphere around my father. However, Paul would have left anyway, he wanted to go to college and to medical school in New York where most of his trust money was being held. But he was not supposed to take my mother and my baby brother Theo with him. Was it his fault? What was his fault?

It was a little after seven when I woke up. I opened the window shades and looked at the small garden with its huge cypress right in front of me and the deteriorated flower and vegetable beds that the previous owner had dug all along the fence up to Monteriggioni's old town wall at the end of my father's property. I would look for a gardener who could plant roses in the spring. The sky was clear, light blue with a hint of an early sunrise pink. It looked cold, certainly below freezing, for the chill had thrust a white crust upon the small grass patch, and icy blisters all around the window frame entwined the glass like a filigree festoon. I quickly got dressed and slipped out of the house for cappuccino and biscotti at Laura's coffee bar: that always makes me feel so Italian!

Via G. Matteotti was empty. Only Mario's dog was standing in front of his master's door quietly watching me as I gingerly walked on the slippery skin that glazed the alley's cobblestones. Laura always opens early. Those who work in Florence or Siena and leave by bus or by car can have coffee on their way out. *Buongiorno!* I said entering the coffee shop, and Laura looked over and responded with *Ciao Anna!* They call me Anna here. I sat at the window and dipped my biscotti into the hot cappuccino—really good! Renzo, the cook from the restaurant, and Giulio, the carpenter from the antique shop, were standing at the bar, silently sipping their coffee, watching Laura empty the dishwasher and fill the shelf above it with the clean cups and glasses. The TV mutely ran morning news, showing the president in a flickering storm of flashlights grinning and nodding and readjusting his tie, and then the Pope waving his arms stiffly stretched in a ceremonial gesture that ended in two white hands sticking out of his richly ornate sleeves; then back to the broadcaster who looked a bit like Sophia Loren. The coffee machine was fizzing and steaming, the windowpanes were all fogged, and I rubbed a little opening into the white mist so that I could peek out to the piazza.

And there I saw my father. Was he already up? So early? He walked along the houses on the other side of the piazza with his left hand sometimes slightly touching the wall, walked upright as if he could see, and I know he wants to pretend that he can. He practices when nobody is around. Yesterday when I entered the living room he had Beethoven's sixth symphony on the CD player and had turned the volume up rather loud, so he didn't hear me enter. I stood at the door and watched him. He seemed absolutely focused. His head moved back and forth, which is how he uses his peripheral vision to find out what's ahead. Slowly he took two steps until his shinbone touched the coffee table, then he stepped back and redid it in one slightly bigger step, repeating this a few times, even with closed eyes, obviously in order to learn precisely how far his foot could reach out without abutting his leg against the wooden tabletop. Then he briefly sat back on the couch, only to immediately jump up as if in a hurry and take this same step without touching the table, a move that he repeated a few times and then took up the next few steps in the aisle towards the rocking chair. He fights for his independence. He wants to prove to himself and to me that he can safely get around. He doesn't want me to worry about him. He made this explicit. The other day his hand missed the glass and the red wine splashed on the table and dripped from there onto the carpet. I rushed to stop it from running farther, and when I quickly, all too quickly, snatched the bottle from his hand—I felt how hurt he was by my degrading move. He first said: Sorry for the mess...And after I had cleaned up he added: Look, this is just a carpet. At the same time, this is a new part of my life, a challenge! I've managed other challenges, and others have managed this one too. So I'll make it, you can be sure of that. I felt bad. It had been rude to run over to him just to protect the carpet. I have to learn to let him do his things on his own.

Looking through the peephole in the clouded window I saw my father passing the closed souvenir shop, barely missing the iron wastepaper box to his right, then going along the church wall touching with his outstretched hand its beautiful hand-cut travertine stones that sent a warm yellow shimmer through the cool gray of the awakening day, and finally he stopped, reaching into the inner pocket of his jacket for his cigarettes, and lit one. Then he walked across the piazza coming right towards Laura's coffee shop. I decided to call him as soon as he entered so that he would know that I was here and nobody would see that he couldn't see me. Father! Everybody else calls him Eddie. Walking across the piazza is difficult because it is paved with big old blocks of soapstone, crooked and uneven—I've repeatedly twisted my ankle when I didn't watch out where I was going—but my father walked like on a red carpet, steadily as if he knew every little edge, dent, or bump on his way, walked with his cigarette between his lips and his hands in his warm fur pockets, and he looked so immersed in his world, so confident, as if he had always lived in Monteriggioni. He walked unhurried, composed and serene, looking even a bit happy, and then he stumbled—must have tripped over the step towards the sweep well—a sudden jolt ripped through his posture, jerked him upwards and forwards, his cigarette and his cap flew off, his hands belatedly exited his pockets and spread ahead to spring the blow and then he disappeared, went down behind the well. Oh my god...!

I jumped up. Laura looked over: Another cappucho? she asked, but I was at the door, and just when I was about to run out to help my father get up and make sure that he was okay, someone opened it from outside, and the door flew in my face—and it was my father walking in. Hi! I said, surprised and rattled, and my father was equally surprised: Oh, he said, I didn't expect to find you here. I thought you were still sleeping! He looked okay, no scratch no blood, only the cigarette was gone. How are you? I asked, still flustered. Fine, he said, let's have coffee! And since you are already up, we could go to Florence and look for some lamps for the bedrooms.

Half a year after my mother had left, my father hired a moving company to clean out my mother's, Paul's, and Theo's rooms, put all their things into big steel containers, and have them stored in the depository of his company at the outskirts of Cologne.

He announced it to me on the weekend before they were to come. Go and see if you want to keep something for yourself, he suggested, when it's put in storage it'll be hard to get to anything. I was shocked because it was so definitive, a declaration that he had given up on hoping for their return. Don't you want to wait till after your birthday next month? I asked. They may come back for your birthday! They may not, my father simply said, resigned or threatening, I wasn't sure. I don't know if I cried or was anxious. In some hidden ways, I think, I was sad and anxious all the time. Sad and desperate that my mother had left, and anxious that my father would lose it, then I would lose him too—what did I know! These adults were no different from us children, I now think, impulsive, selfish, and stubborn. When I wrote Issy a long letter about the whole mess, she sent back a postcard with a single sentence: *Go to boarding school!* What was she thinking? I couldn't leave my father alone, could I? I had to wait for things to get better.

In the meantime I made up stories. I always had my fantasies, but after my mother left, I started indulging in long daydreams. How interesting! My imaginary worlds were like movies with me as the director and main actress. I could sit for hours, it seemed, on the stairs in front of our house, looking out over the garden to the street or stare in a book I had to read for school and simultaneously be in New York with my mother and Theo, or wherever my mind would take me. But I also tried hard to be good and reasonable around my father. I had taken over setting the table for dinner every evening, which

190

was quickly done as it was just for him and me, and warm up what Alma had cooked for us in the morning. My father sat down, usually tired, with dark circles under his eyes and an even darker mood on his mind. He wasn't talkative. So I chatted a little chipper about my day at school. When will you get your year's final grades? my father interrupted me. At the end of March, I said, and told him that our math teacher was pregnant and would be on maternity leave in February, so that I would have a different teacher for the few remaining weeks of this schoolyear, which actually could help lift my grades a bit—with good luck. And then I told him something else, for instance that my best friend Lisa got a little puppy, a poodle, and that she was allowed to bring it into our biology class, and that I had talked with her about how nice it would be if I too had a little puppy, maybe a spaniel, then we could walk our dogs together—and maybe, since Lisa had a female and I would definitively want a male, they too would make little puppies some day; it made us laugh a lot picturing them, I said, because we didn't know what they would look like. When will you get your final grades? my father repeated, and I said again: At the end of March. I understood that he was grieving and couldn't think of anything other than my mother. I too thought a lot about her. But I tried to adjust. You know, I suggested, my hunch is that she just wanted to teach that one class at the Rhode Island School, that's all, and when that's over, she'll come back, and we'll forgive her, won't we? I felt strained, but I tried to show confidence. My father briefly stroked my hand while turning away. Again silence was sitting at our table.

When we all were still together, we used to have the liveliest conversations over dinner. Usually it was Paul who brought up a question, an idea, or something he had read in a newspaper or in one of the philosophy books he liked to study. I think, despite all the difficulties they had with each other, that my father appreciated Paul's intellectual challenges over essential topics, and we all enjoyed these discussions. Now there was nothing interesting left to talk about. Alone with me, no word would spark my father's curiosity to lighten our meals. At night my father drank whiskey and listened to the Bob Dylan, Joan Baez, and Bob Marley, the darker songs of his favorites. Already in my pajamas and waiting for him to come up and tuck me in for the night, I could see through the wooden poles of the stair railing how he was slouching on his rocking chair near the fireplace, slowly swinging back and forth with his eyes closed, in his hand the crystal glass with the dark brown liquor that was supposed to soothe the soreness in his chest. More than once I must have fallen asleep while waiting for him, because the next morning he apologized to me that he had taken so long to come up and told me that he had carried me to my room and finally tucked me in without waking me up. I remember another night when I woke up from some noise, something had fallen down in his bedroom, producing a dull thud, and anxiously listening through the dark I heard him cry, maybe just this one time, I heard him sob, and I walked over and sneaked into his bed on my mother's side and held his hand, and he didn't send me away, instead he slowly calmed down and finally fell asleep without letting go of my hand, and that made me very happy.

But with the moving company about to come on Monday, all hope was gone. I remember how I entered my mother's room, shy, with a gnawing conscience, but also curious. Now I was allowed to look in her closet, to open all her drawers and go through her things—but somehow that felt wrong. I ended up taking only a few items: a black sleeveless mink jacket with a zipper in front that I had always loved and admired on her—maybe I could send it to her some day; a photo in a round mahogany frame showing the smiling faces of Joyce and my mother; her special perfume bottle with the golden rose plug; and from her jewel case a thin golden necklace that she had often worn above her sweaters and that I thought I could wear like she did on special occasions—unless she would want it back later on. I didn't feel like turning everything in her drawers upside down in order to find who knows what. But for a long time I sat on her armchair and thought of what she had written me on a postcard, which showed the Statue of Liberty in front of New York's skyline: Sweetie, we are in New York, and soon you'll come to visit, I promise. Love, Janis. Love, Janis, I thought—maybe she wanted to be my friend from now on. My father too had suggested that I call him Eddie like everybody else, but I didn't like it, it felt odd and wrong. Parents shouldn't be more modern and progressive than their children, I thought. But maybe I would get used to it: Eddie and Janis...

Instead along came Irina. Her long, fuzzy blonde hair was always static, electrically charged, stood up on all sides and moved, if someone walked by, like flimsy feelers that fumbled for anything to attach themselves to. When people gave her a handshake, most often a brief electric bolt popped up between them, and they said *ouch* instead of *hi*. The day I first saw her, just when I came home from school unsuspecting of any news, she was sitting on my chair at the kitchen table scrabbling about something in the big red purse on her lap. She's sitting on my chair! I said right away to my father. He looked irritated. There are four other chairs to choose from, he responded, obviously claiming his own, the fifth currently free one, for himself. So I picked his chair, sat down on it, and defiantly stared at him. My father ignored the move and shrugged his shoulders. This is Ann, obviously, he said to the woman and didn't even bother to introduce her to me. Hi Ann, how was school today, she said airily as if we were old friends. You got a name, by any chance? I responded, and realized that we had started badly. Irina was Russian, had studied German literature in Berlin, then married a bank teller, who had divorced her two years later, and now she was translating the correspondence of an import-export company in Cologne from German into Russian; but really she wanted to be a writer. I love the *MAGIC MAN*, she said, he's cute! My father smiled. I hadn't seen him smile for a long time. Oh…, I thought, oh…! Irina stayed overnight, but not in the guest room. I'll come to tuck you in, my father said after dinner when I went to my room. No need to, I responded. A cherished ritual had ended. My father now wore his shirt collar open, no tie, not even for his board meetings or when he went out with Irina for a dinner party. She liked to wear long skirts or dresses, and I have to admit, she looked stunning, but I didn't like her. I thought she was demanding, sometimes outrageously so, and my father was too patient with her. Alma didn't say a word when the laundry piled up with Irina's stuff, when she left the kitchen a mess, soiled the carpet with the dirty traces from her sneakers after her morning runs along the Rhein in all weather. Your father needs company, Alma explained to me, men are like that. This was the single most uncalled for and dumbest thing she ever said to me. Encouraged by my father, Irina finished her studies in German literature within two years and then decided that she would make a better match with a professor from the medical school, a urologist, who loved Russian poetry and thought she had great talent. Again I was setting the dinner table for my father and me. Let's go to the movies, I suggested, and we went out on Saturday afternoons, and after the movie we had dinner in a fun restaurant.

These were good weeks for us! My father seemed to have more time, and we talked more, sometimes even about my mother. But soon there was Marion, with her wonderful, warm, melodic voice and infectious laugh, a funny giggle that shot up like a silver bullet in a pinball machine and then jumped and trickled down, eliciting further snorts of laughter on its meandering way through the flickering crowd of flippers that could catapult it up again to the top, and as silly as it sometimes was, really, most often we ended up all joining in with her good laughter. But she also wept a lot, in the beginning at least once a day, I don't know why.

She liked mint tea, made from fresh mint leaves, which I came to like too, and she liked to knit all day long and wherever she was, knitted long shawls, bonnets, sweaters, and even blankets in cashmere, mohair, wool, and cotton, in beautiful colors and with very creative designs. She knitted a small blanket for me that I actually still have and use for my afternoon naps. Her knitwear was so artful that my father rented a small shop for her in the old town where she sold her shawls and sweaters, also produced knitting on order, and finally was discovered by a fashion designer who offered to promote her line under his brand name. I don't know why she and my father split up. I was sorry, I liked her, and for a while I still lingered in her shop after school to chat with her, look at her new things, and touch and stroke their soft textures. She usually invited me to pick something for myself, always for free. Your father was so good to me, so generous, she said, take this shawl, it looks good on you, and it'll make me happy if you wear it. She once knitted a sweater for me just the way I asked her to: it was wide and black and reached straight down, ending a hand above my knees, with slim sleeves and a boat neck. I wore it over tight jeans, and it was my all-time favorite! I wish my father and she had married.

Instead Vicki showed up. Vicki was a flight attendant, and immediately I thought that she would get me a cheap ticket to New York! Vicki was there and not there, depending on her strange schedule. She flew long distances, for a while to Australia, then to South Africa, and I thought, as soon as she gets the North Atlantic route, I'll ask her directly to take me along. I didn't like her particularly, but as part of my strategy I behaved. However, my dream didn't come true.

One day Alma broke the news that Theo had died. It was an accident, she said. *What accident?* Alma, who had received a note from my mother, wasn't specific about it. Instead she said that Theo had been in a coma for a week and finally passed away. There was nothing they could do for him, she said. For some reason my mother's letter to me came only a few days later. She wrote: I know how much you loved your little brother Theo, and I wanted you to have the last photo I took of him on his 4th birthday. He was such a buoyant little guy, a smart, sweet, sturdy kid—he gave me so much pleasure—I don't know how to live with missing him so much. The photo showed Theo holding up a water pistol, probably a birthday present, looking simultaneously proud and earnest at the photographer, his mother—and whatever it meant to him that she took this picture, it turned out to be his last. His chest was bare, and someone had painted on it a little heart around the number 4. The picture was taken outdoors, it was summer, and in the background I could see other kids in bathing suits. Maybe they had given him a birthday party in Central Park. I was surprised how grown he looked. Have you seen the photo? I asked my father. I don't want to see it, he said. But it's Theo, he died! I said, puzzled and incredulous over his reaction. I forced the picture on him, pushed it right in front of him at his desk. Too bad, my father said, barely looking at it, poor guy! He moved the picture back to me. Keep it, he said, and that was that.

Later I learned from Issy that it was Paul's accident. Issy learned it from aunt Sabine, my mother's sister, who happened to be in New York at the time of the accident. I didn't know that Issy regularly talked with her on the phone. I had no contact with aunt Sabine anymore. She didn't like my father. Maybe she didn't like me either. Aunt Sabine told Issy what happened: Paul was supposed to bring Theo to the playgroup and had put him on the back seat of his Harley. Had he been driving too fast? He had skidded when turning a corner and had to abruptly make a move to avoid a truck that had parked right there in order to unload groceries for a 24/7 shop. The street was wet from a broken stack of milk containers. Paul's bike swirled around 180 degrees, slipped to the other side of the road, and crashed into the dumpster of a construction company. Paul's right leg was broken in three places, but that could be fixed. However, Theo was so badly injured that he never woke up from his coma. Because of all the milk on the street, Paul wasn't found guilty of reckless driving and involuntary manslaughter; instead the delivery company was sued and eventually had to pay a large sum, probably to my mother. I don't know what happened after that, because my mother didn't make it for much longer. She couldn't get over missing Theo. Half a year later she took a hundred Aspirin and a bottle of sleeping pills and ended her life.

For a long time thereafter I walked through my days like a blown-out candle. I felt dull and empty; nothing could spark my interest. My father didn't talk with me about it. Only once he made a bitter off-hand remark that irked me: She was good at leaving us, wasn't she? His comment stuck in my heart; it kept hurting and ignited endless pleas that I silently delivered to him: She was more than that, much more; she was fun; she was loving; she was witty; but she seemed disappointed, maybe in you, maybe in me too; she seemed lonely; she stopped laughing, she wasn't laughing so much anymore, and she used to be so funny. Why did she stop laughing? What happened? Were you mean to her? Did you make fun of her photography? She was teaching and had exhibitions, but maybe she craved recognition from you? Did you cheat on her? Sometimes she seemed so lonely! I saw her sitting on the stairs to the attic, crying. What is it, I asked her. She wouldn't tell. She said she was fine, but she wasn't. So why didn't I stay with her? I told you that she was crying. Did you do something about it? Why did she leave? Why did Issy leave? Had it already started then? I should have asked her...! It was terrible, my head was spinning endless loops, around and around, as I went over these questions and found no answers and couldn't let go.

Then my period stopped. I was shocked! Was I pregnant? Not that I had ever had sex at the time, but I had a crush on a boy in my class, Roland, or Rolly, as I called him, and we managed to sit next to each other and were sometimes holding hands under the desk during class. So maybe he had a little sperm on his finger, I thought, and it sneaked over to my hand on this occasion, and when I touched myself it wandered up into my vagina and found an egg...This was very unlikely, I knew, but it really scared me. I didn't tell anybody but watched myself carefully in the following months, any sign of morning sickness or odd appetites—actually I lacked any appetite and rather lost than gained weight during this long stretch of uncertainty. At some point my period resumed, simply following its own agenda. I had held my breath, and with a sigh of relief I started breathing again. But I didn't hold hands with Rolly anymore, and he started doing it with another girl in my class.

Then my father and Vicki went to Buenos Aires. The trip had been organized months before my mother's death. My father wanted to find a South American company that would distribute his *FIXIT* products, and he and Vicki planned to take tango lessons. Will it be okay if I go? my father asked me with a concerned look, in doubt or bad conscience. No problem, I said. They left and enjoyed a summer vacation in Argentina, while Cologne froze under the hands of the cold season. I really didn't care. Alma stayed with me while my father was away, and that was all I needed. Maybe not, but that's how I felt at the time.

At night I thought of my mother. This became a soothing habit that helped me fall asleep. Sometimes I still do. She is the good ghost of my dreams. I may see her or just know that she is there. She comes to me, often merely passing by or already being there somewhere, and I love to discover her, and when I see her I feel happy. She is so mysterious. I hope she'll never stop visiting me. Sometimes she enters through a window or steps out of the shadows of the margins where she seems to reside; then she sits down next to my sideboard and arranges something, maybe a bunch of flowers that has fallen apart, the stalks lie on the one side and the blossoms on the other, and she tries to put them back together, and I jump in to help, but then the flowers are gone, and I see her leafing through a book, frantically, as if in search of something; however, the book's pages are all empty, no word, not even a letter—not even a letter! I say, *you're holding the book upside down, you have to turn it around,* and she does, and in fact now the book is filled with writings, but it is ancient Greek, and neither she nor I have studied Greek, so we don't know what the book says. Her long rusty hair is stiff like a shell, an armor it seems, and I see a hairpin sticking in it like a spear. Is she hurt? Is she dead? No, she turns around and smiles at me. Then Paul comes in wearing some old-fashioned combat gear and war-paint on his face. *Hi girly,* he says, and I see that he is holding my ragdoll by its woolen hair; he starts swirling it around, sort of provocatively. I get anxious and look at my mother, but she keeps smiling, now at Paul, who accelerates swirling my rag doll around, and all of a sudden its dress gets caught on the doorknob and the swing rips its head off from its body—*oh no!* I rush over where it lies on the floor, and when I lift its little head I see that it's Issy's, no, it's not Issy, it is Petra, my friend from grade school. But I hear Issy's voice like an echo saying: *boarding school, boarding school!* Now Paul is gone and so is my mother for the night.

My eyes are searching through the dark, and I think of Issy, who now lives as a horse breeder in the Camargue. Halfway through her studies of veterinary medicine in Munich, she went for an internship with a stud in the Camargue, and ended up staying there. The owners of the stud, Monsieur and Madame Menaut, a childless couple, took her in, sort of like their daughter. There are other horse breeders working on this huge farm, she told me, mostly guys, and they all live in small groups of three or four in various farmhouses scattered across five acres. Only Issy lives in the main house with the Menauts. She quit university because she wanted to breed horses. At first my father was adamant: You have to go back to Munich and finish your studies, he thundered on the phone, then you can do whatever you please! Issy didn't. He was annoyed. I paid all this school money for nothing, was his terse comment to me. He knew he couldn't convince her and gave up trying any further. Later my father mused: In our family we are urban people. Who in the world gave Issy this soft spot for country life? It showed that he continued to think and wonder about her. But when Issy finally sent him a photo showing her smiling face next to a white foal's head, he conceded: She seems to have found what makes her happy. That's how he is, stubborn and harsh at times, but then again willing to relent.

I found her decision to live amongst horses exotic. How does one breed a horse? Is Issy present when the stallion mounts the mare...? Or is she more some sort of midwife when the foals are born? When she enters the stable the horses turn their heads towards her and softly snort. They like and trust her. A pregnant mare is restless; she will have her foal shortly. Issy stands next to her, strokes her nose and whispers into her ear. The mare briefly whinnies, stomps the straw, moves back in her small box and then lies down on her right side. Waves of contractions roll along the vaulted dome of her sweat-glistening belly, she's working, huffing, nickering—and then two feet appear under her horsetail, two white feet closely folded together, covered with a thin, white, transparent veil, two hooves followed by their slim legs jutting out like sticks, and the mare keeps undulating and moving, half sitting up, then lying down again—and now Issy moves in and starts pulling, helps the mare by first holding the foal's legs, then cautiously drawing them out, and now there's the head, and then the rest comes out quickly, all covered with shining glaze. The foal is born! It lies in the straw for a moment next to its mother, maybe equally exhausted and surprised, and then it tries to get up, stumbles, wavers, trips and collapses, and again wavers, flailing about, lifting itself up and creasing over while her mother watches and gently nudges and licks it until the foal stands on its four thin legs that are sticking stiffly even though still wobbly on the ground next to its mother's huge body. But then there is Paul! He must have climbed over the barricade, because he is not allowed in. Paul has this mean grin on his face as he reaches out for the pony's tail, and I know he wants to swirl it around as he did with my ragdoll, and I want to scream in order to alert Issy, who is just leaning her head at the mare's neck and doesn't realize that Paul has come in, it is so dark, maybe that's why he could sneak up on her, trap her, so I have to warn her, but I can't scream—I push and press and struggle—and I wake up, sit up in my bed, and realize: this is Tuscany, not the Camargue, it is now, not then, and the morning dawns over Monteriggioni, and I have promised my father to take him to Siena at nine so that we can have coffee at the Piazza del Campo before he has to sign some papers at the notary after ten.

DECEMBER

What if we went to Rome and spent Christmas at the *Hotel Hassler*? my father asked. It was December 24th, 8 AM, and with a cup of coffee and a cereal bowl in my hands I was sitting at the kitchen table opposite him. For a long time Christmas hasn't been part of our family life. But this year was meant to be different. I had planned to get a small Christmas tree that day, a big panettone, and a present for my father, something nicely wrapped in silk paper to give to him over dinner. I even had thought of going to the late-night mass to sing Christmas songs and shake hands with the people of Monteriggioni after the blessings—an unspoken commitment that they would keep an eye on my father when I was back in New York. But Rome was much more fun! Yes, I immediately said, that would be great! My father smiled: You've never been to Rome, and I always loved the city, he said, so let's go! And off we went, enjoying Mozart's horn concertos while riding through the crystal clear morning with its cloudless light blue sky and this pale winter sun that slowly dissolved the fluffy fog cushions between the hills along the highway, grew brighter by the hour the farther south we came, and had warmed up quite a bit by the time we finally stopped in front of the *Hassler*.

The doorman opened my side of the car and respectfully waited for me to get out. *Benvenuto*, he said. I was in Rome! *I was in Rome!!!* It turned out that my father had made a reservation, which he hadn't told me. The receptionist said: Welcome Mr. Stark, nice to see you again, it has been quite a while—two years, or is it already three? Your suite on the fifth floor for Madame with the adjacent double is ready! My father couldn't really see me, but he must have sensed that I was beaming, because he lightly squeezed my hand as the elevator lifted us up to the fifth floor. I'm glad this was the right idea, he said. My bedroom was as big as my whole New York apartment, and the living room was even bigger, all comfortably and elegantly garnished with old-fashioned furniture, lots of green velvet and red plush, silk pillows and oriental rugs, a beautiful flower arrangement on the table next to a bowl with fruit, and a real fireplace in the corner! I would never furnish my place like this, but I was impressed. Don't you want to take the suite, and I'll take the bedroom? I asked my father, but he wouldn't have it. No, he insisted, you'll enjoy it much more than I would, and anyway we'll share the living room. From my window I could look down to the Spanish Steps. I felt like rushing out. But my father wanted to first have lunch at the rooftop restaurant. We got a small round table at the window with a magnificent view all over the city. While I was trying to identify the historic buildings with the help of a card that was placed for that purpose at the window sill, my father chatted with the waiters, whom he seemed to know quite well, because he asked after the health of one's wife and the studies of another's son, and whether the maître de table had been able to finish his house in the Abruzzi…just his usual thing. I didn't care, I was so happy to be in Rome with my father, just the two of us, on Christmas, with no troubles or duties, no sightseeing pressure, as we had agreed, just free to stroll through the next few days and do whatever we felt like doing. Thank you, I said to my father after lunch as we walked back to our suite, this is the most wonderful Christmas present I could think of! My father had his arm around my shoulders, and slightly pulling me closer he responded: Thank you too! Thank you for bringing me back to Rome. I've spent good times here, and I wasn't sure if I would ever make it here again. You made it possible!

Then he withdrew for a nap, and I could finally go out to the Spanish Steps and sit there for a while in the warm afternoon sun and watch people passing by—lovers dawdling along, holding hands, and kissing each other in front of a photographer; students in dark blue uniforms hurrying up and down the stairs immersed in their funny conversations; older tourists stopping to take a breath and a picture before continuing the steep climb. With whom else had my father been at the *Hassler*? Obviously he was well known at this place. Maybe he had taken all his girlfriends to the *Hassler*, but so what! Now it was my time! I watched a small girl in front of the nativity scene, which was arranged halfway down the Spanish Steps; after wiggling for a while back and forth, eventually she managed to wrench her arm from her mother's grip and run over and touch the naked baby Jesus on the haystack; her two older siblings only stared at the display as if torn between their hearts still spellbound by the ancient narrative and their minds already high up in the digital skies. And so enjoying this unusually warm winter afternoon I was glancing over the old buildings alongside the Spanish Steps and their crooked roofs and romantic roof gardens with their luscious lemon and orange trees, and savored this amazing feeling of being in Rome and having time—seemingly endless time to look all over this wide sprawling city with all its people and its history far beyond my reach.

Around four o'clock my father joined me, and we started the afternoon with coffee in the famous *Caffè Greco*. I tried to imagine that Goethe had sat where I was now having my cappuccino, but I got caught up watching the tourists jostling in and out to take pictures with their smartphones. So what do you want for Christmas? my father asked me. This trip is my Christmas present, I protested, that's plenty enough. But he had something else in mind. After we had finished our coffee we walked along the elegant boutiques of Via Condotti with their beautiful displays of leather bags, coats, shoes, and designer clothes. Tell me if you see something that you like, my father said. It would make me happy to get you something here in Rome.

Sure enough I soon spotted a nice sweater that I wanted to try on, and so we entered the store, which welcomed us with a bouquet of white roses in its foyer, and white leather chairs next to small glass tables in front of high mirrors in between sparsely equipped shoe-shelves. A salesperson approached us. I'm Mara, she introduced herself, and offered my father a glass of water before she brought me the sweater I had picked out together with some pants. Oh no, I just want to try on the sweater, I said, but my father interjected: Why don't you try the pants as well, now that we're here! And so I withdrew to the fitting room and slipped into the pants and sweater, to which Mara whipped up a jacket and a silk scarf, decoratively thrown over my shoulder. Gorgeous! she said as I opened the curtain and stepped on stage, and my father chimed in with: You look like Isabella Rossellini! This of course was ridiculous, especially since he hardly could see how I looked. But Mara seized on the moment. Yes, she touted, or rather Isabella's daughter, Elettra Rossellini Wiedeman.—Boy, is she beautiful, she added, leaving it open whom she was talking about. I saw myself in the mirror with my father sitting behind me pretending to look at me after Mara had gone off again. How do you like it? my father wanted to know. It's beautiful, I said. So we'll get it, he decided, just as Mara came back with a long silk dress, which she held in front of me. Why don't you try this on, she said, just for fun. You look so much like Elettra. She wore this last month at a Gala in Milan. I want your husband to see you in this dress! My husband? That's what she thought we were, an old husband with his young wife? My father chuckled but encouraged me: Absolutely, try it on!

And so the game was on. I went back to the fitting room and came out as Elettra Rossellini Wiedeman and asked him: Can I wear this for our New Years Eve party? And he went along and said, Not bad, but I would prefer if you wore something even more dramatic! And Mara walked off and brought something more dramatic, and I stepped into a yellow- and red-colored long satin dress with a shoulder-free top adorned with turquoise feathers—Elettra looks like a luxury parrot, I commented, and my father said: You do look exotic! But I'm afraid you can't wear this, because Miss Stratford wore something like this last year at the Vienna Opera Ball, remember? I was surprised that he would indulge in this silly masquerade, I didn't know that about him, but it was fun to play along, so I continued to star as my father's wife, responding with: Of course I remember, and when she was drunk she ruined it by splashing a full glass of red wine on it! Mara understood that the parrot was out of the question. Off she went and came back with two other evening gowns on her arm, one in black voile with shimmering sequins and long slits from the décolleté to the navel only thinly held together by small clasps, and one in midnight blue laces with a tulle layer that ran long over the carpet, a kind of seductive mist on naked skin. And skillfully she placed two pairs of high heel shoes next to them, black pearled slippers and dark blue satin pumps, and an extra pair of golden and crimson brocade flats as well, all extremely fancy, and I tried them on, and paraded myself in front of my blind father and three big mirrors, eventually with a white mink stole around my naked shoulders, just for the cooler hours late at night. It was truly stunning how I looked! In an understated tone I remarked to my father: Tom Hanks would like this one, wouldn't he? And Mara couldn't help but asking: Do you know Tom Hanks, I mean, personally? My father leaned back and lit a cigarette. Yeah, he is a nice guy, he responded. Oh, he is one of my favorite actors, Mara said. This whole drama was getting a little out of hand, I thought, so I pretended that we were running out of time. What are you choosing? my father wondered. I'll take the sweater, I said. Take the suit as well, he suggested, and perhaps you could find some boots that would go with it. For the evening gowns, I guess we'll need to come back with more time. Mara nodded in agreement. Of course, she said, and quickly returned with an arm full of leather boots, and I ended up with two pairs of boots, a nice belt with a silver buckle, a leather purse, and the suit and sweater, all piled up next to the cash register. I felt dizzy. My father paid and had everything delivered to the *Hassler*.

Boy-oh-boy! I said when we were back at the Via Condotti, that was like in a movie! My father grinned and said: You were a fabulous actress, and we played quite well together, didn't we? Ah, that was fun, wasn't it! Now, come with me, I have one more thing to get you. And he took me by my arm and seemed to know exactly where to go, and was undeterred by the people crowding the street as he steered straight to the close-by *Cartier* store. What are you doing? I wondered, and tried to stop him. Don't be shy, he responded. I want to get you a nice ring. I never gave you a ring, not for your graduation, not when you turned twenty, nor when you turned thirty! Today is the day! Isn't a

211

father allowed to give his daughter a ring, something for life? Still I felt resistant. This all felt too much. You've spent already a lot, I countered, but he cut me off. You spend all this time with me, that's a lot! And tonight I'm in the mood! He entered the store pulling me behind. Was that right? My father knew exactly what he wanted to get me: a trinity ring with a diamond-paved white gold band. He had it all planned out. They had my size. They put it on my right hand's ring finger. How does it look? my father demanded. Beautiful...I mumbled. We'll take it! he said and handed over his credit card. Do you want to wear it? the sales person asked me, and my father responded on my behalf: Yes, keep it on! I didn't say a word. I was moved, incredulous, ashamed, confused, and couldn't really think straight or even say *thank you.*

Hayden, is it okay that I wear my father's ring—the ring my father gave me? I struggle with this. It looks so beautiful, and yes, I want to wear it, but should I? I wish you were here! Would my father have given it to me in your presence? How do you feel about it? Am I just complicated? Anyway, I was exhausted when we stepped out of the *Cartier* shop. It had grown dark, the streets were still filled with lots of people, but the shops were closing. I need a drink, I heard myself saying, and my father said: So do I! Let's have a Campari, that'll give us a nice kick into the evening. And we found a small bar, stuffed with people, but luckily a couple was just leaving, we got their seats, and my father ordered Campari Tonic. I looked at my hand with my new ring that sparkled and shimmered, and I couldn't stop shaking my head. I can't believe you gave me this ring, I said. Well, Merry Christmas, my father responded, which reminded me that I had nothing for him, but when I mentioned it, he said: Your presence is a true gift to me. When did we last have so much time together? I guess I needed to grow blind to deserve this favor again. Was he being sarcastic? I couldn't tell. I'm glad you invited me, I replied, and asked him why he had wanted to get me this particular ring. My father thought for a moment and then simply said: It's a classic, I always liked it. He seemed tired, and for the first time I noticed a strain around his eyes that betrayed his struggle with losing sight. I wish you could see the beautiful things you got me today, I said cautiously, but he brushed me off. I can see them, I did see them—not like you, but good enough! So he wasn't in the mood to talk about his loss of vision.

Later we wound up in a little restaurant, got a bottle of Barolo for our table, shared a bruschetta, had homemade pasta with fungi porcini, a bistecca fiorentina with some roasted vegetables, and finished off with splitting a piece of torta della nonna. Why do I list all these details? Do I have to prove anything? It all felt so Italian, the whole day a Roman miracle!

Then for some reason I started to talk about you, Hayden. I told my father that your mother was from Bologna, that she had studied anthropology in Vienna, where she met your father, and that your first language was actually Italian, even though you grew up and went to school in Vienna. I also mentioned that your mother's name was Anna—to which my father briefly raised his eyebrows—and that she often travelled to Bologna to take care of her old mother, who was sick with arthritis and lived alone, since her husband was killed as a partisan during the war shortly after she was born. My father nodded. We should have come earlier, he said, probably with regard to the American intervention in Italy, but maybe he was thinking of our joint trip to Tuscany and Rome, or he simply felt that it was rather late when we finally left the restaurant.

We were walking through Rome's nightly deserted streets, my father with his hand on my shoulder holding on to me, and I guiding him without being sure about our way back to the *Piazza di Spagna*. The streetlights dimly illuminated the dark cobblestones that seemed to have paved these alleyways forever. Everything here in Rome seems historical, every stone, every corner, every building. Now and then a motorbike, a small car, or a cab passed by, some people were smoking a cigarette, chatting with friends or neighbors in front of their homes. It's amazing how quiet Rome is at night! A white kitten ran across our way and anxiously sneaked under an old Cinquecento to carefully watch us from its hiding place as we were strolling by. Then we turned a corner, and even though I had never been there, I immediately knew where we were. There is the *Fontana di Trevi*, I said, so we are going in the right direction! My father stopped. I can't hear anything, he said. It's empty, no water, I explained, maybe they shut it off for the winter or they are just in the process of cleaning it. My father smiled and seemed to harken. Have you seen *La Dolce Vita*? he then asked, as if speaking more to himself than to me. Do you remember Anita Ekberg walking into the water? Yes, I said, and Marcello Mastroianni follows her. My father nodded. How beautiful that was, he murmured, and his smile seemed to carry him through time glued to this unforgettable image of a mystical moment that wasn't ours—or was it?—but turned him again into this passionate young man in pursuit of this beautiful goddess waiting for him to be kissed under a whooshing fountain of love. A light, sweet scent of music drifted by, originating from an open window or merely from this old memory. My father, still looking at the *Fontana di Trevi*—or did he look at the peripheral me?—shivered. Here we are, he whispered and took my hand, and I saw that his eyes were in tears, Here we are!

Before going to bed I stood for a while at the window and looked all over the illuminated city that lay there quietly in the impressive glory of its history, dome after dome, palace after palace, and the dark universe above! For centuries it looked like this, I thought, even for millenia! How would it be to live in Rome, I wondered? Maybe we could move here for a year, Hayden, maybe this is our city? You would play in a piano bar and teach at the conservatory, and I could do—whatever, something nice and interesting. We would have a little flat somewhere under these crooked roofs, not as elegant as the Hassler, but nice enough, and then we could invite my father to come to visit for the holidays, and we would go to see him once in a while in Monteriggioni…

Suddenly the illumination of St. Peter's Dome fell dark, and then one monument after the other vanished in the night. End of show, it was past midnight. I looked down to the Spanish Steps—where the faint light of the old lanterns still spread a dim shine over the worn-out marble—and there was my father! Was I dreaming? No, there he was, slowly feeling his way towards the Spanish Steps, his arm reaching for the balustrade, and gripping it he slowly proceeded to walk down. What was he doing there? He wasn't even wearing his coat! He would get lost! He must be sleepwalking, I thought. I had to get him! I grabbed my coat, rushed out the door, soundlessly ran along the carpeted hallway, hastened down the stairs, floor after floor, and stormed past the receptionist who jumped up when he saw me running, and out I sallied, and in a few bounds I was at the top of the Spanish Steps. My father was nowhere to be seen. Had he gone down so quickly? I started to hurry down too, skidding on the slippery stones, and halfway through I thought I saw my father at some distance, now at the arm of a woman, both quickly proceeding with their descent. Who was she? Eddie! I called, Eddie! But he didn't hear me or wouldn't turn around. Instead he and his companion were laughing and laughing aloud while swaying and stumbling on, but I had to look at the stairs in order to not fall while running behind them. When I finally reached the bottom of the Spanish Steps the Piazza was empty. Where had they gone? I rushed towards Via Condotti and looked all along this stretch of luxury that now seemed to have fallen completely dead behind iron bars. Not even a mouse would pass through at this hour. Only an empty plastic bag tottered and wobbled along in the cold winter wind. Then I heard another burst of laughter, now coming from the other side of the Piazza. Maybe that's where they went, I thought, and ran past the palm trees towards the end of the piazza. Again I heard fragments of words, some of which resembled the sound of my father's voice...I quickly moved forward, and entering Via Margutta I caught a brief glimpse of a couple just entering a building on the left. I was almost sure that it was my father with this strange woman. Who was she? What was he doing there with her? I sneaked closer to the building and stopped at Number 110, where they seemed to have disappeared behind a heavy wooden door. I touched its doorknob and cautiously tried to push, but the door wouldn't move. Of course it wouldn't. I stepped back a few steps and looked up the dark facade to the three illuminated windows on the second floor—that's where they must have ended up, I thought. Father...? I whispered, Eddie...? A shadow floated past the window, another shadow followed. Then a door next to me squeakily opened, and an old woman stepped out of a dark corridor with a little scrubby dog on a leash. Vai, vai! she murmured, and the dog hobbled out to the empty street while she stood behind in the half open door, just shaking a bit at the leash. The mutt sniffed around the few places close by and soon found a protruding stone worthy to lift its hind leg on. Maybe the woman knew who was living in the apartment on the other side? Buona sera, signora, I said in my best Italian, and only then did she seem to notice me. Startled, she anxiously withdrew a half-step behind her door and suspiciously peered at me. Chi ci vive? I asked her and pointed to the illuminated windows on the opposite building. A brief smile of pride flitted over her wrinkled face. Il Maestro, she whispered, il Maestro! And with a dignified nod at me she withdrew into her house, pulling in the leash with her old dog, and softly closed the door on me.

25th of December. We had agreed to have breakfast at nine in the living room of my suite. The room service knocked five minutes early. I quickly wrapped myself in the bathrobe and opened. Buon Natale, the waiter said, and rolled in the breakfast table. How beautifully everything was set up and decorated; they had even put up a mini Christmas tree next to the coffee pot and the white tablecloth was sprinkled with golden stars. Buon Natale, I said as well, and gave him a special Christmas tip. Since my father wasn't up yet I quickly jumped in the shower and got dressed. We had planned to take a walk at the *Forum Romanum* if the weather would allow for such an excursion, and the sun was shining from an almost cloudless sky. A quarter past nine I was ready for breakfast, but my father hadn't shown up yet. For a while I sipped my coffee and waited. Maybe he hadn't returned from his night at Via Margutta, maybe he was still sleeping in the arms of this strange woman, and I was senselessly waiting for him to show up for breakfast. This idea suddenly annoyed me, and I felt pushed to get up and knock at the connecting door to his room. There was no response. I knocked again and once more, and finally I opened the door and peered into the dim den of his sleep, rather sure that I would find it empty. But there he was, my father, deeply buried in between a load of pillows and a comforter that bulged like a warrior's shield. Standing in

218

the doorway I couldn't even see his head; only his naked foot stuck out, strangely dislocated, it seemed, like a broken pillar, an archeological find from which the covering sheet had partly slid off. Should I wake him up, I wondered, and decided that yes, I was going to wake him up! It was Christmas, we had agreed to have breakfast at nine, and it was nine-thirty. So I grabbed the foot and shook it, but it quickly withdrew and slipped under the comforter. I followed, caught it, and shook it again. Hey! Furiously kicking back at me my father suddenly bounced up and screamed: Are you crazy? What are you doing! For a moment I was shocked, yet I stood my ground. Breakfast is ready! I said. Okay, okay, he grumbled and sank back, bewildered or exhausted. I'm coming in a minute, he mumbled, damn it!

I went back to my suite. I was disappointed. I cut a piece of panettone and spread a big layer of honey on it. I didn't like that my father had yelled at me. I didn't like having to wait for him again. And I didn't like how this day had started. Finally my father shuffled in, unkempt and in his bathrobe. Uhhh, he said and yawned, is it already so late...? I didn't respond, just poured coffee in his cup and waited for him to settle in. I'm sorry, he then said. I didn't get to sleep until late last night, so that's probably why I didn't wake up in time. Should I tell him that I had seen and followed him? I wasn't sure, but then I couldn't stop myself and just blurted it out: You went out last night, I saw you! My father looked at me totally puzzled. Oh, you saw me...he then said, clearly trying to make up his mind what to tell me. Yes, I said, and you didn't even wear your coat! By this my father seemed to be even more taken aback. Well, he then slowly said. An old friend of mine called me on my cell after we got back last night. She happened to be in Rome and just wanted to wish me Merry Christmas. I told her that I too was in Rome. So she asked if we could get together, and since I didn't know if you would like spending time with her, I suggested that she come for a drink at the Hassler. I hadn't seen her in a long time... Actually, it was quite lovely! We were sitting and chatting in the hotel bar till three-thirty. So I didn't need a coat, if that concerns you, he ironically added.

I didn't buy his story. I felt that he had lied to me, at least in part. But I didn't know how to respond. What's the matter with you, my father suddenly erupted. Can't I have a glass of wine with an old friend after my daughter has gone to bed? His tone offended me. I saw you going down the Spanish Steps! I insisted. Baloney! my father barked. I saw what I saw, I defiantly gave back. Well, my father angrily countered, maybe you hallucinated, or maybe you were dreaming! Whatever! I didn't go down the Spanish Steps, neither with nor without my coat, for that matter. There was a tense silence between us while we halfheartedly turned towards our breakfast. Now I was certain that my father was lying. Why else would he be so angry if there was nothing to hide? In my childhood I had come to feel at times that he didn't tell me the truth. I can't recall any particular event—or maybe it usually happened when I asked him about my mother, why she left, when she would return, and the like. He often turned mute or defensive, and when I doubted his answers, he got angry and stubbornly stuck to what he had said, almost as if he wanted to suffocate any further question once and for all and force me to believe that things were exactly as he said they were. This left me befuddled, brooding, and suspicious of him. How strange that he would now react like this, I thought. Still, I didn't want to ruin our Christmas in Rome. So I softened my voice and simply asked him: Who is this friend of yours, what is she doing here? However, to my surprise, my father threw his napkin on the breakfast table. It's none of your business, he thundered, and shaking his head he added: I can't believe it! You act like a cheated wife! I don't owe you any explanation whatsoever for what I am doing! This is totally ridiculous! He got up, clearly shaken, and holding on with his hand to the back of his chair he softly said: You know what? I'm going to lie down again. For me it's early. And it's a holiday. So why don't you go to the *Forum Romanum* on your own. Take a cab. I've seen it many times, and anyway now I can't see it anymore. So what good would it do me or even you if I came along? I'd better sleep another hour or two. If you're back for lunch, we'll have lunch, and if not we can have dinner tonight! And off he went to his room, closed the connecting door behind him, and turned the lock inside.

I was crushed. What had happened? I sat in front of this lovely breakfast that we had hardly touched and didn't know what to do. I had ruined our Christmas Day! First mistake: I woke my father up; he never liked that, and there was no reason to do it. I could have let him sleep for another couple of hours. Second mistake: I shouldn't have mentioned last night. That was really stupid. But then again: why had it made him so furious? I've seen my father with various women, there was nothing new about it. I couldn't understand.

Eventually I got up and left. When I arrived at the Forum it turned out to be closed on Christmas! All year round seven days a week it was open—but not on Christmas! Of course, everything was closed on Christmas, except Saint Peter's. For a moment I thought about going there to attend a mass, just as something special. But I was afraid of feeling overwhelmed with emotions when the organ would play all the classical Christmas songs that I loved to hear in my childhood. How beautiful it had been, how powerful when the organ in the Dome of Cologne resounded—I couldn't afford to be sentimental now. I trudged along the deserted streets of Rome. Every corner was decorated with a bunch of red flowers or some branches of pine trees sprayed with artificial frost. Now and then Santa Claus wagged his finger at me. Dopey! Finally I found an open coffee bar, what a relief! Cappuccino! I was the only guest. The bar man was using the slow morning hour to clean out his closets, whistling an unknown melody. Soon people would come in, their arms full of lavishly wrapped Christmas presents, gathering with family and friends on their way to the big pranzo dalla nonna…

How nice would it be if we had a big family reunion, I thought. We never did. Actually, that's not quite true. When I was little, Oma and Opa always celebrated Christmas with us. Living only a few blocks from us they came over once a week, usually on

Sundays for lunch. But they died early. First Oma died when I had just started school. For some time she had been very sick with kidney cancer. In her final months she was always tired. On her last Christmas with us, she even fell asleep while we were opening our presents. Opa managed two more years on his own, but barely so. Still he refused to join us more frequently, maybe because he was too proud to show that he felt lonesome without Oma, or maybe he preferred to be left alone, so that nobody could interfere when he was dreaming of her. I felt sorry for him. He looked so forlorn. But it was hard to talk with him; his hearing had declined, and he didn't tolerate hearing aids. So I guess I withdrew a bit from him, even while he was still around. He often said he wished he could rejoin Gertrud in heaven, and when he finally died I thought he was happier. Sometimes Aunt Sabine joined us for Christmas, depending on whether or not she was in love with someone at the time and was in the mood for the trip from Freiburg up to Cologne. But then our Christmas gatherings deteriorated. Issy branched off to boarding school, and when she came home for the holidays she behaved more like a guest than a family member. And after my mother, Paul, and Theo had left, Issy eventually stopped coming home altogether. I stayed on with my father and his successive girlfriends. In order to make sure that I had some fun, he allowed me to invite school friends over or go to their homes. But maybe he just wanted to be left alone with his lovers. Sometimes we would watch an old movie on Christmas Eve, a few times we travelled to the Canary Islands, and once we tried out skiing at Zermatt. So I lost the particular feeling for Christmas. But sitting in this empty coffee bar, I wanted it back. For a moment I wished I had a family with two normal parents who would always be at home and reliably organize the holidays throughout the year, Christmas, Easter, Thanksgiving, everybody's birthdays—a safe bet, a place to go, rather than straying through a foreign city, separated from my only parent after a totally unnecessary fight over nothing at breakfast. I looked at my new ring and softly whispered: Thank you. Merry Christmas! I had been unfair to my father. I had been really silly! Yesterday he gave me such a fantastic Christmas present, and today he wanted to sleep a little longer, just that, and I was pissed! In fact, he hit the nail on the head when he said that I reacted like a cheated wife—that remark stung! I had talked about my Oedipal issues in my analysis; I knew how much I'd been in love with him when I was little, so end of story! Or not? Maybe there never is an end to this story. What was I thinking! My father did what he could, he was who he was, and I had to accept him as he was. That's what my mother taught me. Everything else would be presumptuous, arrogant, and selfish! I had no right to blame him for the loss of my family. And actually, what did I do in terms of family? I hadn't even thought of calling Issy! I took out my cell and called her. She didn't pick it up, so I left a message saying that we were in Rome and wished her Merry Christmas. Then I walked back to the Hassler hoping to have lunch with my father.

I'm sorry, my father said. I'm sorry that I got so angry at you this morning. You were right, we had agreed to do something together, breakfast and a walk, and then I bailed out. That wasn't right. Again we were at the rooftop restaurant, which he had chosen because he had a hangover and didn't want to go out, as he explained, and also because on Christmas it would be very difficult to find something nice without prior reservation. My father was thinking of everything. He knows the world! It turned out that he did have a reservation at the Hassler restaurant for what they called Christmas Brunch—so again we got our window table and could make up for our botched breakfast. Good, I thought, let's restart this day. I'm sorry too, I reciprocated, I was stupid, I don't know why. He was sitting there a bit hunched over, looked pale and spent with his face a bit swollen and sagging. He shouldn't drink so much, I thought. It's just that I looked down from my window, and I thought I saw you in front of the hotel—without your coat. But obviously it wasn't you. It's strange that I couldn't let it go, and I was puzzled when I heard these dicey words coming out of my mouth. Oh, my father said, maybe that was me! I walked out of the hotel to wait for my friend and greet her when she arrived by cab. It was such a mild night, and I enjoyed the fresh air. So you may very well have seen me. Now he had admitted that in fact he had left the hotel. But you didn't go down the Spanish Steps? I couldn't stop myself from digging a bit deeper. No, certainly not, he quickly answered. Nothing in the world would have made me do that, exhausted as I already was from having climbed up there after dinner! That made sense. So maybe I had followed the wrong couple...I'm sorry, I reiterated, I thought you lied to me. My father leaned back and said: Why would I lie to you?

Just at this moment a gray-haired lady stepped up to our table and to my surprise remained standing there with a mystifying certainty, tall and upright, while looking at us, calmly albeit somewhat inquiringly. My father, noticing that someone had approached but not seeing who it was, assumed that she was a waiter, because he simply ordered in her direction: Two cappuccinos—we'll take the buffet. It's me, Eddie, the lady responded, I thought we had agreed to have brunch together. So that's what the reservation was for, I immediately understood, and felt my heart clenching. I looked at my father, who clearly was embarrassed. Didn't you get my message? I canceled when Antje came back from the Forum. I had promised her...So you had promised both of us, she said. Too bad, I didn't get the message. I went to Saint Peter's for the Mass and forgot to take my cell. There was a moment of awkward silence. Then a waiter came and offered to bring an additional chair to our table in case we wanted to invite our guest. Yeah, we could do that, my father tentatively said, and asked me if that was okay with me. What could I say? I was a bit annoyed with this interference. I wanted to have this Christmas brunch alone with my father. On the other hand, this lady clearly spoke with a New York accent, which intrigued me. Sure, I said, and put some effort into making it sound nonchalant to cover my inner turmoil.

Something had thrown me off base. I figured she was my father's friend from last night, but she was too old to be one of his lovers. How else were they connected? And why would he allow her to interfere with our Christmas brunch? Had he planned all along to send me off to the Forum by myself and calculated that I wouldn't be back before mid-afternoon? So you are Antje, the lady now said to me, and reached out with her hand across the table to greet me. I took her hand, which felt cool and delicate. I nodded like a child. I'm Teresa, she said and smiled at me. Even though probably in her seventies, she looked quite beautiful. Her big dark eyes were artfully surrounded by an olive-to-golden shadow providing a warm frame to her thoughtful albeit somewhat melancholic glance at me. Her dense curly hair fell down over her shoulders, pointing to a plain but attractive brooch, a ruby square framed in red gold, which was skillfully placed on her thin beige cashmere sweater. I was a friend of Joyce's, she now added, and looked at Eddie as if waiting for him to expand on her introduction. A friend of Joyce—my granny? I was totally surprised! Simultaneously it began to dawn on me that my father wanted to avoid my getting together with her, since he had never told me much about Joyce, and maybe he was afraid that Teresa would be willing to answer all the questions he had always dodged. Your grandmother...? Teresa gave back, now looking equally surprised. She briefly glanced over to my father. Well she wasn't my granny, I explained, I know she was my father's friend—but I decided to make her my granny, maybe because I didn't know much of my father's real parents; they died before I was born.

My father, perhaps trying to contain the upcoming torrent of questions around the Joyce mystery, hastily commented: Oh well, that's a long and complicated story, and asked Teresa if she too wanted to have the buffet and suggested that we all go and have a look at what it offered. So we did—an opportunity to think about how to proceed. I felt torn. On the one hand I wanted to ask Teresa to tell me about Joyce, and on the other hand I wanted to spare my father any further upset after we had just made up from our morning fallout. While I was putting some scrambled eggs on my plate, I noticed that my father and Teresa had a brief exchange at the other end of the buffet. Teresa, taller than my father, slightly bent her head towards my father, who looked up to her as if subtly shaken and simultaneously defiant, indicating both uncanny familiarity and vulnerability as only occur in deep, meaningful connections—not unlike mother-son-relationships. Was she scolding or warning him? Was he beseeching or rebutting her? What were they talking about? Then they split up, my father assisted by a waiter, Teresa proceeding to the bakery basket.

When we all were back at our table, Teresa said to me: I told your father last night that I always hoped to meet you one day. And today is the day. So Merry Christmas! I would love to hear a bit about you. What are you doing—I mean, when you are not travelling with your father in Italy? That seemed a smart maneuver. I would talk a bit about some ordinary things, and my father could relax. So I started out by telling her that I had studied psychology in Berlin, moved to New York a few years ago, and that currently I was a candidate in training at a psychoanalytic institute. She then said that she too had gone through analysis, that it had been a very important experience for her—extremely helpful, she added—and that she too lived in New York. Then she wondered where I lived, and I said on the East side, and she said, I'm on the West side, and then she suggested that we meet some day, maybe for coffee or a stroll in Central Park. Maybe she wanted to let me know that we could address things later when we were both back in New York. At least that's what I immediately thought, but maybe that's what my father thought as well, because he seemed uncomfortable and inserted himself by explaining, quite unrelatedly: Joyce and Teresa were classmates at the acting school, that's how far back they went. But by the time I met Joyce, Teresa had already given up on acting. She had married and was raising her daughter. Is that right, Teresa? Teresa confirmed, but she seemed distracted by his comment, and the whole conversation fell sort of flat. Clearly there was an elephant in the room, but I couldn't figure out from where it came.

So I turned towards the present and asked her what she was doing in Rome. She said she always loved Rome and that's why many years ago she had bought a small flat at the Campo de Fiori, which allowed her to come to Rome as often as she felt like without having to bother with making hotel reservations and packing luggage and the like. I sort of live here in bits and pieces, she said with a smile, it's my second home, my retreat. But my heart belongs to New York, I'm a New Yorker, through and through. I told her that it was my first visit to Rome, and then we chatted some about the must-see sights, and in between I noticed that Teresa looked at my new ring, and I felt like saying, it's my dad's Christmas present, but of course I didn't. Throughout our conversation my father remained rather quiet, and I felt sorry to see him sitting there so isolated, as if excluded from our chitchat, which of course he wasn't. He looked resigned or was simply subdued by his hangover—whatever it was, he didn't look happy. Teresa also seemed to notice his withdrawal and soon announced that she had to leave, but before she got up, she gave me a card with her New York address on one and her Rome address on the other side. Come and see me sometime, she lightly said, I would be so pleased!

In silence we watched Teresa as she was helped into her coat and briefly waved goodbye before she entered the elevator. Her surprising appearance and mysterious innuendoes stayed with us. I was looking over the sun-flooded hills of Rome and thought, now she is walking out there with all the answers I was looking for, and I wondered if my father would finally tell me about her, but he didn't. He seemed to be lost in thought, and I was not to disturb him. What was he thinking about? Finally, partly covering his eyes with his hand, he started to talk, slowly, softly, as if in a daze, spoke almost as if to himself as he gathered the thoughts that strayed through the maze of his mind in search of the words for the story to tell. What was he saying? I couldn't understand everything, but I didn't dare to interrupt and ask him. I felt I needed to remain silent and rather unnoticeable or else he would stop, and I absolutely wanted to hear what he had to say. He so rarely shared what preoccupied his inner world. Tell me, I thought, and listened, listened for a long time. But in the end—I don't know what to think...He spoke like from a dream, far removed in tone yet closely yielding the nightmare it embraced. Was it real or merely fiction? Was it about him or me or anybody I knew? Maybe my analyst would say that I was in denial, but what is that supposed to mean? I'm not denying the facts, if there are any, but in the end the story he told me seemed to be rather his than mine. Despite all the amazing news—I hold that there is something I know about myself that remains untouched by what my father said—yet still, I wonder...

First my father said that he wished he could see me and could look into my eyes. It would be important for him, particularly now, he said, to see me looking at him. Mostly that. Sometimes he is afraid of forgetting how I look, he said, or he isn't sure anymore that the image he envisions when thinking of me is really me, or rather a subtle blend of memories, memories from some diverse moments in his life that cling to him for unknown reasons. These eyes, he said, these eyes that come up at night when he's about to fall asleep...they look at him. All these memories, he said, these memories are eyes in the night. To increasingly be haunted by these fleeting images—and some are not even memories, he said—that really scares him. There is no escape from these images. Since he is going blind, time and again he crashes into something he doesn't see, but that's not the worst of it, he said. He tries to learn to avoid whatever gets in his way, and he is getting better at it. But what he cannot avoid are these images inside—from them there is no escape. All his life he has been on the run, he said, there has always been a sense of needing to escape, he didn't know from what. He never was a dreamer, he said. He felt he was a man of action, an organizer, essentially a simple craftsman, and in order to do the things he wanted to accomplish, he needed to stay, even though he would rather flee. But flee from what? It dawned on him that he never looked at things very carefully. Maybe he couldn't look because he didn't dare to see. He wanted to get away, no matter what, from something—a smoldering menace. But all the things he closed his eyes on stuck to him; now they clog and clutter his mind. All the images he tried to ignore haunt him now that his eyesight is vanishing. They drag him down, drag him towards the past, and he doesn't want to go there. He wants to go forward, he said, forward not backward. He never wanted to look back, he said, and that was a mistake. Now he has to look back, he said, because he has to tell me something. He never wanted to tell me, he said, and he always thought it was in order to protect me. But now he is starting to understand that he wanted to protect himself, more himself than me. When he called me in New York to ask if I would come with him to Tuscany, he had made up his mind to finally tell me, he said. And when we were in Monteriggioni he thought of it many times but couldn't bring himself to do it. That's when he thought that Rome would be the place, and here we are—here we are, he said, and paused for a while, and then he said that he still wasn't sure that I really needed to know, but maybe he had no right to decide this for me.

It's about the beginning, my beginning, he said. Nobody remembers how it all started. That's what our parents have to tell us, my father said, that's what they are there for. He doesn't know much about his beginning, he said, and neither do I, but now he is willing to tell me what I don't know. Maybe it'll give him relief. But he's afraid it'll shock me, and he's sorry for that, he added, and ran his hand over his eyes. Then he said he always thought I have my mother's eyes; it's just amazing how much my eyes are hers, he said, and shook his head in disbelief. That's what he always thought when I looked at him. It even puzzled him at times: Who was looking at him, who was he looking at? Be this as it may, and whomever he was now talking to, I should listen to this. He then said: Once upon a time a sweet little girl was born. Her mother was an actress, and she wanted to call her baby girl Antigone, because in her early years she had been most successful playing Antigone on stage. However, her father objected to the shadow such a uniquely recognized name would cast on his daughter's life and instead suggested Anna. Eventually her parents compromised to Antje. That's how my name came about, my father said, that's how it started: with a compromise. A smile then flitted across his face as he continued. It was the most beautiful moment in his life when I was born, he said. He held me in his hands, and he was just in awe of this little baby, me, his daughter, who looked at him with her big blue eyes, shining and open to him and to all the light that had started to enter her world. As small, wrinkled, and helpless as I was, for him I was simply perfect, he said, a wonderful human being that—to his never-ending amazement—he had fathered. But simultaneously he also felt that I was completely independent of him, a mysterious creature on my own still drifting terms, a little girl who would become a woman, a woman who would live her life—hopefully a good and long life—a life that he would not be able to see to its end—a life that he was supposed to make a happy life. In the minute I was born, he said, he understood that from then on it would always be his most important task to do all he could to make me happy. But what is happiness, he briefly wondered, what is it that makes us happy...? Still, that's what he felt, he then said, that's what he committed himself to, and that will always be so. He wasn't part of Paul's birth, he continued, and it wasn't the same for him when Issy was born. It was with me that he became a father. I made him a father, he said.

And as for my mother, he then continued, this was something that he had to finally tell me: Janis wasn't my mother, he said, it was Joyce who was my birth mother. But Joyce died shortly after I was born. He said, she killed herself, she jumped out of her life, leaving him and me behind. He said he never got over it. He always missed her. And he didn't understand what had taken her out of her life. She so much longed to have a baby, he said, and when she finally had her baby, me, she hardly could hold me or even look at me. She turned away whenever he wanted to put me in her arms. At first she cried and cried, he said, and then she became mute and withdrawn. Maybe she had post-partum depression. They put her on medication, but it didn't help. Her psychiatrist told him that she couldn't be left alone, not for a minute, and he had engaged a nanny who was supposed to take care of me and always keep an eye on her. But then someone rang the doorbell, just that, and in the few moments the nanny went to open the door, Joyce jumped out of the window. She just jumped out of the window…Joyce was a wound that always bled, my father said, and nothing could stop her life from running out of her. Her wound was an abyss, he then murmured, a voracious abyss that swallowed him too—he got hurt and lost in her, desperate, dumb, naked, struggling in her burning chest—a scar of gloom—this was *the wilting flower called necrosis* she sometimes mentioned as if hinting at a secret; it exuded a terrible scent, an etching flame from her breath when she threw out all these poisoned words like praying a bad rosary, bad, bad—they drugged him—made him crawl at her stomping feet—this is what he said, or something like this. He was supposed to be the giant to all of us, he sneered, that's how it looked, didn't it? But ha!—He was a mere slave to her erratic moods, her fucking caprices freaked him out; he was scrunched under her selfish soles whenever a suitor took her for the night, only to throw her in a ditch at the crack of dawn; then he had to pick her up, that was his job, pick her up and clean her up and feed her like a baby. How he loved to do that, really! It proved how dependent she was on him, how much she needed him, how she clung to him. He loved her for that. He hated her for that—that too. But most of all he loved Joyce, my father said, he loved her to the end of his wits. Still, he couldn't help her. For all he tried—he couldn't hold on to her, he said, and then she was gone. Gone forever.

And there I was, he finally said, a baby without a mother, and there was Janis, and Janis loved him, and he loved Janis. Yes, he loved Joyce, but he also loved Janis. Janis was beautiful, my father said, she was simple and clear, and being with her was so easy compared to Joyce, who was always complicated, so damn complicated! What a relief to hang out with Janis, he said, at least that's what he felt at the time. And he wanted me to have a mother, a mother who would hold me, look at me, and care for me. He didn't want me to grow up with changing nannies, he said. So he asked Janis if she would marry him and raise me like her own child. And as young as Janis was at the time, she agreed, he said. For that he loved Janis even more. It was a love different from his love for Joyce, but still somewhat similar—maybe more contemporary, he then added with a smile. Janis was very sweet, he said, and she was reasonable; she had a creative, funny mind, she was hilarious—just a wonderful person! He misses her too, and when he thinks of her it still pains him that she too went away. She stopped looking at him. And she too killed herself. She shouldn't have killed herself! She should have come back to us, he said. He asked her to come back. He didn't beg her, no, but he honestly offered for her to come back. He wrote her many times, but she never answered. Maybe he should have gone to New York to help and comfort her and pick her up after Theo died. He couldn't bring himself to do that. That was a mistake. Anyway, he said, as long as she was there, she was a good mother to me. So perhaps he did this right, he said. In a sense Janis really was my mother, he said, even though she wasn't.—She was and she wasn't.

Here he ended his account, stopped as if to give me time to absorb what he had just shared, but it also seemed as if he didn't want to say more at this point. I was confused and a bit surprised. It all sounded new and strange, interesting and odd, and simultaneously I started to feel that this was the answer to all the questions about Joyce that had plagued me over the years. Had I somehow guessed it all along? I don't think so. Had there been hints from him, from Janis? Had I known it without knowing it? Shouldn't I have been more surprised, and since I wasn't, didn't this mean that somehow I may have doubted all along what my father told me once in a while about my early years? Why had it been so difficult for him to tell me? I had all these questions, but I didn't feel the need for immediate answers. Still I was surprised that I didn't feel shaken. I wasn't upset. I remained calm, maybe uncannily so. I needed time to muse on all that I had heard. What he had told me wasn't an earthquake in my biography—or was it?

JANUARY

When we came back to Monteriggioni there was a big envelope from the notary with forms to fill out and papers to sign, all about my father's property and tax issues for his vacation home. Since my father is now basically blind, it was up to me to read them aloud and fill them out and talk with him about every bureaucratic detail, which I really didn't like doing. However, I had to, not only because he can't see, but also, as it turned out, because he's made me a co-owner of this house! I know, I should have said: thank you! Instead I thought: *you didn't even ask me!* Going through these papers took hours. On our way back from Rome I had decided to finally get to the last sections of my *Oedipus* article; I had thought I would intensely work on the remaining questions to get this project done and over with before returning to New York in February. But now my father needed my assistance. Okay, I said to him, think of all the things you want me to help you with, so that we get them done before I go back to New York! It probably came out a bit harsh, and I noticed that my father slightly flinched, but he just nodded. He had caught a cold—and I couldn't stop myself from saying: See, it's not prudent to go out in winter without a coat, which was stupid.

For the next few days my father felt miserable. He was lying in bed sweating and coughing and sneezing, nothing very serious, just an ordinary cold, but even though he reiterated that I didn't have to do this, I felt like taking care of him. I brought him tea with honey, cooked chicken soup with rice, and several times went to the pharmacy to get him painkillers for his headache, drops to soothe his throat, and whatever made him feel better. Given the circumstances, all of this was fair enough. That's what I was there for. Still I didn't like it. Also, it had been raining for the last few days, and even though it finally stopped, now everything was drenched, and stepping out of the house I slipped a bit and landed with one shoe in the mud of my father's empty flowerbed—yuk! Now on top of everything else I would have to clean my shoes!

The piazza was deserted. Only a big motorcycle was parked near the old fountain. Laura sat alone in her coffee bar and picked her nails. She was glad to get me a cappuccino and have a little chat. I told her that we had been in Rome and that my father had come home sick with a cold. She said that a number of people she knew had gotten this nasty bug, and I should watch out. But how could I watch out when my father was spraying it around with every sneeze and cough and touching everything while shuffling through the house? I asked her how she had spent Christmas, and she told me that her boyfriend Roberto had come up from Perugia where he teaches Italian to the foreign students of the International University, and that he plans to stay till the end of the week. He could give me some lessons, I said, and we both laughed. Laura then told me that her parents liked him okay but were anxious about the possibility that she would decide to move to Perugia, and they were even more afraid that she would prematurely move in with him, since he wasn't committed yet to getting married and starting a family. Why would he? Laura lightly said. Roberto is only twenty-six, and he is ambitious. He thinks of going to Rome to study literature and philosophy. Maybe he'll become a professor or a writer or a journalist. I would like to go with him to Rome. But my parents claim they are growing old, and they would like me to stay here to help them run the coffee bar. It's boring to be in Monteriggioni all the time. Nothing happens in the winter, and all these tourists in the summer.... I can't do this for the rest of my life! I nodded, paid for my cappuccino, and left.

When I came back, my father was listening to Beethoven's String Quartet #16. I recognized it right away, because he had listened to it many times before we went to Rome. Since Beethoven was deaf at the time of composing it, I had thought that my father listened to it to slowly understand what his sensory deprivation would mean to him. But now hearing its last part, *the difficult decision*, it seemed more about getting ready for his planned confession. It was the melody of telling me what I should have known all along. Now I knew. I had always thought that he wasn't just friends with Joyce. (See, Issy, I was right!) I knew they were lovers! But it never occurred to me that they made a baby, let alone that I was their baby! But besides this amazing revelation, what had also slipped out with his words was that his relationship with Joyce had been much more scarring and violent than I had pictured it. Why had he put up with her promiscuity, her egocentricity? He had never hinted at these darker sides. He had always painted her in bright albeit somewhat opaque colors. Now she turned out to have been chaotic, selfish, a cheater, a broken soul, a loose leaf on everybody's stage...! Did I have any of this? Had she handed me down some genes of her depression? Anyway, I couldn't bear to hear this music now, it tore me apart. I rushed over to my father's door, but I managed to stop myself from ripping it open, and instead I briefly knocked and slowly opened it, and then asked him more gently than I felt like if he would turn down the volume so that I could concentrate on my article. Oh sure, my father said, I didn't know that you were already back. I'm sorry! And he reached over to the remote control and softened the sound considerably. Seeing him sitting in his bed so sick and disheveled and so eager to accommodate my demands was terrible! I felt simultaneously sad and angry at him, and still I didn't know what to say or to think. When will we have dinner tonight, he wanted to know. I'm not sure yet, I answered. First I want to do some work. Then I will cook for you. But I may go out tonight, so I might not be available for dinner. I had no idea what to do or where to go, and I totally surprised myself saying that. Oh, my father said, equally baffled, and he seemed to struggle for a moment with wanting to ask me where I was planning to go, but he didn't. Instead he said: Good idea, it's certainly no fun to sit with your sick old father in his small kitchen. I know he meant to say that he was giving me a free evening, but this again irked me: was I his servant or slave or what? But of course now I felt bad. I don't think he meant to send me on a guilt trip, this usually wasn't his thing; still, it worked. How could I leave my poor sick father alone! Let me see what I can do, I said, and closed the door.

I stood in the dark hallway with its white plastered walls and the dark wooden sideboard where the keys to the house and the car were lying next to the telephone, and I absolutely didn't know what to do with myself. Part of me felt like taking the keys and running off, but why and where I had no idea. I could take the car, I thought, and go to Florence or even drive back to Cologne, leave without giving my father further notice, drive all night long with only a brief stop at the Splügen Pass, where I would sleep for an hour or two in the car until the first bakery opened and I would get coffee and a warm croissant before driving on. In Cologne Alma would open the door and let me in, and I would crawl into my bed under the roof and sleep, sleep for many hours, and then Alma, my dear Alma, would pamper me—she would say: here is hot chocolate and a bread with peanut butter, that's what you always liked—do you still like it? Yes, I do, and that's exactly what I needed at that moment, and so I went to the kitchen and got myself a piece of bread and packed it with a big hunk of peanut butter!

Why is it that we eat pizza everywhere in the world but not in Italy where it originated? I decided to change that. On this ordinary Tuesday night in the first days of January Monteriggioni's Pizzeria was rather empty. Three couples were dining on three tables far apart from each other, and one single man was sitting with his back towards the entry door eating and reading a newspaper. Pizza, not chicken soup with rice again! I ordered Quattro Stationi and a beer and asked if they ahad the new olive oil yet, harvested only a few weeks ago. *Certo*, the waiter said, and put bread and a bottle of olive oil on my table. The label showed that it was oil from last year. Don't you have the new oil? I asked again. It's the new oil, the waiter reassured me. No, it's not, it's from last year, I insisted and pointed to the label. It's just the old bottle, the oil is new, he gave back. I didn't trust him. No, it's not, I'm not stupid, I grumbled. I was upset! I love olive oil when it's just come from the mill; I wanted the fresh olive oil, not the old one. The waiter shrugged his shoulders and took the bottle away. I watched him as he grabbed a small dish from the shelf and poured in some oil from the bottle he had just removed from my table; then he brought the bowl and placed it in front of me. They think these tourists can be tricked, I thought, but I didn't say anything. I couldn't look at this guy, because my eyes were in tears, and I didn't know why this stupid thing upset me so much. If only I had taken something to read! I felt uncomfortable sitting alone in this restaurant. I regretted not having stayed with my father. He actually had been fine, quickly accommodating to my going out by deciding to eat in the living room while listening to a talk show on TV. I dipped a piece of bread in the oil, and in fact it was the new harvest, I smelled it even before I tasted it. It was delicious, and I was wrong! Whatever!

And then, I don't remember how it happened, but suddenly this single guy from the other table was standing there with his glass of red wine in his hand, and looking at me with a lovely smile he asked: Can I join you for a little chat? *Can I join you for a little chat!* Hayden, it's very unlikely that I will ever send you these pages, but still, for myself I want to write this down. This guy was immediately likable, and since he had wanted only a chat, we started to chat. Why not? First he said that I looked like a tourist—which was true but not exactly flattering—and then he asked me where I was coming from. New York, I said, which seemed to impress him. He said that he had always wanted to go to New York. He told me he was born and grew up in Siena. Then he wanted to know what I did professionally, and when I told him that I was a psychoanalyst in training, he laughed and said: So you must have an Oedipus complex! Everybody has an Oedipus complex, I shot back. Oh, I thought the Americans don't have it anymore, at least that's what I read somewhere, he responded, and wanted to know if I had seen Pasolini's *Oedipus Rex*, which I hadn't. He said it wasn't Pasolini's best movie but still worth seeing, at least for a psychoanalyst. Then I asked him what he was doing, and it turned out that he was a big fan of Pasolini, he loved his poetry, he had studied all about him in great detail, and now he was trying to put together a script for a movie—not a documentary but a fictional story about his life, titled *Pier Paolo* or perhaps simply *PPP*. I didn't know much about Pasolini. I had only seen *Teorema* many years ago, and when I mentioned it, he said *Teorema* was amongst his favorites. For quite some time we talked about Pasolini, which was really interesting. Having finished my pizza, I ordered Vin Santo with Cantuccini, and he had some Cantuccini with his red wine, and I ordered some more...And we continued to talk about other movies and about Woody Allen, and we laughed, and at some point, in what seemed like an accidental move, his hand touched mine, and this touch electrified me, and I wanted to pull away, but he held it, just put his hand over mine, and said: Nice!— simply that. He smiled, and then he said: Shall we take a ride on my bike? And instead of saying *no*, I said, Where, where would we go? And he said: I don't know! It doesn't matter! Maybe Siena—shall we go to Siena?

And I sat behind him on his big motorcycle, I had no helmet on, but so what, I just wrapped myself tightly in my coat, and he zipped his black, warmly padded bike jacket up and said: I'll shield you from the wind, just hold on to me closely! And the bike's engine howled, blared, and roared on the quiet piazza, the exhaust pipe rattled and belted out, outrageously loud, and I put my arms around his chest, and off we went, slowly at first until we had reached the Superstrada, where we were briefly yanked back when he accelerated to a higher speed, and the wind was rushing at us, and I pressed my cheek into the dent between his shoulders, and I felt so safe and a little crazy but happy, happy, and I thought, *I love you*—whoever he is, I love this guy, be it just for the night—this night that was so clear after all the rain had come down, and we were riding along, we, just two easy riders! In Siena everybody seemed to be already asleep, the empty streets resounded from our thundering bike as we snaked against all rules through the one-way streets of the inner city's circles—and then we arrived at *Il Campo!* Never had it appeared to me so magical! It was past midnight, nobody there, the gaslights dimmed, and the buildings in fading pink and wilting orange seemed to look at us through the windows of a hundred darkened eyes, whisper their secrets, almost inaudibly speak to us from their old family affairs, these myths of blind passion, vicious betrayal, and reckless fraud, revealing the glistening, corrosive trail of incest and murder, envy and jealousy, all of it in a dizzying heart-spell, it seemed, as we slowly rode around its shell, once and twice and a third time, and then he stopped, and turned around, and kissed me. I take you to Siena, and you take me to New York, he softly said. I shook my head, and he kissed me again. Do you want to go to a disco? Do you want to dance? I know some places here that are still open! Again I shook my head. Okay, then we go back, he said, and we rode back.

It had cooled down some more, so I had to press myself even closer to his broad leatherback, and I closed my eyes all the way down to Monteriggioni. At the piazza he parked his bike. Can I come with you? he asked, and when I shook my head, he simply followed me like my shadow, and we entered my father's house, which now is also my house, and without a word we simultaneously took off our shoes and tiptoed in socks through the hallway past my father's bedroom door and into my room. Why not! It had been so long since I was in bed with you, Hayden, and how would I ever know what you're doing on your long tour across the world, and actually we never really committed ourselves to anything before you left. Still it was strange. I wanted and didn't want him that night, and reluctantly I pushed away my meager doubts and laid down. He followed, crept close, his arms pulling and positioning me—and I felt awkward and clumsy, I noticed his strange smell while he was working himself up on me, his body so rough and unknown in its male desire, its urge to perform, win and unload—and what was I doing anyway, an angry lash out, a strange mystery, or what— what? Then I stopped thinking. It wasn't bad, it wasn't good, a bit weird and faintly embarrassing—but so what! At some point *Teorema* crossed my mind, *Teorema* was his favorite...*Teorema*, what was that about...? There was no answer, and no answer was necessary. I fell asleep, and I woke up and trailed off again into the night, a night without dreams, and woke up, noticing his body in the middle of my bed, and I tried to push him over to the side, with no success, he was too heavy, unmovable, this sleeping rock in my bed, so I rolled up next to him again in the curve of his arm, the small spot he left me, and fell back into my wandering sleep.

When I woke up again, I had my thumb in my mouth. What???
I sat up, aghast and ashamed. What was going on here? I had to
do some thinking, for sure! I looked at this man in my bed. He
had a small tattoo on his chest that I couldn't resist touching,
and when I did, he opened his eyes and looked at me. Hi, good
morning, he said, and I whispered back: Let's have breakfast
before my father wakes up. We swiftly got into our jeans and
sweaters and sneaked over to the kitchen. Coffee? Yes! Bread?
No. Cereal? No, thanks. Or a banana? I offered. Okay, he said.
We sat at the kitchen table, unshowered and unkempt, sipping
coffee. There was nothing to say. The rising sun cast a dazzling
shine through the small window. Except for us slurping coffee it
was quiet. How would we say goodbye, I wondered. Did I want
to see him again? I wasn't sure.

Then I heard my father's door being opened! I heard him patting
the hallway's walls on his way to the kitchen, heard his slippers
shuffling on the floor, heard his hand on the doorknob—and
there he was in his striped pajamas, his gray hair standing up
oddly as if from an awful nightmare. Sensing that something
was different in his kitchen, in an effort to find out what it was
he repeatedly moved his head from side to side, where there was
nothing to see, which looked even odder. Hi dad, good morning,
I said, and felt uneasy. I hope we didn't wake you up..? Now
I had admitted that I was not alone. Oh…! my father said, I'm
sorry—sorry for my appearance...Well, since I'm already here,
don't you want to introduce your guest to me? And only then

I realized that we had never exchanged names. It hadn't been important. We were together. I called him *you*, and he called me the same, *you*, and that seemed enough for the night. And just when I wanted to say, this is Pier Paolo, I heard him say: I'm Roberto Collodi, and shifting the banana from his right to his left hand, Roberto reached out to greet my father, who however didn't see this and had already turned away. Well, enjoy your breakfast, Roberto, my father said, and left, softly closing the kitchen door behind him.

Sheepishly we looked at each other. Roberto seemed embarrassed, and I was too, but at the same time I was alarmed by his name. Roberto? Are you Laura's boyfriend...? Roberto raised his hand and put his fingers over my mouth. Shhh, he said, and then: I have to go! He took his leather jacket from the chair back, gave me a weary smile, and left. For a short while I heard his steps on the Via G. Matteotti. Mario's dog barked. Then the morning fell silent again. Ugh, I thought, and felt miserable. What had I been thinking! Why hadn't I wondered what he was doing in Monteriggioni? I should have, could have guessed it! Now I couldn't go any longer for a cappuccino to Laura's. Next time I entered the bar, she would be icy cold, just ignore me while continuing to serve all the other customers; or she would jump at me in a rage, pull my hair, scratch my face, scream at me *how dare you*, cry and howl, call me a slut so that everybody on the piazza could hear it, while Roberto would put on his helmet and drive away.

Then another image flared up: my father standing in the kitchen door in his wrinkled pajamas! How embarrassing for him—and for me to be caught with this man! Maybe he heard us in the night! What was he thinking? I shouldn't have left him alone! I agreed to be with him during these weeks, and then I go out and hook up with a guy! This wasn't how I knew myself. Maybe as an adolescent I had daydreams along those lines, but not now, not now! And then sucking my thumb! I was confused. Maybe this whole thing with Joyce had thrown me more than I wanted to acknowledge. Maybe my father even thought I wanted to punish him with my behavior. I didn't want to punish him! Actually I wanted to continue our conversation. Since Christmas I had waited for him to pick up the thread and tell me more about his time with Joyce, but he behaved as if he had never said a word about my mothers. I didn't want to ask him. He'd said it was the parents' duty to tell their children about their beginnings, hence it wasn't mine to interview him. Nothing had been light between us since Christmas. In the remaining days in Rome I had gone alone to the Forum Romanum. I'd thought of going to see Teresa. I kept her card in my pocket. But I wasn't ready to hear her side of this story. Rather, I wanted to first continue talking with my father. The thought of going to see her without telling my father felt like a betrayal.

I was sitting in the kitchen thinking about all of this, I felt angry, guilty, uncomfortable, and then all of a sudden a different thought went through my mind, a thought that I heard as if spelled out, whispered by another person: *Eddie is sad and alone in his bedroom—he's crying!* Eddie, I thought! A surge of love choked me and made me want to go to him and comfort him and make up with him—but should I? Maybe he wasn't ready for that. Maybe I should wait for him to get up. Then we could sit like two adults and talk together. Still I felt an urge to see how he was doing. Through the dark hallway I tiptoed over to his bedroom and put my ear to his door to listen if he was sleeping or what...? There was hardly anything to hear, but it faintly sounded as if there was a sobbing, very, very soft, and my heart sank, and I thought: I did hurt him, and I wanted to comfort and reassure him, but still I wasn't sure. Maybe he had fallen asleep again and was just breathing rhythmically? So I slowly, slowly turned the doorknob, softly opened his door a crack, and peeked into his dusky den: Wrapped in darkness he appeared to be lying on his back, his head deep in his pillows, his comforter pushed to the floor—lying there like a big torso shrouded under sheets, stock-still, it seemed at first, like a piece of furniture protected against the dust of time with a cloth that gives it a bulky shape, covered, I thought, and motionless, it looked, until I saw something moving right in the middle, something lifting and then sinking again, an indistinct pile or stack alive under thin veil, moving up and down—and transfixed by this mysterious colossus I stared into the half-light of his privacy, stared at what I never should have seen, and ashamed for having crossed this most intimate of boundaries, I wanted to withdraw, but just then the motion suddenly stopped and my father lifted his head out of his pillow, and softly said: Ann?—Ann, are you there? I held my breath, I didn't move, I didn't want my father to know that I had watched him. No way! That would be terrible! Ann...? my father whispered again in the direction of the door. And then since, he didn't hear or see anything, he sank back into the pillows and moved again. Softly I withdrew and closed his door without making the slightest noise.

Back in my room at some point I was thinking of the time when I was seven or eight years old, and our whole family would play games on rainy Sunday afternoons. Usually my parents suggested it when waking up from their nap. They called us, we rushed in, we jumped on their big bed, everybody wanting to catch the best spot. We loved to sit there in a circle, my mother would open the box of chocolates she had on her bedside table, and then we decided together what to play: Monopoly, or a card game, or we produced these silly figures, where one of us would start by drawing a head, fold the sheet, and give it to the next person, who would draw the arms, fold the paper again and pass it on to the next, and so on, with everybody working blindly to produce the surprising outcome that was the point of the game. For instance, I would draw the head of a woman, crease the sheet with the neck sticking out under the fold, and hand it over to my mother who, as it later turned out, continued with a pair of wings instead of arms, just for fun, then fold it and hand it over to my father, who would add a lion's body, then Issy would certainly draw something supposed to look like horse legs—from early on she was obsessed with horses—and Paul of course would grin and finish up by supplying a long serpent's tail clearly representing a penis, which was his big preoccupation in those years, always and everywhere, openly or in innuendos, whether he told a joke, commented on a person, or even when he played with a pencil or picked up a banana from the fruit basket! Anyway, when everyone had made their contribution we unfolded the paper, looked at it, and had to come up with a name or a story for the creature we had fabricated. We called this game *Create A Monster* or later simply *CAM*. Maybe *CAM* was one of those suggestions promoted by progressive educators with the idea that children who create monsters are less afraid of them. But it didn't work for me. I remember that it always gave me a tingling feeling when the paper was unfolded. What would it reveal? It was stupid to be anxious; it was only a silly picture, and Paul usually laughed the loudest when seeing it and came up with the wildest monster stories about it. But today, I think maybe he was even more afraid than the rest of us. Given that he went to medical school to become a psychoanalyst, maybe in the depth of his heart he was equally scared and wounded, perhaps without showing or knowing it. He often made fun of me for looking fearful, and when the story I made up proposed a good monster, not a bad one, he often whispered at me, loud enough so that everybody could hear it: No, this is not a princess turned into an ugly monster by a bad spell, this *is* a devouring giant octopus, a killing snatcher-machine that lures in little girls like you, crushes them into a thousand pieces and swallows them up! Then my father would say: Stop it, Paul, you're frightening her! And my mother would hug me and allow me to move over to her and snuggle under her arm, while Issy would just defiantly stare at Paul and not say a word. Was Issy afraid as well? Maybe we were all anxious little monsters at the time.

At around ten o'clock my father knocked at my door and upon my answer he opened and entered, freshly showered and dressed in his olive green corduroy pants and his soft brown leather jacket over a thin beige cashmere turtleneck. The subtle scent of his aftershave wafted over to me. Moved by my bad conscience like a kid, I got up from the chair at my desk where I had stared at my interview transcripts for the last two hours without being able to work. Do you feel like going to Florence with me this morning? my father asked. I feel much better today, and I was thinking, if you had time and were in the mood we could stroll a bit, go to the market and have lunch at *Camillo's*...What a relief! Great, I immediately said, I'll be ready in a minute. My father brightened, equally relieved, it seemed. Okay, he said, I'll wait for you outside. He left, obviously pleased that I had agreed right away. How wonderful was that! My father was again my father: strong, elegant, and knowing the right words and the right thing to do! I still felt a little anxious but also excited that we would clarify things and hopefully get over our reserve.

On our way to Florence we chitchatted about this and that, politics, a mystery story that my father had read a few years ago and that was coming now to the movies, and his arrangement with the housekeeper, Mario's daughter Adriana, who would come daily to clean and cook while he was there, and twice a week when was in Cologne, just to make sure that everything was alright. We were lucky to find a parking spot close to the Ponte Vecchio. The city was only medium crowded. At the Uffizi Gallery there was a long line of visitors waiting to see an exhibition on the Italian Renaissance that would only run for a few more days. When I mentioned it to my father, he suggested that I try to get a ticket. What would you do, if I got a ticket, I wanted to know, and he said: No problem, I would have coffee at *Gilli's* and wait for you. I was touched by his thoughtfulness. This is my father; he wants the best for me. I could always count on that. However, I didn't want to leave him alone and told him I would try to make a reservation online. We walked through the streets arm in arm, the air was cold and fresh, and after a while it was good to enter the big market hall, which was humming with all the people, who slowly moved along the showcases and chatted while patiently waiting in large groups in front of the stands with vegetables and fruit, meat and poultry, spices or chocolates; in passing I saw a small shark in its impressive entirety displayed in one of the fish booths. I mentioned it to my father, who then tried to get a glimpse of it. All these different smells, he said. At a bar next to a bakery we decided to sit down for a moment and have an espresso. What a nice idea to come here, I said. My father nodded. We have to talk some more, he then said, and I think this always goes better when we are out of the house.

At *Camillo's* my father got us a table in the entry hall, which is my favorite. I love to sit in this first room with its high ceiling and all the pictures on the walls and the shelves with great wines and the big glass cabinet filled with delicacies; I enjoy watching the waiters joking with each other while running in and out of the kitchen and elegantly swinging from table to table in the proud pursuit of their dignified profession: what a pleasure to be served by them! My father ordered a bottle of *Vernaccia* and some sparkling water, and then I read the menu to him. We had time. Even though we clearly had an important and complicated conversation ahead, we were relaxed and in a good mood. When we had ordered lunch, I apologized to my father for having surprised him with a stranger in our kitchen. I wanted to get this quickly out of the way. My father shrugged his shoulders and said: Well, you have the right to a sex life. Yes, I was a bit surprised—in a corner of my heart I may still see you as my little girl, not as a woman who goes out with guys. But it's okay. I thanked him and told him that I felt bad about it, because it had turned out that Roberto was Laura's boyfriend, but he didn't make much of it, just lightly suggested that Laura might not even know about it, or else I would figure out how to deal with her. Clearly he didn't want to dwell on this and had other things on his mind. So I dropped the issue, enjoyed my starter, Swordfish Carpaccio with a lemon sauce, and waited for him to say something.

After a while my father started talking, and while he was carefully choosing his words he appeared pained. Picking up on my going out the night before, he said he was concerned that it was a response to what he told me at Christmas. I was afraid you would leave me, he admitted, like all the others...simply go away or avoid being with me. It scared me. I wanted to talk with you some more, but I didn't know how. All these years I felt protective of your love for Janis. All the memories you had about her as your mother, I wanted them to remain untouched. That was my reason for not telling you about Joyce, I thought. But since I told you—what sticks out most for me is that *I lied to you*! For more than thirty years I made you believe that Janis was your birth mother and Joyce was just a friend of mine. I raised you to stick to the truth, and now I feel like a terrible liar, a coward who betrayed the trust of his daughter. I'm afraid you won't be able to forgive me for that. Maybe I can't forgive me either. I wish I had told you earlier, much earlier, but how early? I don't know...He sighed and pushed away the empty plate from his starter.

Why was it so difficult to tell me, I asked him. A sad shadow flitted across my father's face. You look so much like Joyce, he then said, the way you laugh and sometimes gesture, or just how you throw your hair over your shoulders...She too had a very sweet and tender side to her, and boy, did I love her in these moments when she was fully with me and not in one of her funks...When I met Joyce she was older than you are now, she might have been a little heavier, but she looked nearly exactly like you do nowadays. It was confusing...I mean emotionally confusing. So I think not telling you about Joyce allowed me—I could see you, in a way—like you *were* Joyce. I mean, in my heart sometimes you were Joyce, just a bit, just secretly—I'm sorry, forgive me...

A reincarnation, I interjected, and noticed that it came out somewhat ironic. Well, I knew the whole time that you were Antje, my father hurried to reassure me, and you are very different from Joyce in so many ways! I'm not sure how much I was aware of this confusion. But since Christmas I've been thinking all the time that I just couldn't let go of her. The memory was in my way, the memory of her, and most poignantly her eyes, you have her eyes, and when you looked at me, when I could still see you looking at me—it beguiled me to feel her still being around, her still being with me...

My father paused. I saw how he struggled, and it moved me, even though I felt somehow guarded. Joyce remained your first love, I said, and he nodded and rubbed his eyes with both hands, as if he wanted to wipe her away. Joyce...he murmured, Joyce...! Since I can't see anymore, I see her all the time. I don't want her to come up, but she does. Or is it you? Now I want her to go away, but she sticks with me. Why is that? Haven't I thought about her long enough? Why does this never end? What did I miss? What could I have done differently?—And how did she treat me and why? All these scenes come up, beautiful and horrible ones, things I hadn't thought about for decades, now they sneak up on me and won't let go, they won't go away...

The waiter came, brought us two plates with homemade *linguine primavera* and refilled our glasses with wine. *Buon appetito*, he said. Silently we started eating. Part of me wanted my father to tell me about these beautiful and horrible moments with my mother—with Joyce that is—but I also felt reluctant to ask him and thought, maybe it's better I don't know about this. And as if he had read my mind, my father said: I don't want to burden you with these things, it was long ago, you weren't even born, so let's not get into this.—But I told you many years ago—heaven knows why I did—I told you that when Joyce was very young she gave away her firstborn child for adoption. I thought she never got over missing this child. I thought this loss caused her mood swings or at least contributed to them. I thought if she had another baby, she would forget about this first one and spend all her love and care on her new baby—you. But that's not what happened. She got worse. So sometimes I wished...He stopped and pinched his lips, but I knew exactly what he wanted to say and spelled it out: You wished I hadn't been born. My father nodded slightly. That crossed my mind when she was so miserable, sitting there—totally unresponsive—like a ghost— and after she was gone, and when I was so desperate—alone with you, a newborn baby, and with Paul, who was so difficult...I'm sorry, he said, and I told him that I could understand, and really I felt it!

But I also loved you, my father said, and when I held you in my arms, when I held you—I knew life would go on, you were my future—my future and my past—or the future of my past—anyhow...Again we were silent for a while. I thought of my father and how difficult this time had been for him. And then all of a sudden I thought: Paul knew, he knew the whole time that Joyce was my mother and never said anything! So I asked him: But what about Paul? He was already eight when I was born, he must have known that Joyce—not Janis—was my mother! Why did he never say a word? My father nodded. I don't know if he knew or didn't know it at the time. Most of the week he was at boarding school. Joyce's pregnancy didn't show much, and during the last four months, she was in the hospital in order to avoid a miscarriage. So we told Paul that Joyce was touring with a theatre group. When you were born he was at camp. He came home for just a few hours before going back to school, and I'm not sure that you were there. I think the nanny had taken you to the pediatrician that afternoon. And when Paul came back at the end of the week Joyce had already gone out the window...While I was dealing with all of this, the nanny had taken you to her place for a few days. Then I brought Janis home from art school. So I believe, for him Janis and you came home together. I don't know if he realized...so he might not have known...

I found this phrasing vague. *He might not have known*—are you saying that he knows now? My father confirmed: He knows now. I felt myself getting upset. How come he knows before I do? In order to answer this question my father revealed another secret to me. He told me that when Joyce died, I, her newborn baby, was the legitimate heiress of her condo on 5th Avenue. As my father he had the right to put this inheritance into a trust for me, and he organized the trust in such a way that it would only be knowable and available to me when I had reached Joyce's age on the day she ended her life: that is, at forty-eight years and fifty-six days. It would be relatively late in my life, my father acknowledged, yet still not a bad surprise at that point. He thought that until then he would financially support me if necessary. However, since I had learned about it now, he conceded that if I wished, we could change the provision to make the condo immediately available to me. When Janis, Paul, and Theo went to New York, he continued, I offered to let them live in the condo for free and paid rent on their behalf into your trust account. After Theo and Janis died, Paul stayed there alone, and when he was out of Medical School he took over the payment of the rent. It's a small place but it has a beautiful view over Central Park, my father remarked.

Oh, I know where Paul lives, I said, he invited me over once. I told you that he is a member at my institute, so we are colleagues now. Most people don't know that he's my brother because of our different last names, and we don't tell anyone, for some reason we don't want to make it public. At least I want him to be Dr. Salentino instead. Sometimes it's a little awkward for us. But in all these years since he left he's become almost a stranger to me. So for me he is more like a colleague, one who is higher up in the institute's hierarchy. Anyway, I've seen his place. It's nice!—I had no idea that it was mine...

My father seemed surprised. Oh, you are at the same institute, you see each other? Now I was surprised that he didn't remember. Sure we do. I told you! I even told you that it was Paul who convinced me to apply to his institute for psychoanalytic training! My father still looked puzzled and then said: I don't think so, I don't remember, I can't imagine that I heard it and forgot...I always thought the two of you only briefly spoke on the phone when you first came to New York. Now I was puzzled and in doubt. Had I not spoken with my father about Paul's invitation to join his institute? We certainly didn't speak much about Paul, who had become a non-person for my father, a taboo. But still I thought I had told him...

Anyway, my father continued, your trustee is a lawyer and a good, old friend of mine, Tim Moore; he actually lives in the building where your condo is, just two floors up, and seems to socialize or even be friends with Paul. Janis told me about Tim Moore, I interjected, isn't he the one she came to as an exchange student? Right, my father confirmed. So a few weeks ago when Tim wanted to adjust the rent to the current market level, Paul declared that he wanted to buy the 5th Avenue condo and asked for information about its owner. Tim had no right to talk with Paul about the trust; he was bound to secrecy. But inadvertently something must have slipped out... Paul contacted me, my father continued. For the first time in about twenty years he called me. He asked how I was doing, and then he said it was good to hear my voice! I think it was the first time that he said something nice to me! I was surprised and moved...I suggested that perhaps we could see each other and catch up. And he said that would be good because he wanted to talk with me about the condo! This wasn't exactly the reason I had in mind when suggesting that we meet. Anyway, he said he knew that Joyce was your mother and had bequeathed you her condo, and he knew that this was secret information. Yet he wanted to buy the place. I told him I couldn't sell it to him, it was yours, to which Paul said, if I wouldn't negotiate this with him he would talk to you directly.

He pressured you, I said, that's why you told me! Maybe my father heard my disappointment. That's only part of it, he replied. Since I was diagnosed with AMD I had been thinking about it. If you can't look ahead you can run into something that kills you. Now is the time to put things in order.

Maybe it was as he said, or maybe he put a better spin on it to please me. For a while we were silent. It annoyed me that Paul had tried to blackmail my father. I wondered if Paul had invited me *before* or *after* he found out that the condo was mine. I remember how admiring I was of his place, the gorgeous view and all. I liked it when Paul told me that he had lived there as a little boy with Joyce and my father and later with Janis and Theo, and that he felt really at home there. Still, Paul had also bashed the place, saying that now everything was run down, the pipes were howling, the heating was dripping, the wind came in from the window frames...Was he calculating for a lower price in case he would have to negotiate with me?

At this point most of *Camillo's* guests had left. The restaurant had quieted down, the cooks were cleaning the kitchen, the owner's children were sitting at a private table eating spaghetti and talking with what seemed to be their grandmother. It's nice to know that Janis, Theo, and Paul moved into 5th Avenue, I said. It was generous of you to make this possible for them—despite the fact that they had left us. But why did Janis leave in the first place? Did she feel you were still thinking of Joyce, did she feel she would always be secondary to her? And why did she leave with Paul and Theo, why not with me as well? Was it because I wasn't her child?

My father sighed deeply, pushed himself a bit off the table and, as the waiter just came by, ordered two espressos for us. This is another painful story in my life, he said. I hoped you wouldn't ask me this, at least not today. But since I have committed myself to always tell you the truth from now on: The truth is, I don't know if Theo was my son. Janis said he was at first, but later she wouldn't confirm anymore. At the time I thought she had something going on with Paul. I have to admit, I was suspicious, furious, jealous, I pressured her, and when I wanted to genetically test Theo to determine who was the father, I or Paul, Janis refused. That's when she left me. That's when they left us. At first I thought that was proof enough. Later I wasn't so sure anymore. I thought maybe she didn't know who Theo's father was, and maybe she didn't want to know. I guess I failed and hurt her with my demands. Maybe she wanted me to love her no matter what, and I let her down—after all she had done for me, for you, for us, really…She didn't abandon me! I abandoned her! Later I beat myself up so many times: what difference did it make whether I was or wasn't Theo's father? We all could have lived under one roof. We were a big family—we could have been. Maybe they would still be alive, had I not been such a stupid, stubborn, selfish idiot…Then, all of a sudden, my father's voice broke; he tried to stammer a few more words, then tears erupted, small dry blasts, tearing through the lines in his face; he tried to hide behind his hands and turn away towards the wall, but his back curved and twitched and showed how shaken he was, totally shaken, and I was shocked, and couldn't do anything but wait until his pain seemed to slowly lessen. It was quiet. Most of the waiters had gone. On a small plate the folded bill. Eventually my father lifted his head and show me his anguished face.

We both were exhausted! Slowly we walked along the Arno in the faint afternoon sun, and at some point we just stopped, leaned at the balustrade with our elbows resting on the roundish stone wall and looked out at the river. My father stared at his hands, rhythmically dabbing the fingers of one hand at those of the other, while I was looking at the water flowing downstream, some rowboats passing by, children playing soccer along the waterside, some elderly people sitting on benches watching life around them…I'll come with you to New York, my father softly said. I want to help and support you with the rearrangement of your trust. I want to make sure that Paul doesn't get the better of you. And I want to see Paul—well, I want to get together with him; he's my son—maybe there is still a way we can put our old wars behind us and reconcile, find some peace, maybe even become friends. I would like that—very much...

FEBRUARY

My father was nervous but tried not to show it. After more than thirty years his first trip back to New York! He had upgraded my ticket to business class. Comfortably stretched out, we crossed the Atlantic. After lunch he listened to a concert on his headphones, then fell asleep. I worked for some time on the conclusion of my article, trying to address the difference between fantasy and reality. Many of my interview partners seemed to emphasize their patients' reality. But what can we know about their reality? We just know their tales, and tales are always somewhat fictitious, part of a continuous dream...Hadn't my father dreamt about Joyce for all his life? Hadn't he looked at me and seen Joyce? Isn't that a fantasy? I looked over to him. He was lying in his chair, his eyes closed, his glasses slipped a bit down on his nose, his lips slightly opened as he was sleeping. Was he dreaming?

He seemed to smile a bit. Maybe he was dreaming of traveling with Janis to New York, I thought, dreaming that he had gone with her when she wanted it so badly. Now he's doing it. He owes her. Finally he is ready. Okay, let's go, he says one morning, and Janis is so surprised and excited that she jumps up, hugs him, and dances around in the kitchen. That shows how much she wants it! Finally he gets it! Let's go, even for a few weeks, he says to her. Alma will take care of the kids. And so they go and arrive in New York, and Tim Moore picks them up at the airport and brings them to their hotel—or even better: the 5th Avenue condo happens to be free, so they can go straight there! Jim, the doorman, is still the same! Thirty years older, he has grayed and seems a bit shrunken as he stands behind his desk, but he still has these sparkling eyes, and when he recognizes Eddie and Janis he is so moved that he is tearing up. Shaking his head in disbelief he stammers: Oh, Mister Eddie, oh Mister Eddie! And then he lifts the sleeve of his jacket a bit and says: See this watch that you gave me long ago? I still wear it every day, it still works, and whenever I look at it, I think of you! It is a beautiful day! Central Park is crackling with sunshine, and Janis wants to take a stroll—after sitting all those long hours on the plane, she says, let's go through the park, and Eddie likes that. So they just drop off their luggage and cross the street into Central Park. They choose the sunny paths. Eddie puts his arm around Janis' shoulders, and tightly holding her he keeps the gusts of wind from pushing her tousled tresses over her face. Both feel so young—nearly as young as when they were here last, so many years ago, *unbelievable!* How wonderful, Janis whispers, and

Eddie nods. Would you like to move back to New York? he asks. Maybe, Janis responds, we have to ask the kids, but right now this is where I want to be! Later they visit the Metropolitan Museum to see the new acquisitions of its photo collection—and *surprise*: there is one of Janis' photos hanging—which one?—maybe it would be one of the *Eddie Sleeping* series! They'd bought it and exhibited it in their fabulous photo collection, and Janis didn't even know about it, *unbelievable*! Both she and Eddie are standing there, stunned and totally overwhelmed with happiness! You made it, Eddie says, you deserve it! And Janis wipes off some tears and keeps shaking her head in disbelief. They want to talk to the curator, but he is out that day. So they decide to celebrate and walk over to *Via Quadronno*, their beloved little Italian restaurant on 73rd Street. To Miss Metropolitan, Eddie says when their Prosecco glasses touch, and To Eddie Sleeping, Janis responds, and they are happy to be back in New York. For a while they had felt a little down at home; Eddie had worked very hard on the expansion of his *FIXIT* company; Janis had to struggle to get the funding for her photography courses; Paul had been reprimanded for smoking cannabis in the schoolyard; Ann had been floundering in her classes; Issy had been sick with mumps, and then she broke her arm during her gymnastics lessons; and to top it all off, a storm had uprooted an old chestnut tree in their garden and crashed it onto the roof of their house, which then needed to be fixed—whew!—sort of the normal things a family has to struggle with. But now for once all of this seems far away, and they feel in love again like in their best days. It was so good that they made this trip, they needed and deserved this break, it would turn their marriage around…

Still smiling my father woke up, and turning over to me he looked as if bedazzled by a dream. Would it pain him having dreamt this dream and then realizing that he missed out on living it—everything could have been different, couldn't it? The flight attendant started preparing a little snack before landing. Did you get some work done? my father wanted to know, and when I confirmed he asked: Will you read your paper to me when it's finished? I was surprised and moved by his interest. Then my father asked me to tell him something about Paul: how he looks, how he is, what he does—anything. I'm a bit nervous about seeing him—sort of seeing him, he admitted. So it would help me if you could prepare me, give me a picture, an idea. I wasn't quite comfortable with that but I understood. Well, I said, he's a handsome guy, usually dressed casually elegant; he wears his hair a little longer than most, it sort of falls down to his shoulders, sometimes bound in a ponytail—it makes him look youngish, a bit soft, gentle. He wears some designer glasses, with black frames, fitting to his dark hair. What else...? He's bright, he is considered one of the smartest, has written and published in our field, mostly about developmental issues, because he also works with children and adolescents. I only read one of his papers, it was about a little boy with a gender identity disorder...but now I'm afraid I couldn't tell you much about it. What else…? Paul is rather social, he can be very funny, and the younger people like to be around him. There are some rather conservative analysts in our institute who are skeptical about him, but I can't tell what that's based on—there are always people who find fault with everybody. More recently he seems to have gone through some sort of fight with the chair of the admissions committee, but I was not involved in it and don't know the details.

While I was talking my father listened carefully, and from time to time he nodded a bit as if what he heard fit with some of his own ideas about Paul. Finally he asked me: Is he or was he married, or does he have a girlfriend? I had wondered about that too. Not that I would know, I responded. He seems to live alone at 5th Avenue, but maybe he has someone...We both were silent for a while. Then my father said: Isn't it strange: I know next to nothing about my firstborn son. I met him when he was six, and he left when he was eighteen, so he lived with me only twelve out of his forty years, and still I think I should make up with him. I owe him—but what? It wasn't my fault that I wasn't with him in his first six years. I didn't even know that he existed. Then one day he walks in, and there he is, and he hates me from day one on. I didn't blame him, at least at first I didn't. I understood: he had suffered a shocking loss! He was totally uprooted! Of course he would blame me! Who else could he have blamed, right? But whatever I tried—and believe me I tried hard—I never could win his heart. That I didn't understand. He got older. And then—maybe he took revenge on me, something he felt entitled to but certainly wasn't—or I'm not sure about it. Fact is that he took Janis away. This part of our life can't be rewritten. However, now he's an analyst! He must have thought about our circumstances, he must have understood a bit better and worked through it...But I'm afraid he keeps blaming me for all that was bad in his life. But is it such a bad life? It doesn't seem so. That's why I think, as much as I may have failed him, he failed me too. Yet still I feel I should try one more time. Maybe now we can find each other on a different level. I feel anxious when I say that, it will hurt when I fail—but I'm ready to try.

At JFK Mr. Moore picked us up. In his gray suit, white shirt, and blue tie he looked a bit more formal than I had pictured him, but when he hugged my father it seemed heartfelt. So good to see you, Eddie, he said, and see you here again in New York. That took quite a while! My father seemed equally moved. Well, Tim, in the meantime you came to see me in Cologne, he responded. Then Mr. Moore shook hands with me and said: Nice to finally meet you, Ann. I'm Timothy Moore, just call me Tim. I was sitting in the back of Tim's black Lincoln, and while the two were chatting in the front, I was trying to imagine how my mother felt when she first came here as a young exchange student, not knowing anything ahead, nothing, not how to be away from home, not how to be in New York, and not how to be at the Moore place without Sally—just going towards this blank screen that would be filled by destiny quicker and more fully than she could ever have anticipated...Had she been scared? Had she been excited? Or depressed? I looked out of the window. It was raining. The traffic into Manhattan was slow but at least we were constantly moving.

I wondered how things in my apartment would be. Over the holidays a friend of a friend had stayed there with her husband, and I hoped that they had cleaned up before leaving. But I felt strangely split over the prospect of being back alone at my apartment. My father had accepted to stay with Tim Moore, who also offered a second guest room to me—but I wanted to return to my place. Now I felt I would miss my father! After all these weeks together, I would have wanted him to stay at *my* place. However, I didn't have a second room or a bed for him. I thought he would need me. How would he get around without me? Don't you want to come out with us for a sandwich first and then take a cab to your place later? Tim suggested. I declined. That's not what we had planned. So you'll come for dinner, Tim said when he dropped me off on my street a few steps away from my apartment building because a big moving truck was blocking the road. I walked through the misty rain with my luggage clattering behind me. Now I'm back, I thought, as if the obvious needed to be spelled out in my mind: I'm back. Sadness had gripped me, I didn't know why. Reluctantly I pulled out the key to the building's main door, crossed the lobby with a brief side-glance to the mailboxes, entered the elevator, pressed 7, and trundled upwards. When I approached my door, I saw a wrapped flowerpot sitting in front of it. Who would send me flowers? Was it Hayden? I picked up the gift, opened the door, and entered.

The apartment was cool—of course it was cool! So first I turned up the heat and switched on the lights to make the room feel warmer. The living room looked somehow remote and mute. I'd been gone a long time! I opened the paper around the flowerpot and unveiled a wilted orchid. It must have been sitting there for weeks. When I looked at the address I discovered that it had been sent to an unknown person on the 8th floor. They just missed by one floor, and a lovely gesture went nowhere. I threw the plant away. I felt lonely. Hayden, when will you be back? You never responded to my monthly emails. Are you reading them? How are you doing? You are so far away. What now? I didn't feel like unpacking my luggage. I took a shower, put on some nice clothes, and left my apartment.

When I arrived at Moore's condo, a maid in a formal uniform opened the door and let me in. My father was lounging comfortably on the sofa in the living room with Tim next to him on a chair, both looking like old friends rejoined in good spirits. An open photo album was lying on the coffee table in front of Tim. I looked around, interested in seeing another condo in this building. We are neighbors, I thought, and tried to relate to this idea, but I only felt amazed. My father said: Tim and I indulged a bit in the past. I wish I could see his photos—but at least he described them to me...The photos immediately sparked my curiosity. Can I see them? I asked. Sure, Tim responded. But just when he handed over the heavy, leather-bound album, the maid opened the door, and Paul entered in the company of a young woman with dark curly hair and a fancy silk dress with a wild imprint of big purple flowers on a black-and-white background. Her name, we learned, was Gina. Tim seemed unsure of what to say when his maid asked if she should set the table for five. Gina quickly helped out by modestly replying: I'm happy to stay, thank you. She looked over to Paul with an expectant smile. Paul apologetically shrugged his shoulders and said: Sorry, I hadn't realized when I confirmed for dinner tonight that Gina would be in town. She's an actress, came in from Los Angeles for an audition. I thought—with acting being part of our family tradition, you wouldn't mind if I brought her along.

I felt the sting. I think everybody felt it. I couldn't believe that Paul was doing this. It was the first meeting in years between him and his father, and he was shielding himself with an *actress*! Tim too appeared to be thrown for a loop. He probably had thought of his role as an amiable chaperone for the reunion of our divided family and a mediator for any negotiations, immediate or future ones, in and around my 5th Avenue condominium, not as the host of a social event. Meanwhile my father, apparently not having fully grasped the awkwardness of the situation and obviously taking Gina for Paul's girlfriend—which I didn't think she was—quickly recovered from his surprise and simply said: Hi Paul, it's been a while...Nice that you brought your friend. He reached out to shake Paul's hand, open to expanding his move to a possible hug, but right then Paul busied himself with turning off his cell, so my father's hand stayed hanging in the air, forlorn for a moment—and stripped of its purpose it wandered off, weakened it seemed, towards his head, fumbling there for a bit with his hair, as if it needed to be restrained, and finally fell down and disappeared into his jacket pocket. I think my father meant it when he welcomed Paul and his friend, but I saw that Paul took it as an irony and felt criticized.

What about a gin fizz for the two of you, Tim cut in, we've already started. We all sat down, followed by an embarrassed silence. Then Paul offered an ordinary question: How was the trip? Oh, it was actually quite comfortable, I responded, and in order to start our conversation on more neutral territory, I wanted to continue by saying something about working on my paper, which could have interested Paul, at least remotely from a professional point of view, but Gina jumped in. I hate those long trips on planes, she provided, the air is sooo dry! I always get an allergic skin reaction that stays with me for days. Look, she said pulling up her sleeve and stretching her arm towards my father to show him, It's still red, and it's a week now since I came over from LA! Then, since Paul obviously had told her about my father's AMD, she belatedly seemed to remember and simply added, Oh, you can't see it, and proceeded to move her naked arm towards Tim in search of someone to confirm her little red pimples...I totally disliked this Gina! But my father gently said: Yes, that's a real problem. Have you tried a moisturizing cream? So we babbled along with Gina giving most of the input, my father politely responding, Tim sometimes laughing extra loud, and Paul rather brooding and sometimes surreptitiously leering over to my father, who in turn repeatedly moved his head in order to get a peripheral glance of Paul.

Then the maid asked us to the round dining table. Gina managed to place herself where I actually wanted to sit, next to my father, who was already flanked on the other side by Tim, who had Paul on his other side, so I ended up sitting between Paul and Gina! I love shrimp, Gina offered when the starter was served, they are so much better on the East Coast than in LA! Who cares, I thought, and wondered how we could turn this evening into something more meaningful. Well, it's been a long time since Eddie and I had dinner here together, Tim tried, raising his glass. Yeah, Paul told me, Gina chipped in, ignoring that Tim was just beginning with a toast. Isn't that odd! Tell us, Eddie, why didn't you ever come back to New York? My father seemed to slightly cringe, but he held his ground, softly saying: That's a good question, Gina. But not all questions get to be answered. One has one's reasons, some even unbeknownst to oneself. So we do what we do, and our mind still remains a mystery, doesn't it, Paul? Paul drew a bitter smile. You speak like an analyst, he then said, how could I disagree?

And then happened what sometimes happens: a shrimp slipped off my father's fork, dropped down and disappeared, which he only noticed when he felt the empty fork in his mouth. He looked unsettled, his left hand tapped his napkin in search of the escapee, then felt for it on the tablecloth around his plate, and I would have liked to help him but couldn't reach over my neighbor because she was leaning forward with both of her elbows on the table. So my father said: Sorry, Tim, I'm afraid

I lost something from my fork. I can't see it. If it fell down, I don't want to ruin your carpet...Tim put his hand on my father's shoulder and responded: Don't worry, Eddie, we'll find it later. But Gina screamed: I found it! She reached down at my father's lap, picked up the shrimp soaked in red cocktail sauce, showed it around like a trophy, and comically exclaiming *catch of the day!* she slowly and seductively put it between her lips, kept it there for a moment with its tail sticking out, and then sucked it in, thereby keeping a red speckle on her luscious lips. It was supposed to be funny. Nobody said anything. Then the maid served the main course and refilled our wine glasses.

I was livid! Gina ran the show! Totally full of herself and insensitive to the delicacy of the moment, she just enjoyed flirting or rather making fun of my father, who couldn't see and fully understand what she was doing. From time to time winking at Paul like his secret accomplice, she shamelessly performed her chipper little role—I could have thrown her right out of the window! I felt like shaking Paul—*are you out of your mind*—but I knew that it was better to save than blow the party. I couldn't understand why Tim didn't take the lead; he seemed so passive and helpless! But I too felt clueless about how to shut her up. Paul looked as if he had drawn a blank. Meanwhile my father seemed to withdraw a bit.

All of a sudden Gina calmly said: Look, guys, I understand, it's a freaky thing to sit here tonight after so many years and with so many unresolved issues looming. I went through something like it, many times! My parents divorced when I was five, because my mother ran off with her therapist. They moved from Los Angeles to New Orleans. I stayed behind with my father, who never forgave her and told me about it every day. Of course my mother's new relationship didn't last. After two years she wanted to come back, but that didn't work for my father, no! So for the rest of their lives she stayed miserable, and he stayed miserable. I lived with my father until college and spent my vacations with my mother! No feast nowhere! But worst of all was when I had something special going on, like a major birthday, 10 or 20, or graduation, and both of my parents had to sit in the same room. I could feel daggers flying between them with me in the middle. Whew! I tried to cheer them up, played the funny kid who didn't notice any of the bad stuff that befouled my day. That never worked. I was just thinking of this...When Paul told me last night how nervous he was about seeing his father, I certainly understood what he was talking about. It's not exactly the same, I know, but there is something alike in all people who hate each other because they feel hurt. I like Paul. So I suggested joining him tonight. For me it's just a freaky evening like many others. Tomorrow I'll go back to LA, and I hope you'll make it better than my old folks did. Then she shut her mouth as if she were done for the night.

I was stunned. Gina had hit the nail head-on. My heart was pounding. Tim pinched his lips and looked around from one to the next, and then mumbled something about all divorces being difficult, that his own divorce hadn't been a cakewalk exactly, in particular for his children. Paul stared down at his fingers, which trembled as if they were wired on high voltage. My father, leaning back in his chair, seemed to be thinking about a response to Gina's account. Finally he said: Thank you, Gina, for sharing this. You are right. It's never easy to deal with old hurts. And we shouldn't even try to get into this tonight. We just arrived. I had some drinks. I'm getting tired. Paul and I agreed to spend time together these next few days. So since you'll be leaving tomorrow, why don't you tell us about your audition so that we know for what to wish you good luck?

I think we all were relieved that my father wanted to get us some space here, and Gina too seemed to understand. She immediately started with a longwinded story about having been selected for a leading role in *Desperate Housewives*; however, in a last-minute pitch another actress, who was having an affair with one of the producers, torpedoed her out, probably by blackmailing him. Of course she, Gina, was outraged, not only because she lost this big opportunity, which could have been the breakthrough for her career, but also because she had cancelled another contract when she was picked for the *Housewives*, and all of a sudden she stood empty-handed. When she complained to the producer, indicating that she could go public, he opened a door for her in a pilot in New York, a new comedy series, in which she would play a psychiatric nurse who gets psyched out herself.

I dutifully listened, but I couldn't imagine that anybody was interested in Gina's drama, which sounded like just another soap opera. However, my father got animated by her story; he smiled when Gina made a self-ironic comment, he nodded encouragingly when she seemed to hesitate, he indicated admiration for her straightforwardness, and eventually he turned toward her, put his arm on the back of her chair, and said: That was a smart move! Gina seemed happy. You really understand our business, Eddie, she said, and when he responded with: I mean it, you should fight for this role, you can do it! she leaned over and kissed him on his lips. Thank you! she said, beaming with delight.

I'm not sure that my father expected this award; he seemed a bit uncomfortable with her affection, which I thought was totally uncalled for. But there was not much time to linger, because Gina's cell started chirping in her gemmed purse on the couch. Proclaiming Oh, that could be my agent, Gina jumped up, and as she began to run over to get her purse, she somehow got stuck or entangled with one of her high-heeled shoes between my father's leg and the leg of her chair, and having risen already to her full height, and being in the swing of her move, she toppled, fell with an odd twist backwards, and crashed into the edge of the coffee table. There was a big boom, the other end of the table bounced up, briefly spiked, flipped over, then cracked and splintered into thousand little pieces all over the floor, where Gina had landed in an awkward position. She gasped for air, winced, tried to say something, and kept aspirating Ah, ah, ah...

Her cell stopped ringing. Tim and Paul were at her side and cautiously tried to lift her up while Gina whimpered and whispered: Wait, wait, wait...My father said: Oh god, what happened? I told him, and he was dismayed. I'm so sorry, he said over and over, I don't know what I did wrong, how could that happen, I'm so sorry! After a while Paul and Tim managed to help Gina up. She at first kneeled a bit on a spot that Paul and Tim had swept clean of the shards, then she slowly got up, stood on wobbly, shaky legs, her face pale from the shock, her left hand holding her right arm, which was bleeding from some small cuts. We should call an ambulance and bring you to a hospital, Tim suggested. Gina shook her head. It's okay, I'm fine, I'm okay! She asked for her purse and slowly sat down again next to my father, who apologized one more time, but she wouldn't have any of it. No, no, it wasn't your fault, Eddie, absolutely not, she reassured him, and held herself at his arm, briefly grimacing with pain. Paul handed her the purse. He and Tim kept standing close to her as if ready to catch her should she faint. But Gina composed herself, pushed her hair back, and retrieved the message on her cell. We all silently watched. Then with a rapt smile that broke through her shock-stricken face she declared: I got the part! I'm going to be the nurse! And we all cheered and clapped our hands.

It was the perfect moment to end the party on an upbeat note. Paul said goodnight, and after Gina had reassured him that she was capable of going back to her hotel on her own, he went to wait with her on the street for a cab. Tim offered me his second guest room again, suggesting it might be easiest to spend the night there, since we had agreed to get together early the next morning to talk about the change of my trust. I gladly accepted. The idea of riding home alone and crawling under my cold comforter wasn't appealing. Also, I felt anxious, subtly agitated, as if alarmed without knowing what troubled me. Or is this a thought in hindsight? My father stated that he was overdue for a good night's sleep. So great to have you here, Eddie, Tim said hugging him, you know that you can stay with me as long as you wish; it will always be my pleasure. My father smiled. Thanks, Tim, I really appreciate your hospitality. It makes me feel—well, nearly at home again on 5th Avenue. Then he said goodnight to me and withdrew to his room. The maid had already cleaned the dinner table; I heard her working in the kitchen. Tim waved over to me, Sleep well, Ann. He switched off the lights in the living room. Only the hallway remained illuminated. Goodnight and thanks, I responded, and closed the door to my room. Still too stirred to fall asleep I kept thinking about the evening. Gina's willingness to take the brunt of the awkwardness we brought to the table had given us some space for a new start. My father hadn't shown much of his feelings about Paul, and his generous support for Gina had actually been quite gentlemanly. Paul hadn't interacted much with his father; but given that he used to storm out on him in our early years, the very fact that both were in the same room for several hours could count for a warm-up. Tim hadn't impressed me with any particular strength; he appeared friendly and accommodating, perhaps the best attitude in his position. Altogether I ended up feeling okay with this evening.

Mulling over these thoughts I must have fallen asleep. And it must have happened then that my father secretly stole away from Tim's condo. He must have tiptoed to the front door, silently opened it, slipped out, and equally silently closed it, so that none of us would hear and stop him. He knew the building inside out, the number of steps to the elevator was ingrained in his system, and so was the button for the tenth floor, which he had pressed a million times, tired or excited, expectant or hopeless, alone or with Joyce, or with Paul or with Janis, it had been the key to home for some good albeit difficult years.

And so I imagine him pressing the 10-button without really knowing what his intention is. He just feels this unstoppable urge to go to Paul and to confront him—or whatever needs to be confronted. That's what I think happened. That's how I put it together from the bits and pieces I heard and gathered over the following days. That's what had made me anxious, but I didn't pay enough attention to it. Why didn't I allow myself to be more alarmed by my intuition about the danger lurking through the night? Instead we all thought that we were going to sleep, and that things could wait till tomorrow.

But not for my father! His blind eyes wide open as if to pierce the foreboding gloom, he gets out at the tenth floor, soundlessly walks over the soft carpet that makes his feet sink in deeper and deeper with every step he takes toward Paul's door, finally reaches it, and keeps standing there for a moment, briefly

284

hesitant, holding his breath to hear if there is something to hear, but there is nothing. Is Paul already asleep? He doubts it; and if so, damn it, he has to wake up! My father rings the door bell, *pling-pling!* All remains quiet. *Pling-pling!* Then some noises inside. Paul opens the door a crack and peeks out into the hallway. He is already in his pajamas. Seeing his father, he squints with suspicion, and reluctantly opening the door a bit wider he asks: What's up? Let me in, my father demands, or maybe he doesn't even say a word, just pushes the door open and marches in past Paul, as if this were still his place, even though now it's Paul's, and really it's mine. Whatever. We have to talk, my father says, and Paul, who is annoyed at feeling like a kid in his pajamas, responds: Can't this wait till tomorrow? No, my father says, and feels around for something to sit on. The back of Paul's office chair is the first thing he catches by chance, so he takes a seat where nobody except for Paul should sit, because it's Paul's desk. Paul immediately resents it but doesn't dare to fight with his blind father for his claim, it would sound ridiculous and small-minded; hence begrudgingly he crouches down on the chair opposite his own desk, as if he had been called in to the principal's office to be reprimanded for a misdeed. What's up, he asks again, and the tone of his voice betrays his anger. I'm listening, his father merely says with his face stiff as if cast in concrete and his blind eyes cold as icicles. He's determined to keep his powder dry.

I'm sure my father has traveled to New York with the best possible intentions; he's wanted to make amends with Paul, clear the air, and if possible start anew. But now the old grudges take over. He folds his arms over his chest and decides to silently sit there as long as it will take. So what do you want to listen to, Paul finally breaks the stalemate, and when my father doesn't respond, Paul continues: You want to hear it from me. Here, you can have it: I never liked you. I know that wasn't your fault. In my analysis I've come to understand that. I blamed you for losing my mom. That wasn't your fault. But when I tried to find comfort with Joyce, you wouldn't let me. Whenever I snuggled with her, you looked at me funny or interfered. You wouldn't allow a little innocent boy to feel happy in the arms of a woman. I was always anxious because of you. I felt unwelcome, because of you. For you I was only a bother, an intruder in your lucky life, someone to get rid of as quickly as possible. You made Joyce pregnant, just so that she would get away from me. Then she killed herself, and I lost my second mom. True, maybe it wasn't your fault. Still I blamed you. And then I came to like Janis, my friend, my confidant, in some ways my third mom, and again you came in between us with your damn jealousy. You made our lives miserable, in particular mine. When you threatened to throw me out and never let me see her again, I was desperate. Again I felt abandoned, no one to turn to, and so wronged—I wanted to kill myself. Janis had a sense for these things, she understood even though I didn't say a word. She just knew. That's when we left. Paul is shaking.

My father sits unmoved. Did you fuck her? he asks. Paul stares at the carpet. You don't understand anything, he then says. Was

Theo your son? my father suddenly thunders, and Paul winces at his words as if under a volley of blows. No, he was not, he hisses back. That's what you say, how would I know? my father charges. Paul looks at him with his eyes full of disdain—or is it desperation? That has always been your problem, he then says, you never believed what I said. You undermined everything with your distrust. For you nothing ever was as it was, as simple as that. You had your own ideas, and no one could convince you otherwise. So what good would it do, if I gave you proof? My father pinches his eyes, these eyes that can't see and still need to be squinted into two sharp slits. The thing is, you can't give me proof. And the fact is that Theo was the spitting image of you, you can't deny that! Paul tauntingly laughs. Yeah, he was. But you seem to forget that I was his brother, we happened to have the same father, that's why we looked alike. My father seems briefly baffled, then quickly gets back at Paul: Good move, he derisively comments. Paul looks at him, resigned and pained. He sighs. You know what? he then says, I loved Theo. At times, I too was jealous, I have to admit. Janis was crazy about him. What a great kid he was!—I'll never get it off my chest that he died in that fucking bike accident! Maybe Janis thought that I killed him. I killed them both, what could be worse? Janis couldn't forgive herself that she had allowed me to take him on my bike, and she couldn't forgive me that I had been speeding, or so she thought. It was hell! Today I believe that this wasn't all. She didn't make it as a photographer in New York. She was so ashamed of her ambitions. I think that killed her, too. I guess, in the end, she felt she had nowhere to go.

For a while they are silent. But my father can't let it go. Maybe she was ashamed of having fucked her stepson, he softly suggests. Paul sits up straight. You have no idea what you are talking about, he says. I could tell you, and prove to you what a fucking asshole you are! But I won't. I committed myself to never tell you the one thing you have no idea about. Despite everything, I consider you my father, the only one I have. My analyst thought that I do love you, that I admire you and yearn for your approval. He said I'm just hiding it from myself because it would be too painful to know. Maybe he was right. There were times when I felt it, and then the fog of war between us clouded that sense again. But now, since this stupid paternity issue with Theo is the most urgent concern you have for me—and actually, I find that amazing—my proof is: I've never had sex with any woman. I'm gay. I always have been. Of course, this too would never have occurred to you! My father looks startled, revealing that he never thought about this possibility. Or did he? Was it on his mind when he asked me if Paul was married or had a girlfriend? Only now, as Paul spells it out, does it become totally apparent to him. It's the first time that he instantaneously believes what Paul tells him. Maybe it's because he wants to believe it, that too. But with this proof in hand, he falters, the wrath that had pressured and pushed him whenever he thought of Paul over the years pops and goes flat, and at once he is faced with all he has lost over his stubborn belief that Janis had cheated on him with Paul, which now is exposed as a terrible, terrible misconception. Naked he stands, small and ugly. He wants to say *why didn't you tell me then?* But he realizes that this

288

would mean again blaming Paul for what was his responsibility to wonder, ask, and know about. I'm sorry, he instead stammers, now deathly pale, oh god, how sorry I am…!

Both men remain silent for a long while. Then Paul gets up. He feels the tickle of triumph and makes sure to hide it. Well, maybe it needed to come out that way, he concedes. I'll get us a whisky—and a bathrobe for myself, I'm freezing. My father remains in his seat, but he lifts his head and follows Paul with his peripheral vision. Paul goes into the dark room that once was and now is again his bedroom, puts on a woolen bathrobe, and then walks over to his cabinet to fill two glasses. It's my best, Paul says when he places the glass in front of his father. It's a fifty-year-old single malt: true balm for our sore souls. My father responds with a bashful smile as he takes the glass. Paul briefly smiles as well. To all our hurts and grudges, he says, and my father adds: yeah, may they drown in this malt! The malt is good. The malt rolls through their throats, spreads through their chests, reaches into their arms, tingles in the tips of their fingers, and strokes their bodies from inside. *Aahh!*

If only they had stopped here. It would have been a good moment to build on. It might have opened a new and better chapter for both. They did have the sense that finally this could turn things around. If only they had said *goodnight* right at this point and gone to sleep. It already had been more than exhausting. But my father can never sit with things unfinished; if there is something broken, he needs to fix it right then and there. Thus when the second sip of malt melts on his tongue and warms his tired heart, he asks Paul: So what can I do for you to make up for all that went wrong between us? Now this is a typical question for my father, in this case one of atonement. However, Paul seems to have heard it as his father's old power play, as a move aimed at being in charge again and getting things under control. That irks him. Still, he could have responded with *thanks for asking* or *let's think about it tomorrow*. However, days before his father's arrival, Paul, with his heart full of bitterness and his cranky, vengeful mind full of bad expectations, has thought of something to request, even to demand from his father in order to once and for all put an end to their endless troubles. So when thinking about this encounter with his father, he had come up with an idea that now lay on his mind like a neat package ready to be picked up. And even though they are at the end of their conversation, reaffirmed and ennobled by the old malt, for the first time a tender feeling has come up, a mutual understanding for each other's sore spots, indicating that in fact a new chord could be struck between them, he unfortunately snatches his prefabricated answer and says, in a tone more sharp than he now means it but as hostile as it was conceived: Well, since you have three surviving children, Ann, Issy, and me, you can either sign over to me a third of *FIXIT* and put me on the advisory board, or—maybe even more convenient for both of us—you can pay me off for my share, and you won't have to bother with that part of your life any longer!

I think that right when he spelled it out, Paul heard how dead wrong this was for an answer. However, it was said. And he was too proud to take it back. Stupid pride! Maybe he couldn't have taken it back anyway. It was said, and it killed his father. Just a moment prior, his father had hoped that they were over the worst stumbling block in their relationship; he had sensed a chance to remedy their old wounds, to build new trust and respect for Paul, now seeing and understanding him so much better than ever before, and he was ready to acknowledge how much he failed Paul over the years...Paul's claim ruined it all! It destroyed the delicate progress. Again Paul appeared as the selfish, calculating, hateful kid who would always be out to hurt his father whatever he would try. But he would not succeed, not under my father's watch! Without a single word my father gets up. Paul sits totally paralyzed, simultaneously ashamed and stupidly defiant, so he cannot move. Silently my father goes to the door and leaves. The silver click when the door lock snaps shut shivers in the air. It's strange that this time he takes the stairs, not the elevator. Had he taken the elevator, Paul, who finally manages to free himself from his freeze and runs after his father into the hallway, would have seen from the elevator's floor display that his father, instead of going up to Tim's place, is going down to the lobby. But the elevator isn't moving and his father is nowhere to be seen, he has disappeared, like a ghost, like a vision. Paul stands in front of the closed elevator and wonders if all of this was only a dream. He feels like an idiot. But then again, he doesn't know how long he was caught in his stupor. He thinks that his father probably is already at Tim's. So he shuffles back to bed. Tomorrow he will apologize, tomorrow for sure.

The *EXIT* door has fallen shut behind my father, leaving him right in front of the number 10 that is painted in black shining letters on the fire wall. Is there a moment of doubt, a subtle move to return to the carpeted hallway? Instead my father starts to grope about in the empty staircase that is garishly illuminated by white neon strings running down the naked concrete. Good, at least he can see where to put his feet! His lonely steps echo through the building's emergency canyon where rarely any living soul enters. His left hand clasps the cold iron railing. A dream has shattered: *trusting Paul*—how could he have thought of a new beginning?! A single conversation cannot sweep away a character built over decades! How strange: in Cologne, when preparing to meet with Paul, he had reveled in various daydreams, invariably ending with him and Paul falling into each other's arms with tears, laughter, and relief. He actually had mused on inviting Paul thereafter to the *FIXIT* Board—why not! He would tell his board members that a child-psychoanalyst should be heard in a toy company's decisions. He even brought along one of the rare remaining originals from the *Magic Man's* first edition, in order to hand it over to Paul as a kind of regalia, symbolizing his homecoming to his father's enterprise. He and Paul would sit side by side at the board meetings and discuss their new investments. Of course he, Eddie, would still be the senior, more experienced, hence the superior one of the two and the chairman of the board. But he would tell his son all he knew, and step by step he would turn the business over to him, his successor. But not so! He would not bow to Paul's brazen claim to a third of his company, which basically called for his father's demise! No, Paul would not manage to rip off the hand that one last time had reached out for him. No way! *Rien ne va plus!* My father slowly passes number 9.

How wrong his hope had been, how stupid! It could never have worked with Paul! Paul didn't like him, no matter what. That's what Paul had said. That's what came out of their conversation. And now he can admit it: he never liked Paul either. He didn't want him in the first place. He wasn't asked if he wanted to make a baby, and had Judy asked he would have declined, for sure! With the pretense of passion she seduced him, the naive and inexperienced young man he had been. Single and hitting her biological clock when they met, she had made up her mind to have a baby, without bothering much about a man. Even better without one, she may have thought, so she could be the only one for her child and didn't need to negotiate with a father, who would have claimed a say in his son's education. Paul was the result of Judy's selfishness: gay and mean, a viper like his mother! She bilked him of this child, deliberately hid her pregnancy, and when she couldn't do it any longer she dumped Paul in his lap. Here, you can have him! Destiny played him a bad hand, but now was the time to cut it off. He had no son anymore! Would this make any difference in his life? No! He had lived without Paul for so long, and that's how he would continue until the end. Could he legally cut Paul out of his inheritance?

Maybe he couldn't. But in his will he would make sure to hold him to the necessary minimum. Paul had a good endowment from his mother, so it was only fair to favor his daughters. My father sees number 8 sliding by. His feet now automatically work the descent.

Or he could sign his company over to his daughters in his lifetime! Maybe Issy would be able to buy a ranch in the South of France and finally become independent as a horse breeder. She has been stuck for too long with the people she works for. He should write her a letter and ask if he could help her financially to get on her own feet. It wouldn't be easy. Issy keeps her distance. She has some reservations about him, and he doesn't know why. She rejects Paul, for sure, and maybe she resents her father for never having written Paul completely off. That could be it! At the time when she decided to go to boarding school, there was something about Paul that she didn't want to talk about. But clearly Paul played a role in her decision to leave. She didn't want to see him anymore, she said. At the time he thought they just had their sibling stuff. Kids fight, and Paul was always fighting. For a while he had wondered if Paul had molested her, but in the end he decided that this idea was too horrendous to be true. He never talked with Janis about his concern, and Janis didn't talk much with him about Issy's reasons. Anyway, now as it turned out that Paul was gay, this probably wasn't what had happened between them—but it couldn't be excluded either... Wherever Paul showed up, he caused trouble, damn it! That should finally come to an end, he decides, now at the 7th floor.

How would Theo be now, had he grown up with him? Maybe *he* would have been a son who cared about his father. Then *he* would now be working with him in his company. Smart and energetic, he would have studied law or economics or computer science, all things he could use for *FIXIT*. Paul ruthlessly destroyed that potential! Shame on him!—Had Theo missed his father? Janis once wrote Ann that she hung a photo over Theo's bed showing Ann and Issy standing next to their father; she wanted him to see his wider family. And little Theo in bed was looking at the picture and added himself to the three, placed on his father's shoulders. This is your daddy, Janis would say when she came to pick him up. Your daddy makes toys. When you are grown up you will go to meet him. My father cries. *Theo*, he whispers, *Theo!* And then he thinks of Janis, who had held up a worthy image of Theo's father, so that Theo had something good to dream about. Janis, his funny, sweet and smart little Janis with her great hair, this red fuzzy-head, her freckles around her nose, and her lovely green eyes, green like pistachios... *Oh God!* What a wonderful time they'd had! And how much had he missed her after she was gone! If only he had understood...He should have encouraged her to make *FIXIT* photo-books for children. Maybe she would have felt better about herself. Maybe then she would have stayed. What a painful descent, now passing the 6th floor, which stares at him with its cold and empty face – he can feel it, and it gives him a chill.

He went on this staircase only once with Joyce. There was a power outage in the building. He had brought her to an appointment with her psychiatrist, and when they came back, the electricity was gone. Joyce wanted to sit down in the lobby and wait till the damage was fixed. But the nanny was upstairs with Ann, who needed to be nursed. He tried to get Joyce to climb up the stairs with him, but she simply refused. She shook her head and mumbled over and over: I can't, I can't. The lobby was drafty and loud. The workmen were swearing; they needed to open a part of the wall with a jack-hammer. And he had promised the psychiatrist that he wouldn't leave Joyce alone, not for a minute, so he couldn't run up and bring Ann down. Finally he picked Joyce up and carried her upstairs, floor by floor, with only a short rest at each level, all ten floors. When they finally arrived at their condo, the nanny had left because she needed to go to her classes, and Ann was lying in her cradle crying and crying... And even though his back was killing him, he needed to make sure that Joyce would pump the milk that he could then feed the baby with the bottle. Little Ann was so upset that it took her a long while before she calmed down and could finally drink. He was walking up and down in the living room gently rocking her in his arms, humming a simple song with his dark voice, while Joyce was lying on her bed endlessly twirling a strand of her hair. Oh god, it was terrible! So much easier to go down, now past the door to the 5th floor.

Still Ann had turned out fine. She has her quirks, he thinks, but who doesn't, and somehow they are endearing. Would she be interested in joining him on the *FIXIT* board? He had never thought about it! A psychoanalyst could be good for his company!

She had not yet finished her training, but she didn't even know if she wanted to be a psychoanalyst. So maybe he could offer her an alternative perspective? Interesting idea! Maybe she had waited for him to say something along those lines. He had never considered a woman at the top of his company. Amazing that he could be so old-fashioned while the whole world was changing! But until now he had never thought of retiring, maybe that's why...Ann could be stubborn and sometimes they butted heads, but in the end he could always count on her. When he asked her to come with him to Tuscany, she agreed. He didn't need to beg her, she just said yes. In fact, she was the only one he could ask, and the only one who would always be there for him—will this change once her boyfriend returns? Who knows if he'll ever return, he thinks. But with or without Hayden, if Ann is willing to move back to Cologne, he will have someone who'll take care of him in his old age...And here already is the 4th floor.

When Aunt Margret grew old, boy, was she heavy, heavy like a millstone! Her dementia had destroyed all her faculties except her hunger, particularly for sweets. Her belly had grown out of bounds, doming and protruding from under her slippery nightgowns. When Eddie had to drag her over to the bathroom, she moaned and groaned with every step, and so did he. Watch it, watch it, she screamed in a panic when he lowered her down into the bathtub once a week, a procedure that took all Saturday afternoon, exhausting both of them. Aunt Margret had no health insurance and no money to pay for a visiting nurse. Having finished college, he yearned to go to New York, but couldn't.

He was trapped. After all Aunt Margret had done for him, he couldn't leave her alone. She would have perished. If he left for an hour to get the groceries, and she woke up before he returned, she became completely agitated. So he sat with her through many months, cooked for her, fed her, cleaned her up, combed her hair, cut her nails, read her stories she wouldn't understand but appreciated for the singing sound of his voice, and at night when she couldn't sleep he would hold her hand and allow her another cup of ice cream, vanilla-fudge, her favorite. Yes, he sometimes thought that the sugar might eventually kill her. But he didn't feel guilty about this thought. He did all he could for her. And then one morning she lay dead in her bed, had just peacefully died over night. First he had opened all the windows, and for an hour he had savored the fresh air and the lovely calm sprinkled with the spring birds' chirping calls. Then he had done what needed to be done. But a week later, when he was about to clear out her apartment, in the closet she never had allowed him to open he found a briefcase full of golden nuggets, worth more than $200,000. Oh, how his life could have been easier had he been able to engage some help! But he had followed her rules. As a late reward the money helped him to finally get to New York and shortly after start *FIXIT*, his own company. Number 3 is half peeled off the wall, and his tired feet briefly stumble, but he moves on.

Amongst the ton of junk he had to sift through when cleaning out Aunt Margret's place, he had found boxes with old photos, many of which he couldn't relate to anybody he knew. But there were some pictures of his parents when they were young; nestled in between friends or students they were smoking and drinking and discussing in groups sitting cross-legged on the floor. He too sat down on the floor with the photo box on his lap and studied the faces of his father and his mother and smiled at them almost as if they could smile back at him. There were a few pictures with his mother holding a baby, presumably him, in her arms, but he was so bundled up in these pictures that he couldn't decide whether it was he or any other kid she was holding. Still, he kept these photos and put them in a small handwritten booklet with the title *The Mind and its Freedom* that he had found on his aunt's bookshelf; he wondered if his mother or his father wrote it—because it was out of the question that Aunt Margret would have bothered with thinking about such a nuisance. He started reading a few pages and then decided that he would get back to it once he had left Philadelphia. And now he realizes that he never read it and feels sorry. He wonders where this booklet ended up...Most of the other things Aunt Margret had collected throughout her life went into a dumpster. And he is on the 2nd floor and feels a little dizzy from going round and round, but there is still one more floor left to go.

He walks with his hand slipping over the round railing and his feet gingerly tapping each step. Peripheral shadows are flying along with him like the wings of a bird or of an angel. He is not alone. Someone is there. Someone is looking at him with wonderful eyes, these eyes that come at night and say: *Look at you, my dear, look at you*—and then they go, even though somehow they always stay, as they do now, stay with him all the way down. It'll be all right. There is nothing to be afraid of. Come what may...*just look at you*...and you'll be fine. A wedding is sailing through his mind, lots of people are dancing, Chinese people in a Chinese countryside...they laugh and call him... but then a storm comes up with heavy rain and drowns them all in a dark cloud...Cold hands rip him out of where he had just arrived...and he wants to look, but there is no look anymore. Startled, he makes an uncertain move back, but now he can relax again, for there is a scent drifting by, the scent of a woman, sweet and unique, a scent he once knew and still knows so well... All his life—all he was about—all of it is contained in it...Is it Joyce? Joyce? Look at you, she seems to say, gently smiling and slipping her pinky between his lips. And so looking and searching and smiling he reaches the 1st floor.

The lobby is empty, but Homer, the new doorman, is sitting at his desk reading a mystery story. Do you need a cab, sir? he asks, and my father simply says: No, thank you, I'm just going outside to get a bit of fresh air, that's all. The doorman nods, and my father leaves the building. Cold February winds collide with his heated head. What did Paul say? There was one thing he would never tell him, one thing he didn't know about? What could that be? With his tired, over-tired mind he tries so think of something unthinkable, but there is nothing that would remotely fit the category. Instead, Teresa comes to mind! Teresa knows all there is to know. Teresa could help him figure out how to deal with Paul. Her advice was always wise and valuable. Teresa is

300

on Columbus Avenue! She should be home now. He knows her address by heart. In their early years, he and Joyce often went there for a visit, on summer days walking through Central Park and in winter taking a cab. Teresa is always up late at night. She will welcome him. She will tell him the truth. My father feels energized by this idea that seems like the perfect solution. He steps off the sidewalk to look for a cab with his peripheral vision, a challenge but not impossible, and in order to make himself seen by any available cab that might evade his view, he raises his arm, just as a motorbike turns the corner to swing onto 5th Avenue, racing, for sure, a bit too fast and too close to the curb, and my father's hand hits the biker's face; and even though the young biker reflexively tries to avoid the hit by abruptly branching out with the front wheel, his bike slips away under his hands, driving its back wheel right into my father, whose right pants pocket gets caught on the biker's footrest, which lifts my father up and swirls him around and drags him along a few yards before the whole machine crashes down on him with its heavy weight on the heart in his chest. At some distance the driver picks himself up from the street. He takes off his helmet and hobbles over to my father. Homer, the doorman, comes running out to the street. Together they lift the machine off the dying man. They don't dare to carry him into the lobby. Someone calls 911. Homer calls Tim, knowing that my father is Tim's guest. Tim and I come rushing down. Paul is sleeping in the dark room. The motorcyclist kneels next to my father and cries. My father is lying on the street, a few feet from where Joyce landed some thirty years ago. His eyes wide open, he see the stars twinkling.

He smiles. How nice, he thinks, I can see the stars! And then somewhere up there he sees these eyes in the night, memory's eyes that are now his—eyes looking at you.

PART III

UNFORTUNATE INVOLVEMENTS

Five Hours

SCENE AT NIGHT

It's late at night when I come home after the memorial service for my father. Silence surrounds me like a dreaded fate. I struggle, then I pick up the phone and call Hayden. Tonight is an exception, tonight I can call. *Hayden? Is it you? Can you hear me?* My words slowly thread to the other end of the world—or is it reluctance on his end that grabs time? Then I hear: *Oh Ann—what a surprise! Yes I can hear you, very softly, but still I can hear you.* How distant he sounds. *Where are you?* I want to know. *I'm here,* he says and only then seems to realize that *here* can be anywhere; so he adds *I'm in Buenos Aires.* And after a pause that seems to betray some embarrassment, he asks: *And where are you? Are you still in Tuscany?* He doesn't know anything. He hasn't read what I sent him in January—maybe none of my emails! *You haven't read what I sent you,* I say, and all of a sudden I feel this loneliness that I didn't notice as long as I was writing Hayden, but now it's striking. *My father passed away,* I say, *here in New York.* To this at first Hayden doesn't say a word. Then he says *I'm sorry—I printed them out, I mean your emails, I mean, I'm sorry for your father, I mean your loss of your father.* He sounds like a stranger who mistakenly picked up the phone. *You won't come back to me, will you?* I say, surprised that I am spelling this out in such a matter-of-fact way. *I've wanted to call you for a while,* Hayden stammers, *but I have this recurrent nightmare: We are sitting somewhere, you and I, and all of a sudden your father comes in with a black tie around his neck and a pistol in his hand; he shoots me, and I am dead; then you leave, alone or with your father, I can't tell; the police are after you; I'm dead, but I can see it like in a gangster movie, it's scary; in the end they catch you and put you in prison, in a small cell with nothing but stone walls and a small iron-barred window; then I see you climbing up the wall as if to look out of the window, and I think maybe there is someone out there; but then—you pull your father's black tie out of your pocket, attach it to the iron bars and hang yourself! I see you trembling and twitching for the longest time, and I want to cry out for help, but I can't, because I'm dead, and it makes me so sad, so incredibly sad... That's why—I don't know—I didn't dare to read your emails—Ann, are you still there?—*I don't know if I am—I hang up on Hayden, softly hang up on him, and my last words—what were they anyway?

DR. SHEPHERD

Here I am lying on the couch, and it is my time, but Dr. Shepherd left. When his doorbell rang, I stopped mid-sentence, wanting to give him time to decide what to do about it—if anything at all—but I had thought he would do nothing, would not be available for anybody else because it was my time. Yes, I had hoped he would just stay with me and continue to listen—and now I can't even remember what I was just talking about. It's gone. It'll come back. Thoughts never get lost; at some point they resurge—often as a surprise at inconvenient times. But since the doorbell rang and Dr. Shepherd left, I can only think about what's going on in his house. He briefly apologized for the inconvenience, saying his wife was expecting a new computer desk, which was to be delivered today, and he had to attend to the matter. What kind of desk had his wife chosen? Had they picked it together? Had he talked her into taking this one instead of another she first favored? He certainly wanted her to have the more expensive one. He is so generous. He left.

That was five minutes ago. Or was it eight or ten minutes, ten minutes out of my forty-five? Or actually forty minutes, because he is usually three minutes late to begin, having to do something in his house, and ends two minutes early, having to go to the bathroom, I guess. Makes five minutes plus ten minutes cut out of my time, a third of my 175 dollar-session, how much is that exactly... a third of 150 would be 50, remainder 25, that is seven for 21...It's too complicated, mathematically, and it's stupid.

I don't like that I am thinking this. I want to be generous. I used to give and compromise. But recently I grew fussy—only inside. I'm reluctant to talk about it. It's so different from how I want to be! And given all the money I may end up with when my inheritance issues are settled, it's embarrassing to pinch pennies over a two-minute pee-cut. But that's not it! It's about *my time*! It's about how I'm treated! It's about keeping to the contract! My contract with Shepherd was not that he'd be nice to everybody including his wife and all the deliverymen in the world. My contract was that he'd be my analyst for 45 minutes at a time, period! Instead he chose to be nice. God, he has this lovely smile, which is nice, it is, and who would think he could ever have a mean, selfish thought? I'm sure he doesn't. He means nice and feels nice—pulling me into being nice with him as well: I smile at him even when he is late, and I mean it, because I like him. I allow him to speak on the phone if someone calls during my session, I reassure him that it's not a problem, really it's not; and I say *thank you for telling me* when he spends half of my time sharing with me that his wife is in a difficult patch right now and that he is concerned about her, *you know what I mean,* he says, and I know what he means: He means nice, trusting that I, his analysand, will appreciate that he is willing to let me in on his family, so that I can feel almost like his daughter at his dinner table—only in fantasy, of course.

I heard that in the afternoon his real daughter Abigail will come home from San Francisco, where she is studying anthropology at Stanford and won some famous award, *you've heard of it* he suggested—but no, I hadn't, I'm so unlettered that I hadn't even heard of this distinguished anthropology award, and too bad, now I can't even recall its name, a significant name for everyone except me, which proves everything. I'd better write these things down right away next time he mentions them, so that I can research and learn about them. So his daughter comes in at five, and he wants to pick her up at the airport, that's why he needed to move my session to the morning—the morning of his wife's desk delivery—and he was glad, he said, that I could adapt to his request. If not he would have given me our regular session, and his wife would have picked up Abigail, he reassured me with an audible smile from behind the couch, a smile that wanted to let me know: he would have given me priority over his daughter, had I not said *no problem* and moved all my morning appointments around—I had to change my dental hygienist, my hair appointment, and two of my patients, which of course I didn't tell him, because I didn't want to trouble him with any doubts or else force myself into his afternoon, a time when he wants to be with Abigail. And by bending over backwards to enable Dr. Shepherd to pick up his daughter at the airport, I only reciprocated what I know he would be willing to do for me. Had he not over-extended himself to my needs in the first year of my analysis, when I felt acutely anxious and abandoned when he had to cancel a session or a whole week? It took me by surprise to react so strongly to his absences, because before I started my analysis I felt I was an independent person, more or less...All of a sudden I needed to see him desperately. We came to understand it as a reaction to my shock when Janis left. At the time when we analyzed this, I didn't know how much more complicated my whole story was. Anyway, in these difficult weeks, Dr. Shepherd did everything possible to accommodate my requests by giving me an extra session, or seeing me on the evening of January 1st, a holiday, or taking a phone call on a weekend. I shouldn't have called in the first place, but still he didn't abandon me, he was my savior. So it was only fair to reciprocate on this occasion... and, as he said, and I believe him: he would have been there for my regular session had I needed him to be there. He knows what's right and wants to do the right thing.

My analyst also told me on this occasion that his son John has already arrived from London. John works as an investment broker for a big bank in London. How would I know? Had Dr. Shepherd told me freely? No, I'm sure I asked him, and he was happy to share, because he is a Mensch. He is not as orthodox and rigid as others are. Once he claimed that for an analyst it was easy to simply stick to the rules and much more challenging to walk into the open and risk being more personally involved. He called it modern or contemporary psychoanalysis, and it sounded as if he felt courageous by trying out something new. But what does his adventurousness do for me? I'm too ashamed to admit that more recently I would have preferred a more old-fashioned analyst and be left alone with all his personal sharing. Yet I can feel how much he enjoys telling me something whenever I show some interest in his family, and I like to please him—why not? But maybe he takes what I ask too literally. Or maybe I should stop asking? Why in the world would I ask about all these things?

Meanwhile I also know a lot about his childhood, but this knowledge is confidential, so I can only keep it to myself. Who of my classmates has such privileges? Am I an exception? Or does he tell everybody that much? However, do I really want to know all these things? That's the question that always falls through the cracks when I get derailed and sucked up by his stories. They are interesting, his stories, they show how well he deals with the traps and tricks of fate's deliveries. Could I handle things as well as he does? I'm ambivalent hearing about his accomplishments, but I don't say so. If I said something about it, I'm afraid I would never hear anything anymore, and I'm not sure that I want that either. So I zip my mouth and perk up my ears, shoot! Once, after sharing with me the events of his Thanksgiving party, he all of a sudden turned serious and said: You know, I'm telling you this only to give you an idea of how life in an average, good family can be. You shouldn't despair over thinking that abandonment and betrayal are all there is. Had I really thought that? I don't think so...We did have good times in my family. We too had nice dinner parties, even though it was long ago. I do know how that feels...But now I see the four Shepherds sitting around their dinner table and wonder if Shepherds' dinners are better dinners. Stupid!

Dr. Shepherd's wife is quite beautiful, I've seen her several times at our institute's meetings. Dr. Shepherd, my analyst, told me that she is a good cook, no, she is an *excellent* cook, that's what he said. On top of this she is an artist, patching together decorative quilts—even the New York Metropolitan Museum of Art has been interested, he mentioned in passing—so she was noticed, whereas my Janis-mother never was—which may have been part of why she killed herself, as I think I told him, didn't I?—But the Shepherds are sitting around the dinner table having a good time. First they give a toast to Abigail for her award! Too bad her fiancé was caught up in work and couldn't join her on this trip; the Shepherds like him a lot—he too is now part of the Shepherd family. Nice! Then John tells everybody how much he made in the last quarter, investing half a billion British pounds from his clients just at the right time in the most profitable stocks—*bingo!*—everybody cheers and gives him a high five. Then Dr. Shepherd's wife has a surprise for all, even for her husband: the Met *did* buy one of her quilts, a small one called *Machine Wedding*! Everybody jumps up and hugs and kisses her. *Champagne!*

Only then does the family come around to the actual reason for this gathering: as rumors in our institute have it, Dr. Shepherd is celebrating his 65th birthday! Given his age he looks stunning! Three Shepherds are singing *Happy Birthday to you...*while the fourth looks on brimming with joy, this lucky kid! Then Dr. Shepherd's wife gives her husband a little box wrapped in artfully crafted gift-paper showing a patchwork of family photos. I have only a little something for you, she says with a wink, and Dr. Shepherd is delighted and admiringly holds this delicate package in his open hands. It's too beautiful to be opened, he declares. But after being urged on for a while by his curious kids, he opens it anyway, cautiously trying to detach the paper's edges where they stick together, for he doesn't want to ruin his wife's fancy creation, then lifting up the top and—*hello!*—out of the box he pulls the key to a Porsche! *Wow!* His kids scream in sheer amazement, his wife gently smiles, and he shakes his head in disbelief—*is this possible???* But then everyone gets up and goes over to the window to have a look, and there it is: an elegant, silver-gray Carrera, discretely parked in the shadows of his front yard magnolia tree.

Unbelievable, this story I'm making up here! It's edgy, I can feel it—but so what! Now that my father has passed away, and I'll be rich, I could give Dr. Shepherd a Porsche too! Perhaps he would smile and say, Thank you, but you know that wasn't necessary! I can't believe that I'm thinking this! It does show how annoyed I am that Dr. Shepherd is spending so much time with this delivery. But I won't tell him, for sure. Anyway, he is out fussing on behalf of his wife. Why are these men always so preoccupied with themselves or with something of their own? Isn't Dr. Shepherd supposed to be here for *me*? Well, we have to share. He has his family, and I have mine, and despite everything—it was a good one. But we stopped sitting like this around the dinner table when I was eleven—or rather one year earlier...After Issy had left, we never really had good dinnertimes again—or did we? Yes, we did! Often it was Paul who brought up a funny observation or an interesting topic, which we then all discussed at length, sometimes even over several nights, and he would make sure that everybody had a say in these conversations. When I got sidetracked with what I contributed, and my father would get impatient with me, Paul defended me and made sure that I could finish saying what I meant to say.

Paul...had he really molested Issy? Where did that thought come from...? Were there innuendos, or was it just my imagination gone wild, as Issy always claimed? Would Issy have told me? No! I'm not even sure she would have told our mother. And I haven't told her yet that we have different mothers...I think I'll wait till I see her. It's not easy to convey the whole story, and I want Issy to get the right picture, not just a merely factual or a quasi-sensationalized one: *guess what, Janis wasn't my mother, Joyce was!* That would be cheap. That wouldn't be right. What I learned about my father's early years in New York seems almost more important than the bare fact of Joyce being my birth-mother. In the end this revelation isn't much more than a statement about my genetic fabric, is it?—I wish I could replay every minute of those last conversations with my father. Finally he dared to talk to me, his adult daughter, as a father and as a man who hoped to find some understanding and maybe consolation. He risked telling me how he struggled in his life and how he erred and felt guilty. I'm so grateful for that, and I'm sorry that I didn't tell him how much it meant to me! But I thought we were only at the beginning of a new phase in our relationship, there was so much more that I wanted to ask him...Instead, there were only a few moments of wholehearted truth, and that was the end of it all...

However, these moments will always be key for me, key for how I understand my father. Compared to that gift of trust, really, I don't care much about Joyce. I'm happy to keep her as my granny. Joyce decided to jump out on me. No, that's not fair! She was depressed, hence crazy and not really responsible for killing herself. Anyway, it was Janis who raised me, so she'll always be my mother. I'm sorry that she too killed herself. Issy and I loved her, and I'm sure she knew that, but this wasn't enough to keep her wanting to live on. Maybe she missed my father. He missed her too, that I know! They were both stubborn, and their faith in each other was broken. When my father finally realized that he was wrong and all the terrible pain over the years was for nothing, nothing...

He shouldn't have gone out! Emotionally that whole evening was too much for him, too much! So maybe he purposefully stepped

out and onto the street when he heard the motorbike coming...
Maybe he too wanted to kill himself—I'll never know. When I
called Issy to tell her about our father's death, I emphasized the
accident. It was an accident, I repeated. She didn't say a word.
Issy, are you still there? I asked. Yes, she answered. Will you come
to New York for the memorial service? I wanted to know. She
hesitated and then said: I don't think so.—You won't come!?—
What good would it do and for whom?—He's your father!—Yeah,
he was our father... So get yourself here! I demanded. Will Paul
be there? she asked. What a question! I was all crazed during
that stretch of time, anticipating the organizational frenzy about
getting everything lined up for my father's memorial service in
New York and a week later in Cologne, so I was already on edge,
and then Issy asked about Paul...! I was not ready for diplomacy
and bluntly said: Yes, I guess Paul will be coming, I haven't
asked him. Then I won't, she simply said. Wouldn't you come
for me, *just for me*, so that I'm not alone in this? I screamed
and briefly cried—but then I quickly restrained myself because
I couldn't afford to dissolve with all these events going on. Yes,
for you I would come, Ann, for you always, Issy said, and that
comforted me a bit. What if you made sure that Paul doesn't come
to Cologne, and I'll join you there and we consider it our father's
true burial. It'll be his final anyway—his urn will be placed at the
Cologne cemetery, right? So I will be with you there—but not in
New York, okay? I'm sorry!

I felt partially mollified and—I have to admit—partially relieved.
Her not coming to New York would actually make my life easier.

316

I knew my way around here, and Issy didn't. She didn't even speak much English. So had she come, it would have added another burden to my hectic days. Also, it's true: I wanted to be on my own when I picked up the urn with my father's ashes—it was such a personal thing, and yes, I wanted to have that all for myself, wanted to embrace this moment with all we had shared in these past months...

So I was glad when I was sitting alone in the back of the cab, the urn on my lap, this small gray tin box—so small, so light, containing my whole father...*unbelievable!* I had put the urn in a plastic bag and had wrapped my arms around it, holding it anxiously, firmly, tenderly, I was so afraid that something would spill out from it...Riding on Park Avenue through these long stretches of dark shadows alongside its long wall of gray buildings, disrupted at each crossing side street by sudden jolts of blasting light from the morning sun—rocking and reeling with the cab's starts and stops at each traffic light and occasionally bumping into a sudden, unexpected pothole, thus thoughtlessly swinging in the back of this old cab with nothing to do for as long as the journey would last—nothing but holding the urn—for the first time I cried; tears, an unstoppable stream of tears, washing my eyes away, drowning my view and my world, running and rolling down my face and all over, inside and out—silently, mute or hushed, dropping, tickling and doodling over my icy fingers clasped around the cold urn...I was crying, and it felt good, good to feel how unfathomable this sudden disappearance was, how unbelievable and unacceptable. He, who had been here, right here, alive and well a few days ago with all his undefined future in his heart, now wasn't anymore, not now, not tomorrow, would never ever be with me, never when I wanted to see him, when I needed him...erased from life, gone from this world, gone, forever! It was over! He had disappeared somewhere behind the unknowable, invisible line...

Over and over in these past days I had thought that I shouldn't have brought my father to New York, shouldn't have left him alone. He needed my hand to be safe, and I let it go. But why did he sneak out that night, why? Couldn't he wait to talk with Paul? Had he tricked us by pretending to go to sleep while planning to escape, or did he follow a spontaneous intuition, an idea that had sprung on him and forced him out of his comfort zone? I'll never know. Maybe he kept standing behind his closed door listening to how the bedtime noises in Tim's condo died down, and when all had been quiet for five minutes he tiptoed out. Was Paul so important to him? Or was it the ever-nagging question of whether or not Janis had cheated on him with Paul? Fact is, he didn't wait. He forgot everything else, dropped all caution, didn't think of me, gone was his promise to help me with reorganizing my trust—in the end all he wanted was to confront or redeem Paul. It cost his life! For nothing, nothing!! And so he ended up as a powder in a box on my lap! How dumb! He left me angry, devastated—left me missing him for the rest of my life, feeling betrayed and cheated out of what he owed me: *yes*, he owed me a stretch of good mature years, collaborative, open years with mutual trust, years of his aging wisely with me as a caring partner in his life...He took this away from me! This is what I resent! Not that he hid the truth about my mother, Joyce, so be it! I can understand that he wasn't sure when to tell me, and after a while he was afraid to tell me at all. But that he didn't make sure to stay alive so that we could have shared our struggles, our hurts, our longings...Had we had time to talk with each other, just more of those long conversations during dinners and walks and evening hours, I would have been able to grasp his dreams and memories, those memories that looked at him when he walked in the dark, these eyes that followed him through the night... But maybe I was not supposed to know my father's dreams, his hopes, his wish for love...maybe they were supposed to remain private. I have my private thoughts as well. He's gone.

What else is new! He always did what *he* wanted to do! He could be so inconsiderate! He had an idea, and off he went with it, no matter what! He didn't care how hard we pleaded: *Stay with us! —Can't I first finish this? —Give us a bit more time! —We would rather go somewhere else. — Didn't you promise...?* No, if he wanted something else, he did something else, just walked out on us—maybe not unlike Dr. Shepherd. In the first years after my mother had left, I wanted to visit her in New York. I wanted it so badly! Each summer I pleaded to go to New York to see her. No! If you want to go to New York, you can just stay there, he threatened. But how could I have just stayed there? He was angry with Janis and took it out on me, certainly sometimes. Had he allowed me to see her, maybe I could have brought them back together...that's what I wanted, I wanted them back together. Instead they stayed apart. For what?!—Today would have been my father's birthday: today we wanted to celebrate at the *Gotham Bar and Grill*, maybe with Tim and Paul or just he and I, and instead he ran his bullhead into the ground! What a shame!

At home I put the urn into the original cardboard box of the *Magic Man*. This box was the right place for him to be. I looked at it as it was sitting on my shelves with the *Magic Man* sitting on top of it and said: *Hi Eddie!* He didn't respond. It was the end of magic. When I told Dr. Shepherd about it, he said: Your playfulness shows your ego strength and creativity! I'm sure he wanted to say something nice and supportive, but I felt anything but playful!—And now I'm thinking of this one Saturday morning when I threw the *Magic Man* out of my window. Was that playful? It scratched the roof of my father's car, then it fell on the lawn. My father was just coming out of the house to drive to his office. He looked up and saw me standing at my window watching the scene. Why did you do this, he asked me. I couldn't tell. I was shocked and defiant without knowing about what. Anyway, I refused to pick it up. Pick it up, my father demanded, but it was as if I was nailed to my spot at the window, I didn't make the slightest move, didn't say a word, certainly didn't pick it up. You will not get your allowance until you've picked it up, my father declared and drove off. Still, I didn't pick it up! The next day it rained, and the *Magic Man* kept lying on the lawn, face down, and got all wet. Pick it up, my father demanded, but it was as clear as nothing else in my life that I would not pick it up, never ever! Days or weeks later the *Magic Man* disappeared, sort of magically left the lawn, maybe Janis or Alma picked it up and threw it away, and without further comment after a while my allowances resumed, and we didn't talk about it anymore. But now I wonder, what was that all about? Had I been angry? I can't feel that. I can see myself standing near the open window and sort of thoughtfully throwing it out. Thoughtfully—what had I been thinking about? Maybe I wanted to find out if the *Magic Man* could fly, if it would fly out of the window like *Spider-Man* in order to do something good in the world and then fly back home to me. Maybe I didn't want to accept that he had simply banged into my father's car and then plopped onto our lawn. How ordinary, how dull! No magic at all! Or maybe I had somehow understood on that very day that if you fly out of a window, it's over. I couldn't play with it anymore! This *Magic Man* was gone! How strange that my father didn't understand! Maybe Janis did.

Yes, that's what I was just talking about when Dr. Shepherd left in order to open the door for his wife's delivery, the end of magic. Is it okay if I go, he asked, and I said: Oh sure! What else could I say? Say whatever comes to mind! I looked at him as he walked past the couch. The back of his shirt looked damp and shriveled, wrinkled from sitting all these long sessions with his many patients, wrinkled also from moving around in his chair. I often heard him shifting his arms and legs when I was silent for a while. Was he impatient with me? Uncomfortable? Funny, once he told me something that had happened in the middle of a session with another patient: he said that for some reason he leaned far back in his chair, and by doing so he knocked over a big vase that was sitting on the floor planks next to his bookshelf; the vase broke and the water spilled all over his carpet. The water had been sitting in this vase for about a week, it wasn't so fresh and clean anymore, whereas the carpet was fresh, actually brand new, put in only a week before this accident, and now it had this big, ugly, stinky stain on it. Of course when I came in, I saw it right away and asked about it. I guess all his patients asked about it, you just couldn't ignore it. The whole event must have been discombobulating, embarrassing, and quite uncomfortable for him, even though, I guess, many analysts spill things over the years, preferably coffee! These things happen. Good for him that he poked fun at himself! But then again, it made me think about why he had leaned so far back? I knew exactly where this vase had been sitting, and I considered it almost impossible to even reach from where his chair stood. So what had been going on in this session? Was he just fidgeting around because his patient was so boring that he needed a little exercise? Or had he tried to pick up a book or something from the shelves behind his chair, stretched out his arm calculating that he could secretly grab the desired object and play with it a bit or silently read without his patient noticing that he was cheating on her with something else, and when he was almost there and could nearly touch it with his fingers, suddenly the vase turned over, fell, and broke—and gone was all secrecy! Of course his patient must have turned around and wondered. I too wondered silently through most of that day's session how he might have explained his unexpected movement to his patient. But in the following days he repeatedly referred to his mishap, ironically bemoaning the new carpet, and I guess we all—I mean all his patients—felt a bit sorry for him...Of course, he understands our bad moves, and we want to understand his. That seems fair, and we can forgive each other. Still it's not good. I did notice for a while that in some sessions, rather than talking about a bad dream or an idea I had been bothered by, I would talk about something he had told me from his life or childhood, thus my qualms didn't have to come up. Or did they anyway? I don't know. But I think he is a bit like my father, who despite his strength always let me know that he needed me to comply with his ideas and adjust to his needs, and so I did. It's my issue. And now I'm doing it again.

When Dr. Shepherd walked by the couch, I could see that his gray hair had thinned out on the back of his head. I never noticed it before, most likely because I rarely if ever saw him from behind. His bare scalp shimmered through in pink. That happens when we grow older. We? He once mentioned having written about a patient who amongst other things was upset because she was losing her hair in a very stressful situation. When he said it, I immediately worried about my own hair. Was I losing mine as well, stressed out as I was already then, let alone now? Was he, sitting behind me, all the time looking through my curls at my naked scalp—while I was talking about the things I struggled with? At home I looked in the mirror and made sure that the back of my head was still densely packed and covered with hair. It was. If I were to lose my hair, then not now, and not during this analysis! These things happen much later in life, after fifty or sixty, if at all. Maybe Dr. Shepherd was apprehensive about his bald spot, and maybe that's why he mentioned something like this.

Dr. Shepherd left the door a crack open. Now one of the workmen, schlepping the bubble-wrapped desk towards its final destination, briefly glances through the crack into the office. How embarrassing to be seen lying on Dr. Shepherd's couch at 10:40 in the morning! Defiantly I stare back. In an instant he disappears in the dark of the hallway. An overloaded hat tree blocks half of my view of the staircase where the pulling and pushing of the bulky monster is in full swing. Dr. Shepherd directs the event with both arms like a conductor: A bit more to the left, a bit up, he shouts, no, not there, watch out—the picture over there, look at me, try it like this, here, like this, look at me—up, up! How do these workmen feel being ordered around? It's not the first obstacle that they've dragged up a flight. They are used to nervous clients and just stay calm. The client can say and behave as he pleases because he pays. Can I? Dr. Shepherd just wants to be helpful. How excited he is! He's a character, some say. What would I say...? He is my analyst—but now after three years I wonder: is this still analysis? It's as if I've run out of steam, I don't feel that I'm making any progress, rather, at times, on the contrary...

In the beginning I was miserable, actually more miserable than I had realized before getting on this couch. I was in a state

324

of suspense. I had my Ph.D., had enrolled as a post-doc at Columbia, but I didn't know much else. I had just ended it with Max after five heavy years. I loved Max, but he was depressed. He dragged me down. I tried hard to lift him up, which he resented and resisted most of the time. It was exhausting! Why had I chosen to be with a depressed man? I tried to get him into therapy, but he refused. He felt he didn't deserve to be with me, and in the end he succeeded. I left. At first I thought I could finally breathe again. But then I too felt depressed, plunged into a thicket of guilt and loneliness. I thought if only I could kill myself, this pain would stop...but this was the one thing I knew I could never do, never, not to my father, not to Issy or to Alma or to my friends. So I had to get out of everything that reminded me of Max. I had to take care of myself. That's when I decided to go to New York. My father didn't object. He even said: Good idea, try it out!

I hadn't told him that I had googled Paul, first just out of curiosity, but then I contacted him. Paul was quite enthused to hear from me. For the first time in years we met. He invited me to lunch at the *Grand Central Oyster Bar*. I was nervous and excited. Only a day earlier I had arrived in New York, and now I was standing in *Grand Central Terminal* with all the rushing and running around me, this huge station, and everybody seemed to know exactly where to go, everybody except me...He was a bit late. When I saw him, I was surprised because he no longer looked like my rough big brother, the guy I remembered, no, now he was a handsome man, cool, sophisticated, a guy to have a crush on. His shining black hair had two silver streaks at the temples—had he dyed them? I was impressed, in awe. This is my brother! We hadn't seen each other in years, he seemed strange albeit familiar. We ended up talking for three hours. At the time I was still rather unhappy. He suggested that I apply for psychoanalytic training at his institute, saying it would be good for me, given our complicated family history and certainly a good addition to my post-doc time at Columbia. And later when I was accepted for training and had to start a personal training analysis, he said: Dr. Shepherd is great. Everybody raves about him. Try him out.

So I went, and I liked Dr. Shepherd. He was nice, easygoing and accommodating, and I said *yes*. Then I plunged. It was as if I had opened a can of worms that were crawling out and all over me, and there was no escape. I needed my sessions, I needed my analyst, and I had a lot to tell. I think in the blackest of my days, when I felt nothing would ever change, somehow my analyst managed to lighten up my inner world. Was it that he threw in an idea of his own that intrigued me and helped me out of ruminating on my miseries in endless circles? I felt I could hold on to him. I could talk to him, and that already helped! The thought of staying in New York and becoming an analyst grew more realistic. But after about a year and a half things slowed down—I don't know how that happened, but I ended up talking about things Dr. Shepherd was more interested in than I. Was that transference?

Now I feel stuck. Maybe it's a transitional phase. Or maybe my analyst isn't so great after all? Could I say this? He would certainly say: Of course you can! But would his reassurance do? Wouldn't I have to understand why it is that I feel I cannot say what I think? This makes me angry! Could I openly unleash my anger at him? He would say: Of course you can, and you should, don't be inhibited! Easy to say! Once I got angry, openly angry at him for always being late, running over with a patient he saw before me on Wednesdays, thus cutting into my time—again another few minutes gone. I know, it's petty. But one day, to my own surprise I exploded, demanding my time in full! And instead of welcoming or simply accepting my outburst—what an accomplishment, I thought—he told me that this patient was in so much pain, felt so badly, and needed him so much that I had to understand...What? I don't have to understand anything about your other patients, I yelled at him. What a mess!—The whole thing led to nothing, and we returned to being nice with each other, which made me feel better. I like him, what can I do... I'm tired! Maybe I'll take over some function at *FIXIT*. As soon as all the legal issues are clarified I will decide whether I will return to Cologne for good.—Why would I think this now? Do I think I can fix all that went wrong, all these lies I lived with? I can't fix anything! And what about my condo on 5th Avenue? Shall I sell it to Paul? Shall I keep it for myself? I would like to live with a view of Central Park, who wouldn't? But would I like to move into Joyce's place? Shouldn't I start over, more modestly, more on my own, more real?

Now the workmen are trampling the floor in the room right above me. Their voices are muffled. They seem to push some furniture around, maybe in order to make space for the new object. Then everything falls quiet. Now they're admiring their work. No, the shifting and banging continues. Someone opens the window. They must have gotten hot on the job. What if I just got up and left, without saying goodbye? It would feel good, but it wouldn't be me. So I keep lying here, one foot over the other, my hands folded over my chest where I try to hold things together, and wait. The next patient has already arrived. I hear her walking up and down in the little waiting room—not a good place for exercise. She always does this, comes about fifteen minutes early and never sits down. Her high heels hammer the wooden floor as if she wants to make me hear that her time is coming up. Not so fast, lady! I still have ten minutes to go—or eight with the pee-cut. Now the workmen trample down the stairs, Dr. Shepherd shouts, Thanks a lot, the front door bangs shut, and in he comes huffing and puffing. Sorry, I'm really sorry. It took so much longer than I thought. Are you okay, he asks, and looks concerned. Sure, I say, no problem! Relieved, he gives me one of his great smiles and sits down in his chair behind the couch. Maybe we can make up the time some other day or something, okay? he suggests. *Or something*, I wonder but then I think it's not important whether we do or don't. It's not about a few minutes, more or less. I made good use of my session anyway. I had my thoughts, and maybe at some point I will talk with him about them. It's fine..,I say, and somewhat unplanned I continue: While you were gone I was thinking of my father. Today would have been his birthday. We had planned to celebrate it at the *Gotham Bar and Grill*, and I've decided to go there tonight. I will have dinner on my own and think about him. It's not so different from how it often was: we planned to do something together, and then he got a different idea in his head or was distracted by somebody else, and he skipped out on us. He used to come back. Now he won't. I wasn't prepared for that. But maybe that's how life is...*You're never prepared for the end!* That could be his final lesson. Can I take it? I have to! I get up. It's six minutes before the end of my time, and Dr. Shepherd is a bit surprised because he usually ends my sessions three minutes early, not six, so he scrambles to get up from his recliner before I open the door. Good bye, I say and send him a smile before walking into his waiting room. His next patient gawks at me. His phone rings. I close the door behind me and leave, go past his front yard where the tulips are starting to flower, yellow and white tulips, go to the street where the cars are honking and people are coming out from the subway station, opening their umbrellas because it's starting to rain, and I smell the fresh air of spring.

CHRIS

Reluctant yet still determined, Anouk Bossard entered my office, hardly putting one foot in front of the other, while her big gray backpack, hanging down her right arm, which awkwardly stretched towards me as if posing a unwieldy question, seemed to almost drag her into the room. Anouk appeared small and thin but sturdy; her tousled brown hair sparked off her white freckled face with its light blue eyes searching for me in a cautious though curious way. Hi, she said with a transient smile and slight blush. Can I drop this here? She hesitated, and I said: Sure. With a soft dark plop her backpack landed on the wooden floor.

When she had called a few days ago, I felt reluctant to take on a new patient. Only a couple of weeks earlier I had returned from Cologne to New York, and I didn't even know at that point if I wanted to stay here to finish my training, let alone settle down for good with an analytic practice. Nevertheless, something in

Anouk's request to *simply talk with me for a limited number of sessions* had intrigued me. Is there ever any limitation, once we start looking inside, or is this limitation just the closed door that we are about to open? Maybe I was becoming an analyst after all, I thought, and maybe over time I would grow what one of my supervisors calls *the third eye,* this uncanny sense for special albeit rare moments when an unspeakable world briefly flares up with almost intuitive clarity, only to be shrouded, often for years to come, into the layers of obscurity that relentlessly unfold from the shadows of our own and our ancestors' pasts. She would make it, I thought. How could I tell? Immediately I liked her.

I leaned back in my chair and watched how Anouk, kneeling next to her backpack, opened and closed the zippers of its various pockets to dig around in their depths, obviously in search of something—a something that turned out to be a tissue, into which she thoroughly blew her nose, then crumpled it up and stuffed it back into one of the slots to be finally zipped shut. She got up and sat down in the chair opposite mine—there nervously wrenching her hands while seemingly thinking about how to start. The blue of her sweater matched her jeans, all simple and clean. Her feet were warmly wrapped in fur-lined leather boots.

I won't stay much longer here in New York, she began. At the end of September I will go back to Zürich, provided I'm accepted for a job I've applied for—which I hope will be the case. So I've only a few months left—and I'm not planning to use them all up here—anyhow, time is running short—and I don't know what to do—and I can't think this through on my own—that's why I'm here! She kept quiet, and I remained silent as well, thinking that she had started with telling me that she was leaving.

I was in analysis when I was sixteen, Anouk continued after a while. This is not what I'm looking for right now! I just want to talk to you. I heard that you are German. Perhaps that'll make things a little easier for me. I'm Swiss. I grew up in Zürich. But I don't want to speak with you in German. I am in New York right now. This is not where I belong—neither is what I want to talk about...I'm afraid I'm not making sense. Anouk looked at me slightly puzzled, so I said: You want to talk to me without using the language we're coming from. She briefly smiled. It's complicated, she said. I'll try to give you a brief introduction, and then—you'll regret having agreed to see me...

Defiantly she betrayed how vulnerable she felt, and for a moment I saw myself as a four-year-old standing at the fence of our garden with my bare feet on the warm dry summer lawn, one fist clenched around the rough wooden planks, the other firmly holding Sasa, my dear rag doll, both of us surrounded by the flickering air and the silence of noontime crisscrossed by the bumblebees that kept humming and reeling over the luscious blue of the cornflower beds. I was waiting for my mother to come home—a memory timeless and meaningful, for unknown reasons imprinted forever. I don't remember what had happened that day, and maybe it was nothing to point my finger at, but it could be that for the first time I felt a crack in my life lacerating the ground I had been building my endlessly fascinating days on, a crack that slightly separated me from naturally being in the world. Could all of this crumble and break down beneath me? At the time I guess I was just a little anxious without knowing why. But now I wonder: had I heard something I wasn't supposed to hear or sensed something to the effect that Janis wasn't my mother? How confusing! I thought she was gone, and I waited for her to come back down the street... Would she? *Ann,* I was called from the kitchen, *lunch is ready!* And still lost in my dreamy thoughts, I went in, and my mother was standing near the stove, her cheeks red and shiny from the heat of making blueberry pancakes for Issy and me...

I looked at Anouk who seemed to be thinking hard, furrowing her brows, twirling a strand of her hair. She won't take much time here, I thought, but she doesn't want to be rushed, and I wasn't in a rush either. So I just listened as she told me that last week she had turned 22. For the first time she hadn't seen her parents on her birthday. She had called them, she said, and it was fine. She loves them and sometimes misses them here in New York, but most of the time she doesn't miss them so much! Was that right? They always loved and supported her, she emphasized, characterizing them as good people, reasonable, modest in their ambitions, amazingly tolerant with regard to her moods, and accepting that she wants to do things her way. I had some wild years as a teenager, she said, and I was cured from being outrageous by my first analyst. That was helpful, but then again—life seemed so flat: always doing the right thing right, always ending up in the order of days-as-usual, always sort of paddling with average speed in the middle of the mainstream... Ugh! That's why I came to New York. I wanted a different life. I wanted to be on my own. I had applied at the Art Institute for a program in graphic design and was accepted. My parents transfer money to my American bank account on a monthly basis. So I can live here as long as it'll take me to graduate.

My phone rang and the answering machine kicked, in producing the mechanical sounds of recording an unknown caller. It could be Aaron, I thought, the chair of the progression committee, who was to come back from his trip to Athens and had promised to give me feedback about my second case report. Anouk seemed to notice and wait for the machine to stop while thoughtfully stroking the back of her left hand. I'm in a terrible dilemma, and I don't know what to do, she then said. I saw that she was struggling to withhold tears, and when I kept silent, she told me that she often thinks of going away to never return, she would forget about her earlier life, and at some point all she could say about it would be like telling a dream without knowing whether it was real or not. Anouk looked up from her hands and straight into my eyes. Yeah...I said.

Anouk sighed. But why would I want to sever all ties to my parents? I feel so bad about it, so ungrateful! They did nothing wrong! I'm their only child. They arranged their whole life around me. My mother stopped working as a physician to become a stay-at-home mom and raise me. My father declined a career opportunity as a judge at a higher court in Geneva only to allow me to stay in Zürich and remain at the school I loved, where I had my friends. And now I'm gone, leaving them behind...My mother feels too old to restart in medicine and wonders what to do with the rest of her life, and my father is where he is, and that's okay, but not great...If I think of my parents, I feel bad! I take their money to live the comfortable life of a student in New York—and secretly I think I would never want to live like they do, never! That isn't right!

Anouk looked down on her lap, shrunken, it seemed, and hovering over some dark thoughts. The afternoon sun had broken through the clouds, pouring its pale spring light over the desk and lighting up the small clay copy of a Greek Sphinx that Paul had given me as a present when I became a candidate at the institute. Once it had fallen to the floor when I was in a hurry; part of its face had broken off, which actually made it look even more antique.

I'm pregnant! Anouk suddenly punctured the silence. You are the first person I'm telling this to. I took the test twice. I'm pregnant!—That's my biggest problem. I don't want this child! I don't want a baby, or certainly not now. I'm too young to be a mother! So what can I do? I don't want an abortion. I'm not against abortion in general—it's just that I cannot do it. When I think of all the photos I've seen of young fetuses—I just feel it's not right...this little guy...I can't do it. So what other options do I have? Shall I have the baby and give it up for adoption? I can't do that either...And then Anouk told me of a daydream she has been having for the longest time, in which her parents aren't her real parents, they only adopted her. She sees herself being dropped at the doorstep of an orphanage in the early morning of March 18th, which is her official birthday; so she would be a bit older than people think she is, she tells me. Her mother—in her fantasies she pictures her as short, barely 17 years old, scared but also tough—scurries by, anxiously looks around to make sure that nobody is watching her, then opens her coat and the black sweater beneath it, and cautiously pulls her baby out of the warmth of her body's cavern; and she, the baby, looks at her mother with blurry eyes, sees her waning face silver from the crack of dawn, sees her flickering eyes-in-a-hurry, her twitching cheeks, her pinched lips, and she doesn't understand—she must have been nursed only a few minutes earlier so that she wouldn't cry too soon— and now, where is her smile? Instead, her mother removes her headscarf, a dark red woolen cloth, nothing fancy though solid material, tightly wraps it around her baby to protect her from the cold winds, and before she puts her down on the doorstep, she kisses her tiny forehead, kisses it many times, and her pounding heart hammers all the words she will never get to say to her little daughter onto her small chest, where Anouk can still sense them, even right now...Just that and no tears, no tears, Anouk emphasizes.

Then her daydream takes a wild turn. Her mother hears a noise that shocks her, she jumps up and runs to the side of the

336

doorway, and through the early morning fog two men in black overcoats, black hats, black glasses, old bullyish men—they are coming, looking right and left while pointing with their pistols in every direction, small pistols, whose silver sparks slit the dew-bearing air like flashes of lightning. Briefly their pistols look at the infant, but they can't see her in the shadow of the deep door's alcove where she is hidden, safe and sound. The men's black capes move by. Mother is gone. The men follow the scent of the Milky Way. Then a door opens, two hands pull the baby in, and she is in a different world, forever.—This is the core of my fantasy, Anouk says as if she is just awakening from it. Maybe it's just a movie that I've seen once and forgotten, or a combination of several movie scenes. Anyway, this daydream is home for me, familiar and mysterious, it's exciting...When I'm in this scene I have lots of thoughts: Who are these men? Is one of them my father? Why do they persecute my mother? Where did she flee? Was she safe or did they eventually find, rape, and kill her? Or did they enslave her, make her clean the floors of their homes, or raise the kids of their official wives, or deliver their stolen goods to obscure middlemen? Why did my mother drop me at the orphanage? Did she not want me? Did she feel it was too risky for me to stay with her? Was she sick and about to die? Did she want to save my life from the ruthlessness of these pistols? So many questions, and each time I find new ways into this mystery, each time it seems that I'm almost there, close to the answer of my problem, the end of the enigma...but never quite yet. The final scene is prosaic: the Bossards come along and adopt me. They have long been waiting for a newborn baby, and I am as newly born as they can find. They put me in a little basket, put the basket into their little Volkswagen, and drive me home to be my mother and father. And that's what they are, my parents! In reality I don't doubt it—but in fantasy I do. In my first therapy I talked about these daydreams, and my analyst said they expressed my separation anxieties. That seemed to make some sense. Still I keep fantasizing. And now I'm pregnant and don't want this child, but I can't give it up for adoption—it would be like walking right into my daydreams...It scares me! This makes me so mad! I'm stuck!

As I was listening I was thinking that I did grow up with a mother who wasn't my real birthmother and who adopted me, a variation of Anouk's daydream or family romance, as Freud called these elaborate fantasies. But I don't remember ever having thought that my mother wasn't my mother... The family romance I had written down for Hayden didn't exchange my parents, I just made up the stories of their lives. It was my father who changed my story...My father—Anouk hadn't talked about the man who would be the father of her baby...This is a difficult moment in your life, I noted to Anouk, who had sort of rolled up in the chair, embracing her knees with her arms, slowly rocking back and forth while seemingly brooding. Have you talked about it with the man who got you pregnant?

Anguish seemed to strain Anouk's posture. Chris is my other problem, she then said. *A big problem...!* I love him, I really do.

He is my first real love...And then Anouk told me about Chris, who she met at her Art School. He wants to become a stage designer. He is incredibly creative, she said. He's my age, he has lots of ideas, some pretty wild, and I like that about him! I first noticed him as he was coming down the hallway...The floor was shining from the morning sun, so glazed and mirror-like, it looked as if he was walking on water or on ice, I just saw his black silhouette against the shining floor...and he kept coming and looking at me, and then sat down right next to me, saying: You are Anouk, I know you are, and I am Chris, and I want to get to know you. That's how straightforward he is—or used to be. He just took my breath away! She said that part of her wanted to give him a snappish response and run away, but she didn't. Chris is sexy, erotic, sensual, he is so totally in his body, how can I say this...she smiles a bit. When he moves the atmosphere around him seems to crackle, he radiates pleasure, the pleasure of moving, and he is so unaware of it...When he touches me or puts his arm around me—it really electrifies me. I'm so attracted to him that I can barely stop myself from touching him. I've never thought that it could be like this...We used to spend a lot of time in bed, not only sleeping and having sex, but also eating, reading, discussing, and studying in bed—and when we felt like it—we just rolled over...

It only took us two weeks to decide that we wanted to live together. My apartment was bigger than his, so he moved in with me. Chris threw his few belongings in his comforter, knotted its corners to a big bag, stuffed it into his car, and there he was! He liked to cook dinner, and I did breakfast. Everything was easy. What if we write a movie together? he suggested one day, and I was all for it. We started spinning the story, it was fun, I got caught up in the growing plot...and suddenly he dropped the whole thing, all of a sudden he didn't feel like it anymore. Why? Let's put it to the side, for now, he suggested. He had so much to do, other things, his coursework, an internship he wanted to apply for, and so on. I was a bit disappointed, but okay, I thought, fine, we can pick it up some other time. But that's how it goes time and again. He has an idea, we start on it, progress, and then all of a sudden and with no good reason, he drops the whole thing. I was flabbergasted. Why didn't he finish anything? There was no answer, just his need to get out. Then he was ready to graduate, had all his coursework done, great grades, just the final piece was missing, and...No, I said to him, not this time! But yes, he dropped it! The deadline passed, and he hadn't signed up for his finals! Why, what's wrong with you? I screamed at him. Don't be stupid! You're ruining your life! You're nearly done...I fought with him, I wanted him to talk and explain it to me. He couldn't. I just want to be your lover, I don't want to be your man, he said at some point. What? What is that supposed to mean...? Instead of an answer he cried—for the first time he cried, actually he sobbed, and I thought, he really has a problem. So I emailed my former therapist in Zürich, and he found me an analyst in New York. Go, talk with him, I said to Chris, you can resolve this. It took a couple of weeks to convince him, but then Chris went and eventually started with analysis.

Life went on, and Chris got all into his analysis. He told me how amazing it was, how great, how important, indicated how much he discovered, how smart his analyst's interventions were, and I was preparing myself for the announcement that he had dropped out. I was really waiting for it to happen, but it didn't. Instead Chris became a bit withdrawn. For hours he would play his guitar in his room, or he would go to the movies but without me—and we loved to go to the movies together; and he started to travel on weekends, to see an old friend or visit his parents, no big deal, even though I missed him—still I wondered...Things grew more distant between us, and maybe we had been too close anyway, but the lightness of life was gone. I assumed he was working something through in his analysis, and meanwhile I focused on making progress in my classes. He remained sweet and friendly, but still I missed his hugs, his affection, and I missed having sex with him. We did have sex once in a while, but it wasn't as great as it had been... Also, Chris moved out of our big bed, he now sleeps on a crummy sofa he bought at the clearance of a theatre's storage. He's become a bit prickly. Sometimes he doesn't even like me to touch him. I've asked him: What's wrong? and he says: Nothing, leave me alone! He's started to stay out overnight during the week, mostly on Mondays and Wednesdays. Where were you, I asked him when it first happened. Just give me some space, will you, please, was his terse reply. It was as if he couldn't wait to get out. Maybe this was just my perspective. But what was going on? I had all sorts of fantasies: Was he on coke—or other drugs? Was he having an affair? Most of all I thought: Now I am the one who has been dropped! How could it be any different? This is how everything went in Chris' life—so now it must be my turn. But I thought his analyst would know, he would work it through with him and not let him enact the whole wreckage again.

Still, one Wednesday I couldn't stand it any longer. I decided to follow him. He left around six o'clock saying he wasn't sure when he would come back. As soon as I heard his steps on the stairs I snatched my coat and softly sneaked behind him. When I came to the street I just caught a glimpse of him as he turned the corner, so I could easily catch up with him and follow with some distance. It was really weird, like in a detective movie. I felt bad but also excited: now I would find out...We walked for a long time. Chris likes to walk, he has crisscrossed all over Manhattan and rarely takes the subway. Following him I got tired and clammy from a freezing drizzle, but I stayed hard on his heels. Finally somewhere in SoHo he entered some Irish pub. I looked through the window and saw Chris steering towards the back of the room. As I couldn't see where he was going, I entered the pub and peered over to the booths in the back of the room—and there, at one of those tables, was Chris. He was sitting with a man who was talking with him, and at first I thought, this is a friend or colleague, but then I noticed that this man was holding Chris' hand—*a man holding his hand?* The man laughed and turned Chris' hand around, putting his fingers in Chris' palm, and I thought he was playing a psychic, making a fortune-teller joke—but then he picked up Chris' hand and kissed his palm! I couldn't believe it! What I saw seemed so beyond my imagination. I looked away and then looked back anew. And that's when I realized that the man who held Chris' hand was his analyst! At least he looked like his analyst! Chris and I had once run into him in a Starbucks, and he had briefly introduced us, so I had seen him—quite a handsome man in his forties, very warm and welcoming...I liked him. Anyway I recognized him, and I got confused...hot, shocked—I don't know what...I thought *this cannot be, no, it can NOT...!* Part of me wanted to rush over and confront the two. Part of me felt threatened as if I had gotten myself into big trouble. And still another part of me kept thinking that this was *verboten*, impossible—hence it wasn't real, I'd misunderstood... Simultaneously I thought I had to protect Chris, immediately I thought he needed my help. But if I wanted to help him, I had to first cool down! I had no idea what to do...I left the pub. For a while I stayed lingering at the entrance. The street was crowded, there was an opening at a gallery nearby, people were going in and out, smoking cigarettes and drinking wine on the street, so nobody cared why I was standing there. Occasionally I glanced through the window...I guess I was still hoping I was wrong. But the scene remained the same. At some point the man leaned over and kissed Chris on his lips, and I was shocked. I felt as if *I* had done something wrong, something shameful—spying on them like a *Peeping Tom*—yuck! I turned around and left.

I couldn't sleep all night. I tried to figure out how to confront Chris. All I came up with was blaming him for cheating on me with a man—*with a man!* I needed to talk to someone, urgently, yet it felt too dangerous to tell anybody! My heart was racing in overdrive! At six in the morning I left and went to my gym. I ran for an hour on the treadmill. Then I felt better. Fortunately, I wasn't home when Chris returned. I had decided to not say a word, not yet. I wanted to follow him one more time. Maybe I had been spooked, just seen some stupid vision or something... On Friday I said I was planning to spend the weekend with a friend in the Berkshires—which was a lie. Oh, good, he said. I took my backpack and left. But at the next corner I waited for him to come out. Isn't that horrible to eavesdrop on your own boyfriend? Anyway, I had to know! Sure enough, half an hour later Chris came out, and he nearly walked past me, could have seen me, but he was so in his own world—I guess he didn't see anything around him. This time he crossed Central Park, walked for about half a mile on 5th Avenue, and then all of a sudden he disappeared into the entrance of an apartment building. I waited to see if he only had briefly gone in to ask the doorman for something and would come out shortly...but he didn't. After half an hour I left. I had taken the number of the building. Back home I googled his analyst and found both his office address on Madison and his home address on 5th Avenue; the number was the one I noted.

Anouk kept silent for a moment and I froze. *No!* I thought. *Do not let it be Paul, let it not be Paul!* Many analysts live around 5th Avenue and have offices on Park or Madison, dozens of shrinks—how many actually? I felt the urge to ask Anouk about the building's number, but I stopped myself from doing so, and I didn't want to hear it, that too! So I continued to wait, but the shock had chilled the temperature of the room, sending goosebumps all over me. Anouk wasn't looking at me, she was sitting upright, pale and stiff, like a chunk of chalk approaching the story's end line. Only her right hand's fingers ferociously pulled and plucked at the cuticles around her nails.

I had already missed my period for the second time, she softly continued. At first I thought that can happen, the body can skip a period, particularly in times of stress. I thought I had taken my pill regularly...I was nervous—but actually more about what I had seen... I spent the weekend in a funk. All these thoughts and images...! When Chris returned on Monday morning I confronted him right away. I told him that I had followed him twice and knew that he was with his analyst! Chris was shocked. Are you going to leave me? was the first thing he anxiously asked me. I don't know, I said, tell me what's going on! That's when he told me that he thought he was homosexual—or rather bi-sexual, he explained, because he also loved to have sex with me. But sex with a man was something different, he said. He called it *phenomenal*, said he had never allowed himself to think about it, but in his analysis it turned out that all his difficulties resulted from the repression of his homosexual longings; that's what his analyst said and it was a powerful discovery, a life-changing revelation...He said he was unsure whether it would be transitional or grow into something major, something lasting... While talking Chris had this eerie glow in his eyes, and a horny smile kept breaking through whenever he talked about this man, his analyst...I had the hardest time looking at him! But I had committed myself to letting him tell me as much as he could, and despite the shocking news, it felt good to finally talk again matter-of fact! I don't know if I loved him at this point, but I certainly cared about him. Eventually I said: *But he's your analyst!* Just that, because it seemed so evident that this whole thing wasn't okay. However, Chris just responded with, Yeah, I know, that's a little unusual, and declared that there have been cases of real love occurring between analyst and patient. He said Paul—that is, Dr. Salentino, his analyst, because now of course they are on a first name basis...

As Anouk spelled out Paul's name my heart jumped into overdrive. I didn't want to hear one more word, but Anouk continued to talk precisely and without mercy for herself or for me, I couldn't tell. Was she aware who she was telling this to, who I was? It didn't seem so, hence I felt I had to stay calm and at least end this session with a neutral stance. Anouk shook her head. Paul told Chris there were always exceptions; he listed a number of people, analysts and patients, who had gotten married. One rule doesn't fit all, he argued. Chris said he wasn't thinking of getting married to Paul, but he feels Paul really loves him! Paul told him that never before had he loved someone as much as he loves him; never before could he feel so connected and understood as he feels with him; Paul thinks they are soulmates, they are made for each other...Chris said that Paul weeps and laughs with him and gets aroused simply by seeing him, and that makes Chris feel good about himself. Paul told Chris that for an analyst this kind of love is not without risk, and he asked Chris to not tell anybody about their relationship, because he could lose everything, for which he wasn't quite ready yet...However, Paul reassured him that all those concerns would pale in comparison with this love, and he would give everything, everything to be with him—but maybe he didn't have to...Chris said to me, I can feel his love, and I think I love him too!

Anouk shook her head. Chris said he knew that this was hard for me. And the strange thing is, he doesn't want me to leave him, he begged me to give him a bit more time to figure this out. Chris asked me to not tell anybody, because it would be devastating for Paul and for him if anybody knew. I would kill myself if I lost him now...Chris said. It's all so new, so important and so confusing, please, give me some time! That's what he said and at that point Chris cried, and I cried too, because we were in such a mess, and I felt so enraged and alone and all...I couldn't say a word, I wouldn't have known what to say, I just kept shaking my head, as if I could shake this whole damn thing off...Finally he said: You sent me to Paul, it was you who urged me to go and see him, and I did. Now I'm in your hands: I will live—or die if you won't bear with me till the end of my analysis! Then he went over to his room and rolled up on his sofa.

Anouk looked at me. I lowered my eyes, avoiding hers, just stared down at my hand, which seemed to move in slow motion over the chair's armrest, stroking the black leather that was brittle and wrinkled from being used for many years, worn down by my colleague, Dr. Meredith Adler, who had worked here all her life, and now as she had grown tired, she had limited her practice to a few hours a week and allowed me to share her office. Could I talk with her? With whom could I talk? One of my supervisors was out of town for the next couple of weeks; the other was a friend of Paul's, so I couldn't bring this up with him. Dr. Adler seemed to be trustworthy; maybe she would give me advice? But she was from a different institute...No, what Anouk had told me was confidential. She was my patient, even though I now regretted having accepted her! It would have been better had Anouk revealed her story to somebody else—anybody but me. Paul is my brother, I thought, I shouldn't even hear this!

I didn't know what to do! Anouk continued. Chris begged me to let this affair go on—he even calls it *analysis.* His threat to kill himself, if I betrayed his secret to anybody, is outrageous, and I don't have to accept it. Actually I don't think he means it, it's just theatrical. Still, I don't want to risk it. He is in such a state of mind that I think he could do anything. Last week he bought an antique pistol—a pistol! What is that for? I demanded, and he just said, it's cool, and put it on his desk. He wants to use it as a paperweight—that's what he claims, and I don't even think that this old pistol would work, but still...At the same time I feel I need to help him out of this mess, it's insane! It's not even that I absolutely want him back for myself, I don't know about that, maybe yes, but I definitively don't want him to be fucked by his analyst!

I cringed when she said that. Would Paul really do this? The enormity of Anouk's accusation made me wonder...Was she bringing me a true ethical complaint, or was this merely her fantasy gone wild, an expression of her jealousy of Chris' analysis? After all, it was *she* who was here as a patient. Was it part of her pathology that she wanted to sell me Chris as a patient or Chris and Paul, two men—maybe all of this was an outgrowth of her adoption fantasy that had been reinforced by her pregnancy—or maybe she wasn't even pregnant...?

So I'm in this terrible bind, Anouk went on, I'm muzzled, and I'm angry, actually I'm mad as hell! I wouldn't hold off for a second to file a formal complaint against Dr. Salentino, I don't care about this guy. However, I care about Chris, and Chris is madly in love with Paul. He's totally dependent on seeing him every day! This whole thing is sickening! For days on end I have wracked my brains, and didn't know what to do about it. But then a few days ago I got an idea! I had made some flip remark to Chris, something like: why don't you just move in with your analyst? Chris didn't even get my irony. Instead he responded as if to a serious suggestion! He said that right now he couldn't move in with Paul because Paul's apartment is owned by his sister, and he wants her to sell it to him, so he avoids anything that could interfere with this plan. Chris also told me that Paul believes his sister will go back to Germany, once she has finished her training at his institute. When he said this, I saw my chance! I understood that his sister is an analyst! I tried to look you up but couldn't find you under the name Salentino. So I emailed my analyst in Zürich, asked him about a German-speaking analyst in New York, casually mentioning Dr. Salentino's sister, and two days later he sent me your name and contact information. I thought if I came to you as your patient, what I tell you is confidential, so you can't talk about it to anybody else, right? On the other hand, if Paul really is your brother, you would want to straighten things out with him, right? I have no idea how you could do this—and I wouldn't even care to know about it, because I want to keep my promise to Chris to not tell anybody that he is having an affair with his analyst. So in the real world I haven't told anybody. But I do want something to be done about it! That's why I came to you! I want you to help me—*please, help me—help us!*

Anouk had tricked me! She had dumped her problem in my lap! I felt shocked, deceived, assaulted, and I struggled with wanting to point this out to her, accuse her of not having been upfront. A surge of anger briefly choked me. I had to think this through before saying anything about it. I needed time! Meanwhile our session drew to a close. So I said: It's a difficult and serious situation...There is your problem with Chris, and then there is your problem with your pregnancy...

Anouk interrupted me. I was just thinking about it. I feel so relieved, now that I have told you about the whole mess. It's good to not be alone in this...I think it's a bit like when I was a kid and had some trouble, and I didn't want to tell my parents... But when I finally did, what a relief, and usually it all worked out well. So suddenly I thought: I could tell my parents that I'm pregnant. I thought—maybe my mother would want to have my baby, raise her or him... now since she has nobody else to care about...and my father has always been great with kids. Anyway, I thought: I can tell them, I really can. She smiled at me and added: Guess that's already a good outcome of our session, isn't it?

Now she wants to give her mother a baby, I thought, and clearly there was more involved than we could address in the remaining minutes, but I said: You want them to adopt your baby. Anouk looked a bit puzzled, and since she didn't say anything, I asked her if she wanted to make another appointment, so that we could continue to think together about all she had brought to me. But to my surprise Anouk shook her head. No, not right now... I'll mail you a check for today's session, and if I feel I need you, I'll call you, I promise. Thank you for your time. We got up. Skillfully she threw her backpack over her shoulders, walked towards the door, but stopped there, and as if punctuated by a sudden idea she turned around, came back, and stretched her right hand towards me: As Europeans we can shake hands, can't we? We both smiled. Yes, we can! I confirmed, and took her hand, which briefly pressed mine. Goodbye, I said. Bye, she responded, and walked out with steady steps as if knowing where to go from there. A small silver whistle attached to one of her backpack's pockets was bobbing and swaying with each of her movements.

DR. CRAMER

Dr. Alexander Cramer practices psychoanalysis in one of those New York garden apartments that are accessed via some steps down from the street level to the side of the building's main entrance. Walking through Manhattan I often look at them, see their windows either darkened and dusty like old forgotten cellars, or illuminated but covered with curtains impenetrable to the curious eye, and then I wonder, who might be living there? Dr. Cramer isn't living in the basement; it's only his office. (I don't want to go there.) Maybe a century or two earlier the space of his office housed the owner's servants, who needed to stay close enough to be called at any time, day and night, but still remain outside the family's space to keep the necessary distance and privacy for both parties. Psychoanalysts are no servants, their answering machines can be called day and night, but they certainly should keep their distance and privacy and offer their services only during their scheduled hours. Maybe the current owner of the building rented out this walk-down space to Dr. Cramer (I don't want to see him), or maybe Dr. Cramer *is* the owner and lives in this elegant, impressive townhouse, which seems to have been renovated recently. Everything looks new and fresh: the facade is painted off-white, doors and window shutters shining black, brazen doorknobs glittering like golden eggs. The stamp-size front garden with its bunch of planted daffodils—all the same size, densely packed like brigade soldiers eagerly showing off their white helmets to the street's pedestrians—is fenced in with turn-of-the-century style wrought iron, painted the same black as the shutters and so clean that I think it must be dusted daily—anyway, everything here is breathing the air of solid craftsmanship and financial power. (Maybe it was a mistake to make this appointment.) Through the first-floor window I can see a huge Gobelin tapestry hanging on the wall, two old-fashioned armchairs next to a round table with a yellowish alabaster shade lamp, all arranged a bit like in a museum even though it's most likely the living room. Three graceful branches of a delicate orchid full of white blossoms artfully meander from the silent windowsill through the cultured atmosphere of the interior towards the light of our dubious days.

If Dr. Cramer lives upstairs and works downstairs it would be convenient for him on rainy days: using an in-house staircase, he wouldn't even have to unfold his umbrella. However, on sunny summer mornings it would cost him a deep sigh to trudge downstairs and be crammed all day into his basement office, listening for endless hours to the misery of his wealthy patients (the not so wealthy ones are sent to the candidates). Slouched in his chair, Dr. Cramer may be aware of his nagging back pain; to distract himself, his eyes involuntarily may wander out the window towards his street-heaven where hundreds of legs are marching, ambling, running, hopping, or dancing by—which is pretty interesting and sometimes even exciting. I would think that over the years, he's gotten used to identifying and naming some of these legs, just privately, and when he recognizes them strolling along, he silently says *hello* to them or *good afternoon*, depending on the time of the day. (I still could walk away...)

Dr. Cramer looks like a nice guy: wild white hair, big and bushy, and an old-fashioned mustache; he is always dressed in a gray suit with a vest carefully buttoned up and nicely displaying the golden chain of his watch that sticks in its special little pocket next to his heart, from which he pulls it out when he thinks *it's time...*; also, he always wears a white shirt with golden cufflinks and a big bowtie in seasonal colors, now probably yellow and orange, because it's spring. The only break with the past he displays is his choice of fancy high-end sneakers (I hear they qualified for the New York Marathon), which really seem to jump out of the whole picture as if they wanted to escape his large feet and run away from this heavy man and his grave demeanor (and so do I).

Three years ago I was in his office for one of my admission interviews (and I hadn't thought of ever returning). It's nice and small, furnished almost completely with mahogany, still-life oil paintings on the walls, a big soft Persian carpet covering the floor, and the couch looks like a copy of Freud's original: very Vienna. Dr. Cramer (who I now feel so reluctant to see) emigrated from Vienna when he was very young, people in my institute whispered, so his Vienna couch makes a lot of sense. There is an adjacent waiting room, or rather a drop-down niche, established right next to the entry and exit door, where people can hang their coats before perching themselves on a tiny chair, which I noticed had a broken spring while I was sitting on it three years ago (let's see if he has fixed it in the meantime).

Quite unusual for this time of year, it had been freezing overnight, and by a hair I'd slipped down the sloped stairs, not having noticed their icy coating, because I was briefly fascinated with a decorative pompom tree sitting in some kind of a rustic copper pot next to the scuffed-off stone lion that is watching whoever approaches Dr. Cramer's office; the needles of the evergreen were frozen and their ball-shaped pompoms sparked icicles in all directions, making the plant look like a gang of white hedgehogs settled there on a mysterious mission. Fortunately, I got my hand on the railing, but the sudden threat of losing my balance jolted me. (Was speaking with Dr. Cramer the right thing to do?)

For several days I had been struggling with a strange aversion to making this appointment, and still unclear whether it was a good idea or not, in the end I did it, mostly because I thought I should—but should I really? Ever since I had agreed to this early morning hour, I had been preoccupied with formulating various excuses, some of which quite exotic for a late cancellation. However, I hadn't followed through with any of them, had ignored my inner voice to *not* see him—instead this morning at 6:30 AM I lowered my head and went to meet my obligations. Dr. Cramer is one of the oldest and most prominent members of our institute, and he is its Ombudsman. He is not the chair of the Ethics Committee, which is Dr. Miller, an old classmate of Dr. Cramer, as we all know. Dr. Miller is much more likable than Dr. Cramer; however, due to their different functions I chose not to go to Dr. Miller, because he might have tried to talk me into filing an official complaint, which I hope to avoid by speaking only to Dr. Cramer. Our institute's ethical procedures seem to me such a complex and obscure juristic cobweb, I'd rather not get caught in it…Still, I thought I should talk with the Ombudsman, as a compromise of sorts, because the whole situation was so confusing, and I didn't really know what my obligations were. Had this meeting with Anouk been therapy or merely a consultation? Was a consultation as confidential as therapy? Did I have to report a relative, my own brother? Was I as a candidate under all circumstances required to talk with somebody from the institute? What would that do to Paul, and to me? I wasn't sure about any of these questions.

On top of all I was afraid that I had transgressed a boundary, because I hadn't been able to stop myself from calling Paul. The day following Anouk's session I had called and demanded to talk with him. He was a bit surprised and said he had come down with the flu, but if I didn't mind visiting him in the evening at home he would be happy to talk with me. He opened his door dressed in Jeans, a sweatshirt, and a large woolen scarf wrapped twice around his neck, obviously sick but curious and seemingly in a good mood. Did he think I'd come to tell him that he could have my condo, since I would move back to Cologne? Instead I confronted him with the fact that he was having a sexual relationship with his patient Chris. Paul was shocked! His hand clenched the armrest of his chair as if he needed to find some hold. Don't...don't...he stammered, looking away from me, his face crestfallen, his shoulders sunken, a pathetic little boy. Paul...I said, devastated to see him so deflated by my statement, and I realized that I had hoped he would reassure me that *it wasn't true*. It was true!

It became a long and painful night. We both drank too much whiskey, at some point I had to throw up, and in the end I slept on his couch because I wouldn't have been able to safely return to my apartment. What a night! I regret having had any alcohol at all, because my recollection of what Paul told me is blurred, and I cannot clearly draw the line between his account and what I made of it. While some of what he said stayed crystal clear in my mind, I cannot remember what exactly he stated as facts and how he tried to trivialize them in order to nullify their gravity. But what I did take away from this long night with Paul was this: He is totally in love with Chris, madly and desperately in love with him, more in love than ever before, he said time and again. He told me that despite being liked and even idolized by lots of people, many beautiful women and even a few gay men, he had felt alone all his life, deeply alone. He said he had tried many times to break out of his solitude: he wanted to be close with the colleagues he admired; he entertained flings and dated women as well as men—but it all felt empty, all his efforts went nowhere—before he met Chris. Chris changed everything! Chris was different. Chris was smart, sweet, funny, sensitive, and sexy, that too, but that wasn't even the main thing, Paul asserted. Chris had a tremendous presence, he was so present, *unbelievably there*...! Chris was all he wanted to be with, if possible 25 hours a day! Paul said he loved Chris more than he would love any alter ego, if that proved it...And Chris needed him, desperately needed him, Paul claimed. Chris needed his help in working through an excruciatingly traumatic childhood; he needed his guidance in channeling and growing his creativity, because *he is a genius,* Paul said with a desperate look, beseeching me to believe him. Without me he is lost, he stated, lost in this world, lost with this Swiss girl who doesn't understand how special he is, who just wants to make him an ordinary school teacher. Paul went on and on, with no interest in hearing whether I saw things differently or had anything to say to all of this. Don't, don't take this away from me, Paul repeatedly said, I don't know what I might do to myself, really...Without Chris I don't feel like going on—my life would be so empty—it would be unbearable, please...

I was appalled to hear him talk like this. Having pleaded for more than an hour, eventually he stopped, as if he had used up all his good arguments, and the ensuing silence felt like an enormous relief. After a while I said: Don't you think you need analysis to work this through? Don't you think that this is a little sick...? Paul briefly sneered, maybe only for a split-second, before he responded—angrily or discouraged, I couldn't tell: I was in analysis for half of my life...and you think I need some more of it? What could I say? We both held our tongues, crushed by the terrible weight of this mess, filled with a sense of helplessness, a threat that somehow harked back, far back to our childhood, and strangely enough it made us real brother and sister again, moved us closer than I had felt to him in decades, and I reached out and took his hand and didn't let it go, and Paul shyly glanced over to me and briefly gave me a bashful smile, and in that moment, as he was exposing his dependency and need for my protection, for the first time I could sense Paul's love, a love for me that Janis had always claimed to be there and I had always doubted; this love became strangely palpable, and I felt bad that I hadn't understood it sooner nor ever reciprocated...

You know, Paul softly said, and withdrew his hand to reach for the whiskey bottle, in one of my analyses I came to recognize that unconsciously and up into my adult life I had held on to the belief that you were my little baby daughter. It sounds totally crazy—but not from the perspective of a child's fantasy! When I came home from camp and Joyce was there with you as this newborn baby, I thought it was ours. I thought she and I had made it because we loved each other, that's what I felt, we really did! They said, if two people love each other and are close, they can make a baby. So I thought, maybe it happened. Maybe on that one Saturday night when Eddie was at some business dinner, and Joyce had crawled into my bed, and I don't know if I only dreamt it or if she really let me touch her, her breasts and her private parts and all...I believe it was real—then we both fell asleep...we slept together. After that she went away. I was convinced Eddie had banished her because he was angry with us, even though he claimed she was traveling with the theatre. When I saw her again some months later just coming back from camp, Joyce had this baby on her lap, and I immediately thought: *we made a baby that night!* I knew that pregnancies took a few months. *I was so proud!* Nobody celebrated with me, not even Joyce, but at night I prayed a little prayer for you...This sounds ridiculous, but when I retrieved this memory, I could feel it again, *it was the most wonderful moment of my life!* You, my little Ann-baby, you were the most precious thing I'd ever seen...And after Joyce had jumped out of the window, I silently promised to myself to make sure that you would be fine, always fine...Of course all of this got more or less repressed. Janis showed up and took over, and for many years I sort of forgot that Joyce was your mother, not Janis. I know, I was mean to you, as mean as every brother is to his sister. But I'm sure I would have defended you against anybody who would have dared to hurt you, all without knowing that the unconscious reason for my wish to protect you was my infantile belief that I had fathered you. It's silly, isn't it? But you can see that my analyses did bring some insight about...

I was taken aback by his confession, felt like withdrawing and being trapped. Why had he told me? Didn't he realize that I was his sister, not his analyst? I wished I hadn't learned about these fantasies...and I wished he hadn't betrayed his night with Joyce to me—if it was true at all—how ruthless to let herself go in Paul's bed, a monster devouring this little boy with his curious fingers and his stupid, eager soul—my troubled brother...In whom could he have confided such a shameful treasure? What a heap to be urged on him, dark and bittersweet—how confusing! I watched him now tending to his sniffles, and felt sorry for him.

After a while Paul said: I'm not telling you this to coerce you into silence now—or maybe I am... But what I meant to say was: I loved my mother, I loved Joyce, and I loved Janis, they all were my mothers. I hated Eddie for most of my life—even though I also admired him, and I did feel protective of him... There was something I knew about him that I never told him because it would have been the end of him...Sometimes when I was furious, I felt like throwing it into his face...! But I never did, not even in our last conversation, the night he died! For a while I wracked my brain: *did it slip out despite my resolve*? Did Eddie walk into that bike because I told him...? But no, I didn't tell him, I did not! And I won't tell you either. Maybe you think that I'm just making this up. What I'm trying to say is that I'm not just bad, a lost cause, a bad apple, a bad character, someone who needs to be cast out and away...

Over the years when we had no contact, I missed you. I would have liked to just call and chat with you a bit. After Janis had passed away—*without a note of goodbye, imagine, not a single word!*—I felt totally lost. I had my colleagues, my friends, but at the same time I had nobody. Then Chris came along, and everything changed. All of a sudden I had a focus. I knew what I wanted. My whole love went to him as if he was a powerful magnet, inescapable and solidly there. *Wow!* Only then I woke up and could be fully in my life! Never before had it happened to me with any patient. I'm a good analyst. I always held the boundaries! That was never a problem for me. But with Chris it was something different, totally, absolutely different. Please, believe me! It can happen! Maybe it's a once-in-a-lifetime moment...I've finally found what I yearned for my whole life. From the outside it must sound horrible. In formal terms, it's an ethical violation. I know that very well! But how can true love be a violation? Think about it! Think well before you decide. I'm in your hands now. If our colleagues learn about it, they will tar and feather me and drive me out of the institute. Do you want that to happen? Do you want them to name and shame me in front of everybody? Do you want me to lose everything?

When I left the next morning, left without having seen or spoken to Paul, who was still sleeping when I silently closed the door behind me—but maybe I should have left him a note?—I was incapable of thinking any worthwhile thought. Down on the street the normality of life on 5th Avenue felt simultaneously strange and reassuring. I carried my splitting headache into a Starbucks and sat there for an hour brooding over a cinnamon muffin without even touching it. Eventually the coffee woke me up. I would have to find a way to spare Paul the worst and still talk with someone from our institute, so that they could do something to help with this terrible situation. What would happen to Anouk and to Chris and to Paul and finally to me? That's when I came up with the idea to talk to our Ombudsman, and despite all lingering doubts, I showed up for my appointment with Dr. Cramer, even a bit early.

The minutes seem to barely creep ahead while I'm anxiously sitting in this narrow waiting niche, staring at Dr. Cramer's office door and rehearsing in my mind what I've decided to tell him. Finally the door flings open, and there he stands, tall and almighty and smiling like a fox. Well good morning, Dr. Stark, why don't you come in? I enter with guarded steps and sit down in a deep leather chair opposite his slightly higher armchair—and notice a smudgy dust cloth clinging to the top of his backrest, obviously left there by the cleaning lady. The tissue box next to me is empty. Funny that I would notice such unimportant things in a moment gravely laden with fatal powers! Calmly and attentively Dr. Cramer looks at me and waits. So I start and say exactly what I have prepared: I'm coming to you as the Ombudsman of our institute. I'm having a very general and sort of hypothetical question. If I were to see a patient for just one session, and she told me about a boundary violation, would what she told me have to remain confidential between her and me, or would I have to report it to our Ethics Committee?

Dr. Cramer remains silent for a little while as if trying to decide carefully how to respond, and then starts out by explaining some of the procedures and technicalities of an official complaint, in contrast to a consultation with an Ombudsman, which latter would remain basically informal, he says. You are in a difficult position, he then adds, and it must have been his empathic attunement to my inner turmoil, conveyed with these few words that sound as if they're coming from a good father who knows what to do and will right all wrongs, that I tell him against my precautions everything about Anouk's session with me, Paul's situation with his patient Chris, and my visit with Paul. Dr. Cramer listens, sometimes slightly nods, expressing seriousness and concern in a neutral way, and I feel held like by a helping hand. After I'm done he remains silent for a while and then starts to speak.

Yeah, it's a bad situation, quite bad. I knew you would be coming, I was waiting for your call. I had heard about it. We hear a lot of things...People talk. People have eyes and see, they notice, and then they talk...Your brother is a character, quite a complicated character! We've always known that. Charming and smart, one of our best, I have to say. He's written some quite amazing articles—really good, profound. I've been teaching some of his papers in my seminars, outstanding...! And since he is teaching at NYU his students apply to our institute for training. A remarkable guy, no question about that! Still, it's serious, I agree with you.

I am a bit surprised that he obviously knew already about Paul's situation and feel a bit relieved that I didn't betray anything new to him, but then all of a sudden the warm glow in Dr. Cramer's eyes turns sharp and piercing, it seems, as he continues: Still, I do wonder a bit, Dr. Stark...what actually is it that brings you here *today*...or maybe I should say: what brings you here only now, that is rather late, if I may say so? His question puzzles me. It's only been ten days since I saw Anouk...What do you mean...? I ask. Well, Dr. Cramer says, now that it's too late...A few days earlier we might have been able to do something, probably not much at that point, but who knows, we certainly would have tried...But now since this young man, Dr. Salentino's patient, has chosen to kill himself...

He killed himself? The soft, shrill scream of my question wrenched itself away from my effort to stay calm and composed.

Yes, he killed himself in some kind of Russian roulette, Dr. Cramer explains. It's not clear that he meant to kill himself, so we can't blame his analyst or anybody really for that. He seems to have played with an old pistol, put it to his head, and his girlfriend was scared and tried to wrestle it out of his hands. In order to prove that this was not more than a theatrical gesture, he pointed the pistol at some corner, pulled the trigger, and nothing happened. But when he put it again at his temple and pulled the trigger—there must have been an old bullet in it, even unbeknownst to the seller, a guy in a small antique shop; he has been interviewed by the police and could convincingly claim that he had no idea there was a bullet in this pistol. Anyway, the poor kid was dead on the spot! You didn't know that?

I am devastated. I see Anouk in her anguish, and see Paul in desperation, and I feel the cascading pain I unleashed: I told Paul, and Paul told Chris, and Chris surely faulted Anouk, and Anouk probably blames me and herself for Chris' death. Why hadn't Anouk called me? Obviously she'd lost all trust in me. How terrible, I whisper, oh god, how awful!

Dr. Cramer thoughtfully nods and gives me some time to grapple with the bad news. Then he says: Well yeah, it *is* awful! Too bad for this young man! He seemed to have been just kidding around, and one never should kid around with a pistol! Of course we analysts might wonder about the deeper meaning of this suicide, but that will remain our mystery, the doubt we have to live with. However, all in all, this whole thing can't have come to you as a surprise! We both know that your brother molested you as a child, right? So there is a deep flaw in his character that extended itself to this prohibited sexual relationship with his patient, which was abusive and unethical, no doubt! Too bad that the character flaws of this smart and highly gifted man obviously weren't worked through with his analyst—who by the way was not the best of our guild, I must say. It will forever escape me why someone as clever as Paul chose Dr. Hemmington—may he rest in peace!—as his training analyst...he wasn't special and wasn't even smart, that was well known. So I guess there was already a lot of resistance in Paul's choice of his training analyst—a resistance that wasn't resolved even in his second analysis, I'm afraid...

366

I'm startled. Paul didn't molest me...I interject. Of course he did, Dr. Cramer claims, you told me about it in the sessions we had some years ago, didn't you? I don't remember, I counter, I only came here once for an interview, and I don't think that I said anything like this. I may have said that I wondered if he molested my sister, but frankly I doubt...Dr. Cramer briefly looks puzzled but quickly recovers. Yes, right, he molested your sister—and if I didn't hear it from you, I must have heard it from someone else...Anyway, amongst us and despite the fact that he's your brother, Dr. Stark: *what can you expect from such a character?*

I'm totally thrown! Is he telling me that someone else talked to him about Paul and Issy? That could only have been Paul. Who else would know? Had Paul confided in Dr. Cramer? Or had one of Paul's analysts or Dr. Shepherd talked with Dr. Cramer about Paul? I should leave right away! Look, Dr. Cramer continues, there's the rub—and you are a young analyst, a colleague, if I may say so, hence you are able to have some analytic thoughts about what I'm asking you now...He pauses, closes his eyes as if to better concentrate, and leans his head on the backrest right next to the smudgy dust cloth, which, pulled in by the cushion's slight indentation, starts to slowly sink or creep down onto his white mane, settling there feathery and unnoticed while Dr. Cramer curls his lips saying: Just in general and sort of hypothetically, Dr. Stark, if you knew that a young woman managed to get accepted for analysis by the analyst of her brother—just hypothetically, as I said—and this young woman who had kept her mouth shut as long as bad things were going on, and only after—*after!*—all had ended in a tragic death, approached you with an ethical complaint about said brother, a complaint of quite horrendous proportions, wouldn't you wonder about her motivation? Wouldn't you wonder whether an old sibling's rivalry had carried her in? Consciously she may very well be convinced of doing nothing other than the right thing, the ethical thing, which is to protect her brother's patients from further harm. But unconsciously—*unconsciously!*—she may—*may!*—be driven by revenge, a powerful wish to destroy her brother, to pay him back for all he did to her, or to her little sister for that matter, *and* for her own shortcomings—interesting word, isn't it?—*shortcomings* and disadvantages she felt she had to endure throughout her childhood *because of him.* This is all hypothetical—I said that—but how would *you* think about it?

I feel hot and cold. I regret having made this appointment. I am confused and furious. Is he saying that Dr. Shepherd is Paul's second analyst? Paul had never told me with whom he was in analysis, and I never asked him, nor did I tell him that I had ended up on Dr. Shepherd's couch. Anyway, if this was the case, Dr. Shepherd shouldn't had taken me in analysis, and Dr. Cramer shouldn't be telling me! That's what I say: I'm not sure that you should tell me that Paul and I have the same analyst...Dr. Cramer opens his eyes in surprise. Oh, I'm not saying this, not at all! I said: *hypothetical, just hypothetical!* What I was trying to get you to wonder about is this: you want to throw dirt onto your brother, isn't that right? You want to polish him off with this foul suspicion—it's a mere suspicion, because don't forget: whatever is said, we never know what really happened; people have their ideas, their fantasies, they think and feel something that isn't there; but for them it's there all the same, and it may very well be there—anyway, now you want to bring these charges, now that it would be to no avail, for what it's worth...And you are his sister! You can't tell me that you don't have feelings for your brother, some of which may not be so pretty...old feelings never die, they sneak up on you, even when you're analyzed—Paul just proved it again, didn't he? So I want to ask you: don't you have to wonder if this old stuff plays any role in wanting to bury your brother under a load of shame, something that would kill him professionally, I mean really kill him for all time...?

I am shocked and outraged and can't get a grip on this conversation. You make me very uncomfortable, I say. Dr. Cramer smiles. Good, he responds, that's all it needs. We know when something is uncomfortable we have to first think and analyze before we decide and act. So let me introduce a further hypothesis: what if Dr. Salentino, let's say, following the wake-up call of his little sister, had decided to consult with me or anybody from the Ethics Committee, seeking to remedy the situation, for instance by referring his patient—who, by the way, didn't file a complaint, and only he would have had the right to do so, that's another crucial point—so what if Paul had sought to send Chris to another analyst, something that Chris might not have wanted to accept, who knows if that played some role...And what if Paul himself had decided to go once more into analysis in order to figure out how in the world he could have become so crazy—because that's what this kind of love for a patient would be, mere craziness, right?—so what if all of these wise steps to remedy the situation already had been put in motion, and then first this poor guy fires a little bullet into his head, and then all of a sudden, with a delay of say two weeks, you come in to throw a handful of dirt on your brother...I'm not sure how I would think about it, are you?

Is Dr. Cramer telling me that Paul has sought his advice? I haven't talked with Paul since our painful conversation, but maybe knowing that I knew, Paul panicked and tried to right the situation and do the unavoidable...? I am upset, I can't think clearly. Dr. Cramer is accusing me of wanting to hurt Paul. This is crazy! This totally twists my intent! And all the news that he is springing on me under the disguise of hypotheses, confidential steps that Paul might have taken and that I am not supposed to know about—or am I? And then, all of a sudden I hear myself saying: You have a dust cloth on your head! I say it with some malicious undertone, and in fact I catch Dr. Cramer by surprise. What? he utters, clumsily feels up by his head, pulls the smudgy dust cloth off his white mane, and looks at it with big eyes. Ha-ha! he then exclaims, and carefully, as if it were the evidence, places the dirty rag on the side table next to his chair. Good for you, Dr. Stark! This one goes to you, he adds with a chuckle, immediately realizing that my remark is meant as some kind of tit-for-tat response.

For a while we both keep silent. I am exhausted, and maybe he is too. Then Dr. Cramer softly says: I know, this is all very confusing. I apologize, I've been a little rough on you. These things are never a cakewalk. I remember, when I was a young analyst at this institute, we had a case of a sexual boundary violation. One of our training analysts slept with his patient—a candidate at our institute. He did it over several years, and his patient seemed to have gone along with it—at least she didn't file a complaint. Maybe they too thought that this was a special and unique love; maybe she was ashamed and afraid that if this came out, it would be the end of her training. Shame and anxiety are the big rulers in such cases. However, despite all secrecy, at some point it did come out—it always does! I can't remember how, but that's beside the point. Someone from our institute, perhaps a friend of this colleague, may have warned him that something was brewing...So before any ethical investigation could get started, he resigned, left the institute, and there was nothing we could do about it in retrospect. Needless to say, the affair with the patient ended under no good terms. I don't know the details, there were many rumors at the time, not worth remembering, I suppose. The candidate ended her training and left the institute; she became a journalist and a fervent critic of psychoanalysis. And what happened with her analyst, our former colleague? He was ostracized! Nobody would remember ever having said anything appreciative about this man. Everybody claimed to always have known that he was a loose cannon. In retrospect we are all smartasses, aren't we?—Nobody wanted to be in contact with him any longer. Those who were closer to him were in a terrible dilemma. They felt betrayed by their friend, but abandoning him felt like betraying him. For many years our institute ached under the loss of this colleague and the silence that fell over his ethical violation. At the time many thought there was no good way to resolve such a breach of boundaries. As you know, because of the transference situation, sexual boundary violations are always incestuous, Oedipus lashing out, and that's what makes them so repellent. Our institute only slowly recovered from this catastrophic failure in our midst; maybe it never fully did. Maybe there remained a dirty stain on our culture, some hidden complicity, an unconscious rebellion against the rules—*the law of the father*, as the French like to call it—that could have contributed to Paul's deficient analysis...If so it would burden us all with a collateral guilt. Today, many years later, I sometimes talk with my friends about it. Some of us, in particular Dr. Miller and I, have spent many hours thinking about how we, most of all our training and supervising analysts, could have done it differently. We haven't found conclusive answers, but there is something we agree on: in the aftermath of this disaster we analysts lost our analytic attitude, which requires a minimum of empathy that everybody deserves. In retrospect we can see that this colleague was crazy, *love-sick* we may call it. And doesn't craziness deserve some analytic compassion, reflection—care? This is not about protecting our colleague.

First of all we have to be concerned about the patient. However, the colleague I'm talking about was no predator. He had a good reputation. But at one point he snapped and stopped being an analyst. He mistook the patient's and his own desire for real love. He sailed off into unprotected waters, didn't realize that the secrecy with which he shrouded his affair was showing him a red flag, a clear sign of doing something unacceptable. Too bad that he didn't try to get help. Or maybe he asked someone who was also prone to snubbing the rules and mistaking transference love for the real thing...Anyway, what saddened many of us was that this one crime cost our colleague his life as an analyst. Maybe that's how it is: we have to live with the consequences of what we've done! However, as much as we turn away from a boundary violator, we cannot turn away from ourselves. We were the ones who had nothing else to offer than expulsion, and that's a little shabby for a psychoanalyst, isn't it?

Dr. Cramer doesn't look at me. As if lost in his thought, he picks up the dirty dust cloth and folds it carefully into a small package, which he then places back on his side table. Then he pulls his golden watch out of his vest pocket, looks at it and says: Unfortunately, our time is up. A lot remains to be thought about. I understand that this whole thing is hard on you...Anyway, I'm glad you came in, Dr. Stark! Goodbye now. Goodbye, I say and walk out. The day has warmed up. The pompom tree's icicles have melted, its green needles are fluttering in the morning breeze.

TERESA

How often had I thought of Teresa's *come-and-see-me-sometime* invitation, reluctant though to take her up on it. And the longer I delayed contacting her the more towering she grew in my imagination as this intriguing woman, radiating clarity and warmth together with an almost aristocratic reserve, which attracted and intimidated me. Still, that wasn't it...

Then Tim Moore called and wanted to discuss some more recent and future issues, as he cryptically indicated, and I went to see him. He offered me an elegant leather chair in a corner of his spacious office overlooking Lincoln Center, and while his secretary was placing two espressos and two glasses with chilled water in front of us on the low cast-iron coffee table, he started to chat a bit about how much he loved the Metropolitan Opera, where several of his clients perform, which then led him to share some funny anecdotes about them, nothing confidential, as he reassured me, it had all been in the media—but I wasn't in the mood. Instead I nervously waited for him to tell me what he wanted to tell me. Now I'm nervous all the time, I realize, even when I don't quite notice it, I'm tense, as if I'm constantly waiting for the other shoe to drop.

Finally Tim turned serious, declaring that he was in a somewhat awkward if not impossible position. And as if to first establish and ascertain his own defense, he started out by emphasizing that ever since my father gave him the power of attorney over my trust, he had worked for the best of my interests. Okay. When Janis, Paul, and Theo arrived in New York, he helped them settle down in my Fifth Avenue Condo; and after Janis had passed away, he negotiated a new lease at a fair market price for Paul. I knew all that and grew impatient. Then, Tim said, sometime later Paul asked him for legal advice, nothing big, and he saw no problem in helping him. They met a few times, and Paul's case was quickly resolved. But they kept talking, and eventually they became friends, slowly, very slowly, Tim said, as if pace was an argument. Paul had always been a bit of a loner, he continued, so Ben and he often spontaneously invited him for brunch or dinner, and Paul gladly accepted. He liked to cook with Ben and loved to play chess with Tim, they had good conversations...Paul is an interesting guy, Tim said with a melancholic undertone, and allowed himself to get a little carried away, vaguely indicating something about having fallen in love with Paul or the other way round, Paul with him, I couldn't tell, and maybe I misunderstood, but it sounded as if they had had an affair, with the consequence that Ben broke up with Tim and moved out—after so many years in which they had been doing so well, Tim said, showing signs of regret, but things happen, he murmured all lost in reminiscence, and I didn't say a thing—I didn't want to know that Paul had broken another heart. So I just looked out of the window and saw the big poster in front of the Met announcing *Don Giovanni*, and I thought I should finally go to the Opera one of these days, now that I could afford to pay for a good seat.

Tim noticed that he'd lost me and apologized for his digression. He continued, admitting that he hadn't told Eddie about his being friends with Paul, because he knew that Eddie and Paul didn't get along, and he was afraid Eddie would have demanded their friendship end, which would have been impossible for him at the time. Of course he knew that there was the potential for a conflict of interest as my trustee and Paul's lawyer/friend, but he thought he could manage...I tell you all of this because now I'm right in the middle between you and Paul, he explained. Then he informed me that Paul had moved off of 5th Avenue and left New York.—No, I exclaimed, where did he go? Tim said that he was not authorized to tell me. But he's my brother, I interjected, I need to know! Tim seemed to hesitate before he said that he didn't know exactly where Paul went, he just had his new email address, which he couldn't give me. But he has patients, a full-time practice! He can't just leave!

Tim seemed to feel how upset I was. He gave me a concerned look and continued to tell me that Paul had closed his practice as well and had asked him, Tim, to hand over a list of his patients to a senior analyst at his institute, so that a group of colleagues could organize the referrals. Now I was totally horrified! He didn't even tell his patients in person...? He went away without saying goodbye? I was furious! I was devastated! This all felt so wrong...wrong, wrong, wrong! Tim moved a bit away from my anger and said: I'm sorry, Ann, I really am!

This will never end, I thought, I'm in the middle of an awful disaster, and on top of it all I've involuntarily co-created it. Had I not talked with Paul, maybe Chris would still be alive, and Paul would still be in town, and his patients would continue their analyses with him instead of being confronted with the fact that the one person they had trusted the most was suddenly gone—a loss as sudden, radical, and incomprehensible as death... and maybe Paul was dead, maybe he had committed suicide— feeling he didn't deserve to live any longer, he'd put a heavy stone around his neck and plunged into Hudson River never to come up again—or ashamed to his bones, he'd jumped from the George Washington Bridge in the blackest pit of night with no eyes around to see him—all alone he'd leapt out of his life after making arrangements with Tim that no one other than him would ever know about! No, that couldn't be, that wasn't Paul! Rather, he had panicked and run off like a murderer rushes from the scene of a crime. Was he so afraid of losing his license through an ethical investigation that he'd selfishly decided to sneak away, disappear, and restart his analytic practice elsewhere? But maybe Paul, heartbroken over the loss of Chris, had gone mad with fear and desperation, thinking his days were over...How is he? I finally asked.

Tim seemed again careful in choosing his words when he answered: As far as I know he is doing okay. He called me last night, and he seemed—let's say: well composed. I'm not sure that I should tell you this, but yes, he is willing to adapt to his new life...What does that mean, I wondered, what new life? Can he just go elsewhere and shake off the shambles? And why had he not written me a word? Had he mistaken my silent departure in the morning after our last night as a sign that I didn't want to have anything to do with him? But that's not what I said, and not what I meant! No word for me? I tried, but Tim only shook his head. Please, tell him to contact me!

Instead of a response Tim said: There is something else: Paul asked me to represent him in all issues regarding his inheritance at the opening of Eddie's will, and I agreed to help him in that way. This is not directly related to your trust issues, but you see that it can get complicated, and so we have to think about how to handle these things...*We have to think about it?* Why hadn't *he* thought about it first? I was appalled! How could Tim allow Paul to snatch him up, he, who was *my* trustee and was supposed to work for *my* interests? What a mess! And Paul had coldly calculated to cash in on our father's inheritance! But after all that happened, did he still deserve anything at all? To pay out his share of *FIXIT* could break up the company, something my father wouldn't have wanted and certainly not for Paul's sake! I hadn't thought that through, but I had been musing on a vague idea about the three of us, Paul, Issy, and me, somehow agreeing to continue *FIXIT*, perhaps with me running it, should I decide to return to Cologne. And this option—*my future!*—could be thwarted if Paul wanted to cash in on his share. Maybe Paul should be excluded from inheriting anything at all! I needed legal advice on that, but now of course I couldn't talk with Tim anymore, not about any of these thoughts. I would have to get my own lawyer.

I have to go, I abruptly said. Tim gave me an insecure look but didn't object. He simply handed me an envelope. These are the keys to your 5th Avenue condo. You may want to go there and look at it, he suggested, there is no rush, but eventually you'll have to decide what to do with it, and of course I will help you, anytime, if you want...I took the keys and got up. I'll be in touch, I said. Good, Tim responded, and then added: By the way—I think you've met Teresa. She was Joyce's oldest friend, she became your father's friend, and I know that Paul was very close to her over all these years. Maybe she knows where Paul is...

And so I left thinking again of calling Teresa. Would she tell me? But why would I even want to know where Paul went? Now I'm so angry that I want nothing to do with him. Yes, I want to elbow him out of my father's inheritance! I would split it between Issy and me, and given all I did for our father, actually *I* am the only one who really deserves anything. Issy basically just called

379

our father on his birthdays and on holidays, and Paul had no contact with him over all these years—he may have even killed him in their last conversation—who knows what really went on between the two of them! In fact it was only I who always cared for our father through the years! So I should at least be privileged. Yes, all of a sudden I clearly felt I should be the one to decide about *FIXIT* and all the rest...! This thought jumped into my head like a mean, vengeful demon flashing a knife, ready to bump off brother Paul with a good volley of stabs...Yes, I had to fight him off, I thought, were he ever to return from hiding in *Bongo Bongo Land*!—Still I wanted to know where he was.

And so I finally called Teresa, who immediately invited me for tea. It was a beautiful Sunday at the end of April, and I briefly thought of bringing her a bunch of tulips but then decided against it—next time. She had left her door a crack open so that I could enter right away. Teresa? I called into the narrow hallway, and she immediately responded: Yes! Please, come in and then lock the door twice, I'm back here in the living room. The hallway was cluttered with bookshelves on both sides, an overloaded coatrack and a small chest of drawers with keys, gloves, letters, and some figurines on its top and a golden-framed mirror above it.

Teresa was sitting in a small wing chair, her legs up on a footstool wrapped in a woolen blanket. Next to her was a round table with a small lamp spreading its warm light onto a Chinese tray with two cups and a bowl of cookies.

Excuse me for not greeting you at the door, Teresa said with a friendly smile. A few weeks ago I had a little stroke, not too bad. I'm recovering. I'm not a quick walker right now, that's all. She looked much older than I remembered her from our brunch on Christmas in Rome, when I thought she was in her seventies—now she seemed to me well into her eighties. Oh, I'm sorry to hear that, I said, maybe I should have come at another time...? It's fine, Ann, she responded, just have a seat and pour us some tea. Is tea alright with you? What a lovely manner! I filled our cups with tea, sat down, and looked around. The room was small yet seemed spacious with nothing in it other than more of these densely packed bookshelves all around the walls and a small desk containing a laptop, a manuscript with a pair of glasses on it, and a white mug filled with pens and pencils next to an old-fashioned black telephone. Along the shelves several small spotlights were switched on, casting white circles on the beige Berber carpet that covered most of the wooden floor. I had just crossed Central Park in bright sunshine, and here Teresa needed electric lighting all day long, because the only window in this room looked straight onto another apartment building opposite a narrow street, leaving not more than a short-angle view onto Columbus Avenue. Maybe the sun never reaches down to Teresa's seventh floor and it's always darkish here, I thought. Still, Teresa's place offered a light and calm atmosphere, and as if I had finally arrived at where I needed to be, here and nowhere else, without being able to say why, I started to cry. With no particular thought in mind, tears were welling up, somehow beyond myself. I can't recall where my thoughts strayed. Teresa was comfortably sitting between her pillows, and I felt she would give me as much time as I needed.

Paul left town, I eventually said, and Teresa nodded. Yeah, it's a tragedy, all that happened—what a shame, she responded, clearly saddened but as if she had thought everything through. Are you a writer? I suddenly surprised myself asking her as I was looking again at the manuscript next to her laptop. I'm a literary critic, Teresa responded, but right now I'm enjoying writing a virtual autobiography—so yes, I'm also a writer, I suppose. Her modesty felt natural. The notion of a *virtual autobiography* intrigued me, and I asked her about it. Well, I'm not so much interested in what really happened in my life, I know that, she responded. I'm more interested in exploring what *could have* but did *not* happen even though I thought about and wanted it, opportunities I missed, efforts I shunned—that sort of thing. How would things be different now, had I made other choices? Of course this could be an endless project, if I tried to take it to all ends, but I won't. I portray my life more like a movement of awareness radiating to all sides—that's the virtual part—while returning to and passing again through certain crossroads along the trajectory of my life—and that's the autobiographical part. So it'll be an anatomy of skipped potentials, if you will, a revival of earlier thoughts, fantasies, and imaginations, all of which is an amazing experience...Teresa looked at me as if to make sure that I understood what she meant. Interesting, I said, and felt intrigued.

In some ways it is a continuation of my analysis that ended twelve years ago, Teresa continued. I wouldn't be able to write this book had I not gone through this long process that allowed me to finally understand myself. What an adventure! In fact, my analysis was one of the best things in my life! I was surprised how hard it was to talk about certain things that I had thought about a lot—still, to spell them out was sometimes very painful; and I was amazed to retrieve early experiences, ideas I had totally forgotten about, and to recognize how they had shaped my view of life. My analyst was a wonderful woman, quiet, sensitive, smart or rather wise, with a warm sense of humor. I trusted her, and I loved working with her. It helped me to finally come to grips with the things I had struggled with so long. A few months ago I read in the *Times* that she passed away at age 98. I miss her. I had often thought of going back to her for a few more years, simply because it was so interesting to explore my thoughts with her; she knew how to listen and how to respond... It's unlikely, but once in a while I think of getting on an analytic couch again someday.

Teresa's voice was a little hoarse, and as she continued to speak I wondered: was she briefly tearing up, mourning her analyst? Or was her voice worn off by her age, or had she just recovered from a recent cold? Nothing felt harsh in her way of talking to me—on the contrary, there seemed to be some forbearance, a gentle caution in weaving her tale as if she was speaking to a little girl, and that's perhaps what I felt like: a child expecting to hear a sage reciting some ancient myth.

Here she had lived, this old lady, for most of her life, sixty-some years, here, since she had turned twenty, and Stavros, her husband, two decades her senior, had carried her over the threshold after a beautiful wedding party in Central Park. *Oh, how much I love you!* Her white dress was sprinkled with green from the grass and red from the strawberry cake they had eaten without using spoons or hands, just with their loving lips, and as they plunged into the sweetness of their love's feast, everybody had applauded and laughed heartily. Then quietness fell over the newlyweds as they dropped their shoes and threw off the bridal veil and the silver bow tie before falling onto their bed, exhausted but so happy: from now on, forever Stavros & Teresa Castellanos.

With that her acting career had ended, closing the door to the path she had meant to stride with grace towards glory, but leaving it open for her best friend Joyce, who continued to rehearse her roles with her, and to carry whatever was on top of her life and stage—love and lust, passion and pathos, fear and fury—into Teresa's calm and more pondering world, enlivening the latter while offering respite to the former, because Joyce was always in need of a soothing voice. Joyce practiced her roles with me, here at this table, Teresa said, knocking on the wooden top and making the china jingle. She was sitting right where you are sitting now, she murmured, looking at me with a glimmer in her eyes as if I were Joyce, who had just flown in through her window and sat down in order to practice with her once more, maybe for her last performance. If you were Joyce, *now* I would finally tell you all I never told her. I would feel, *now you need to know the truth*. The truth hurts, it's never comfortable, which is strange, isn't it? So maybe all truth is tragedy…

In this case it's a tragedy in three acts, Teresa mused, and turned back to a time when Joyce in the beauty and glaze of her youth, and urged by grand expectations, was restlessly meandering through her days, hungry for opportunities and eager to play the roles thrust upon her by mighty or handsome men in the name of art, poetry, and experimentation. Her life was play, and Broadway was her world, her only dream come true. Joyce was struggling, but she was happy whenever she was on stage. She worked hard, really hard, and it started to pay off. She was the only one from her acting class who got offers, sometimes even two at a time, so that she could pick and choose, while her classmates were happy to grab whatever they could catch on the fly. Joyce was ambitious. The more she seemed to make it on Broadway, the harder she worked!

Then the pregnancy! What a shock! What to do? And as Joyce despaired over the collapsing range of her options, time and again running into a dead-end of her imaginary self, and Larry, the originator of her unwanted fertilization, wavered between ridiculously priding himself for having fathered a child and furiously accusing Joyce for not taking better precautions, a silent fantasy crept up in Teresa's mind: what if *she* adopted Joyce's child? Later she would have her own children, for sure, but why not this one now? She never said a word about it, not to Joyce, not to Stavros—not even when the baby was born after twenty dolorous hours of labor, during which Teresa had held Joyce's hand, rubbed her back, and dabbed the beads of perspiration from her face, over and over, until with his mother's strenuous scream the baby rushed out of her and made his own first scream, sharp and shrill, a piercing call—and Teresa had not responded, not even then! She had watched Joyce, spellbound by her baby, her eyes wide open, absorbing and assimilating all of him in an almost defiant move of appropriation as time stood still for half an hour or so, truly still—and yet ran out. Maybe too fast! There, in the brutal white of the delivery ward, while waiting for a stranger from the adoption agency to enter and disrupt their lives, Teresa silently struggled with saying to Joyce: *Give him to me! Let me be his mother!* Could she say it? What would that do to their friendship? *To say, or not to say: that was the question!* Could her wish have preempted—or would it rather have encouraged Joyce to claim: *He is mine! I want to keep him!* None of this materialized. No word was spoken. The agency person came. Teresa took the baby from Joyce, held him and saw him closely for the longest fraction of a minute, an image that remained with her as an unforgettable token, always retrievable and once in a while imposing itself with shocking clarity to her inner eye; and as she held him, she saw this little heart-shaped mole on his left foot, right below the big toe, and kissed it in a spontaneous gesture of delight... Then he was gone.

Why didn't I say it? Teresa marveled, and she kept marveling over this question ever since. Even after her daughter Penelope, called Penny, was born, she thought that Penny could have had a brother to play with, and was sorry for having deprived her little girl of this source of joy and companionship, her *virtual brother*; and certainly after Penny died from Leukemia at age eleven, and Teresa missed her, missed her so sorely, it felt like a double-loss as she also missed the boy she could have raised as her own, he, who would have been her comfort yet was not more than her *imaginary son*; and when after several miscarriages her growing age and increasing concerns for her health required her to give up trying to conceive, once more she missed him, *her lost son,* because that's what he had become in her mind, the first-born, who kept asking: *why didn't you keep me?* It might have stopped hurting, had she ever mustered the audacity to talk about it. But she treated these ideas as thoughts for the birds and blamed herself for being tenacious. Also, she didn't want to sadden Stavros, who wanted so much to give her another child and tended to blame himself when things went wrong. Only in her analysis, late in her life, could she say it aloud. I should have adopted Joyce's son!

That's what my analysis did for me, Teresa explained. It brought these things to life and then to rest. She sipped some tea and asked: Am I upsetting you? I just shook my head, being in the middle of a dream that I didn't want to end, a dream about Joyce and her fragile moods, her deep, unfulfilled yearning for something that spurred her performances to breathtaking heights and dizzying downfalls, a nerve-racking roller coaster that wore everybody down, her friends, her colleagues, her stage directors.

The second act starts right at the moment when Joyce gets badly panned for her performance as Jocasta in *Oedipus Rex*, Teresa said, and this coincidental merger of theatre and life is still stunning to me! Joyce, very unhappy about the criticism, is afraid her career is over, even thinks of killing herself if this turned out to be true, and at this early momentary low point of her career, in comes Eddie! He shows up, and miraculously Joyce gets over her wounds of public shaming, calms down, turns more sweet-tempered, more reliable, more tolerant, more able to work on rehearsals—it is as if her better self emerges, finds firm hold and settles down in her relationship with Eddie. He loves her, he supports her, and he shields her from all that isn't good for her. She calls, and Eddie is there, unobtrusively there to help, almost as if it isn't he but she herself who can get things done and get what she needs with her own faculties and skills—that's part of the miracle that folds its hands around both of their minds: Eddie makes Joyce feel better about herself, which makes him very happy. Does she love him? Well, yeah, as much as Joyce can love someone. She is grateful for him being at her side. Initially, Teresa has concerns about this relationship with Eddie being so much younger than Joyce; but wasn't Stavros about as much older than she? So who is she to make a fuss about that age difference? Instead she takes a deep breath and says to Stavros: *Good for them, Joyce and Eddie!*

Stavros and Eddie hit it off right away. They develop a deep connection, perhaps not unlike the father-son relationships that both missed out on when they were younger—Eddie having grown up solely with Aunt Margret, and Stavros, whose son from his first marriage had returned with his mother to Greece, to the light over the Gulf of Corinth and the mysterious shadows of Mount Parnassus, where she had opened a small hotel for the visitors of Delphi, and he had grown up to become an olive farmer, never interested in returning to see his father, visit New York, or renew his American passport. Long ago, long gone! Stavros and Eddie are eager to make up for all that. On Sunday mornings they run together in Central Park. They go fly-fishing in the Catskill Mountains. Stavros invests half a million dollars in the production of the *Magic Man*, and it's not only out of gratefulness but also for his economic know-how that Eddie invites Stavros to sit on the Board of *FIXIT.*

Then, two years into their friendship—and Teresa is still amazed that it took her so long to realize it—one summer weekend, the four go together to Westhampton Beach, and while being immersed in a heated political discussion that pounds its long trace of feisty footprints into the sand, Teresa suddenly sees the heart-shaped birthmark on Eddie's left foot! The foot is naked, and it is there! She sees it! That particular shape! How many people in the world have a mother's mark looking like this and exactly at this spot? Tell me! She is speechless! Oh my god, she thinks, and the heated debate around her falls silent, and she can only think: *he's her son, he's her son—Eddie—he's her son!* After a while Stavros notices Teresa's withdrawal and says, I think we've lost Teresa—guess we've exhausted the topic! Teresa stands still and is on the brink of blurting it out, when Eddie looks at her and gives her the sweetest and most innocent smile asking: okay, Teresa, what would you like us to talk about? You tell us!

She can only shake her head, she's mute. Had I adopted him, we would not be in this situation now, she thinks, and keeps shaking her head, indicating that she doesn't want to say anything. They turn around and stroll back. Stavros puts his arm around her shoulder and she snuggles at his side, needing his warmth and strength to think this through, my god, think this through before saying one single word! The walk back isn't long enough to think it through, she needs more time, days and weeks, and still she can't come to a convincing conclusion. What to do with this shocking discovery? *To say, or not to say: that is the question!* If she tells Joyce, will she destroy the one love-relationship that makes her happy? If she tells her, will Joyce be so upset and outraged with her that she will turn away from her? And if she tells Stavros, will he be so disgusted with Joyce and Eddie that he will break with both and lose his new filial friend? Will her word destroy all the four of them and all they now enjoy together?

Teresa is tortured by these questions and sinks into bed with pneumonia while Joyce gets herself into *A Streetcar Named Desire* and travels as Blanche around the country, a journey requiring lots of trips by bus from city to city, lots of moving in and out of hotels, and lots of brief rehearsals. Joyce is so preoccupied that she lacks the time to call Teresa, what a relief! In her bed Teresa races through feverish dreams, trying to flee from having to watch how Joyce struggles to hang herself with the beautiful silk scarf that Teresa once gave her as a present, but wherever Teresa turns, Joyce is right in front of her, wobbling on a chair with the scarf around her neck— *help!*—and Eddie is glued to the background and makes no move—*help!*—and Teresa wakes up, all agitated, and Stavros strokes her hand and tells her that it was a nightmare, just a nightmare! And it is a nightmare! Even if she doesn't close her eyes, which she is now afraid to do, she always sees Eddie's blue eyes trustingly looking at her, sees the sweet smile of this kind, earnest, and steady young man, who wants nothing but to make things right for Joyce and bends over backwards to accommodate her erratic personality—and should all of this have been in vain, even turn out to sound the death knell for her? What will the truth do to them once their love has turned into horror? Will they commit suicide? Can they still find a way into a mother-son relationship after all the erotic passion they've mutually enjoyed...? Will they lose each other again? But what if Teresa keeps her secret? What if she lets them continue to have what they have—will they remain happy? So far only she knows!

Joyce returns from her exhausting tour, and Teresa has recovered from pneumonia without having come to a conclusive answer yet, but the four of them resume their mutual visits and beloved routines, and the longer they are doing this the less these questions seem in need of a quick answer. It is as if this poignant discovery subtly pales, fades into something familiar and transparent, a *human condition*, almost beyond anybody's control—not quite so, if she really thinks about it, but she has to think about other things as well, so why should she bring this up? Joyce and Eddie enjoy each other, and in the end, who knows whether Joyce really is Eddie's birthmother, maybe there are two people in this world who happen to have the same mole without having anything to do with each other. Eddie might just be Eddie.

Is Teresa talking about my real father? Or is this just fiction, a tentative edition of her life? You see, Teresa says, virtual autobiography reaches into lost land, it is driven by guilt, grief, and yen. Would I have told them what I saw, had I anticipated the third and final act of this tragedy? Yes, I'm sure I would have! But then again, why would I have drawn the line then and not sooner? What kind of morale is that?

Through Teresa's window I could look into an illuminated apartment in the building on the other side of the street. A man and a woman were walking back and forth between the kitchen and the dining room, cleaning the table after an early supper they had unknowingly offered for me to watch almost as a distraction from Teresa's haunting tale, and after all was done, the man and the woman left the room, they disappeared, and I thought they went into their dark room to make love...

That's what Teresa tells me: Joyce needs to make love, because this is what reassures her that she is still desirable; and Eddie wants to make love in order to give her a baby, hoping it would lift her depressive moods, because he thinks that the reason for her misery is the loss of her firstborn son. Who would have thought that it would work? Teresa was silently concerned about this possibility, but given Joyce's age she quickly dismissed it. Eddie didn't care about Joyce's age. Replacement was the remedy! He just kept trying and hoped eventually it might work. And, surprisingly enough, it did, Joyce became pregnant again! Actually, she was rather shocked and not at all sure that she wanted this baby. Eddie was more enthused and urged her to try keeping it. He pledged his support whenever necessary. He promised her that her career wouldn't suffer; on the contrary, he suggested, she would thrive to new highs once she could add maternal depth to her repertoire. In the end, that was the most convincing argument for Joyce. But she demanded to keep it secret for as long as possible. So Teresa didn't know about her pregnancy until Joyce had to go and stay in the hospital in order to hold on to the fetus, and then of course it was already too late. *To say, or not to say: that wasn't the question any longer!* All Teresa could do was to seal the truth in her chest and hope the baby would be healthy!

But to her own surprise, Teresa couldn't bring herself to visit Joyce in the hospital. When Eddie had first called her with the news, she was totally taken aback! She managed to wish good luck and lightly promised to soon pay Joyce a visit, but she knew right away that she couldn't make good on it. She could hardly even think of it! A deep abyss had opened between her and her friend, and there was nothing that could bridge her fear and aversion to looking Joyce in the eyes and seeing the dome of her pregnancy. In real life there was always something else going on. More often than previously, Teresa helped out with taking care of Paul on the weekends, which was a great relief for Eddie, and he thanked her for it. Thus her devotion to their friendship seemed to continue. However, she couldn't talk with Joyce. Again and again Eddie called Teresa, reminding and eventually outright begging her to contact Joyce—but Teresa couldn't do it, she couldn't! She certainly tried. She sat down next to her phone, determined to make this call, she even wrote down some light-hearted words to say to Joyce, but she never called her! Next to the abyss of shame and disgust, an insurmountable wall of guilt had risen around her, and this wall was as tight as the secret it enshrined. The truth had become a towering prison with a lone inmate, Teresa, shackled by not having disclosed to Joyce what she had known all along and what she would have owed her: the truth. What a betrayal of her oldest friend! How could she have left her in the dark?

She never saw Joyce again, and never again did she speak a word to her. Joyce couldn't understand! Had she offended Teresa?

Was Teresa sick? How could Teresa be too busy to visit her in the hospital—even once? Eventually she concluded that Teresa was jealous and hurt that she, Joyce, could have another baby while Teresa had tried and always failed. Eddie told Teresa about Joyce's allegation in one of his last efforts to bring her to visit Joyce, if only to correct this false interpretation of her absence. But Teresa didn't. It pained her that Joyce would think so, but she silently welcomed this rather benign supposition as a way out. May she be seen as the jealous one—it seemed a minor price to pay for hiding the awful truth. It was the darkest time in Teresa's life.

When Eddie called to inform her of the birth of his daughter, she could barely aspirate some congratulatory words into the phone. Stavros went out with Eddie that night. Over a nice steak-dinner they emptied two bottles of wine and talked men's talk, while Joyce and Teresa, each on her own, their eyes wide open into the night over Manhattan, worried about the baby's and their own futures. Had Joyce ever known or guessed who fathered her daughter? Did she care? Did she suspect and hide it? Why would she have come up with the idea of calling her little girl *Antigone*? Didn't that tell it all? Eddie vigorously objected and modified the name to Antje, so maybe he too almost knew and hence so fiercely denied that his baby girl was an *Antigone*—not just Antje.

Teresa thoughtfully shook her head, all lost in her past that she was spreading out in front of me. But what was she talking about, and who was this all about? Maybe she was talking about Joyce, my granny, but she couldn't possibly be talking about me...Or was she? No, it's not about me, it's merely fiction. Still, the end of this tragedy doesn't play out on stage. After having briefly glanced at her newborn baby daughter, Joyce falls into a state of utter absence. They call it *post- partum depression*. It'll pass, the midwife says. It's the hormones, the doctors suggest. It's a girl, and it was supposed to be a boy, Eddie thinks, that's what it is...But so what! She may be the wrong child, but he still loves little Ann, he instantaneously does, whereas Joyce doesn't want to even touch her and recoils whenever he puts the baby in her arms. More and more she withdrawals, and eventually she takes flight in the empty wings of an imaginary castle, where she is wandering from door to door, a lost soul, a tired bird, vaguely tapping on closed windows, a hopeless gesture without much meaning, maybe not more than a recurrent reflex after an endless line of failed attempts, *tap-tap, tap-tap*—until one day she sees a *school bus* down there, in yellow, with big black letters on its side-panel reading *s-c-h-o-o-l—b-u-s*, and it's a long, long while ago that she has last seen this school bus, and she gets all excited, the window opens, and she rushes down to reach it before it's gone...

Through the crash hole in the splintered glass the winds are howling horribly, boisterous rain scourges and wheezes in, pouring gray puddles onto the white leather sofa, a draft slams a door shut, and in comes Eddie, who stands there, a letter in his hand, and howls, howls his horror over the crash of his doomed world, howls out into the bleeding sky. It was in the living room. It was right after she jumped. It was because he forgot to take his keys, and the nanny went to open the door for him. *It was his fault*. Stavros said it was *not* his fault, it was because Joyce was too old to have another child, her baby girl took her life, *it was her fault*, but of course it wasn't her fault either. And Teresa hadn't spoken to Joyce nor seen her when she was so depressed, and that may have been part of it, or at least she could have averted the worst, thus *it was Teresa's fault*, wasn't it? Who knows! The day after the jump, Stavros asked Teresa: Would you want to raise Joyce's girl? Teresa only shook her head: *no—no!—NO,* she almost yelled at him. I was just asking, Stavros mumbled.

Anyway, Eddie would never have given his baby away! He loved little Ann, and to his utmost surprise, only a few days after Joyce's death he surged out of the thin but all-pervading fog that had clouded his mind during all these years, these difficult years with Joyce, and started to clearly think about the future. His good pragmatic side kicked in. He thought of Janis. Would she agree to try life with him and his two children? He liked her already, and he felt he could eventually love her. So if she loved him and his children, together they could start over. Yes, they would make it, he felt—but not on 5th Avenue, impossible, and not in New York, no! When Stavros heard that Eddie wanted to move to Cologne, he tried every argument to talk him out of it. Nothing helped. Eddie, Janis, Paul and Ann left before the fall winds had swept the last leaves from the lawns of Central Park. Stavros broke with Eddie and never talked with him again.

Only Teresa kept in contact. Once in a while they saw each other when she travelled to Europe. It was as if both wanted to stay connected with their shared past, albeit without ever touching it. And so at last Eddie had become Teresa's son anyway, sort of. They sat together in Europe's hotel bars, restaurants, and street cafes, and they talked together about work, art, and life, everything except the very personal, intimate issues, just as most mothers talk with their sons when they are grownups. As if bound by an unsaid pact, they never spoke about Joyce, Paul, Ann, or Stavros: these four people remained taboo in their conversations. It took Teresa many years before she dared to transgress this silent prohibition and ask Eddie this simple question: *How is Ann doing?* Eddie responded: *Fine, she is doing very well!* And when Teresa added: *I hope to meet her sometime...* he said *yes*, but it never happened—not before last Christmas in Rome.

There is no tea left in our cups. The cookies are untouched. The lights in the apartment opposite the street have gone out. Have I fallen asleep? Have I just dreamt it all? No, this isn't my dream. But where is Teresa? She seems to be gone—maybe she went to the bathroom? I too need to go to the bathroom. So I get up and go through a door, which leads to a small dining room with an

398

adjacent kitchenette, all neat and clean, and then I open the next door, but this isn't the bathroom either, it is Theresa's bedroom with a queen-size bed, two side-tables with dimmed lighting on it, a framed wedding picture on the one, a photo of a gently smiling older man on the other, next to which a man's dark suit is hanging on the outside of a closet. Hadn't Teresa told me that her husband died fifteen years ago after a lovely evening they'd spent first going to a Broadway show, then having dinner at their favorite restaurant, then slowly strolling home, arms linked, and finally they had gone to sleep as usual—*good night my dear*—and in his sleep Stavros, ninety-two years old and still a very interesting man, had died, quietly, peacefully, and maybe in the middle of a beautiful dream...Had she kept his suit hanging there all these years? Had she needed his male presence to continue through his fine broad-shouldered jacket? Or did she have a boyfriend, a new lover who had settled into her life, appreciating the maturity and warmth of her personality, the riches of her mind, and also the sensuality and responsiveness of her body, a man her age who soon would come here to sleep with her? There is a strange noise under the bed as if something is moving, perhaps a cat...or what? I bend down and look under her bed, and there I see Teresa, shrunken, a tiny dwarf, sitting there, strangely waving her hand, as if she were saying: *get out of my bedroom, leave, go away!* And this makes me so mad, all of a sudden I'm full of rage, and furiously I scream at her: *I'm not Joyce, I'm Ann, Antje, do you get it, finally get it? So why did you tell me all of this? Why did I need to know? Did it make YOU feel better to finally have said it? And what am I supposed to do with this now? Shall I be disgusted for the rest of my life over my granny being my mother, my mother and my granny—or what? Why didn't you leave it alone? Why didn't you keep your secret, once you'd decided to make it yours, even though it never belonged to you? So why did you stick it to me now? I don't want your secret! I don't believe your story! It's fabricated, it's fiction, nothing else! And it's your fault, your fault! You ruined my family! You've ruined Joyce's and Eddie's life, and now you want to ruin mine! I hate you, I hate you all! I hate you for planting this story in my head, I won't allow it to grow, I will chop every little offshoot down, hack it short, do you understand, do you hear me? Go away, you go away, you...!* Teresa squints under the barrage of my words; she pulls up her knees to her chin and protectively holds her arms over her head, realizing that I am out of my mind and am about to senselessly beat up on her and pay her back for all that her lack of courage has done to us...I'm exhausted, I'm sweating, I sink down on her bed, spreading my arms and legs; circles are dancing at the ceiling and I am pulled up and sucked in and am circling around with them, twirling around and around, and I'm getting all dizzy, but there is no way out of this, no way, never ever...

I'm glad you came, Teresa said after what seemed to have been a long silence separating our worlds and reestablishing us as the two strangers we are to each other, the two who just met. I know, what I told you is a lot, she admits. But I believe you can handle it. Had you not called me I would *not* have reached out to you, but you did. You came because you wanted me to tell you something, so I decided to tell you. I don't know whether this was right or wrong or too early. In the past I waited, and then it seemed too late. Tonight I may have another stroke that could mute me forever. That's why I decided not to wait. My whole history taught me it is better to know than not to know the truth. The late albeit complicated answer to my question is: *it is better to say than not to say*. I thought that as a psychoanalyst, you would agree. That's why I told you. I believe you should know and live with the truth.

I looked at her and knew she was right. This was the moment, this was my chance, and maybe my only one. Did my father know? I asked her. Teresa averted my eyes and seemed to think for a moment before she responded: I don't know for sure, but I think he didn't. He received a letter from the adoption agent the day Joyce jumped. At the time he thought this letter could have saved her life. But it would have killed her one way or other. Eddie said he didn't open the letter, so I don't think he knew, because I never told him!

Somehow it comforts me to think that my father didn't know—know...what!—How hard is it to think it, let alone to spell it out, this terrible word—Teresa didn't mention it, not even once did she say that Eddie committed incest! But that's what it was—and for him to know—he might as well have committed suicide—did he? So now I'm the only one in my family who knows? I wondered. Teresa shook her head. No, Paul knows, and he's known for a long time. Two days ago, just before he left town,

Paul came to visit me, not only to say goodbye, but also to tell me his secret. There was another letter from this adoption agent that arrived a day later at 5th Avenue. It seemed to have been a copy of the one your father received at his *FIXIT* office. Paul picked it up with the mail, and for some reason he kept it for himself. He didn't open it right away, it slipped into his things and got sort of forgotten. Eventually though he opened it, and then he realized what it was. It shocked him, he said, but at times it also justified his contempt for his father. Still, he always felt he couldn't tell Eddie, it would have destroyed him—and that's not what he wanted. But before he left town, he wanted me to know about the secret connection between Joyce and Eddie. He asked me if I had known. I pretended that I hadn't. I denied it! I feel terrible about it. I lied to him. I don't quite understand why, and I regretted it immediately. I think he would have appreciated my honesty. Anyway, he left it up to me to tell you or not tell you. He was sure you would come to see me; he said: *She's rather alone here in New York, so she will need you. Tell her or don't tell her. You'll know what's best! You always make the right decisions!* He had no idea how wrong he was. So secrecy goes on. He doesn't know that I knew it all along. And now when you see him again, you may tell him or not, it'll be up to you to decide.

Night had fallen and I made moves to leave, so Teresa added: Here, I have something for you. It's from Joyce—actually it's from Joyce's grandmother, who gave it to Joyce's mother, who gave it to Joyce when she went to New York to become an actress. If you want to come to see me again I will tell you

402

everything Joyce told me about her mother and her grandmother, which should be your maternal great-grandmother or...I'm getting confused here. But since we never know what the future holds for us, I want to give it to you now. She handed me a small paper box, and when I opened it I saw the golden brooch with the red stone she had worn at our Christmas brunch. You wore this in Rome, I said, and she smiled. Yes, actually I anticipated seeing you at the Hassler, and that's why I put it on. I noticed that you looked at it and thought it would look nice on you. Joyce gave it to me when Penny died, because for some reason Penny loved this brooch, and she decorated every person in her drawings with this special brooch. Joyce gave it to me so that I could wear something Penny loved. It was a sweet gesture. I can still see her wearing it, always placing it at the right spot, with style and even a sense of cheekiness—she had an unusual sense for beauty, quite special...Now it's time for you to have it. I thanked her. I was moved but didn't quite know yet what to think of it. I'll come back soon, I said. That would be lovely, Teresa responded, and waved goodbye.

HAYDEN

When I entered the lobby, Homer, the doorman, got up from behind his desk, where he had been working at his computer. Good morning, Ms. Stark, he said. I haven't seen you since that terrible night...my condolences! I thanked him, and as I was foraging in my purse to dig out the key to my condo, I found myself fighting a sudden surge of tears. Homer seemed to notice. Softly he said, Mr. Moore let me know that you would come one of these days to look at your condo. Shall I take you, or do you know your way...? His words felt like a warm hug. I'm fine, thank you! I responded. Homer handed me a card and explained: You can call this number day and night, there will always be me or someone else to respond. How nice, I thought, and stepped into the elevator, which he had opened for me. Thank you! I said again, and he answered: You are very welcome!

Then silence. The old elevator slowly sauntered upwards. A sweet scent like from an old lady's perfume lingered in the small mahogany box. Perhaps there were people in this building who still remembered my father and Joyce when they first came here, I wondered...*The elevator carries a maximum of three people*, I read on the brazen panel with the shining buttons for the building's 18 floors. They all touched number *10*—Joyce, my father, Paul, Janis, and maybe even little Theo...and now *I* touched it as well. I ran my fingers over the polished star with the number *10.* Then the elevator abruptly stopped, the door slid open, and I stepped out. The hallway lay silent, its lights were dimmed. Nobody heard me as I went past the doors of my unknown neighbors. In front of my own door I suddenly felt like a thief. To use this key for the first time was like intruding into someone else's place, a bit exciting and as if forbidden. What if I caught someone in there by surprise...? Nonsense! This condo is mine—at least on paper! Will I ever appropriate it? Will I ever live here?

With a soft click the door opened to the small foyer that extended its reach into the big living room—now completely empty. What a lonesome space! There was nothing! I hadn't expected it to be so empty...As I walked towards the living room my footsteps creaked on the naked wooden floor. The wallpaper looked run down with the blank squares of lost pictures darkly framed by the dust of time. Was this the wallpaper once chosen by Joyce or Eddie? Had Paul just painted it over and over? Parts of it were ripped off or loosened, so the walls would all need to be stripped. Maybe something ancient will emerge under these layers of former lives, a drawing that little Theo had slipped into a crack, a secret he had buried there and then forgotten? Or a note from Joyce's lover, something he wrote down for her before he vanished from her life? Or even some trace from a previous owner...? All these people who had lived right here, would I now be the next in line...?

The door to the dark room was half closed, and when I pushed it open, I heard a soft tinkle—*surprise*—a small silver whistle was hanging on the inside doorknob! Paul's silver whistle! He always carried a silver whistle, either on a leather band around his neck, on his keyring, or clipped to a belt loop of his pants. I don't know what it means to him...Had he forgotten it or left it on purpose, as a gift for me? I picked it up. I blew the whistle. The shrill sound gave me goosebumps—instantaneously it opened up all the sadness within me. *Paul! What did I do to you...? What did you do to yourself...? What did we do to you...? What did you do to us?* All these questions...! With the whistle in my fist I turned around, momentarily looked into the bathroom—yellow spots on the marble desktop over the sink, the silver frame of the mirror chipped off at the edges, a brownish oval stain baked into the enamel coating of the bathtub right where the faucet was dripping...all of it needed to be fixed! Only briefly I glanced into the bedroom that had been Paul's study, a small room with a small window, an opening more for air than for light, looking onto the brick wall of the neighboring building less than ten feet away, just enough for the iron fire escape.

But all this light in the living room! I stepped to the middle window and looked out over Central Park. Here they had been sitting, my father and my mother, watching people enjoy a stroll or head towards the Met or the Guggenheim in all weather and seasons, day and night—life in Manhattan. Here they were sitting with a glass of wine, talking about this and that, present affairs, future plans, and then without really knowing why, Eddie would turn the conversation to the far removed past, yes, almost as if he was looking for something of his own in Joyce's memories. That's what I'm thinking now. That's how I think it could have been! And Joyce liked to step into the treasure trove of these early years when she was young and antsy with anticipation, thinking *oh, what will be*...when she woke up in the morning. How little money she had in those days! She would sneak into the premiere parties on Broadway just to eat her fill; and she would serve tables in a French restaurant and secretly slip into her bag what the customers left behind until she got caught and was fired. These things felt so hard when they were happening, but how much freedom there was, how much hope, how romantic to have lived that life—and now...?

Then Joyce would have another glass of wine and talk about Larry and his art, and the artists around him who got together every night, mostly to drink and smoke pot and babble about whatever; but they never came to see any of her performances on Broadway, imagine, not once, she told Eddie, and sneered about Larry, who would fancy that she could fall in love with him, but what was he thinking! Unbelievable! And when she got pregnant, just by accident and out of the goodness of her heart, he behaved like an idiot, really! However, she was so young at the time, unbelievably young, and when she later thought about it, much later of course, she sometimes regretted not having kept the baby and raised her son. Despite it all, maybe she could have managed, she mused; and Eddie would be highly attentive and a bit spellbound, and pour her some more wine to hear some more of these old stories as they moved and changed with her wavering memories. Where might he be *now*, Joyce would wonder, what might he be doing *now*, she would marvel, and how might he look *now*, she would ponder. And then she would describe the little baby that she had given birth to, his dark wet hair, chubby cheeks, little clenched fists, big head over his slim body—*now* for sure he's tall and slender, she would intersperse—and most of all his big eyes, big blue eyes, Joyce would emphasize, and his eyes looked into hers as if diving deep—but babies are shortsighted and can't really see, she would add, and still she was convinced he saw her as well as she saw him—so well did she see him that she could claim: *I would recognize him amongst a million people, immediately!* And Eddie would sit there, his heart pounding for no discernible reason, he thought, or did his eyes see more than he knew they did? Maybe it was subtle, as if his skin was merely responding to something subliminal,

408

something like a strange electricity, an aura around Joyce, a subtle flurry of vibes that she brought into the room as soon as she entered and that maybe only he would sense and notice when it was there, amongst a million people he would sense it, like a scintillation or an aroma, unique and still elusive.

Sometimes when Joyce had finished talking, Eddie would try to tell her in return how Aunt Margret had raised him with the mindset of a decent middle-class person, taught him to be an orderly, reliable good student, and when Joyce would yawn, he would move over to stories about his more artistic parents, episodes he couldn't remember but had cobbled together from the bits and pieces that Aunt Margret had provided, and scenes that Eddie's fantasy had made up: two bohemian writers, existentialists in the grip of their romantic albeit dark visions, lost in the cracks of the restrained habits of those self-righteous times. Approvingly Joyce would nod and say: *We are tarred with the same brush, that's why we love each other*. What was that supposed to mean?

Joyce could be my mother, Eddie sometimes thought, and as if picking up on it, Joyce would say, *my son would be about your age, isn't that funny?* It made her giggle, because it was so funny. When was he actually born? Eddie wanted to know. I can't remember exactly, Joyce would say, I'm so bad with numbers! 1952, she then decided. But the week before she had said 1950, and the following week she was sure it was 1951, so Eddie never quite knew—or did he anyway? There were moments when he thought she was like his mother, and this idea almost killed him. Not once would he consider incest, no, his thoughts would never stumble towards even the slightest degree of concreteness. However, to imagine that his mother could have been as lost, fragile, and restless as Joyce was, deeply saddened him! Maybe what I do for Joyce, my father did for my mother, Eddie may have thought, and that's how everybody looks out for somebody. We help out where we can, which is a good thing. Then his thoughts may have moved on to wondering: How would it be with Joyce later on, let's say in ten or twenty years? Would he still feel attracted to her, or would her aging body turn her into a sickly woman, an Aunt Margret, who needed to be taken care of—ugh, this again...? Quickly he would push these images out of his mind. Maybe I'll be dead long before then, he may have thought, so why worry now?—But see, father, you did worry. In some of your more quiet nights, you may have guessed that Joyce was your mother, she could have been, and as it turned out, she was! You had this thread in your hands, but you dropped it, you didn't want to know. Or did you? Or maybe the adoption agent called you for a follow up a few days after she had sent the letters. Then you knew! Did you? And if you did, how would it have been for you to live with this truth all the time and all alone? How would you have decided to not tell anybody, and most importantly to not tell me? Were you too ashamed of yourself, or too worried about me? Or did you choose to forget?

I opened the window, a fresh breeze rushed in, and I looked down, the whole way Joyce went down after her jump—what a dizzying abyss! Homer was standing on the street, just having stopped a cab for a man who seemed to live here; he lightly tapped Homer's shoulder before getting into the cab. Someday I will meet a man, a man about my age, we will go out on dates, we will love each other, and eventually start thinking about having children, and then he will ask me about my family. What can I say...? Shall I say: my mother committed suicide, I was raised by a lovely stepmother who also killed herself, because my one half-brother Paul killed my other half-brother Theo, of course unintentionally, but how unintentional is anything anyway—and would I then top this already gruesome account by confessing that my father, who was a decent, cultured, caring, responsible, interesting, and successful man, who all in all raised me well and supported my development every step of my way...would I then say that he fathered me with his own mother—of course unknowingly, but how little can we ever pretend to ourselves to not know anyway—so that this woman turned out to be at once my mother and my grandmother, which made my father simultaneously my oldest brother—Eddie? How sickening! How confusing!

I closed the window and sat on the floor. It all felt so miserable, so complicated, so impossible! Will I remain alone with this for the rest of my life?—But my past is not all I am! My family is not all I am! I am who *I* am, or am I not? I'm more than the child of an unconscious incest! I'm more than the bland caretaker of my father! I'm more than a sister who threw dirt on her brother. I am many other things...I am 32 years old, I am alive, I am a psychologist, and I want to have a future with a man, raise children...With this history I should become a psychoanalyst after all...

Then I saw something that first appeared to be just a shadow on the wall, but too solid for a mere shadow, and as I stepped closer the shadow turned into a picture frame hanging in a niche behind the window—it was Janis' photo of the little girl sticking her tongue out at the customs control officer at JFK, the first photo she took when she arrived in New York! I hadn't seen it in so many years! Did Paul miss it when he moved out in a hurry? Or did he leave it here for me? I looked at it closely. What a defiant look! Behind her back she held her rag doll that was hanging head down from her right fist. What was this little girl thinking? Was she afraid the customs control officer would not allow her doll into the country? He grinned, or did he threaten her by baring his teeth? I remembered exactly where it hung at home: next to the front door over a small shelf where we used to drop our keys and the mail. After Janis had taken the picture with her, my father replaced it with a small mirror. When going out I used to look into this mirror and briefly stick my tongue out to myself. Now I had this picture back. *Hi Janis! What an insubordinate little person you were!*

Janis...she'd been so quiet and careful in her way of handling the practical things in our life. She had a dry and safe attitude

412

about almost everything: making meals, helping us with our homework, organizing family events...She was patient with us when we were late, when something broke, when we forgot: she accepted that these things happen. She only grew angry when we interfered with the three hours a day she reserved for her work, for going out with her camera to take pictures, or working on the enlargements of her photos in the dark room, or preparing her seminars, or strolling through the galleries to see the new exhibitions in town. I always thought, I'm a bit like she is, I inherited her calm attitude towards life, and this remains true, even though I don't carry her genes. She knew the whole time that she wasn't my mother, but she never made me feel that, she became and really was my mother—and she'll always be my mother even though she went away...

The doorbell rang. It was Homer with a big bunch of flowers, fortunately delivered in a vase, because there wouldn't be a vase in this empty place. What a surprise! Thank you! I said, and again teared up, overwhelmed by this lovely gesture, whoever did this. Do you need anything else? Homer asked me. No, I'm fine, I really am, I reassured him. He smiled and left, closing the door behind him. In the kitchenette I ripped off the paper. White lilies, big, beautiful lilies! I put the vase in the middle of the empty living room floor. At once the room didn't look so empty anymore. Then I opened the small envelope and read the card: *Welcome to 5th Avenue! May these flowers indicate a good start! Tim.* It just made me cry. Everything makes me cry these days! Wasn't that sweet? *Welcome to 5th*

Avenue! May these flowers indicate a good start! Tim. Maybe he felt sorry for having become part of this mess. I looked at the lilies. Eventually they would fill the whole condo with their strong sweet fragrance!

On my fifth birthday my father brought me a little bunch of small pink roses. I was so proud that my father would bring me roses! I had seen him giving roses to my mother on their anniversary, and it was the only time he brought me roses. That day he also invited me to go out with him for an ice cream. I wore my new blue-and-white-striped summer dress and my white shoes without socks, I still remember every detail, and I felt I could never be happier than that! My joy wasn't even ruined when a scoop of chocolate ice cream dropped from my cone onto my lap. *Nobody is perfect,* the ice cream vendor said, and gave us a bit of mineral water to wash it off. It remained a beautiful day. When we came home, my mother had set the table for my birthday party, nine friends! I always had these lovely birthday parties, every year. Issy was different. She didn't like parties. Instead she usually picked one friend and went with her to a museum or to the zoo or to do something smart that my mother would prearrange for her...

My cell phone rang, I looked at the display, it was Hayden. *Hayden...!* I hesitated to pick it up, but then I did it anyway: Hello? Ann? Hayden! For a moment we both were speechless and felt awkward. Well, I'm back, Hayden then said, and since I kept waiting he explained: I'm back in New York. I came a

414

week ago. Currently I'm staying with Keith. I first wanted to fully arrive here, settle back into the city before calling you... Actually, I wasn't sure if you still want to see me...Do you? Did I want to see him again? It seemed so long ago that I was with Hayden, I didn't quite remember how it was to be with him if not complicated, but my heart was pounding. It's been so long...I said. Yes, he agreed, it's less than a year but it feels like ten. Was there anything I blamed him for? Maybe he had been right not to read my emails, or maybe he had read them in the meantime...? I wanted to ask him about it, but at the same time I didn't want to bring it up. Had he felt uncomfortable reading them, had he sensed something strange in the way I invented my past and later described my time in Tuscany? I hadn't sent him all of them, but even the pieces I emailed him could have revealed more of the underlying secret than I realized at the time. Now I wasn't so sure I wanted him to read any of this at all. But then to my own surprise I said: I'm near Central Park right now. If that works for you, we could meet—let's say—at our usual bench near the lake, do you remember? Hayden immediately responded: Sure, I do. That's actually perfect. I'm at the Apple Store, so I could be there in about ten minutes. And before pondering this idea any longer, we had a date, and off I went.

The summer breeze felt nice and freeing. Crossing 5th Avenue I nearly stumbled across a miniature poodle's leash when the little creature discovered a mate on the other side of the street and suddenly coming from my left darted straight ahead, only to abruptly stop, maybe belatedly realizing the size of this big

415

brown boxer that stood still, ambiguously prick-eared and softly growling, whereupon the amatory dwarf turned and quickly ran back to my right towards its old mistress. Oops! The dog owner apologized, unwound the leash around me, and scolded the little barker before walking on. I entered the park. What a great view and feeling, sun, warmth, and the freedom of leisurely time! I wished I was on rollerblades, swinging along with the joggers and bikers, easily speeding up against the wind and the weight of all memories...

And then I heard him call me from behind: Ann? I turned around. It was Hayden. Hayden...He smiled broadly, and I smiled too. Are you on your way to our bench? Can I walk with you? he asked. I nodded and felt confused. I'm so surprised, I stammered, all of a sudden you are here! Hayden looked funny as he stalked stiff as if on stilts, with his hands stuffed into his tight jeans pockets all but barring them from reaching out for me. Yeah, it does feel sudden, he agreed. Time is a strange companion... In these past months there were moments when I felt I couldn't wait to see you again; and there were others when I was sure I would never see you again. And even though it's been quite a while since I left New York, now that I've been back for a week, it almost feels like I was hardly ever gone. I was nervous about seeing you, but also curious. I itched to call, but I also wanted to think about how to reconnect. So I decided to give it some time before ringing you up. And now I have, and a few minutes later we're walking together in Central Park. It's as if the meantime just collapsed, totally amazing, isn't it?

416

Here he was again, Hayden, with his little philosophical quirks! Two policemen on high horses were riding past us, then turned left at a fork and disappeared behind the bushes. So much can happen in a year, I said. Hayden looked at me seriously. Very true, he said, and pointing to a beverage cart on his right he added: Wait, I'll get us some water. I watched him as he went over and talked with the soft drink seller. He wore the blue-and-red-checkered shirt I had given him for his birthday last year—had he picked it on purpose today or just by chance? The sleeves were rolled up to his elbows. The skin on his arms was tanned, a black sports watch had slipped below his wrist. He wore his brown hair shorter than he used to, it sparked off his head to all sides...He looked more slender, fitter, even younger, not eleven years older, rather my age—he looked really good! Hayden...!

He came back with two bottles of water and handed me one. Thanks! Silently we walked on, for a while surrounded by screaming children kicking a yellow ball along our way. Walking next to him, it was as if I was touched by a memory—or was it just a feeling of something familiar? I opened the bottle and drank a bit of the icy cold water. We arrived at our bench, and since an old couple was sitting there with two open lunch boxes at their sides, obviously intending to stay for a while, we strayed from the shady path, strolled out onto the lawn into the full brightness of the day, and lay down far away from everybody else, I on my back with my arms under my head, and Hayden next to me on his side, his head resting in his hand. He was looking at me—or was he just looking through me at something back in time? I closed my eyes, I enjoyed the sun's warmth on my face, and all I wanted was to listen to Hayden's soft voice as he started telling me about his summer in Buenos Aires in the middle of our winter.

It felt like he was living on a different planet, Hayden said, a strange place somewhere between an exterior and interior world. It was the time when he had these nightmares, he explained, the time when I had last called and hung up on him, which he hadn't really understood. But maybe I had sensed something about him, he wondered, because he was for a while in a state of mind that could easily have destroyed him—but in the end it didn't. Part of it may have been that he and his friends had grown a little tired of each other, he mused. After so many trips and concerts and being together all the time, they felt worn out, rather listless, and their improvisations had become increasingly uninspired, almost routine.

In Buenos Aires the audience was great, people seemed to like their gigs, so it went a bit better, but altogether he felt run down. Yet he loved strolling through the city—what a great city, and what good people, really good, beautiful inside and out...! Then the last evening: The performance of their final piece has meandered its long way through all the instrument's solos, and the last voices have died down under friendly applause. Mike, the trumpet player, suggests having a drink in one of the nearby tango clubs, just to chill out before going to sleep. It's a simple location, nothing touristic or fancy, an ordinary place where the local people go to dance. They order a bottle of wine. They watch the people on the dance floor. Nobody feels like talking. When the bottle is empty, Andy, the drummer, suggests going elsewhere, he doesn't like the place too much, he says. The others agree. Hayden wants to stay. He enjoys watching the dancers, and he doesn't care so much about drinking. Okay, the others say as they get up to leave, see you tomorrow, breakfast at eight.

Hayden stays sitting at the bar and looks over to the dance floor. A small band of elderly men in dark suits plays classical tango, serious and professional. They've been playing here for decades, he thinks, always here, night after night, five days a week, growing old together! He doesn't want to grow old with his buddies, no! His eyes follow the dancers as they move around the floor. How sophisticated these tango steps are, how skillful! The dancers walk, turn, link, dive, rise, and swirl around, every step accurate and right...an almost meticulous mastery of passion, poignant and powerful yet tightly restricted. Looking at them, a mysterious desire moves Hayden, something he faintly recognizes... Then his eyes catch a couple on the periphery of the crowd, both outstanding dancers: he a short stout man probably in his sixties, mustached with black-rimmed glasses and black shining hair glued to the back of his round head, a dark pinstriped suit and a tie in screaming red over his white shirt, in close embrace with a young woman, maybe in her early thirties, a bit taller than he, with short black hair and a white headscarf artfully wrapped around her shoulders over a tight black dress slit open along her left thigh. They dance with their eyes closed, all lost to their imagination, totally in sync with themselves and out of touch with everybody else. Not even once would they bump into any of the other couples around them! They dance as if they were all alone. They've done this forever, they always do this, they may not have much else to share, but this they have, their tango, their devotion, their language, their dream. He holds her, a firm grip around her upper body, which leans on his chest, and with her cheek on his she seems to surrender all self-determination to the fate of his unforeseeable will…

Hayden feels strangely provoked by their mastery. After three pieces there is a break. Everybody quickly returns to the tables to have a sip of water or wine. Hayden watches how the man brings the young woman to a table in the back of the room, there briefly indicating a bow as she sits down. Then he leaves, disappears in the crowd. Maybe they don't know each other. Or maybe he's her man. The woman is sitting with her face towards Hayden, her eyes cast down to the glass of water, which she slightly moves back and forth between her white hands, unreadable in her apparent absentmindedness. The music starts again, and everybody quickly gets up to dance, only she keeps sitting, refuses when asked for the next dance by another man, simply shakes her head without even looking at whoever proposes, just stays put, a lone figure amidst abandoned tables. Hayden is tempted to go over to her, but he can't dance tango. He has nothing to offer. She seems unsettled, as if swayed by sudden thoughts disrupting her mood, and when the third piece starts she gets up, takes her purse and comes over to the bar as if she has made up her mind, comes and sits down right next to Hayden.

The bartender pours her a glass of red wine. Hayden says *hi* and introduces himself, whereupon she writes on a piece of paper *Hi, I'm Angela, I'm mute.* She moves the paper over to him. Hayden is a bit shocked. He's never met a mute person, and immediately he thinks that the conversation will be all on him. So he starts telling her that he doesn't understand much about tango, but he finds her a phenomenal dancer, and in order to validate his judgment he admits that he watched her dancing for quite a while. *I know, I'm not blind*, Angela writes on her paper to show him. He's a bit taken aback. Was that harsh, a reproach? He hadn't noticed that she was watching him too, and now he doesn't know if she was offended. So he changes the subject and tells her a bit about his band, the concerts, and the good experiences with the audience in Buenos Aires. She listens and smiles once in a while, a sad smile, it seems. He feels curious about her. So he dares to ask her what she is doing when she isn't dancing tango. Angela hesitates for a moment and then writes on her paper: *I can't go home tonight. Can I come with you?* Hayden is flabbergasted, and even though he feels attracted to Angela, it wouldn't have occurred to him to sleep with her. But when she asks him, there is no question, no question at all, that he will invite her in and go with the flow...

His hotel room is small and neat, cleaned by the staff. She doesn't seem shy or embarrassed. There is nothing impulsive or driven.

It is as if she's thought it all through, knows what she wants, and he wants it too, quite naturally. Doesn't he think of me? Maybe he briefly does, but there he has already entered an unknown space where mundane concerns are removed and don't count. It's all about the embrace and all she sees behind her closed eyes. Show me! She doesn't. Hayden didn't say whether or not he slept with her, but I believe he did...She rubs her knees against his, links her calves with his, presses her cheek on his, clasps his arms, chases his heart, submits to his lead, and he—is he still in amazement, stunned to the point of disbelief, mystified by some ancient tale, emerging like a dream come true? He can hardly catch his breath. It's true. It's now. And it's over before his eyes can create an image of what really happened. The next morning she is gone. Gone...He stumbles downstairs to the breakfast area where his friends are already sitting with their hands around their coffee cups, their bags and instruments heaped up in a corner. Hey, hurry up, we have to leave in ten minutes, our plane is at 11:30, they say, shocked to see him so unkempt and in his boxer shorts, a wrinkled t-shirt sticking to his sweaty chest. I'm not coming, he mumbles. What? I'm not coming, I'm staying here! There is a brief exchange, anger flares up, Ralph the guitarist is swearing, Andy gives him a punch on his back, everybody finds good reasons to convince Hayden otherwise, but Hayden remains unreceptive. Finally Mike says: If you're not coming now, if you're blowing off our commitments in Caracas, we're done—hear me?—done for good, finished! All right then, Hayden says, that'll be it! He gets another cup of coffee and climbs up to his room. His friends are devastated. Has he gone crazy? They

422

continue to debate leaving as planned or staying to give Hayden time to change his mind. They end up missing the plane and have to struggle to get another one in the afternoon. Several times they bang on his door. Hayden doesn't respond, doesn't open, just remains in his room, at times asleep, at times staring at the ceiling, where no thought emerges and nothing explains to him this endless stream of images fleeting beyond comprehension.

In the evening he finally gets up, releases a sandwich and a coke from a vending machine on his floor, and steps out into the warm summer night to sit on the stairs of the hotel entrance, chewing ham and cheese and watching people go by. She didn't leave a note, nothing, just left while he was asleep. Okay. Not okay. Okay. He has extended his stay for another week. He will extend it indefinitely after that. Night after night he goes to the tango club, sits at the bar, watches the dancers—waiting to see Angela. It takes a week before she comes back. On Thursday, again on Thursday, she shows up, sits in the back of the ballroom, and again her partner comes, same dark suit and red tie, just looks at her from afar, and she gets up and follows him. They dance three rounds of three dances. Then she disappears. This time she leaves first while her dance partner is still digging in his pockets for some coins for the waiter. Hayden notices that Angela has seen him, but she ignores him. No sign of recognition. Not even a fleeting hi, or who are you after all... Shall he leave, follow and rejoin the band, return to New York? Hayden stays. She will come back, he thinks. It's this man who doesn't let her go. He's too old for her, definitively too old.

Night after night he walks over to the tango club. It becomes his job to go there. He gets to know every inch of the bumpy road, thrown up by the bulky roots of the sycamore trees. He learns to watch his steps. After a while the street feels like home, the hotel feels like home, the club feels like home—home is a mysterious world. Not that he would think all the time of Angela. No, he has started to pick up composing. During the daytime he's sitting at the small desk next to his bed and working on a rhapsody he's had in mind for quite a while. Now is the time to write it down. Nobody interferes. Nobody knows where he is. He writes. Downstairs in the lobby there is an old piano that he uses once in a while to try something out even though it's not well tuned, but he can correct in thought what he hears when hitting the keys. Every evening he goes to the tango club, always, despite the fact that Angela comes on Thursdays only—only on Thursdays! She never takes much notice of him. But he does, and looking at her he tries to imagine who she is.

Eventually Mateo, the bar man, realizes that Hayden is looking for Angela—if it is still Angela he is looking for, it seems so, but he doesn't know. A strange lady, Mateo says, she never talks; she isn't really mute, she just chose to not talk anymore, strange bird! Why would she not talk, Hayden wonders and watches her, eyes closed, in close embrace with her dance partner, devoted and surrendered to his every move. You are not the first, Mateo mentions as if to casually warn him, but Hayden doesn't care if he is the first or anybody. He watches her, and his composition grows, while his sense of himself slightly dissolves, allowing for a looseness and a wish for more looseness, a vague conviction that giving up on who he thought he was would be the price for creating something new, his composition, which sounds more and more like a melancholic mix of the Italian *Bella Ciao* with Vienna coffee house music and Argentine tango—somehow the tango had invoked it, but it was about the song his mother hummed day-in, day-out: *alla mattina appena alzata*...and tucking him in at night she would sing it to him: *una mattina mo son svegliato*... Why were you always singing that one, he had asked her later, and she had responded, oh, my mother used to sing it, it's a partisan song, a song for my father...and now it's playing in his head ...*ho trovato l'invasor...che mi sento di morir*...

Of course, reality knocks at his door. His dwindling finances first require him to move up to a smaller room under the roof with no air conditioning. It's hot, the bed sags like a hammock, the small table totters. But he continues to work his night and day shifts. Long since has he given up expecting Angela to come over to him ever again, and to his own surprise he is fine with it. Maybe it's not about her, or maybe he has accepted that she belongs to the pinstriped man, her dance partner, even though he's never seen them coming or leaving together. But who is this man, and what are they together? One evening he asks Mateo. Do you know who they are? Mateo raises his eyebrows. Nobody really knows them, he then responds, they don't live around here, probably they are from another part of town. And after a moment of hesitation he adds, people say she is the infant of one of the *desaparecidos*—you know, under the military dictatorship...A while ago there was something about her—or some woman like her—in the news. She refused to learn who her real parents were...

Hayden goes back to his hotel and starts to feverishly research every detail he can find about these stolen babies. He reads many stories, dives into individual tragedies, leftist women kidnapped, tortured, and murdered, their babies cut out of their pregnant bodies, babies born in prison, declared dead and given to families in the military service. The air over Buenos Aires grows thick, sticky, and clouded with these tragedies emanating from the horrors of injustice. People were scared. People looked the other way. Hayden looks at Angela dancing with her partner. Maybe she is this young women who refused to be DNA-tested in order to hold on to the parents she grew up with? When she finally relented to the full force of truth, she was presented with a man she'd never seen before, her real father. He was her father? As much as she empathized with the pain of this man, who had never given up on searching for his daughter, she couldn't abandon her real/fake family. At their first encounter her real father brought her a photo of her real mother, who had disappeared; and he brought her the white headscarf of her late grandmother, who had walked around the Plaza de Mayo every Thursday till the end of her life. The article mentioned that her real father invited her for tea at his home, which was the same home where he and his wife, her birthmother, had lived before she was abducted; but it didn't say whether his unnamed daughter accepted his invitation. It is also unknown whether she

426

still lives with her fake parents or is on her own now, neither here nor there, in between and alone. Hayden wonders: is Angela the young woman he read about? And is her dance partner her real father, with whom she dances every Thursday night, dances without a word in close embrace? Or did she separate from her fake parents but continue meeting the man who she loved as her father in this remote tango club every Thursday night—on Thursdays, that would have been her condition honoring her grandmother—reunites with him for a short embrace without words and then leaves to an unknown location?

Hayden's composition stalls. An image emerges that starts haunting him deep into his nights and into the heart of his dreams: Angela would hang herself with the white headscarf of her real grandmother or with the red tie of her father. Unable to resolve her conflict, her wavering feelings would tie an ever-tighter knot around her soul, increasingly strangle her mind, and paralyze her moves, those beautiful moves she had reserved for her father, the father who wasn't, and in the end she would offer them one more time in her last tango to whomever the man she embraced had turned out to be. Then she would strangle herself, and Hayden would not be able to rescue her.

These thoughts really possessed me, Hayden said, and I couldn't do anything about them. First I tried to mention something along those lines to Mateo. He turned away. Then I couldn't go anymore to the tango club on Thursday nights because I was afraid *not* to see Angela—meaning that she would have killed

427

herself. Or did *I* want to kill her because I was so enraged that she would continue to dance with her father, the fake or the real one, and ignore me completely—but what's the difference anyway? I knew I only had made it up, but still it was more powerful than I. Eventually I understood that Angela wasn't my problem. I don't know what role I played in her life, and I'd rather not know. It's not even clear to me what role she played in my life. Actually, I was upset that I could get so swept up that I would abandon everybody, you, my friends, the band...Maybe I need to embark into psychoanalysis to figure that out.

Anyway, not being able to work on my composition and not having to look out for Angela, I had no reason any longer to be in Buenos Aires. Also, I started to rot. My finances hit bottom. With the little I had left, I picked myself up, booked a flight to Vienna, and visited my aunt. Somehow I felt like going home, seeing the places where I grew up, visiting the few people there I'm still in contact with. I was so confused! I needed time. I had long conversations with my aunt. She told me about her brother, my father, and what she knew about my mother and the times of the war and her regrets for having fallen for Hitler, which she is still ashamed of and quite incredulous about. She also told me stories about me as a little boy and showed me photos I hadn't seen before. I'm glad I had this time with her; she is getting old. She's slowed down, needs to rest on each floor when she climbs up to her sixth-floor apartment. But she is well connected and has friends who look after her. She told me not to worry about her. In order to make some money I played in a piano bar four nights a week, the usual things: *Strangers in the Night* and *As Time Goes By*...but sometimes I smuggled in one of the *canzoni populi*, the old *Bella Ciao*, or a piece of my unfinished rhapsody. Eventually I felt better. I noticed that I was looking around again, feeling interested. I enjoyed going to the *Hawelka*, having a *Melange*, reading the newspapers, and getting involved in all sorts of conversations with all sorts of people... And I thought again of you. That's when I decided to go back to New York. I missed you. I wondered where you were. I hadn't received any email from you for a while, and I worried that you had ended it with me. But I had not. I wanted to see you. I wanted to know what had happened in your life—besides the death of your father...I want to find out if we still can make it together after all...Shall we take some time to talk? There is so much I want to talk with you about!

I looked at Hayden and felt some relief and some hope—it surprised me. Yes, I said, I'd like that. And I'm not so clear about my story either...Hayden smiled. Oh, good, he said, maybe we can help each other sort things out. Let's go, I suggested. We got up and crossed the lawn all the way down to the lake. A fresh wind had picked up. I was in New York, it was Monday, June 28th, life would go on, one way or another...and there was Hayden, right next to me.

Also By Cordelia Schmidt-Hellerau

and

IPBOOKS.net
International Psychoanalytic Books

DRIVEN TO SURVIVE makes a compelling case for the recognition of our mind's constant strivings for self- and object-preservation. It also offers a new understanding of aggression in the service of our preservative and sexual drive activities. Numerous clinical examples show the relevance of these conceptual shifts. *DRIVEN TO SURVIVE* was a 2019 finalist of the American Board & Academy of Psychoanalysis Book Prize.

"Cordelia Schmidt-Hellerau has given us a work of deep scholarship and original thought. Fully engrossing and forceful in presentation, it is a bold and necessary reworking of Freudian drive theory. Her new formulations will reshape our thinking and our way of listening."

—Daniel Jacobs, MD, author of *The Distance from Home*

"This is a sharp, courageous, innovative and thoroughly documented exploration of one of the most problematic, unresolved and disputed areas of Freud's theory: preservative drives as part of the death drives. Cordelia Schmidt-Hellerau develops a revolutionary approach to the topic that leads to an unexpected, substantive metapsychological revision, a remarkable change of clinical perspective, and further considerations of cultural assumptions. Her convincing proposal gives us a new vision in psychoanalysis."

—Stefano Bolognini, MD, IPA Past President

Driven to Survive is a book that can make our impossible profession closer to possible. This is so because it throws a new light at a forgotten, often almost unnoticeable dimension of human strivings, the daily struggle to survive. Showing with many clinical examples how the needs of self- and object-preservation, as well as their neglect and pathology impact our patients' lives and treatments, it gives the therapist a new sense of what awaits to be addressed, explored, and understood. Reading it is like having a good session, in which a dark background brightens and new perspectives come into focus.

—Arlene Kramer Richards, EdD, author of *Psychoanalysis: Listening to Understand.*

CPSIA information can be obtained
at www.ICGtesting.com
Printed in the USA
LVHW082345230121
677318LV00045B/819